J.M. Hall is an author, playwright and deputy head of a primary school. His plays have been produced in theatres across the UK as well as for radio, the most recent being *Trust*, starring Julie Hesmondhalgh on BBC Radio 4. His novels, *A Spoonful of Murder*, *A Pen Dipped in Poison*, *A Clock Stopped Dead* and *A Brush with Death*, are about retired primary school teachers who turn to sleuthing.

A BRUSH *with* DEATH

J.M. HALL

avon.

Published by AVON
A division of HarperCollins*Publishers* Ltd
1 London Bridge Street
London SE1 9GF

www.harpercollins.co.uk

HarperCollins*Publishers*
Macken House
39/40 Mayor Street Upper
Dublin 1
D01 C9W8, Ireland

A Paperback Original 2025
2

First published in Great Britain by HarperCollins*Publishers* 2025

ISBN: 978-0-00-860696-1

Set in Bembo by HarperCollins*Publishers* India

Printed and bound in the United States

To Sandra, a wonderful teacher

PART ONE

Nice chap but nobody likes him

CHAPTER ONE

Saturday 14th June

From the Instagram feed of Chelsey Barlow:

Today will be all about cleaning ☹

Chelsey would always remember the weather that morning, that terrible Saturday morning, as being gloriously lovely – the real start of that summer's heatwave people would say afterwards. As she'd driven down the leafy lanes to Hollinby Quernhow, the sky had been completely cloudless; the trees, drowning in green, stood out in sharp enamelled contrast.

Not that any of this had been uppermost in Chelsey's mind as she'd approached the village in her mum's rattly old motor. Her mind had been dominated by a different image entirely: herself the night before at Yo-yo's, in her new pink top, clutching a WKD Blue cocktail and looking not unlike Kim Kardashian. She didn't care what anyone said, that lip enhancement had been worth every last penny! Not that anyone *had* said anything – that was the problem. Only *five* likes on Instagram: her mum, her sister and three mates. *Nothing* from Charl or Nat, for all their selfies and exuberant declarations of friendship. And nothing from Josh. Okay, he and Nat were A Thing but she knew for a *fact* it was more off than on, and he'd been talking to her for nearly half an hour whilst Nat was off dancing with that lad from Harrogate.

Driving into the village she became aware of the usual sinking, trapped feelings. She'd have nothing worth posting for the next six hours, unless bin bags and spray cleaner were suddenly on trend. Which, unless one was Mrs Hinch, they were not.

Whereas most people would have admired the cottages of honeyed stone or whitewashed stucco, for Chelsey they represented only one thing: cleaning. There were four holiday lets in the village on her boss's books – four to clean top to bottom in the seven hours between the 10 a.m. check-out and 4 p.m. when the new guests could take up residence. And it was a tough shout, no two ways about it. The fact they were all in the same village meant that it was *just* about doable but it was always a close-run thing. On more than one occasion Chelsey had found herself frantically finishing off the last house as the new holidaymakers waited outside in varying degrees of impatience at being deprived of the first few minutes of their stay.

What made the whole day so unpredictable was the state the previous tenants left the property in. The overwhelming majority were okay: waste bagged up, towels in the bath, bedding bundled on the beds as requested. But sometimes, *sometimes* . . .

Chelsey knew she wasn't the tidiest of people, ask her mum; but honest to God the state some people would leave the place in – bottles and glasses all over the shop, smeary finger marks on every surface. And the toilets – even her brother used the loo brush, for God's sake! Then there were the more serious occurrences – that time when there'd been an inch of muddy silt at the bottom of the washing machine – or those acrylic paints all over the bedding. And that basque! Hanging like a bat from one of the light fittings! That she *had* posted on Instagram until her boss Jax had told her to take it off smartish. And it only took one such incident – one mess, stain or spillage – in any of the four properties to throw the whole day out, into a nightmare of hurry, rush and stress.

That awful day when no less than three of the houses were in such a state, her mum and her brother had to be dragged in to help.

Today she was going to start, as she always did, with the Snuggery: a square, stone outhouse conversion at the very western edge of the village, owned by Mr and Mrs Hilton. The Hiltons lived in the adjacent barn conversion (named appropriately enough 'The Old Barn') and let out the Snuggery for a weekly sum that left Chelsey feeling winded. She always started her cleaning there, because at just four rooms it was by far the smallest of the properties she cleaned and consequently never had children or large parties staying.

She turned into the gravelled driveway, which lay between the two buildings, one short and squat, one long – like a cow and its calf she always thought. All at once she found herself sharply braking, making the tub of sprays and polishes slide off the back seat. One of the main house's wheelie bins had been left, a lone sentinel, *right* in the way of her designated parking place in front of the Snuggery.

Chelsey sighed in impatience. *What was that doing there?*

For a second – only a second – she was tempted to park by the main house, but, as always, memories came back of the time when that bitch Mrs Hilton, with her hard, expressionless face and tight jodhpurs, had given her a right doing for blocking access to her four-by-four. And even though the black four-by-four was absent, she wasn't willing to take the chance.

For all that, she thought as she parked up, she actually preferred Mrs Hilton. Mr Hilton, his toothy smug grin in that plump face, was always ready to point out some misdemeanour with her car or her cleaning or even her grammar. Not that she normally saw either of them in the fifty or so minutes it usually took to clean the place.

She got out of the car and moved the bin back to its spot, faintly puzzled. Why had the bin not been put back? One thing about Mr Hilton, he was a right stickler for putting back all the various waste and recycling bins from the two properties in their *exact* spot – more than once she'd been the unwilling recipient of a lengthy lecture on the subject.

Bin replaced, sprays, bin bags and gloves collected from the car, Chelsey found herself pausing. It really was a lovely day. The grey wall of the Snuggery was swamped in thick white blossoms, which made her think of weddings or picnics in the fields – not several hours of cleaning other people's crap. By the front door she could see a couple of charity bags, no doubt full of Mrs Hilton's designer cast-offs. She felt a sudden bleak little stab. Twenty-three and working three jobs, none of them amounting to much. When Mum and Dad were twenty-three, they'd been married two years and living in the house in Carlton Miniot. The prospect of actually owning her own home seemed as remote to Chelsey as winning the lottery. She thought again about the cost of renting out the Snuggery and shook her head at the unfairness of the world.

Come on, Chelse, no point in moping. That's what Mum would say. If she got done smartish here she could maybe grab a selfie by those white flowers. See if *that* got a response from Josh.

The first thing that hit her on opening the door of the Snuggery was the smell of cleaning spray – sharp, fresh, floral. This boded well. Unless there'd been some major catastrophe somewhere, and the scent represented some token attempt to put it right . . .

She went into the kitchen, always the place with the greatest potential for domestic devastation. Today it was spotless, the draining board bare, the floor swept, the hob sparkling in the morning sun, which was streaming in through the mullioned windows. Chelsey's first thought was there'd been some mistake – had the Snuggery even had any tenants during that past week? But no, the hospitality tray (Yorkshire teabags, Hambleton gooseberry jam, two garden centre café scones) was empty, and there was a light on, on the dishwasher. It seemed whoever had been there had followed Mr Hilton's entire irritating litany of laminated instructions – *please leave cutlery IN the dishwasher; please empty the rubbish into the CORRECT coloured wheelie bin.* With a lightening heart, she headed for the living room. At this rate all she'd need to do was change the bedding – she could be out in twenty minutes.

This is what was going through her mind as she opened the living room door and her life changed forever.

The lines of the hoover on the dove-grey carpet were one detail amidst the immaculate cleanliness that would haunt her nightmares for years to come.

Mr Hilton was seated on the slate grey velveteen sofa. He was wearing a smartish grey jacket over a checked shirt and orange tie. And he was dead.

Chelsey knew it instantly. There was something unmistakable about the utter stillness of his body, and there was everything about the way his head was thrown back, flung back, as if howling with laughter. Or just howling. And his *face*. That *look* on his face, milky eyes wide, toothy mouth agape.

Chelsey had seen one dead person before in her life: her Nanna Renee in the hospice. She'd looked exactly as if she was sleeping, wrinkled hands folded neatly on the snowy coverlet. There had been such a beautiful feeling of peace. That lovely Jamaican nurse had opened the window 'to let the soul out'; afterwards she had gently placed a flower on the pillow next to Nanna Renee's head. But here, in the living room of the Snuggery there was no feeling of peace whatsoever. Here there was ... anger ... *outrage* – fear even. Any released soul would, Chelsey instinctively knew, be battering at the closed window with the force and fury of an angry wasp.

All at once adrenalin exploded through her body. With a great gasp Chelsey ran out of the Snuggery and into the lane outside on legs that didn't seem to want to work properly. If it had been Acacia Gardens, where she lived in Thirsk, there would have been *someone* around, cutting the grass, unloading shopping, chatting over the fence – but here the idyllic village street was deserted and drowsy in the morning sun. Her fingers, usually so adept with a phone, felt fat and clumsy as she attempted again and again to dial 999. As she waited for the operator she felt a further pang of panic – what should she ask for? Police or ambulance? She was pretty sure Mr Hilton *was* dead – but what if he wasn't? Would she be in trouble for getting it wrong?

In the event she didn't need to ask for either, by the time she'd finished gasping out her story the operator had decided for her and told her to wait outside – for police or ambulance she wasn't entirely sure. Standing in the deserted lane, Chelsey shivered. Despite the heat she felt icy cold but knew she didn't dare go back to the car for her jacket.

And it was as she stood there that she realised there was a second thing wrong with the scene she'd just witnessed. It had been driven out by the sight of Mr Hilton. It wasn't that it was exactly *wrong* – not in the way a dead body was wrong (her shivering intensified) but it *was* odd. Different.

Sinister.

She shivered again. How long would whatever was coming take? She remembered the idea she'd had of taking a selfie by the flowers and posting it on Instagram. And suddenly she realised on some deep, sad level that she would never post on social media again.

CHAPTER TWO

Tuesday 8th July

From the Hambleton Five Parishes Newsletter:

As temperatures soar, all five of our churches will be open for people to pop in and take sanctuary from the heatwave. Please remember to keep the doors SHUT as our feathered friends also like to cool off – and they aren't too fussy about the mess they leave behind!

From his post at the front of All Saints church, Pickhill, the lanky, bald man in the baggy designer suit frowned down at his tablet.

'Cut Neville Hilton in half,' he said confidently, 'and you'd find the word "education" stamped through him like Blackpool Rock.'

Behind him the Reverend Mare – vicar of All Saints (and four other churches) – gave a well-practised smile of mirth tinged with sadness. From a gilt easel surrounded by waxy white lilies, an enlarged image of Nev Hilton smirked toothily out at the congregation as if acknowledging the speaker's words.

The speaker – identified on the glossy order of service as Chris Canne MBE, CEO of Lodestone Multi-academy Trust – raised his eyes to scan the assembled mourners. It was then he saw the three ladies of a certain age sitting some five rows back. One wore a worried frown; the second, in a wispy black outfit, was adjusting a black pillbox hat; whilst the third – the one with a grey bob and large glasses – lowered her gaze and bowed her head as if in silent prayer. His eyes flicked uneasily back to the iPad. 'He was a man for whom education was a passion and is, quite simply, a *massive* loss to the profession.' His voice sounded noticeably less certain.

Head bent, Thelma was not praying but considering what Chris Canne was saying about the deceased. Her thoughts spooled back to probably the last time she'd seen Neville Hilton: that staff night out at the Busby Stoop, some years ago now, for her head teacher Feay's retirement party (hence the presence of spouses and partners). Nev Hilton had been sitting at her end of the table with his then-wife Jax, who had been Thelma's classroom assistant at the time. Thelma could picture that same toothy smirk, hear that rather whiney voice droning on. What was it they had been talking about? Something that led to him making some rather contentious political point – completely oblivious to the fact that those people he wasn't boring, he was annoying.

It hadn't been so long after that, she remembered, that he and Jax had split up. Looking round the church of All Saints, blessedly cool on yet another scorching July day, Thelma found herself wondering about the late Neville Hilton. Aside from the huddle of men and women in expensive suits (obviously Lodestone Education personnel) there didn't actually seem to be *that* many people, certainly not locals. She contrasted it with the funeral of her friend Laura in that very church the previous Easter. Then the church had been packed, people standing at the sides . . .

'Neville Hilton was someone who will be greatly missed,' said Chris Canne MBE sombrely.

Will he? thought Thelma.

★ ★ ★

Yes, thought Pat, Chris Canne had *definitely* clocked the three of them and was *definitely* shooting uneasy glances in their direction. Was it seeing the three of them again after that last, awkward encounter, or was there another reason? She shifted in some discomfort. Despite the cool of the church and the wispiness of the various black layers (her 'Kate Bush get-up', as her son Liam termed it) Pat was feeling uncomfortably warm. The black pillbox hat felt like a hot clamp on her head. She wouldn't have bothered with it had she not been painfully aware her roots needed touching up.

'All of us at Lodestone Multi-academy Trust were impressed by Nev's professionalism,' said Chris Canne – very definitely NOT looking at Pat.

Professionalism? Like Thelma, Pat found herself remembering Feay's leaving do. What had that silly argument been about? Brexit? Neville had been so irritatingly dogmatic. Pat remembered her husband Rod's fixed smile and repeated kicks under the table. And then talking with Nev's wife in the ladies'.

'Nev just doesn't know when to shut up,' Jax Hilton had said in her usual airy tones.

Like Thelma, Pat recalled it hadn't been that long before the pair had broken up. Or more accurately, Jax had broken up with Nev. Of the many, many break-ups Pat had seen over the years, this had been one of the more amicable ones – a load of cheery assertions from Jax by the photocopier about *growing apart*, life being *the play not the rehearsal*, before smartly removing herself off to a flat in Boroughbridge.

From what Pat had learned through the Staffroom Grapevine there didn't *seem* to have been anyone else involved. And it was very much one of Jax's defining qualities, tiring of something and moving on – something Pat had seen happen with various diets, multiple gym memberships, and now her marriage. Presumably there *had* been some tension, some sadness – though it was difficult to imagine anything removing the smug smile from Nev

11

Hilton's face – but notably Jax had never bad-mouthed him and now the former Mrs Hilton even had the cleaning contract for the man's holiday flat, which presumably meant some ongoing contact with her ex.

Pat looked across to where her one-time colleague was sitting three rows back, her trademark brassy blonde ponytail sprouting energetically from the top of her head bouncing slightly as she dabbed at her eyes. Ten days ago, Jax Hilton (she'd never shed her married surname, Pat noted) had rung out of the blue, with a breezy assumption bordering on an insistence that Pat *would* be as sad as she was and *would* naturally want to pay her respects. The forceful tones had rather reminded Pat of the way Jax would sell raffle tickets at the school summer fayre, effortlessly shifting book after book. Looking round at the half-empty church she could only assume Jax's call had been part of an attempt to drum up support for the service. Pat shifted slightly; it really was uncomfortable in this outfit. She couldn't wait to get home, into her shorts and T-shirt and into the garden. Assuming a certain bronzed somebody hadn't nicked her favourite sunlounger to top up that improbable tan.

'In the short time we worked together, all of us at Lodestone were impressed by the sheer work ethic of the man.' Chris Canne always was one for going on, Pat remembered, discreetly readjusting the pillbox hat. 'We all saw him as something of an educational *powerhouse*.'

Educational powerhouse? Again, Pat remembered that evening at the Busby Stoop. *Bellend* had been Rod's pronouncement.

The third woman of the trio, grey-haired, in the smart but decidedly well-worn black dress, wasn't solely there at the prompting of Jax Hilton. Liz was there because her husband, Derek (sitting next to her now, discreetly holding two of her fingers in his left hand), had felt it only right he should be there to represent the Thirsk and Rievaulx Rotarians. As branch treasurer, attending the funerals of members seemed to be something that fell into his remit, along with the stewarding of the Thirsk fun run and selling raffle tickets outside Tesco. And of course it had felt absolutely right that, as his wife, Liz should accompany him – especially taking into account her one-time connection with Jax.

Like her friends, Liz also noted the empty pews. Derek's sentiments of solidarity and support were obviously not ones widely shared by other Rotarians. She also regarded the smirking image on the easel. A heart attack, Jax had said when she'd phoned to tell her about the funeral. *Gone just like that*. Had it been Liz's imagination or had there been something *else* in that airy, bossy voice, some darker undertone? Maybe some other medical factor had come into play? Instantly she felt her mind flying gloomily off to her meeting later on that week. *Always* with these meetings she was *so* apprehensive before – and afterwards felt so *unremittingly* flat. Still, it had to be done.

As though reading her gloomy thoughts, she felt Derek's grip on her two fingers tighten. Liz sighed and sternly forced her mind back to the service. On the front row she could see the person who Pat had identified as the second Mrs Neville Hilton. Standing in her glossy, tight-fitting purple-black dress, with her ramrod posture, she put Liz in mind of a tightly closed tulip. *Hard*. Her face and expressionless mask of make-up and Botox had left Liz with the odd feeling that one sharp tap would dislodge the whole edifice, like one of those Venetian masks, sending it clattering to the tiled floor.

From the tone in his voice, and the way the Reverend Mare was stirring, Liz sensed that at long last Chris Canne MBE was winding down to a close. 'Put simply,' he said, 'Nev Hilton was a top guy.' As the Reverend Mare walked to the lectern, Liz found herself pondering the words. *A top guy?* Like her friends, she remembered the pompous figure holding forth at the Busby Stoop . . . no *malice* in him, but such a strong sense of his own views. She remembered that immortal phrase of her late father, one used by both her and Derek when talking about Neville Hilton that morning.

Nice chap but nobody likes him.

After the service the sparse congregation milled in the vicinity of the stone porch of All Saints, waiting for the emergence of the coffin, marking the start of Neville Hilton's last journey on this earth: the short drive to Maple Park Crematorium. Like the rest of the countryside that summer, the graveyard was bleached and dusty after nearly four weeks of blazing sunshine and little rain; the various stilettos and designer trainers of the Lodestone group sparked little puffs of sandy dust.

Whilst Derek gravitated to the couple of fellow Rotarians, jackets over their arms, Liz, Pat and Thelma retired to a discreet distance under the shade of one of the gently rustling trees by the honeyed stone wall.

'So,' said Pat bluntly, removing her black hat (roots be damned). 'What was *that* all about?'

'I'm wondering,' said Liz, 'why the funeral was here and not in the church at Hollinby?' She made a grab for her bag, and a balsam tissue. Standing in this graveyard was doing nothing for her hay fever.

'There *is* no longer a church at Hollinby,' said Thelma. 'It was deconsecrated a couple of years ago.'

Pat shook her head impatiently. 'I don't mean where the funeral was but who was at it,' she said. 'Or rather who *wasn't* at it. There was hardly anyone there!'

'Most of the Rotary lot were away on holiday,' said Liz. 'At least that's what they told Derek.'

'There's the group from Lodestone,' pointed out Thelma. The three looked over to the huddled group. Chris Canne had his back to them.

'That's something else,' said Pat. 'Is it me or is Chris Canne avoiding us?'

'He certainly looked surprised to see us,' said Liz, blowing her nose.

'I did say "hello",' agreed Thelma. 'But he didn't seem willing to talk. Though of course he could just be embarrassed about the last time we met.'

There was a brief pause as they all remembered the scandal involving a certain member of the Lodestone Trust personnel they'd been involved in uncovering.

'I wonder,' said Liz, 'if there was maybe some issue with Neville at work?'

'Some murky goings-on?' mused Pat. '*Neville*?'

'He'd only been there ten minutes,' said Thelma. 'According to Chris Canne.'

'And all those lilies,' continued Liz. 'Don't you think they were a bit OTT? There's so many lovely flowers at this time of year – and a lot cheaper. Remember all those daffodils at Laura Barton's funeral?'

'Nev would have been on a fair old whack if those Lodestone suits are anything to go by,' observed Pat. 'And apparently the fuddle's at Ainderby Golf Club. No expense spared according to Jax.' At the mention of their former colleague there was a significant exchange of glances.

'I suppose what I'm wondering,' said Thelma, 'is why we're here.'

'Because Jax "asked" us,' said Pat. The inverted commas round the word 'asked' were audible.

'I don't understand,' said Liz frowning.

'Jax was very insistent I came,' said Thelma.

'And me,' said Pat. She looked at her friend. 'You think maybe she wanted us here for a particular reason?'

Thelma nodded. 'The thought did cross my mind.'

Liz remembered that dark undertone in Jax's voice. She had a sudden nasty feeling she might be committing herself to something she'd much rather not.

'But *what* reason?' she said worriedly. She could feel another sneeze coming on.

Thelma nodded to where a blonde ponytail could be seen making a purposeful passage through the graves towards them.

'I think we might be about to find out,' she said.

'I'm completely gutted,' said Jax emphatically. On her unspoken but unmistakable bidding, they had relocated to a more discreet distance from the other mourners, next to a pile of pungent, crawling grass clippings and the last resting place of Fred Webster. Beyond the yew trees, a combine was making dusty progress across a baking beige field.

'I tell you' – she looked at her three ex-colleagues – 'I've been in absolute bits since it happened. But it's Chelse. She's the one I feel sorry for.'

'Chelse?' asked Liz politely.

'The girl who works for me. She's the one who found him. *Terrible*, she is. Won't go to clean on her own anymore – me or her mum have to go with her, poor love – and with twelve holiday lets to do on a Saturday, it's a complete nightmare.'

'It must have been very upsetting for her,' said Thelma drily.

'It was more than that,' said Jax darkly. The three looked at her, wondering what could possibly be more upsetting than coming across a corpse.

'It *was* a heart attack?' asked Pat bluntly.

'Oh, yeah.' Jax nodded vigorously. 'Nev had been having all murmurs and stuff even when we was together. Used to worry me half to death. But you know him – he wouldn't be told.'

'What was it that upset Chelsey so much?' asked Thelma.

'Apart from finding a body on the sofa,' said Pat.

'Two things.' Jax lowered her voice and looked round at the three. 'Nev – he weren't one for getting scared or owt. He wasn't sensitive, not like me.' Here Pat hurriedly converted a snort into a cough. 'But according to Chelse, the look on his face . . . *terrible*, it was.' There was a pause when no one – not even Pat – thought it appropriate to point out that a sudden heart attack was unlikely to result in an expression of calm serenity.

'And the other thing?' prompted Thelma.

'Excuse me.' The voice that broke in was both abrupt and rather harsh. They looked round to see the advancing black-purple figure of the second Mrs Hilton.

'Ffion.' The ponytail gave an agitated flick. 'I want to introduce you to Thelma, Pat and Liz – they used to work with me. They all wanted to pay their respects like.' Jax spoke in a nervous rush, and all at once the three realised the reason for their discreet relocation.

'We're so sorry for your loss,' said Thelma earnestly, if not strictly truthfully.

Ffion nodded perfunctorily, was that a gleam of antipathy in those hard features?

'Does any of you own a white Fiat?' she said. 'Only it's blocking in the hearse.'

Liz's hand flew to her mouth. 'I am *so* sorry,' she said, sounding as guilty as if she'd managed to stumble into the grave itself. She stiffened and emitted two sharp, horrified sneezes.

'It's okay,' said Ffion grimly. 'Only if you could shift it.'

'I'm going now,' said Liz, fumbling for more tissues as she set off as rapidly as she could in her black court shoes, followed at a distance by the second Mrs Hilton.

'So go on,' said Pat. 'What was the second thing?'

'We really can't talk here.' Jax frowned after the retreating figure. 'You *are* going to the fuddle, aren't you?'

Both Thelma and Pat instantly and emphatically shook their heads; both began evoking appointments and commitments, but Jax spoke quickly over them. 'Don't apologise, it's fine,' she said (making both of them feel the need to say sorry). 'I'll come across and see you. You do still meet at the garden centre on Thursdays? I'll see you all then.'

'But what was it?' said Pat. 'What happened?'

Jax shook her head. 'Something inside the holiday let where they found him,' she said. 'Something really weird.'

She looked round uneasily as if expecting the second Mrs Hilton to make a reappearance.

'In what respect weird?' asked Thelma.

'The police thought nothing of it, and neither did Ffion – but then she never sets foot in the place. But I know that holiday let, inside out.'

'And there was something wrong there?' Thelma prompted.

Jax nodded, eyes still roaming around the churchyard. 'It's been done out right tasteful,' she said. 'I mean one thing Nev did have was an eye for colour schemes. And the living room – where they found him – it's been done out in greys: grey sofa, grey walls, all set off by a crimson carpet.'

'So?' said Pat.

'It was one of the walls,' said Jax. 'When Chelse went in and found Nev, she noticed someone had gone and *painted* it.'

'Like graffiti?' said Pat.

'No.' Jax shook her head emphatically. 'No, they'd painted a line. *Someone had painted a bright yellow line down the back wall.*'

CHAPTER THREE

Thursday 10th July

From the Thirsk Garden Centre website:

Beat the heat and find relief with the delicious range of mouth-watering smoothies in our café! Our current fave is raspberry and mint!

'*Yellow!*' said Liz, for what must have been the third or fourth time.

'According to Jax,' said Thelma – also for the third or fourth time. 'A vertical yellow line, going from top to bottom, right in the middle of the wall.'

Liz frowned, shaking her head. 'It just doesn't make any sense.'

Her perplexed gaze roamed abstractedly round the Thirsk Garden Centre café as if seeking to draw reassurance from the summer normality. The patio doors were flung wide to the morning sunshine but most people had chosen to sit inside, out of the direct glare and intense heat. The place was bright with the pastel colours of summer T-shirts: yellow, lavender, pink, echoed by the displays in the Edinburgh Woollen Mill. Sun hats were on tables or poking out of handbags like large floppy flowers and many a reddened upper arm was in evidence. 'Better get used to it!' the *Look North* weatherman had said only that morning. 'This is our new normal, folks!'

'Just because it doesn't make any sense to us, doesn't mean there isn't a reason behind it,' said Thelma calmly.

'It's probably nothing,' said Pat, aiming her coral-pink handbag fan discreetly at her cleavage. 'Just Madame Jax getting her knickers in a knot as per. There's got to be some perfectly logical reason behind it.'

'Such as?' said Liz, still frowning worriedly. She could sense a sneeze brewing. This morning her head felt especially muzzy and bunged up.

'He could have been redecorating.' Pat's tone was impatient, dismissive, as if men were found dead in front of painted walls every day of the week.

'On a Friday night?' said Thelma mildly.

'He might have been trying out colours,' said Pat airily, waving the fan. 'That's what we do – we get those little weeny pots of paint, just to see what they look like.'

'Jax didn't mention pots of paint or anything like that,' said Thelma stirring her coffee. 'Or that Nev had been wearing painting things.'

'Anyway,' said Liz, 'surely the way you use those sample pots is in patches – not great big lines?'

'Who knows what went on in Neville Hilton's head,' said Pat dismissively, shutting off the fan and returning it to her bag. 'Here's a thought – maybe he'd done that one line and the thought of all the upheaval involved caused him to – you know . . .'

She made a discreet but unmistakable gesture with her pastry fork.

'Of course, we don't know how ill Nev actually was,' said Thelma.

'Derek said he seemed fine at Rotary,' said Liz. 'But that's Rotary.' There was an unspoken pause as all three reflected on their experiences of all-male gatherings where it was perfectly possible for someone to be at death's door without exciting any particular attention.

Thelma looked at Liz. 'What time did Derek say Nev left the Rotary meeting?' she asked.

'About six thirty,' said Liz. 'And it'd have taken him about twenty minutes or so to drive back to Hollinby.'

'*Six thirty?*' Thelma frowned. 'Isn't that a bit early to leave a Rotary meeting?'

'The meeting hadn't actually got started,' said Liz. 'According to Derek they were all gathering in the Wheatsheaf, and Nev got a phone call, said he had to leave and headed off.'

'What bothers me,' interjected Pat, 'is why Jax Hilton–Shally wants to see us again – after strong-arming us all into going to the funeral . . .'

The three friends exchanged eloquent glances that said all there was to say about their ex-colleague. Back in the day Pat had nicknamed her 'Shally' – short for '*Shall I leave it with you?*' During the times they'd all worked together at St Barnabus Primary School, that had been Jax's special skill – getting others to sort out any problems that should come her way. Jammed photocopiers, unmanned playgrounds, miscreant children (especially the latter) all would all be brought to staff by Jax accompanied by a bright, conclusive 'Shall I leave it with you?' And now all three had a nasty feeling that the former Mrs Hilton viewed the death of her ex-husband in the same way: a problem that needed *sorting*. Sorting by someone other than herself.

'And we have lift-off,' said Pat in an undertone as the blonde ponytail appeared at the entrance to the coffee shop. 'Get ready to Stand Firm, ladies.'

'I've not heard anything more from the police.' Jax had been sitting with them some one and a half minutes and had not even touched her coffee. Another of Jax's traits was her ability to Cut to the Chase.

'You were expecting to?' said Pat.

Jax fixed her with a look of offended widowhood. 'We *were* married,' she said in gently accusing tones, which successfully glossed over the whole issue of her defection. 'Of course I want to know what happened.'

'Do the police think there was maybe something untoward about Nev's death then?' asked Liz.

Jax nodded vigorously, ponytail bobbing on the top of a tight-fitting ensemble of spearmint and pink. 'The police don't. But *I* do. One hundred and fifty per cent I do.'

'Why?' asked Thelma, ignoring the dramatic but inaccurate maths.

'I saw him,' said Jax, 'just the week before he died. And he were *fine*. More than fine.'

'Heart attacks often come out of the blue,' said Pat.

'What I want to know,' said Jax, 'is what brought it on in the first place.' Her tone was dark despite the warmth of the day. There was a chilly pause, broken only by an explosive sneeze from Liz.

'You think there was more to it?' probed Thelma.

'All I'm saying is, according to Chelse, the look on his face was *terrible*. "Jax," she says to me, "Jax, I can't get it out of my mind – that look!"' She took a conclusive sip of her coffee. 'Not only that, there were something else that was odd—'

'You mean apart from that yellow line on the wall?' asked Pat.

Jax nodded. 'Apart from that. Why was Nev there?'

'Because it's his property,' said Pat mildly.

'But why go in there at all?' said Jax. 'It's a holiday let, not his home.'

'Maybe whoever was staying in the outhouse had a problem with something?' said Liz reasonably.

The ponytail swept dismissively from side to side. 'There was no one there,' she said. 'According to the woman across the road, the person staying had had to leave early. Some crisis at home – so she'd gone that afternoon.'

'And you think that whatever happened was something to do with the yellow line on the wall?' ventured Thelma.

Again, that firm nod. 'One *thousand* per cent. It's *got* to be. The way Nev was staring at it. Chelse swears it wasn't like that the week before, so why had someone done it?'

'You've spoken to Ffion?' asked Thelma. 'Maybe she can shed some light on it?'

Liz felt an embarrassed flush, remembering the tight, dark figure glaring at her as, sneezing madly, she'd manoeuvred her car out of the way in a many-point turn.

'Ffion?' Jax's eyes rolled expressively. 'She's full on with her horses, that one. Not interested in the holiday let one iota. She left all that side of things to Nev. You could paint the whole flat sky blue and pink with yellow dots and she wouldn't notice. She said it must have been done by Nev at some point, but Chelse and I know that's not the case. Like I say, Chelse swears it was the first time she'd seen it and you can hardly miss a thing like that.'

'Did Ffion have anything to say about Nev's heart problems?' asked Pat.

Again, that dismissive flick of the head. 'I asked her point-blank – had he been ill – and she just shrugged. But unless Nev had suddenly grown a mane and four hooves I don't reckon she would have noticed one way or another. And the thing is—' There was something in Jax's tone that made Liz look up, Thelma stop stirring and Pat pause, Melmerby slice halfway to her lips. '*There's something else.*'

'What?' asked Liz anxiously.

'Ffion told the police she was away in Carlisle on some horse do. *But people are saying she wasn't.*'

Jax looked squarely at her three ex-colleagues. 'I know you probably think I'm being OTT, but he was my ex and I did care for him.' Her voice was strong, almost defiant. Were those tears in her eyes?

There was a pause.

'So, what is it you want us to do?' said Thelma gently, ignoring Pat's stony expression.

Jax looked at her, once again the brisk, efficient person who could work their way through a pile of laminating faster than anyone else in Key Stage Two.

'I want you to see if you can find out what happened,' she said. 'Ask around a bit. There's some festival in the village this weekend. I thought you could go along, talk to people—' The reluctance on all three faces was plain to see as Jax continued speaking quickly. 'Look, you're *good* at this stuff. *Everyone* says so. We all heard how you sorted out that business with them anonymous letters at St Barney's. And found out about what happened to poor Mrs Joy.'

The three exchanged glances. The circumstances surrounding both those events had been complex and intensely personal to all three of them; in stark contrast none of them had so much as seen Nev Hilton for years. Thelma was opening her mouth in an attempt to put this as tactfully as she could, when she saw Jax's eyes widen in recognition at a point somewhere over Pat's shoulder.

'Chelse!' she said. 'We're over here!'

Springing Chelsey on them unannounced was, they all later agreed, something of a master stroke of manipulation on Jax's part. Sitting there clutching a mango and peach smoothie, the girl looked painfully young and vulnerable. She reminded all three ex-teachers of a child starting in a new class, wide-eyed and unsure in a world suddenly unfamiliar and hazardous, and although they all felt annoyed with Jax, that didn't diminish the sympathy they felt for the girl. They regarded her awkwardly, unsure what to say.

Jax, however, had no such qualms. 'Go on, Chelse,' she said firmly. 'Tell them what you told me, about finding Mr Hilton.'

Chelse nodded obediently and took a deep shuddering breath; the hands clutching the glass shook. 'Sorry,' she said brokenly. 'Sorry—'

24

'You've nothing to be sorry about,' said Liz gently but firmly. 'I can't imagine what a horrible experience it was. *Anyone* would be upset.'

Chelsey nodded. 'I just keep seeing him there,' she said. 'On the sofa, with that look on his face.'

'Chelse love,' said Jax. 'You need to get your head round it and move on. Now come on, these ladies haven't got all day.'

'I can't stop thinking about it,' said Chelsey, her voice distressed. 'Could I have *done* something? Stopped it from happening somehow?'

'*Chelsey*,' said Jax with the air of a zealous paramedic. 'Get a grip, love.'

Liz glared at their ex-colleague. 'Anything can bring on a heart attack,' she said to Chelsey, passing her a balsam tissue. 'At any time. Really, there's nothing you could have done.'

'Liz is absolutely right,' said Thelma in a tone she'd used so many times over the years with upset children. 'The police said he'd been dead for hours.'

'The police—' Chelsey seized on the word. 'They kept asking me the same questions, over and over again, like they thought I *knew* something.'

'They have to do that,' said Pat soothingly. 'It's how these things work.' She was feeling a complex mix of emotions: annoyance with Jax, sympathy for Chelsey, plus a very strong urge to simply walk away and check out the sale in the Edinburgh Woollen Mill.

Chelsey nodded and blew her nose.

'Come on, Chelse,' urged Jax. 'Tell them about finding Mr Hilton.'

'Never mind that for now,' interjected Thelma smoothly. 'Tell us about when you arrived that morning. Whether you noticed anything odd.'

Chelse visibly relaxed and even looked a bit less stricken. 'Not really,' she said. 'Just that Mrs Hilton's car wasn't there, but she often goes away on a weekend with her horses.'

'So, you parked up—' prompted Thelma.

'That's right. I was in a hurry because with four places to do you need to get a shift on. And – *oh*—' She stopped herself, frowning. 'There was one thing—'

'Go on, lovey,' encouraged Liz.

'It sounds silly,' she said apologetically. 'But I had to move the wheelie bin.'

An investigating police officer could well have dismissed this event but Pat, Liz and Thelma were not investigating police officers and knew all about the potential significance of wheelie bins, moved or unmoved.

'You don't normally?' asked Pat, growing interested in spite of herself.

Chelsey shook her head. 'No. Mr Hilton always puts it out on the street on a Friday night; he used to tell me all the time how he'd do it straight away every time he got back from his Friday-night meeting. Made a big thing of it, he always did.'

There was a pause. All three women could well imagine Neville Hilton making a big thing of putting wheelie bins out.

'There's trade waste collection on a Saturday,' said Jax authoritatively. 'It's different from normal waste. A load of holiday cottages use it but you have to remember to put your bin out where they can see it.'

'It hadn't been put out like normal; it'd been left in the driveway blocking the way to where I park,' said Chelsey.

'So, you moved the wheelie bin and went inside,' prompted Thelma.

Chelsey nodded. 'It were clean,' she said. 'Spotless. Everything washed up and put away, nothing left out.'

Thelma frowned.

'What?' said Pat.

'Some of the messes I walk into,' said Jax importantly, '*disgusting*. Proper animals some folks.'

Thelma ignored this. 'Did you notice anything else?' she asked.

'Just the body. Sat there, eyes open.' Chelse's voice shook and Liz covered her hand with her own.

'I can't imagine how horrible that must have been,' she said to her.

'Forgive me for asking,' said Thelma. 'Did you happen to notice what Mr Hilton was wearing?'

Chelse frowned. 'Just normal clothes,' she said. 'Well, normal for him.'

'He wasn't,' said Thelma, 'wearing painting clothes?'

'Oh no.' Chelse shook her head. 'Nothing like that. Jacket and trousers – not a suit – and a checked shirt and a tie.'

'Just the sort of thing he'd wear to Rotary,' said Liz.

'And this yellow line?' Thelma asked the question almost casually.

'Oh yeah.' Chelsey frowned, eyes once more fearful. 'That. I've no idea what *that* were doing there.'

'What was it like?' asked Liz.'

Chelsey frowned. 'Well, it were yellow,' she said. 'And it were a line. I don't know what else I can say really.'

'What shade of yellow was it?' asked Pat, by now thoroughly engrossed.

'Pale,' said Chelsey. She looked around and nodded to a woman in a primrose-yellow top sitting at a table across the café. 'About the same shade as that lady's T-shirt. Maybe a bit paler.'

'And thick?' said Thelma. 'Or thin?'

'I dunno really.' Chelsey looks confused. 'I mean not *thin*, thin – but not thick either.' She shivered, eyes widening. 'It was *weird*,' she said. 'I didn't like it.' She half closed her eyes. 'I've been dreaming about it,' she said. 'Like I'm somewhere normal – and suddenly there it is on the wall . . . *a pale-yellow line . . .*'

The trio watched the two figures retreating across the rapidly filling café, Jax with a proprietorial hand between Chelse's shoulder blades.

Thelma looked grave. 'In cases like this,' she said, 'it's always the innocent who suffer. Finding Neville like that – it's something that'll always stay with her.'

'Poor lass,' said Liz. 'Poor, poor lass.'

'Never mind "poor, poor lass",' said Pat. 'Madame Jax Shally just wants to have her cleaner back up and running.' She looked grimly at her friends. 'The phrase "thundering cheek" comes to mind.'

'What was she playing at?' said Liz, blowing her nose in exasperation. 'Bringing the poor lass here like that and making her go through it all over again?'

'And then expecting us to go and investigate what happened,' said Pat. 'Who does Ms Shally think we are – a Miss Marple tribute band?'

'It's that lass that bothers me,' said Liz. 'She's never going to get over it, thinking she's responsible in some way.'

'Well, if you want to go trawling round Hollinby Quernhow Village Festival this weekend, fill your boots,' said Pat, finishing her Melmerby slice. 'I have other plans.' Her words were firm, her mind filled with the glorious prospect of a weekend with just her and Rod in the house. Padding round in her favourite faded sundress, reading in the garden, maybe binge-watching that new season of *Real Housewives of Tampa Bay*.

'I'm not saying we should get involved,' said Liz hastily. Her weekend was also full. Her grandson Jacob was staying over and Liz had a nasty idea he planned to go through her food cupboard and weed out what he termed 'unsuitable food'. Forestalling and ensuring there was at least *some* food left would take both time and patience.

All at once they both became aware that Thelma was saying nothing. Saying nothing but stirring her coffee in that very familiar way.

'*What*?' said Pat with a long-suffering sigh.

'I'm so sorry,' said Thelma. 'I was just wondering.'

'Wondering what?' said Liz.

Thelma looked at them. 'A couple of things really,' she said. 'According to Chelsey the flat was left spotless – but then Jax said the person staying there had had to leave in a hurry. Surely if you were called away by some crisis, you wouldn't stop first and clean somewhere that would be cleaned anyway?'

Pat shrugged. 'Some people are like that,' she said. 'It's a point of honour to leave places cleaner than when they found them.'

'What was the other thing?' asked Liz.'

'It was something Jax said. Why did Neville go into the holiday flat?'

'There could be any number of reasons,' said Pat dismissively.

'But why didn't he put the wheelie bin out first?' Thelma's words seemed to cast a chill across the warm room. They all instinctively felt there was something odd about that misplaced wheelie bin.

'Chelsey said he always put the bins out when he got back from Rotary,' said Liz slowly. 'But he didn't.'

'So, what stopped him?' asked Thelma.'

'A heart attack?' said Pat pointedly.

'No,' said Liz, 'if you're feeling ill, you'd go into your own house – not a holiday let—'

'Exactly,' said Thelma. 'So the chances are he was fine when he got back – and for whatever reason didn't put the wheelie bin out *because of something that happened*. And that's what made him go inside the holiday let. And now I think on it, there's a third thing.'

'What?' asked Pat uneasily.

Thelma steepled her fingers in thought. 'Derek said he left Rotary early because he got a call . . . So, who was the call from – and why did it make him go back home – but not into his own home?'

CHAPTER FOUR

Friday 11th July

Met Office weather forecast:

Exceptionally high temperatures across parts of England and Wales now updated to extend into Monday.

'Summer.' DS Donna Dolby blew out her broad cheeks expressively. 'Bad idea.' She cast a grim glance round the garden centre café, which looked much as it had the previous day, the sun hats, the T-shirts, the open windows. It was even hotter today. Already the temperature was nudging the mid-thirties and outside the pylons over the cattle market stood stark against the dazzling blueness of the sky.

'You wouldn't believe the number of things that kick off at barbecues,' she said.

'You're busy?' said Thelma politely.

'Is there a vowel in the month?' The police officer's gaze lighted on an elderly couple eating an all-day breakfast; she regarded them impassively for a moment as though considering the possible need for a taser. 'Anyway.' She turned back to Thelma. 'How are things with you?'

The gaze she gave was shrewd and questioning, the sort of gaze that, Thelma realised with an unexpected stab of panic, could see straight through *any* form of pretence. She felt an unwelcome flush of shame. *Get a grip!* Surely DS Dolby couldn't know about what had happened to her?

'Fine,' said Thelma. 'Just enjoying this beautiful weather.'

Donna regarded her, face expressionless. 'Your hubby still on with his vicar-ing at the college?' she asked. Thelma smiled at this description of Teddy's former vocation.

'Actually, he stopped working in Ripon last year,' she said. 'He's now working as a delivery driver.'

Donna slowly nodded. 'Interesting.'

Thelma smiled again; initially she'd been against Teddy's unexpected change of career to a delivery driver for Wait A Minute Mr Postman (known as WAMMP) but these days the thought of her husband sailing serenely round the postcodes of Ripon and Thirsk, windows wound down, *The Best of the Goons* playing full blast, brought an envious pang.

'So . . .' DS Donna leaned forward on her elbows. 'There was something – or rather someone – you wanted to know about.'

'There was,' said Thelma. 'Thank you.'

DS Dolby retrieved a notebook labelled 'Let's Smash This!' from her battered leather shoulder bag and flicked it open.

'Neville Hilton,' she said. She looked at Thelma. 'What I'm about to tell you,' she said in the careful, deliberate tones she always used during these sessions, '*is* in the public domain but even so I'd appreciate it if you didn't share it with all and sundry.'

'Of course not,' said Thelma gravely.

She regarded Donna's broad face and bleached blonde hair not so much with affection exactly, but with esteem. It was undeniably useful to have this contact in the police force, but as ever the encounter felt a tad too formal to be termed a *friendship*. Indeed, she wasn't at all sure on what basis their relationship actually worked. From time to time, they'd meet up and from time to time Donna would share information with Thelma – whether this made them friends she was uncertain. The speed at which Donna would respond to her requests was always gratifying. She thought guiltily of Contralto Kate in the choir and her ongoing woes with her disabled parking space – three weeks on and still no word from the police – yet here she was a mere twelve hours after sending DS Dolby that tentative text.

'Neville Hilton,' said Donna again. 'Sixty-two, found dead at the holiday let adjacent to his residence in Hollinby Quernhow, having been dead, according to the pathologist, between twelve and fourteen hours. At the time of his death, he was alone; the tenant of the holiday let had left earlier that afternoon and his wife – Ffion Hilton – was at some horse-riding event in Carlisle. He'd been last seen at a Rotary meeting around six thirty where he'd seemed fine but of course that's not unusual in cases like this.'

She paused to fan herself with the notebook, before continuing.

'The autopsy revealed the cause of death to be a massive heart attack; according to Mrs Hilton and medical records, Mr Hilton had been under supervision for a number of years. No signs of anything suspicious or untoward.' She shut the notebook and looked at Thelma. 'Or *are* there?'

'Apparently,' said Thelma. 'He was looking rather terrified when he was found.'

Donna nodded unconcernedly. 'A not uncommon feature of a sudden heart attack,' she said. 'Anything else?'

Thelma took a deep breath and told Donna about wheelie bins, Neville's sudden recall to the property and a yellow line appearing on the wall of the holiday let.

DS Donna nodded again. 'Granted these might all be relevant factors if the death was suspicious in any which way. But it wasn't. Mr Hilton obviously came back from wherever he'd been; maybe saw a light on in the holiday let or something, went inside and kaboom.'

'A light?' said Thelma. 'At seven o'clock on a sunny June evening?'

'Or a window open or *something*,' said Donna uninterestedly. 'And as for that yellow line.' She shrugged. 'Maybe he was planning to redecorate?'

Thelma nodded. 'Thank you,' she said. 'You've been most helpful.'

Donna nodded back. 'You're very welcome, Mrs Cooper,' she said. For the first time the trace of a smile cracked those grim features. 'However, *should* you find out anything—'

'Anything like what?' said Thelma innocently.

Donna fixed her with a broad, professional gaze. 'Oh, you know – vanishing charity shops. Anonymous letters. Anything like that. You know where I am.'

The combined blast from the coral-pink handbag fan and an altogether larger tabletop variety ruffled the pages of Angela Hartnett's *Summer Suppers*, open at courgette and hazelnut salad. From the sweet spot where the two blasts of air met, Pat regarded the slender, tanned girl in the mint green shorts who was photogenically perched on her oak kitchen table.

'That's *such* a shame,' she said to her.

'I know!' Tiffany-Jane looked mournfully at the pyramid of brightly coloured toilet rolls she was in the process of photographing. 'Poor Lin and Mex! They were such a *strong* couple!' She sighed and took a volley of shots with her phone; Pat could almost see a line of broken-heart emojis forming in the air above the girl's burnished gold head. 'I am *beyond* gutted!' She swapped round the orange dotted and the blue striped rolls and sighed as she considered the effect. From across the room Larson, the dog, eyed the lithe figure warily.

Pat felt considerably more than beyond gutted – *beyond* beyond gutted. She regarded her eldest son's girlfriend. Tiffany-Jane was undeniably a sweet enough girl, as she'd said so many times over the past few weeks to Liz and Thelma. Pat just happened to find her exhausting. She regarded the toilet rolls. *Beyond* exhausting.

It had been some four months since Justin and Tiffany-Jane had been forced to relocate from their glass-and-steel flat in Manchester to Pat's spare room in Borrowby. It was a common enough feature of these straitened times; what her various trashy magazines termed the 'back to the nest syndrome'. Because the sad simple fact was whatever consultancy and influencing employment Justin had and whatever influencing Tiffany-Jane did, it was no longer enough to fund life in Salford Quays. Justin, after several optimistic but ultimately heartbreaking weeks of Chasing Opps and Nailing Meetings had resorted to working at a call centre in Northallerton. (Strictly short-term, folks!) Tiffany-Jane, however, had resolutely avoided 'leaving her path' (as she termed it) as a social media influencer and spent her days Creating Content – which seemed to involve taking delivery of and photographing a bewildering assortment of items from wrist straps to non-organic muesli. How she made any sort of living from all this was beyond Pat, but a combination of her ten thousand followers (TEN THOUSAND!) and a series of perky, bright images of Tiffany brandishing these various items managed to somehow net the girl a thousand-odd pounds a month.

Although naturally dismayed at this turn of events in her son's life, Pat had rather looked forward to getting to know his girlfriend. Tiffany-Jane had proved such a refreshing change from Justin's usual parade of high-maintenance, high-octane women, collectively termed by Rod as 'Les Misérables'. Indeed Pat had hoped this eloquent, motivated and yes, friendly girl might be the one to add some permanent shape and purpose to her son's enthusiastic but rather aimless existence of motivational talks and podcasts. She only really knew Tiffany-Jane through her various social media posts (Ms T.J. Rox!) – but now, after nearly four months of living under the same roof, Pat felt she hardly knew her any better. Such conversations as they did have were short, chirpy exchanges with all the depth and brightness of – well, a social media post.

Pat had envisaged a series of bonding family meals but what with Tiffany's ultra-healthy diet (kale seemed to feature largely) and Justin's erratic work patterns (evening shifts seemed the norm) this hadn't happened. Indeed, much of the time, Pat felt herself in sympathy with Larson the dog, who though amiably tolerating the various coos and scratches on the ears nevertheless spent his days warily avoiding this new house guest. Tiffany was slim, Tiffany was fit, Tiffany was wholesome in a way Pat definitely wasn't and there was something about the bright, energetic presence that made her crave carb-heavy pasta, reality TV and Prosecco. Lots and lots of Prosecco. Which is exactly what she'd planned as soon as Tiffany-Jane had announced this spa weekend at an eco retreat as a hen party for Lin and Mex. Quite who they were Pat wasn't altogether sure, beyond the fact that as a couple they self-identified as pansexual and were totally sound. But totally sound or not, something had happened and the spa weekend was off.

'What a shame,' said Pat again, thinking of bacon muffins and *The Real Housewives of Tampa Bay*. 'You were so looking forward to your weekend away.'

Tiffany-Jane, however, wasn't listening. She was frowning slightly, one pale pink nail resting on her plump lower lip.

'*Or*,' she said with a growing energy that made Larson stir uneasily in his basket. '*Or* don't get down, *get right back up*!' This reference to one of Justin's more irritating podcasts did nothing to improve Pat's gloom.

'What do you mean?' she said warily.

'I mean! OMG!' Tiffany jumped up in excitement. 'I mean, how about *we* have a spa day *HERE*? Saturday? Just you and me, Pat?' She smiled eagerly, the whites showing all round those honey-coloured irises.

'Here?' said Pat weakly.

'I've some mango facemasks to endorse! How do kale

smoothies sound? Followed by Pilates and a binge-watch of this totes amazeballs new lifestyle show?'

'Oh wow!' said Pat. 'I'd love to! That sounds *brilliant*.' She smiled the awkward smile people use when getting out of something they don't want to do. 'The only thing is, I promised Liz and Thelma I'd go to this village festival thing with them.'

The table fan turned and ruffled the image of courgettes and hazelnuts anew. 'Tell you what,' she said. 'Why don't you join us for supper? There's always plenty – it's nothing spectacular, just some salads.' She had a sudden vision of her, Rod and Tiffany, sat round the table, laughing, clinking glasses in an impromptu toast or two.

'Pat, I'd love to,' said Tiffany. 'Only the thing is, Justy and I are seeing some friends over in Harrogate.'

'That's fine,' said Pat. She was aware Tiffany was beaming the exact same awkward smile she had just used herself.

'*Et voila! J'accuse!*' cried Harvey, pulling from his plastic crate a packet of chocolate digestives, with the air of Hercule Poirot unmasking a villain. There was an audible gasp of dismay from the pre-diabetes awareness group.

'Just two of these bad boys gives you over *half* your daily recommended amount of fat and sugar!' said Harvey, smiling eagerly round the stuffy room.

'Fookin' hell,' said Zippy Doodah in an undertone. The two women flanking her – 'the coven' as Liz privately called them – nodded in grim sympathy.

Liz stared sadly at the offending packet. Not because she was such an ardent fan of chocolate digestives, but to be told by someone so young in such bald tones how potentially damaging such things were to those with elevated blood sugar levels left her with the bleak feeling of mortality closing a clammy hand round the back of her neck.

Of course, it was nothing short of miraculous that the

beleaguered NHS was still able to provide such sessions – but miraculous or not they were undoubtably something of a trial. Liz was obviously not the only one to think so. The group, which had started out with some thirty-plus members, had steadily dwindled over the past three months to a hard core of six or seven. It probably wasn't helped by the fact that Harvey (or 'Happy Harvey' as Zippy had dubbed him) addressed the whole question of ageing, weakening bodies in the same way Liz used to emphasise to her six-year-olds the importance of cleaning one's teeth.

She tore her gaze away from the biscuits, recalling far-off staffroom days when a plate of them would appear on Friday breaktimes, marking the glorious start of the countdown to the weekend.

Get a grip, Liz! Things with high fat and sugar were to be avoided and that was that.

The group seemed similarly deflated – even Zippy Doodah and the coven, who could normally be relied on to find a riotous reaction to everything, were looking glum – a marked contrast to their raucous, almost rude laughing earlier on when Harvey had attempted to demonstrate the process of sugar absorption using sock puppets.

'I can't do without me choccie digestives,' said one sadly.

Harvey smiled a bright restorative smile of salvation. 'Yes, but there's always a low-cal substitute to find!' he said. 'Captain Carrot Sticks coming to a fridge near you!'

'Fookin' hell,' said Zippy Doodah again.

Liz regarded the wide-mouthed woman sitting across the table with her usual feelings of irritation. It was bad enough she had to cut all these things out of her diet without all this incessant commentary from Zippy and her coven. The usual feelings of unfairness welled up inside her. Why should *she* – Liz – have to watch her blood sugar levels? She who had remained a steady eight and a half stone these past thirty years? And there was Zippy Doodah at least twice her weight, whose idea of five-a-day seemed

37

to consist of potatoes and cider. And that ridiculous name! Well, to be fair, half that ridiculous name. She'd introduced herself in the first session as Zippy, a childhood nickname due apparently to a resemblance to that wide-mouthed puppet off *Rainbow*. It was Pat who added the 'Doodah' and the name had stuck indelibly in Liz's mind ever since.

'Okay, peeps!' said Harvey. 'That's a wrap! Keep up those steps—' Here he brandished his NHS Fitbit. 'But remember to keep well-hydrated in this scorchio weather and I'll see you at the next sesh when we'll be immersing ourselves in the intriguing world of food triggers! I'd say maybe *the* most important session so far.'

'More bad news,' said Zippy Doodah in an undertone.

Stepping outside Thirsk Library, Liz had to shade her eyes. Despite the fact it had gone eight thirty, the sinking sun was still strong, casting long, lazy shadows; the sky above the rooftops was an unburnished pale pink, fading into a seashell blue. It was an evening to feel mellow, but Liz didn't feel mellow, she felt unremittingly flat as she always did after these sessions. Plus, despite the lateness of the hour, she could feel what she termed a 'pollen throb' behind her eyes and in her sinuses. Checking her phone, she saw there were no calls so presumably Derek had survived his evening run without succumbing to the heatstroke he had been fearfully predicting. She needed to text Thelma to let her know definitively she wouldn't be accompanying her to Hollinby Quernhow tomorrow. What was her friend playing at, talking to DS Donna like that?

Across the still evening she could hear the marketplace clock chiming eight. Just time, she supposed, to nip to Tesco to replace yet more things with low-sugar substitutions – though no doubt she'd need to make another visit after Jacob's planned blitzkrieg on her food cupboard. Plus, she needed to pick up a new paintbrush for treating Billy's bench at the allotments. She sighed again and without enthusiasm fished for her car keys.

'It's still fookin' red hot.' Zippy Doodah appeared, peering suspiciously at the sunset and clutching a thick cardigan round her in a way that made Liz break out into a sweat. 'I'll need to sleep with the windows open again.'

Liz smiled thinly and unlocked the white Fiat. 'My forsythia's crying out for some rain,' she said.

'Anyway,' said Zippy, 'it was a good do I thought.'

Liz felt puzzled; this seemed a rather odd way of referring to that evening's session. (Sugar: one lump or several?) 'What Harvey said about salad cream really made me think,' she said politely.

Zippy Doodah gave a grim bark of laughter. '*No*,' she said. 'Not Happy Harvey. I mean Nev Hilton's funeral! I saw you and your friends there in church.'

'I'm so sorry,' said Liz in genuine surprise. 'I didn't see you there. I'd have said hello.' Which she would have. Probably.

'I was at the back.' Zippy's tone held a curious qualification, as if she'd been there but only on certain terms. 'I live in Hollinby and wanted to pay my respects like.' She gave a dour chuckle. 'I saw you trying to get out of the way of the hearse.'

Liz's lips thinned in embarrassment and annoyance at the memory.

'You weren't at the wake,' said Zippy.

'No,' said Liz, pointedly getting out her car keys. 'I had to get off.'

'You missed a good do.' A faraway look came into Zippy Doodah's eyes and her voice dropped to an appreciative monotone. 'Vol au vents, crab pâté, these little meringue thingies. And I tell you something, I didn't put any of *that* in my food diary!' She nodded grimly and Liz looked instinctively over her shoulder as if expecting Harvey to bear down on them with a wide smile and a sugar-count chart.

Zippy looked at Liz. 'So how come *you* knew Nev Hilton?'

'My husband knew him through Rotary,' said Liz. 'And I knew him slightly through working with his wife – his first wife.' She came to a stop, aware that Zippy was giving the sort of stare that made her wonder if her blouse had come unbuttoned. 'It was very sad,' she added uncertainly, wondering what it was she'd said.

'Sad and sudden.' A definite timbre of something significant had entered Zippy's voice and all at once Liz felt if she had to, she could always go to Tesco first thing tomorrow.

'It was a heart attack I heard?' she said.

'That's what they said.' Zippy's gaze didn't falter.

'Do people think maybe it wasn't?' ventured Liz.

'I don't know,' said Zippy Doodah, who obviously felt that she did. 'After all, the police should know what they're talking about. What people are wondering is what brought the heart attack on in the first place.' There was a pause and despite the heat of the evening Liz shivered slightly.

'Surely anything could,' said Liz, remembering her words to Chelsey, 'if the heart's not that strong.'

Zippy nodded. 'Including a screaming row with his wife.'

'A *row*?' Liz frowned.

Zippy nodded. 'According to Judy Bestall.'

'Judy Bestall?'

'Lives in the village. She was walking her dog past the house and heard them – going at it hammer and tongs. Fair screaming at him she was.'

'She? You mean Ffion?' An image of that taut black and purple figure rose in Liz's mind and she felt a sneeze brewing. What was it Thelma had told her earlier? 'Didn't she tell the police she'd gone away? Some horse do – Carlisle or somewhere?' she asked.

Zippy Doodah rolled her eyes. 'She might well have done. All I'm saying is, according to Judy Bestall, at seven o'clock the night Neville died, Ffion Hilton was in their garden screaming blue murder at him.'

CHAPTER FIVE

Saturday 12th July

From the Hollinby Quernhow Village Facebook Page:

> VILLAGE FESTIVAL UPDATE: Due to the heat and the lack of numbers, the children's sports event has been replaced by a Fun Paddling Pool Challenge.

'I'm a bit bothered.' Liz fumbled in her bag for a tissue; her gung-ho curiosity of the night before had faded sometime in the hot small hours as she'd vainly tried to find a cool part of her bed. 'I mean if Ffion *was* shouting at Nev—' Her worried comment was broken off by an explosive sneeze.

'What's to stop her coming and shouting at us?' finished Pat, taking a bite of millionaire's shortbread. 'What I'm thinking is if she's been lying to the police, and it's all round the village, surely someone's going to say something to them?'

'If Ffion *has* been lying,' said Thelma mildly.

'You think she wasn't shouting at him?' asked Pat.

Thelma shrugged noncommittally. 'That's what we're here to find out,' she said.

Liz blew her nose and tried not to stare too longingly at Pat's rapidly melting cake. 'I don't know,' she said. 'It just feels like we're, well, nebbing in—'

'Which is because we *are*,' said Pat through a mouthful of chocolatey crumbs. 'Anything to get Ms Shally off our backs.' She looked round the rather sparsely peopled village green. 'What bothers me is exactly how we go about nebbing in. There's not many people about for a village fete.'

They were standing in the shade of one of the oaks fringing a village green. Across the road in the car park of the closed and boarded pub a brass band could be heard discordantly tuning up, rather outnumbering the actual visitors. At first glance Hollinby Quernhow had looked idyllic: bunting and stalls brightening the browning twin triangles of grass that formed the centre of the village, with more stalls outside the individual houses. The archetypal English fete on an archetypal English summer day. Closer inspection, however, revealed a somewhat different story. The main feature of the festival – like so many other village festivals – was that locals were free to run their own stalls outside their houses, a system that worked very effectively in most places. Hollinby Quernhow, however, where almost every other house was a holiday let or second home, was not most places. Here the net effect was too few stalls, spread widely and awkwardly – too few beads on a too long string. And – glaringly apparent to Liz, Pat and Thelma as ex-teachers – was the marked lack of the *young*. There were only a couple of chocolate-stained toddlers, very few youngsters pitching wildly at the stacked tin cans and no teenagers moodily showing off on the Whack-a-rat.

'But the stalls outside the houses are going to be manned by the people who live here,' said Thelma. 'And I did notice there's a couple of stalls down towards the end of the village where Neville lives—'

'Lived,' corrected Pat, scrubbing chocolate off her sticky fingers with a napkin.

'But are people going to want to talk?' persisted Liz. 'I mean a stand-up fight between husband and wife? And then the husband *dies* – it's a bit of a personal thing.'

'Are you kidding me, Liz Newsome?' said Pat, fishing for the coral-pink handbag fan. 'In a village? I'm surprised there isn't a display stand about it, even if hardly anyone lives here.'

'If there *was* a fight,' pointed out Thelma.

'You think Zippy Doodah got it wrong?' said Pat.'

'She's not what I'd call reliable,' said Liz, casting uneasily about as if the mere mention of her name could somehow conjure up that mountainous presence.

'What I mean,' said Thelma. 'It's all hearsay about this "argument". Your friend – she didn't actually see this row herself?'

'She's not my friend, just someone from pre-diabetes awareness,' said Liz firmly. 'And she heard about it from someone called Judy Bestall – *she* was the one who saw it.'

'Exactly,' said Thelma taking a final sip of her lemonade. 'Hearsay. And we all know how these things get blown up.'

There was a pause as they considered the truth of Thelma's words, remembering various times over the years when the most apocalyptic of tales had turned out to have a much tamer reality behind them. Screaming rows that were in fact tense words, cases of measles that turned out to be slight temperatures, that famous time when a burning building proved to be merely a pan of unattended playdough.

'So what's the plan?' said Pat, stuffing the napkin in her bag. 'Find out if Ffion was telling a load of porkies to the police about not being in Carlisle?'

Thelma nodded. 'And see if we can find out a bit more about Neville. What people here thought of him.'

Liz and Pat looked at their friend; even in the baking afternoon heat she looked as calm and self-possessed as ever.

'What are you getting at?' said Pat.

'I mean,' said Thelma. 'If Ffion was screaming at him loud enough for people to hear, it'd be interesting to know *why*.'

Some ten minutes later, the band were striking up the theme to *Jurassic Park*, to rather desultory applause from some two dozen wilting onlookers. Outside the white stucco cottage – the Old Post Office – an elderly man and an elderly woman were presiding over a plants stall. With his black visor and her red sun hat, they put Pat in mind of the figures on a weather house. She flashed the man one of her best smiles as she cast her eye over the various yoghurt pots of drooping seedlings.

'These look great,' she said enthusiastically, having no idea whether they did or not. If only Liz was with her.

'It's the watering that's the beggar,' said the man. He looked gloomily up at the blazing sun. 'The rain butt's been dry for three weeks now. If it keeps on like this, I'm going to lose half my planters.'

'I keep telling him,' said the woman. Was she one of those people who sounded perpetually exasperated or was it the effect of Pat's smile? 'He needs to be using the bathwater.'

'And I keep telling *you*,' said the man, 'no way am I heaving great buckets of bathwater through the house.'

The woman looked at Pat, raising her eyes as if to say, 'What can one do?' Pat extended the smile to the woman and decided now was the time to cut to the chase.

'I was thinking how lovely all the gardens were looking when I came through here last week,' she said. 'Only I was going to Neville Hilton's funeral and didn't get a chance to take a proper look.'

The look shared by Mr and Mrs was both immediate and significant. 'You knew Nev Hilton?' said Mrs, trying (and failing) to sound casual.

Pat nodded. 'I worked with him – well, his wife. His *first* wife. But of course, I knew Nev . . .' She paused, aiming the coral-pink hand fan at her neck. 'A bit of a . . . funny onion.' The inflection in her voice was expertly pitched. Pat was getting the non-too-subtle feeling that here were two people who relished a bit of local gossip and she wanted to signal that whatever gossip there was, she was well up for hearing it.

'A funny onion?' said the man. 'I'd put it somewhat differently.'

'Donald,' said his wife, but rather perfunctorily, Pat thought.

'Jean,' said Donald. 'Don't give me all that guff about not speaking ill of the dead. You know as well as I do that that playing field would be up and running if it wasn't for Nev Hilton putting his spoke in.'

Jean looked wistfully at Pat. 'This village used to have a cricket team and a football team. Some of us were thinking that if we could get the field sorted, get them going again, it might bring a bit of life back into the place.'

'And Nev stopped it?' asked Pat.

'His Lordship objected,' said Donald. 'The field's behind his house, see. Big letter of complaint to the parish council. His back gate gives on to the field, says it's a security hazard, too much noise – like there aren't some right old hullabaloos coming from that holiday let of his!'

Pat seized her chance. 'Like the one going off the night he died?' Again, that expert inflection in her voice. Again, significant glances were exchanged.

'*That* wasn't anything to do with the holiday let,' said Jean. 'That was Neville Hilton himself. Out in the garden for the whole world to hear.'

'I'm not surprised the man had a heart attack,' said Donald. 'I certainly wouldn't fancy my chances against her.'

'By her you mean his wife?' asked Pat.

Donald nodded. 'The not-so-merry widow herself.'

'But didn't she tell the police she was in Carlisle?'

'She might well have told them that,' said Jean. 'But according to Judy Bestall, she was out in the garden giving poor Neville a right old doing.'

Donald nodded in confirmation. 'It's a foolish man who attacks Ffion Hilton,' he said.

'*Attacks*?' said Pat. '*Neville* was attacking his wife?' Pat pictured that smug figure with the toothy grin.

Both of them nodded. 'Fair going for her he was,' said Jean.

Pat was having great difficulty picturing this. 'And this Judy saw it?' she asked.

'It's not what Judy saw as what she heard,' said Jean. She paused dramatically. 'First of all, she shouts out, "*That'll teach you.*" And then she screams at the top of her voice, "*Have pity on me.*" You don't say that unless someone's doing something you want them to stop, do you?'

'"*You need to go to a charm school!*"' The plump lady nodded avidly at Liz. 'Then she says, "*For pity's sake!*"' She cast a nervous glance at the honey-coloured barn conversion directly across the lane. 'And now—' Her voice changed, became sadder. 'And now she's on her own like me.'

Liz regarded the lady with feelings of sympathy. With her pink sparkly head covering and her thick Birmingham accent, she struck Liz as somewhat out of place in Hollinby Quernhow and indeed as rather lonely. The eagerness with which she'd struck up conversation spoke of someone for whom chatting was the breath of life, and yet something she was not getting much of a chance to do. Her house, 'SidrahNick', a long, low amalgam of what looked like three cottages joined together, stood at the quieter end of the village, directly opposite the Hilton residence just before the lane looped out into the fields. The woman's stall was the only one for at least four or five dwellings, and seemed as lonely as its stallholder. Liz looked at the woman, who she guessed must be Sidrah. And Nick? The woman's wedding ring, plus the poignant collection of men's bric-a-brac and prominent Cancer Support collection bucket told their own sad story.

'And this argument took place in the garden?' she asked.

'According to Judy the dog walker lady.' Sidrah fanned herself vigorously with a Haynes motoring manual. 'She was walking her Whisky at the playing field at the back.'

Liz wondered how Ffion had had the nerve to lie so blatantly to the police. Panic perhaps? Years of dealing with miscreants in her class had taught her people were apt to tell the most obvious whoppers when faced with their wrongdoings.

'But you didn't see this row?' she asked. Surely from here any altercation in the garden of the Old Barn, or even in front of the adjacent Snuggery would have been hard to miss?

'No.' Sidrah shook her head regretfully. 'No, I'd have been Zooming round then. I usually have a catch-up Zoom with the people who work for me round six thirty, just to finish off the week. Of course, if I'd been out in the garden—' She cast a loving glance towards the neat ranks and rows of vegetation flanking the side of the cottage. From there, Liz reckoned, she'd have an almost flawless view of the comings and goings at the Old Barn.

'It is a lovely garden,' said Liz looking at the expertly tended plants, and unlike Pat there was genuine admiration in her voice. 'You're having better luck with your forsythia than I am.'

Sidrah nodded, all at once her face eager. 'It's keeping up with the watering,' she said. 'I'm just crossing everything hoping they don't bring this here hosepipe ban in.'

'You and me both,' said Liz with feeling. 'But you're keeping on top of things so far—'

'I've always loved my garden,' said Sidrah. 'And now it gives me something to do of an evening.' Her voice sounded suddenly lost and her gaze lingered over the table with its silk ties and the men's hairbrush set.

'It was so sad about Nev Hilton,' said Liz. 'It just goes to show you never know what's round the corner.'

Sidrah gave a heartfelt nod of agreement. 'Ain't that the truth.'

'And to have a row like that just before he died!' She felt rather bad changing the subject like this, but at the end of the day there were things she wanted to find out, and there was always the chance Zippy Doodah could appear, or indeed Ffion Hilton.

'I wonder what on earth it could have been about?'

'Summat big, it must have been.' Once again Sidrah's face was eager. '*For pity's sake* – that's what Ffion was shouting – and you don't say that unless you're thoroughly hacked off.'

Liz wondered. To her it seemed a rather restrained choice of words for someone who was really angry. 'I wonder what it was he'd done?' she said.

Sidrah shrugged. 'It could have been anything,' she said. 'Always chuntering on about something Nev was – people parking, cutting down trees, all that kerfuffle about the playing field. And bless him, he would never admit he was wrong in any way, shape or form.'

'So, he wasn't popular?' said Liz.

'I wouldn't say *that* so much,' said Sidrah. 'I mean there was no actual harm in the guy. It's just no one actually liked him very much.' She was about to say more when the hollow clop of hooves made her look up, eyes widening in alarm. 'Hello, Ffion,' she called with the false brightness of someone rapidly changing the subject.

With a thrill of fear Liz turned to see the taut, ramrod figure of the second Mrs Hilton, advancing in stately fashion down the lane atop a vast brown horse. With her look of stony detachment, she put Liz in mind of a general leading her troops into battle. Ffion nodded briefly at Sidrah and would probably not have even noticed Liz had it not been for the two loud sneezes she gave vent to. The woman's eyes slid over to her and disinterest shifted into a puzzled frown of recognition. Hastily Liz turned away, taking a sudden interest in some rather hideous stripy socks.

'Does she have a stable at the Old Barn?' Liz asked when she was sure that the disdainful figure was out of earshot. Sidrah shook her head.

'No. There's these stables at the edge of the village on the Marley Road. It's where she works. I don't mind saying' – she lowered her voice conspiratorially – 'she can have a right temper on her. And she's been right funny lately, ever since Nev died.'

'She's likely upset,' ventured Liz.

Sidrah shook her head. 'I know for a fact a couple of people have called round to see if she was okay. I mean I was only too glad to see people after my Nick passed. But apparently, she all but shut the door in their face.'

'Grief can take people in different ways,' said Liz gently. She looked thoughtfully down the lane where the disdainful figure on the huge horse had disappeared round the corner.

Sidrah rolled her eyes. 'If she *is* grieving,' she said. 'Funny sort if grieving in my book.'

'Do you think,' said Liz, feeling another sneeze brewing, 'she was lying to the police about being in Carlisle?'

Sidrah nodded. 'She must have been. But having said that I don't know how she did it.'

Liz frowned. 'Did what?'

'Well, she must be a bit of a magician.' Sidrah glanced uneasily in the direction of the disappearing horse. 'The camera doesn't lie, does it?'

'I'm sorry,' said Liz. 'Camera?'

'I have CCTV,' said Sidrah. 'When I heard what had happened, I had a look to see if she *had* come home. I usually see her if I'm in the garden. Hard to miss her, that ruddy great tank she drives. But when I get on the Zoom – well, as my Nick used to say, a helicopter could land in the garden and I wouldn't notice.'

'So, you checked your CCTV?' prompted Liz.

Sidrah nodded avidly. 'That's the odd bit,' she said. 'Nothing and no one came to the house until Nev gets in. So, either Ffion must've been in the house all along or she had a cloak of invisibility.'

In the distance the brass band had stopped, leaving only the soporific hum of insects. Unlike her friends, Thelma wasn't

49

actually talking to any stallholders. Instead, she was standing in the overgrown playing fields at the back of the Old Barn, seeing what she could see of the property behind its thick hawthorn hedge. At one time the Old Barn had been exactly that – a barn – but now, like so many agricultural buildings, it had been handsomely and expensively remade into an embalmed version of its former self. What had been utilitarian gaps in the walls for light and access had been remodelled into features of stone lintels and deep-set glass. The doors that had once admitted livestock and machinery were now imposing oak barriers studded with iron.

Taking care to avoid the nettles, Thelma moved closer to the hedge into which was set a tall black gate, which was actually more of a door, with one of those old-fashioned latch handles. She tried peering through the unkempt hedge, where she could just make out the vague shapes of buildings. The Old Barn and to the right of it a squat square building – presumably the Snuggery where Neville had been found. Was the gate open? Would anyone notice if she took a quick look? She stepped back, unsure, and sent up a quick prayer for guidance.

'Are you looking for summat?' The voice was grim and belonged to a large woman with a dour face sporting, in spite of the heat, a thick brown cardigan and orange pedal pushers. Beside her stood a tiny chihuahua dog; both were regarding her accusingly.

'I'm here for the village festival,' said Thelma.

'Well, you won't find it *here*,' said the woman with dour satisfaction. 'In fact, you'd be hard put to find much of it *anywhere*. I said to people, "Why bother with a community festival when there's no fookin' community to speak of?"'

'There seemed to be some people,' said Thelma mildly.

The woman snorted. 'The tea tent's from Leeds, the cake stall's from Boroughbridge and the brass band's from the other side of Darlington. And if you're wondering why it's all gone quiet, the tenor horn's passed out from heat exhaustion.' She nodded with grim satisfaction.

'Oh dear,' said Thelma and, nodding politely, turned to go.

'I saw you at Neville Hilton's funeral,' said the woman, and such was the command in her voice that Thelma found herself stopping in her tracks. 'You're friends with that Liz whatserface – her who goes to pre-diabetes awareness.'

So, thought Thelma, this must be the famous Zippy Doodah.

'I am,' she acknowledged.

'And you knew Nev Hilton?'

'Yes, I did,' said Thelma.

'So, you know this was his house?' The voice was now heavy with suspicion.

Yet again, Thelma nodded. 'I do,' she said.

Zippy Doodah fixed her with an uncompromising look and Thelma realised that here was no fool and that this was one of those situations where evasions and half-truths were going to cut very little ice. 'Actually,' she said, 'there's a couple of us – myself, Liz – who are a little concerned about Neville's death and were wondering what it was that really happened that night.'

Zippy Doodah said nothing but regarded her searchingly for a long moment, as if coming to some decision. Finally, she spoke. 'As you've no doubt heard, a row is what happened,' she said. 'How Judy Bestall was walking her dog right here and heard everything?'

Thelma nodded. 'Is there any chance that I could speak to this Judy Bestall?'

Zippy Doodah gave a grim snort of laughter. 'You'd have a job,' she said. 'She's gone to her daughter's in Malaga, not back for at least three weeks. I said: "Judy, love, you're wasting your money; it's hotter here than it is there."'

Three weeks? Thelma sighed inwardly. Was she going to have to wait three weeks before finding anything else out?

'But she told you about the row?' she said to Zippy.

Zippy nodded. 'A load of shouting, according to Judy. Fair bellowing, she was.'

'And this was his wife?'

'Who else would it be?' There was a restrained note in Zippy's voice that made Thelma wonder what she was thinking.

'And did they often argue – Neville and Ffion?' she asked.

Zippy considered. 'Not that I heard,' she said grudgingly. 'But she's a sullen madame, is Ffion Hilton. Not that I ever have much to do with her. And she's someone who does herself no favours. A few of us locals went round after Nev's death – to see how she was doing – she all but told us where to go.' She shook her head and it suddenly struck Thelma that despite the gruff exterior here was someone who was rather isolated in this non-community of holiday lets and second homes.

'Why do you think she was shouting at him?' she asked. Zippy gave Thelma a look heavy with significance.

'I've no idea,' she said eventually. 'If, of course, it *was* her.'

'You think it might have been someone else shouting at him?'

Yet again Zippy shrugged. 'I've no idea. I wasn't there,' she said dampeningly. 'Oh, and if you're wondering about this here gate' – she nodded at the black door set into the hedge – 'I can tell you Neville keeps it locked. Used to tell anyone who'd listen how it's fastened with two padlocks and three bolts.' To demonstrate her point she grabbed the latch and gave a dismissive shove.

With a gentle whine the door swung inwards, giving a perfect view of a blank wall of the Old Barn and that small, squat building with wide windows that was the Snuggery.

CHAPTER SIX

Sunday 13th July

'Liz Newsome – just because the woman clocked you from her horse, it does not mean she's out to get you.' Pat sounded weary as she fanned her shining face with her floppy white sun hat. Once again, the patio doors of the garden centre were wide open, but today this only served to make the interior almost as hot as outside. The young lad stacking trays of dirty crockery from people's Sunday brunches was bright pink under his apron and black T-shirt.

'You didn't see the way she looked at me,' said Liz, fumbling for a tissue. The pollen count seemed to have gone up a notch overnight and her itchy eyes felt like they must be bulging from her head.

'According to Jean and Donald, she's like that with everyone. Both Sidrah and your pal Zippy Doodah said how she was turning people away when they were calling to see how she was. Anyway—' Pat fished the coral-pink fan from her handbag and leaned back in her chair, allowing the cool draught to play over her face and neck. 'So we're thinking Mrs Neville Hilton the Second snuck into the garden via this back door? Then let rip at Neville and . . .' She let her words tail off as she made a discreet but graphic gesture with the fan.

Liz emitted two worried sneezes. 'And then lied to the police about being there,' she concluded, blowing her nose.

Pat looked across at Thelma who was writing in her old green mark book. 'You're being very quiet,' she said.

'I'm sorry,' said Thelma. 'I was just jotting down everything I saw, I didn't get the chance before church. Now—' She looked up 'What was it you heard again?'

'There was some argy-bargy in the garden, and Ffion shouted have pity or for pity's sake or some such at Neville,' said Pat a trifle impatiently. It was so hot she had neither energy nor appetite to eat her Melmerby slice, which wasn't like her at all. Thelma nodded, and considered a moment. 'Does none of that strike you as odd?' she said eventually.

'Not particularly,' said Pat. 'Why should it? People say all sorts when they're upset.'

'And we're only hearing what people heard from this Judy person,' said Liz.

'Exactly,' said Thelma. 'That's my point *exactly*—'

A shrill cascade of trills broke into the moment and they all wordlessly looked at Thelma's phone, sitting on the table next to her iced mango juice.

'Jax Hilton,' said Thelma.

'Jax Shally,' said Pat. 'Ringing for the third time. Turn it off.'

'It might be important,' said Liz.

'Or,' said Pat, 'it might be "*Hi. How are you getting on with solving my ex-husband's death? Shall I leave it with you?*"' Her mimicry was spot on and the other two smiled.

'I can't turn it off,' said Thelma. 'Teddy's going to let me know when he's likely to be finishing his Sunday deliveries. We're planning an expedition to the pick-your-own.'

'Rather you than me in this heat,' said Pat.

'Anyway,' said Liz. 'Go on with what you were saying.'

She eyed Thelma's drink. How many sugar cubes were in a glass of mango juice? A lot, she guessed gloomily. They'd had a rather nice mango drink at home but following Jacob's blitzkrieg it had been summarily replaced with bottles of sparkling water.

'Well,' said Thelma. 'There's a couple things that strike me about this altercation. First of all, there's the question of *where* it took place.'

'In the garden,' said Pat.

'But no one saw it in the garden,' said Thelma. 'Judy Bestall only heard it. She was in the back field, remember – she couldn't have actually seen anything much through that hedge. But remember, too, it was the first of the hot days so in all likelihood the windows would have been open.'

'So, this row was happening inside?' said Liz. 'That would make more sense.'

'You wouldn't row with your wife outside,' agreed Pat. 'You'd get them inside the house then give them a roasting.'

'No,' said Thelma. 'Not in the house. The Old Barn is set back from the field. If they'd been in the house, Judy might have heard raised voices but not made out the words.'

'The Snuggery!' said Liz.

Thelma nodded. 'It's right next to the back hedge – and one of the living room windows directly faces it.'

'And it's where Neville was found dead,' agreed Pat. 'Okay, so let's say Neville was arguing with Ffion inside the holiday flat.'

'But why were Neville and Ffion in the Snuggery and not the house?' said Liz, fumbling for a tissue.

Thelma gave them a look they knew well – her 'denouement look' as Pat termed it.

'If it was Ffion,' said Thelma.

There was a pause as these words sunk in.

'But surely this Judy said she'd heard Ffion?' said Liz.

'She heard a woman and assumed it was Nev's wife. But she didn't see her. And Ffion had gone off to Carlisle on some horse event, remember.'

'So she told the police,' said Liz darkly, remembering the stony-faced figure on the horse.

'People didn't seem to think so,' said Pat.

'She could've lied,' said Liz. Both a liar and a murderer? She shivered.

'But did anyone actually see Ffion?' said Thelma. 'That's the question. Everyone's saying she lied to the police, but the police would've checked her story. And there was an event in Carlisle that Friday. I looked it up – it started at eight thirty so Ffion would have had to leave Hollinby at six thirty at the latest.'

'Maybe she got there late,' said Pat.

Thelma nodded. 'That is possible, but when you look at the fact this row was in the Snuggery, you have to at least consider the possibility it might have been someone else.'

'Who?' asked Liz.

Thelma shrugged. 'That,' she said, 'is the million-dollar question.'

'Maybe a burglar?' suggested Liz. 'Nev saw something wrong, maybe the door open, went in and confronted him?'

Thelma shook her head. '*Her.* Judy assumed the voice belonged to his wife, remember.'

'Her then,' said Pat. 'You can get female burglars.'

'But remember the phone call Neville got at Rotary,' said Thelma. 'Calling him back to the house. You wouldn't get a burglar doing that – and you're less likely to have a total stranger screaming the odds at you.'

At that moment there was another burst of sound, this time a tinny version of the theme from *Flashdance*. Pat rolled her eyes, retrieved her phone and pointedly turned it off.

'Thank you and goodnight, Ms Shally,' she said. 'So where were we?'

'If it wasn't Ffion, who was Neville arguing with?' said Liz. 'And why?'

Thelma patted the green mark book. 'The only clues we've got are what was said—'

'And that's all second hand.' Pat gloomily gave herself another fan with the sun hat. In response, Thelma turned the battered green tome towards her friends, who both smiled faintly at this remnant from their former life, conjuring benign ghosts of spelling scores, dinner registers, lists of readers. On an empty page of the squared paper, Thelma had neatly drawn two columns.

'What Judy Bestall heard, and repeated to others, falls into two parts,' she said, pointing to the page. Her neat, clear-varnished nail indicated a sentence written at the top of the first column in her neat, rounded teacher-script. *That'll teach you.* The nail moved to the second column where was written: *Have pity on me.* 'That's what Jean and Donald said Judy heard,' she said.

'But how can that help?' said Pat. 'They were just repeating what this Judy Doody told them.'

'No, they weren't repeating,' said Thelma. 'That's the whole nature of hearsay. The mind of the listener picks up on the detail that seems important to them.' Her friends looked at her blankly. 'Remember Margo Benson's chimney?'

Light slowly dawned.

'Everyone was up in arms,' said Liz slowly, 'because someone thought they'd heard Margo say she was walking around with the flu.'

'When all along,' said Thelma, 'it was her chimney flue that was blocked.'

'I don't see how that helps us there though,' said Pat.

Thelma turned to Liz. 'What did Sidrah tell you Judy heard?'

Liz frowned. ' *"You should go to a charm school"* and *"For pity's sake"*,' said Liz.

Thelma nodded, writing furiously.

Thelma turned the book round again and the three friends looked at the neat handwriting. In the first column was written: *That'll teach you* and *You should go to a charm school*; in the second: *Have pity on me* and *For pity's sake*.

'I think we can guess the first part,' said Thelma. 'If you take the words *teach* and *school*.'

'Education!' Liz's triumphant cry made people on adjoining tables look round in surprise. 'She was saying something to do with education!'

'Nev worked for Lodestone Trust,' said Pat slowly.

Thelma nodded. 'And before that he was a head teacher – and an Ofsted inspector.'

'So, this person – whoever they were – was shouting something about education,' said Pat. 'But what about the other part? *Have pity on me – for pity's sake?*'

Thelma frowned. 'That's the bit I'm struggling with,' she admitted.

'Whoever she was, she must have been asking him to stop doing something,' said Liz. 'Have pity—'

'For pity's sake,' said Pat. 'That's not asking anyone to stop anything—'

'It's how the words were spoken that doesn't match,' said Thelma stirring her mango juice. 'Judy Bestall was quite clear the tone was angry – shouting. You don't generally beg for mercy in angry tones – and you'd tend to say, "for pity's sake" if you were feeling exasperated, not angry.' She sighed and took a sip of her drink. 'And of course there is always the possibility it was Ffion shouting at him after all.'

'Well, we've got somewhere,' said Pat. She thought for a second. 'I could always email Chris Canne at Lodestone. See if he knows anything about Neville. Maybe that's why he was looking so uneasy at the funeral.'

'And I could talk to Becky Clegg at St Barnabus,' said Liz. 'She used to work with Neville when he was a head teacher over in Northallerton.'

'That's if we want to,' said Thelma calmly. The three looked at each other. There was a lot to be said for just letting the whole matter slip into that vast catalogue of the strange and unexplained.

'It's that lass, that Chelsey,' said Liz eventually. She faced her friends, resolutely dismissing any thoughts of a scary woman on horseback. 'It's her I keep thinking of – her feeling like it was her fault in some way.'

'Exactly as Ms Shally expected you'd feel,' said Pat tartly.

Thelma stiffened. 'Talking of.'

They all followed her glance. Yet again the brassy ponytail was threading its way through the slicing beams of sun, atop an ensemble of emerald green and a glittery gold sun visor.

'I tried ringing but you weren't picking up,' Jax announced, sitting herself down. 'All day I've been saying to myself: I wonder how they got on in Hollinby yesterday. So' – she looked expectantly round – 'how did you get on in Hollinby?'

Liz and Pat watched as Thelma gave a brief but circumspect account of their trip to the Hollinby Quernhow Village Festival. All three were feeling (yet again) ambushed, and at the same time instinctively reluctant to share much of their thinking. There was the unvoiced certainty that, however vague their theories, there was a pretty good chance they'd end up plastered across Jax's various social media platforms within the hour.

As Thelma finished, Jax nodded. 'I said to myself: *Jax, there must've been something going off.* You don't just drop down dead like that. And there's Ffion screaming in his face.'

'If it *was* Ffion,' said Pat.

'Who else would it have been?' said Jax. There was a slightly loaded pause and Thelma put a protective hand on the green notebook. 'I've always said to myself, *I've an odd feeling about you,*

Miss Ffion,' said Jax. She sighed a long deep sigh. 'I don't mind telling you, this whole thing has proper shook me up.'

'How's Chelsey?' asked Pat in a pointed tone, which was totally lost on Jax. The brassy ponytail shook glumly. 'Terrible,' she said. 'A right state. And there's me having to do all me Friday and Saturday holiday lets on my Jack Jones.'

'Has the lass seen anyone?' ask Liz worriedly.

Jax rolled her eyes. 'She finally gets in to see the doctor – but you wouldn't believe the waiting list for counselling. Nearly a year! I said she should go private but she's not got that sort of money. No, the only thing that'll put Chelsey's mind at rest is if we can tell her exactly what happened to poor Nev.'

She looked at the three friends. The three friends looked back.

'What had you in mind?' said Thelma noncommittally.

'What someone needs to do,' said Jax, 'is physically go into that flat. See if there's anything they can find out. Something to take to the police to prove Ffion was lying to them.'

There was a pointed pause, marked by a suppressed sneeze from Liz.

'What about the people staying there?' asked Pat. 'They won't be happy to have us all traipsing in.'

Jax shook her head. 'She's cancelled all the holiday lets, so the place is just sitting there empty. And, anyroad, I have to do a clean in there – the place hasn't been touched since they found Nev. I just need someone to come in with me.' She looked at them appealingly, ponytail bent in supplication. 'I'm like Chelse, I just can't face going in there on my own.'

'I'm going to St Barnabus to talk to Becky Hunter,' said Liz firmly.

'And I'm going to Lodestone to talk to Chris Canne,' said Pat equally firmly.

Jax turned her stare on Thelma. 'Come on then, Thelma,' she said. 'How about it?'

CHAPTER SEVEN

Monday 14th July

Text sent from St Barnabus Lodestone Primary Academy to parents:

Our end-of-term picnic and bouncy castle WILL take place today, but children MUST come wearing sun hats and with sunblock ALREADY applied.

It was blessedly cool in the converted church that formed the headquarters of Lodestone Academy Trust; from high up in the vaulted ceiling, vents were discreetly breathing gusts of chilled air. As Pat approached the panelled door with its tasteful crimson nameplate, she heard voices from within. Unsure, she paused. Surely the receptionist had said to go straight on through? Tentatively she knocked. The door opened, and Chris Canne's flustered face appeared.

'Pat,' he said, ushering her in, 'I'm just finishing a Zoom call.'

Following him in, Pat could see his office had changed since her previous visits. Then the walls had been adorned with multiple pictures of children working, now these had all gone and the white walls repainted a restful lemon colour. One of these walls was totally dominated by an enormous flatscreen, the size of something to be found in a small art-house cinema; this was currently showing a mosaic of headshots with attendant glimpses of backgrounds. Chris smiled distractedly at Pat and waved her into a seat, before addressing the screen.

'Okay, folks,' he said brightly, 'I reckon that's just about a wrap. And it's fifteen minutes off the magic hour of one o'clock. I'm guessing that no one's had the dreaded Ofsted call?'

The various faces shook their heads or gestured with a thumbs up. Chris gave a relieved smile.

'In which case,' he said, 'everyone have a *brilliant* summer! And if you could all ping your Audits of Readiness across to Jared by close of play, we can get them across to Bun so she can work her magic ready for us to hit the ground running come September!'

The faces began blinking out of existence one by one, until only one remained filling the entire screen, a woman with red earrings that caught the sunlight that was streaming in from her right-hand side. Her background stood out as a vivid contrast to the others, with their rather anaemic collection of bookshelves and noticeboards; this woman faced the world against a backdrop of vibrant red and orange drapes.

'I meant to say earlier, Bun,' said Chris to the woman, 'I've been hearing such great things about these Ofsted readiness sessions you've been running in our schools.' Pat thought she could detect a slightly nervous timbre to his jovial tones. 'And vis-à-vis any Ofsted action planning – there's totally no pressure whatsoever. It's the end of term next week so we can easily park this till September.'

'I'm going to be totally honest with you, Chris.' The woman's deep, contralto voice resonated out into the office. 'I'm finding all this constant harping on about Ofsted readiness more than a little disconcerting.'

Chris pulled nervously at his collar. 'Understood,' he said, nodding. 'One hundred per cent do I see where you're coming from, Bun!' He took a deep breath, Adam's apple shifting uneasily.

'But at the end of the day, surely it's about balancing the needs of the school with government expectations, isn't it?'

'But is it?' Bun sounded dismissive. She was as striking as her drapes, a bright orange scarf twined in her hair, eyes heavily ringed with kohl eyeliner. She put Pat in mind of a book she used to regularly read to her class: *Hey, Mrs Kohl Panda, what can you see?*

When the woman shook her head, her deep red earrings winked in the sunlight. 'Chris, I think you have to ask yourself: are we about educating children or are we about passing Ofsted inspections? Because sometimes I *wonder*.' Abruptly she clicked off her screen and the face was replaced by the corporate logo of Lodestone Academy Trust.

'Bun Widdup,' said Chris with a rueful smile as he turned to Pat. 'A real force of nature and a gifted school improvement planner. Like all of us, she finds Ofsted a challenge.'

'I remember what a strain it all was,' said Pat. 'And that was just in one school. I can't imagine how it must be with the number of schools you have to oversee.'

'Twenty-seven,' said Chris. 'Eleven of which are in the Ofsted window. But we know we won't get any this week – and with so many schools breaking up on Friday we're off the hook until September.' His face broke into a sunny, relieved smile. 'Anyway – brilliant to see you, Pat. Thanks for coming in – and so quickly! You're looking great!'

'So are you,' said Pat politely. This wasn't strictly true – there were noticeable purple smudges under the man's eyes. As if calling out the social lie he vented an enormous yawn.

'I'm so sorry,' he said. 'My nights are somewhat broken at the moment.' He swivelled his laptop round to show a screensaver of his husband, Tony, holding a very determined-looking toddler with beautiful almond-shaped eyes and a ferocious jut to his chin. 'Meet Oskar,' he said.

'How lovely,' said Pat warmly. 'How old is he?'

'Just fourteen months,' said Chris, biting off another almighty yawn. 'Excuse me!' He shook his head vigorously as if trying to wake himself up by sheer force of will. 'We're on with routine embedment. All the manuals agree it's important to establish those sleep parameters, but I don't mind admitting it's a struggle.'

Pat found herself biting her lip. 'I'm not sure toddlers do sleep parameters.'

Chris nodded his way through yet another yawn. 'I was sorry not to get to talk properly to you all at Nev's funeral,' he said awkwardly.

'Well, we all had to hurry off,' said Pat diplomatically. 'But that's why I'm here now. Nev Hilton. There's something a bit odd I want to ask you about.'

Chris Canne nodded as if his worst fears were being confirmed. 'Oh God,' was all he said, but his manner forcibly reminded Pat of that other time when he'd been faced with the news of misdemeanours going on at St Barnabus's school. Obviously there was some story there, but then she'd already guessed as much from the sheer speed with which he'd responded to her email that morning, asking her to come in as soon as she possibly could.

'Why? Had something happened with Neville?' she asked, reflecting her suspicions had been right.

Chris looked at her, as if trying to make his mind up about something. 'You go first,' he said.

Puzzled and curious, Pat briefly outlined recent events: the overheard shouting, the stricken look on Neville's dead face, and that mysterious yellow line. When she'd finished, Chris didn't look quite so uncomfortable.

'I see,' he said. 'Or rather I *don't* see. And I don't think it can have anything to do with what happened here. I don't think so.'

'What *did* happen here?' asked Pat.

Chris looked at her cautiously, almost appraisingly. 'If I tell you,' he said eventually, 'you must promise to keep this to yourself. Even though the guy's dead, he still has rights – or his widow does.'

Pat nodded, intrigued. 'Of course,' she said. Telling Thelma and

Liz didn't count, not really – and surely Chris must realise she'd share this with her friends.

Chris Canne took a gulp from his steel water bottle. 'The thing is,' he said replacing the top, 'the thing is – if something untoward had happened to Nev Hilton – well – I wouldn't be at all surprised.'

Even in these glossy days of corporate education, St Barnabus Primary Academy was looking especially polished, Liz thought. Walking through the hot, heavy corridors of her former workplace, she noticed how every display had been crisply and immaculately labelled, every surface pristine. There was none of the endemic clutter schools generate, especially towards the end of the school year – orphaned pumps, discarded reading books, lidless felt tips. But surely the school was breaking up for summer at the end of the week?

'It's all looking very smart,' she said to Linda Barley in puzzled tones.

The office manager rolled her eyes. 'It's amazing the effect the word Ofsted can have,' she said, opening a door labelled 'Documentation Hub'.

'Is the school due an inspection?' Liz had to fight down the instinctive flutter that the dreaded 'O' word had brought, firmly reminding herself she was retired.

Linda sighed. 'Our Ofsted window is well and truly wide open,' she said, fanning herself. 'However, come one o'clock I reckon—' she glanced at her watch '—that'll be us clear until September, fingers crossed. Just in ten more minutes. So, you wait here, lovey. Becky'll be down with you in two secs.'

Left alone, Liz looked round the room – a small space that she remembered as being used as something of a dumping ground by the PTA. Now cleared of dusty tombola prizes and bags of polystyrene cups, it was dominated by a smart conference table and shelves. Lots and lots of shelves crammed with a profusion of ring binders, folders and magazine boxes, each one bearing a neat, printed label – *School Development Plan, Minutes of Governor's Meetings, Latest Policies A–F.*

'Welcome to the War Room.'

Liz turned and saw Becky Clegg, the head teacher, standing in the doorway, a smile fighting her habitual frown. Her face was slightly flushed in the heat, her frizzy red hair tamed by a series of brilliant green hair slides.

'*War room?*' said Liz. Becky nodded.

'As decreed by Chris Canne and the trust, God love them. It's where we're to have every last scrap of documentation that Ofsted could possibly want. All schools in Lodestone Trust due an Ofsted have to have one.'

She walked forward and gave Liz a brief and uncharacteristic hug.

'It's good to see you,' she said and flopped down in a chair the way energetic people do, slumped back and outstretched legs reminding Liz as ever of her old Raggedy Ann doll.

'I remember how stressful it all was,' said Liz. 'Waiting for the Ofsted call to come.'

Becky nodded. 'It's like waiting for an exam,' she said, pouring herself a glass of water from the jug on the table. 'Only you've no idea when it will be or what the questions are.' She held the glass against her forehead. 'There's literally thousands of things they could ask you about.'

'And you're expected to have a full and detailed answer for each and every one,' finished Liz.

Becky nodded wearily; she seemed to be wilting in the heat. 'Everyone's been hoping and hoping they won't come until September. Every Monday morning we've all been like cats on hot bricks in case the call comes, but if I'm being honest I'm wishing it was all over and done, so we can all enjoy our summer.'

'I completely understand. It's very good of you to find the time to see me,' said Liz. 'I know what the end of term is like even without Ofsted hanging over you.'

Becky smiled and took a thirsty gulp. 'I always, *always* have time for you and your friends after what you did for the school – and for me.'

Liz nodded, remembering that whole nasty business of the poison pen letters – that horrible, creeping tension in school. Surely waiting for Ofsted couldn't be as bad?

'Anyway.' Becky's voice broke into her train of thought. 'How can I help you?'

'Neville Hilton,' said Liz simply.

Becky took another gulp of water and eyed her thoughtfully. 'I'd heard he'd died of course,' she said. 'And I had half a mind to go to the funeral but we were full on here.' She gestured absently round the War Room.

'You worked with him, didn't you? In Northallerton?'

Becky nodded. 'He was my head teacher at Bullamoor Park.' She looked at Liz. 'So d'you think there's maybe something odd about his death?'

Liz flinched somewhat at Becky's characteristic directness. It was a very sudden conclusion she'd jumped to – and one that was very close to the truth. How much should she say?

'Why d'you ask that?' she said, stalling for time.

Becky shrugged. 'I don't know, it just seemed a bit sudden, him dying like that,' she said. 'He wasn't that old and' – her face broke into a smile – 'I know you and your friends!'

Liz decided to ignore that. 'I'm interested to know what he was like to work for,' she said.

Becky nodded thoughtfully, considering. 'He could be fine,' she said. 'Or he could be an absolute *nightmare.*'

Chris Canne looked earnestly at Pat. 'What I'm going to tell you is totally confidential. HR would roast my you-know-whats if they knew I'd spoken about this.' He leaned back in his chair, plaiting his fingers as he remembered. 'It was back in February, when we were appointing for the job, and Nev was on our short list,' he said. 'He was a strong candidate – excellent application, good references – a few years of being an Ofsted inspector under his belt. And then three days before the interview I got a call from Ken, the CEO at Quays Academy Trust. He said he'd heard there were some disturbing things about Nev that maybe I should look into. And then later that day Chantelle from Finefare Academy rang me, saying much the same thing: disturbing rumours I might want to find out more about.'

'What disturbing rumours?' asked Pat. Chris shook his head unhappily. 'That's just it,' he said. 'No one seemed to know. Just ... something we might want to check out. Naturally we got HR onto it, but they couldn't find a thing. A couple of complaints about a couple of the Ofsteds he'd led, but that's par for the course with an inspector.'

'Did you not find out who was starting these rumours?' asked Pat.

'No one seemed to know,' said Chris. 'Everyone we spoke to had heard them from someone who'd heard them from someone else—'

Pat nodded. For all its flatscreens and state-of-the-art media, this world of corporate trusts wasn't so very different from the world of the primary school staffroom.

'Believe you me,' said Chris, 'HR were all over it like a rash,' he said. 'IT, safeguarding, the lot. But there was nothing we could find, so in the end there didn't seem any reason we couldn't go ahead with the appointment – especially after the other candidate dropped out ... But ...' He tailed off, frowning.

'But you always wondered?'

Chris nodded. 'Especially after I got to know Nev. I mean the guy was a hard worker, no two ways about it ...' Again his voice tailed off.

'But?' prompted Pat.

'Well, I did hear some of his inspections got a bit fraught – one in Ossett, one in Fulford – a place in the North East called

Pity Me of all things. Some of the names of these places – we've currently got a Gallows Lane on our books!'

'These inspections,' prompted Pat, bringing him back on course.

'Yes, a bit problematic.' Chris nodded. 'Blood on the walls—' He realised what he'd said and stopped short.

'But surely you get that with inspections?' said Pat.

Chris nodded. 'Oh yes, all the time. But then, when he came to work with the team here—' Again he stopped.

'He didn't get on with others?' hazarded Pat.

Chris spoke slowly. 'Nev Hilton was not a people person. He rubbed more than one person up the wrong way.'

Pat remembered that long-ago night at the Busby Stoop. She looked at Chris who was gazing worriedly at the ceiling.

'I always wondered if this might come back to bite us,' he said, almost to himself.

'But it hasn't, has it?' said Pat. 'Not that I can see.'

Chris nodded. 'Do you think something happened to Nev – I mean that night – when you said someone was shouting at him?'

Pat shrugged. 'The police seem satisfied it was a heart attack.'

Chris nodded again, shoulders relaxing. At that moment the door opened and a young man Pat had met once before, Jared Keen, came bouncing in, eyes wide.

'The call has come!' he announced dramatically, completely ignoring Pat.

'Not Ofsted?' Chris half rose, eyes also wide. 'I thought we were in the clear? It's well after one!'

'Wagon Lane,' said Jared. 'They've only just let us know.'

Chris groaned, briefly closed his eyes. 'Wagon Lane,' he said to himself. 'That's all we need at the end of term!'

'I'm getting the inspection team over there now,' said Jared, retreating to the door. 'Jacky Southwart's down in Barnsley. She's going to hotfoot it over there post haste.'

'Pat, I have to go,' said Chris.

Pat, who in this moment was very grateful to be retired, merely nodded.

After Liz finished her account of what had happened at Hollinby Quernhow, Becky took a thoughtful sip of water. 'When I think of Nev I always remember that old saying: intelligence is knowing tomato is a fruit . . . wisdom is knowing not to put it in a fruit salad,' she said.

Liz frowned. 'Neville was intelligent but not wise?' she said.

'He had no sense of how *other* people might be feeling,' said Becky. 'Or if he did, that wasn't important as long as what *he* wanted to happen was happening. It was either his way or the highway, if you get my meaning.'

'But surely,' said Liz. 'Surely you *need* that as a head teacher?'

Becky nodded. 'I'm not saying you don't need to be decisive,' she said. 'It comes back to what I was saying about wisdom – it's what you're decisive *about*.' She gazed at the slab of glaring blue sky visible from the window. 'There was this one time at Bullamoor Park. Our improvement officer had said school needed to improve its attendance scores, so we introduced this rewards system and the kids took it really seriously – I mean really seriously. And there was this one child – she had the day off to attend her grandmother's funeral, but Nev refused point-blank to be flexible about it. The child wasn't in school, so the child could not have her attendance point. There was no end of argy-bargy. It even made the *Northern Echo*.'

Liz nodded. 'So, he was someone who annoyed people.'

Becky nodded. 'Having said that,' she said, 'I mean I don't think he ever meant any actual harm. I honestly don't think the man had a mean bone in his body.'

Maybe not a mean bone, Liz thought, but plenty of obstinate ones. 'So, you couldn't think of anyone who'd wish to attack him?' she said.

'If someone had landed him one in the pub, I could see that,' said Becky. 'But for someone to actually turn up at his house and scream in his face . . .' She shrugged. 'Mind you' – she glanced at the shelves and shelves of ring binders – 'I could imagine him being a bit of a nightmare as an Ofsted inspector.'

'Oh?' said Liz.

Becky frowned at the assembled files on the shelves. 'He wasn't very experienced. He was only a head for what – barely three years? – before he did the inspector training. You see, because of being short-staffed they've been taking on more and more people who haven't got so much experience to be inspectors. You should see some of the comments on my head teacher WhatsApp groups. I'm just praying we don't get one like that.'

The door was abruptly flung open to reveal Linda Barley looking at her watch. 'Five, four, three, two, one, and it's one fifteen!' She gave a little cheer and punched the air. 'Summer starts here!'

Becky stood up, relief palpable on her face in spite of what she'd said earlier, and turned to her office manager, suddenly brisk and business-like.

'Can you tell all the staff please, Linda? Perhaps nip down to the bakery, get some buns? And order the skip for tomorrow. Tell the staff they can start stripping displays and clearing out. Oh, and remind them there's the final Goal Enabling with Bun Widdup Zoom at three fifteen.'

Linda nodded and was gone, leaving Liz briefly wondering what a Bun Widdup Zoom entailed. She stood up. 'I'm going to let you get on,' she said.

'I can't see I've been much help,' said Becky. 'About Nev. The thing is – and I know this sounds horrible – but I just can't see anyone caring enough about him in the first place to do him any actual harm.'

* * *

The afternoon traffic coming out of Leeds was heavy, and even with the air-conditioning on, the air inside the Yeti still felt thick and stuffy. Outside the car everything felt thick and soupy with exhaust fumes. Crawling up Scott Hall Road, Pat felt too tired and heavy to put her tangled thoughts into any semblance of order. What had she actually learned? Those rumours. But *what* had Nev really done to provoke them in the first place? Something that would give anyone any sort of motive for harming him. But what?

The person walking down Scott Hall Road, deep in thought, gave Pat a jolt of recognition but it was that strange thing of seeing a familiar face in an unfamiliar context and as such she didn't immediately recognise Tiffany-Jane.

A very subdued Tiffany-Jane . . .

What on earth was she doing in Leeds? Why was the energetic, motivated Ms T.J. Rox looking so tired and grim? And – and somehow this was the most shocking thing of all – why was she without make-up?

CHAPTER EIGHT

Monday 14th July

Voice of the Vale, Thirsk FM Radio: Today's beat-the-heat tip!

Hey, hot Thirskians! Today's the ideal day to defrost that freezer! And save all those lovely chunks of ice . . . Put them in a bowl in front of a fan – and voila! Your own home air-conditioner!

About two hours later, Jax's cherry-red hatchback could be seen zipping down the lanes to Hollinby Quernhow.

'I could tell Nev hadn't been happy for a while.' Jax smartly changed gear and the car roared accordingly. 'I used to be sat there talking to him and I'd think: *You're not happy.*'

Thelma clutched her seatbelt and tried to focus on what Jax was saying, as opposed to how she was driving. Ideally, she would have driven herself and met Jax at the Old Barn – but things were far from ideal. Again, she thought of the letter that had been awaiting her when she arrived home yesterday and was now sitting unopened in her desk drawer.

No . . . ! Focus on the task in hand, Thelma!

'So, you were still in touch with Neville then?' she said,

reflexively pushing with her braking foot as the car nipped round a bend in the road.

The ponytail nodded vigorously. 'He used to come and chat to me if I were the one doing the Snuggery that week. Have a coffee.' Her voice darkened. 'He was always on his own on a Saturday, on account of you-know-who being off with that horse. Like she supposedly was the night he died.'

'You think Ffion wasn't in Carlisle like she told the police?' said Thelma.

'What she told the police and what she *did* are two different things, I'm thinking.' The ponytail bounced dismissively as Jax angrily changed gear with a clash and a roar. Again Thelma's foot flexed. Time to change the subject.

'Just before Neville started working at Lodestone, he was an Ofsted inspector, wasn't he?' asked Thelma. 'Was that his only work, do you know?'

'It was enough. Wakefield one week, down south the next, up north the week after that. I used to say to him: "Nev, for God's sake slow down."' She sighed and finally, blessedly, slowed down herself as the first of the houses appeared. 'Up and down the country like a blumin' yo-yo, bless him.'

Thelma sighed inwardly. The task of finding one particular person who Neville Hilton had upset seemed to be rapidly taking on needle-in-haystack-like characteristics.

Although lengthening, the shadows were still harsh and sharp in Hollinby Quernhow main street. The deserted main street. There was none of that afternoon bustle you get in even the smallest of places – people delivering leaflets, walking the dog, children coming from a school bus. The place looked to be asleep in the late afternoon sunshine . . . No *not* asleep, Thelma thought, *dead*. Despite the heat of the afternoon she shivered as it suddenly struck her that in a place with so few actual inhabitants the village wasn't such a bad place to stage some kind of dark deed.

With a business-like scrunch of gravel, Jax smartly brought the car to a halt in front of the Old Barn.

'Right.' Jax turned off the engine. '*Right*,' she said again – but she didn't move. For all her brisk tone, she seemed in no particular hurry to get out of the car.

Thelma looked at the empty driveway. 'There doesn't seem to be anyone here,' she said.

'There isn't.' Jax unclipped her seatbelt. 'Ffion's off at the stables today – she always works till gone six on a Monday with late riding lessons.'

Thelma frowned at this. 'Maybe we should come back when she's here?'

'Tuesday, Wednesday and Thursday, I've Helmsley and Masham ladies; Friday, Saturday I'm flat-out with the holiday lets,' said Jax. 'It *has* to be today.' She wrenched open the car door. 'Anyway, Ffion wants me here.'

'Did she say so?' asked Thelma.

'Not in so many words, but the place hasn't been touched since the other week. I bet it's in a right old state.'

As Jax sorted out cleaning materials from the boot of the hatchback, Thelma looked around uneasily. Jax seemed confident enough, and of course there must have been times when she cleaned with neither Mr nor Mrs Hilton being there . . . but even so. To give herself something else to think about, she walked over to the wheelie bin, now standing flush against the wall near the kitchen door. It was easy to see where it would be put for collection, the spot by the gate was delineated by a small, neat sign: *Blue trade waste wheelie bin HERE.* Neville's work no doubt. She walked towards it and stopped in a place where she reckoned the bin would foul the driveway. *Yes.* Turning round, the squat square structure that was the Snuggery was in plain sight. What could be more natural than leaving the bin here if someone were to call you from the front door of the holiday let?

'Oh my God!' Jax's voice cut into the still afternoon, shrill with outrage. Thelma quickly moved to where she was examining a stack of filled charity bags heaped willy-nilly near the front door.

'Well, she hasn't wasted any time,' said Jax, poking in a bag. She straightened, holding up a tie, like a huntsman displaying a kill. 'Nev's Rotary tie – and him only dead five minutes.'

Thelma could see the younger woman was upset and so refrained from pointing out that in fact Neville had been dead for the greater part of five weeks, and that clearing the possessions of those who have left us was one of those enforced, heartbreaking chores that follow in the wake of death.

'That's really upset me,' said Jax plaintively. 'I mean I know Ffion's always bagging up her own stuff and leaving it out, but I thought at least she'd have taken Nev's into the shop herself instead of leaving it out here like it's rubbish.'

'Come on,' said Thelma, gently leading her away. 'Let's do what we came here for.'

Standing on the threshold of the Snuggery, Thelma was struck by that feeling common to holiday cottages lets, the sheer impersonality of the place. No stack of mail jumbled on the hall table, no coats crammed on the pegs, no bags and boots dumped in the hallway. Like so many of the properties in Hollinby Quernhow, the Snuggery was a house but by no means a home.

'Okay . . .' The word was drawn out and there was an uncharacteristic waver in Jax's voice and Thelma became suddenly aware that her friend had not moved since stepping inside the hallway. Indeed, the ponytail was distinctly on the droopy side and a slight tremble was detectable in the hand clutching her plastic bucket of cleaning materials.

'Why not let me go in first?' said Thelma gently.

'I'm just being stupid,' said Jax.

'Not at all.' Followed by Jax, Thelma led the way from room to room – bathroom, bedroom and kitchen – opening windows as they went. The kitchen was especially immaculate, all gleaming glass and steel. On one of the granite worktops stood one of those knife blocks that looked like marble, but were somehow magnetised, four knives glinting in the afternoon sun. It was a make familiar to Thelma through Teddy's delivery work and now she looked more closely at the four knives ... Shouldn't there be *five*? But before she could pursue the idea further Jax's voice broke into her thoughts.

'Chelse said how it had all been left clean.'

Thelma felt puzzled. If Chelsey had specifically said the place was clean, then how come Jax was so insistent the place needed cleaning? Unless Ffion had specifically asked her? She remembered her previous thought: why was the Snuggery so clean in the first place, when its occupant had apparently left in such a hurry? These were the thoughts in Thelma's head as she followed Jax to the living room.

Again Jax stopped.

Thelma laid a hand on the younger woman's shoulder. 'There's absolutely no need for you to go in there,' she said.

'I need to do this,' said Jax.

Thelma nodded and opened the door.

Again, it was the smell that hit them first – musty and stuffy with the merest disagreeable hint of something chemical, but not like any sort of cleaning product ... and something else. In normal times the lounge would be a cheerful sunny room, where the afternoon sun would shine in great dappled beams from the left-hand windows. Now the light poked a finger between closed curtains, highlighting a thin patina of dust covering a state of mild chaos: chairs had been pushed back higgledy-piggledy, a coffee table propped against the wall giving free access to the sofa. The sofa. Grey and opulent, with one gaping white gap where a cushion had been removed. Jax stared at it.

'That'll be where they found him,' she said, her voice quiet. 'They'll have had to bin the cushion because of what happens when you suddenly die.'

Thelma, no stranger to sudden death and its unfortunate physical consequences nodded, was again aware of that faint disagreeable odour. Her attention was focused on the walls. Three of them were dove grey, contrasting pleasingly with the rich red carpet ... but on the *fourth* ...

The line was a pale, vanilla-yellow line, an eerie highlight and a striking contrast against the grey of the wall and red of the carpet. It was about eight inches wide, raggedly uneven at the edges, decidedly amateur-looking when set against the refinement of the rest of the room.

'And you're sure this line wasn't there before?' she said.

Jax nodded adamantly. 'When I last saw that wall, it were just like all the other walls,' she said firmly. 'And Chelse swears the line wasn't there the week before Nev died.'

She turned her head away from the room, suddenly blinking back tears.

'Look,' said Thelma, setting the coffee table down on the carpet. 'Why don't I clean in here? You can do the rest of the house?'

Jax nodded. 'I'm sorry,' she said. 'There's something about being in here I just can't get my head round.'

Left alone, the first thing Thelma did was pull the curtains and open the windows, breathing in relief as the musty air began to dispel in the warm draught. She crossed again to look at the wall and its line. Looking closely, she could see it had been painted with uneven, hasty-looking brushstrokes, with patchy smeared edges. She had hoped that seeing this line close to, it would remind her of something, make sense in some sort of way – but it didn't. Still, seeing it in the context of the room, she supposed she could understand why both the police and Ffion had dismissed it; it didn't look particularly sinister – just *odd*. As if someone had started to decorate but thought better of it.

Taking out her phone she took some photographs, thinking furiously. Chelsey had been adamant it hadn't been there the Saturday before, so it must have been painted at some point in the week leading up to Neville's death. Who had been staying in the holiday let then? Of course, the line could have been painted in the short interval after they'd left, but before Neville arrived home. But *why*?

She stood back facing the wall, with a strong feeling there was something else she needed to see but wasn't. She shut her eyes. *Father, open my eyes*, she prayed. *Open my eyes to see – if there is anything TO see . . .*

She suddenly became aware of some evenly spaced holes, each about a foot apart, running along the top of the wall. Had they held pictures at some point? Surely, they were a bit high up for that? Standing on a footstool she could see they'd been drilled fairly recently – before or after the line had been painted.

She stepped back again, until she felt the backs of her calves brush the sofa. She started. There was something about sitting in that cushionless white gap she found highly distasteful. She took half a step forwards and caught her leg on the coffee table, which wobbled . . . The can of Mr Sheen fell with a startlingly loud clang and rolled away across the floor. Heart pounding Thelma stopped to pick it up – and caught sight of the scrap of paper.

It was a fragment, one straight edge, which looked as if it had been torn off a larger sheet. On it was a symbol of some kind . . . a five-pointed shape, a sort of hybrid between an asterisk and a stick figure.

What was it? Even though she couldn't place it, it was familiar. She knew she'd seen it before somewhere . . . But where?

The elusive thought reminded her of another elusive thought she'd had earlier in the kitchen. Slipping the paper in her pinny pocket, she retraced her steps to the gleaming room. She looked again at the magnetised knife block with its four knives. *Four* knives. Where was number five?

It didn't take long to track it down; it lay glinting and sinister in the top of the dishwasher. The machine hadn't been emptied and the contents sparkled clean – three dinner plates, a tureen, and three teacups. *Three* plates? Had the occupant of the Snuggery been entertaining friends?

The noise of scrunching wheels broke chillingly into her ruminations. Looking out of the kitchen window she could see a black, tank-like four-by-four pulling up next to the cherry-red hatchback. With its battered fenders and spatters of mud it looked as grim and business-like as its driver.

Panicked, Thelma flattened herself against the kitchen wall, out of sight. What to do? She didn't for one minute share Jax's airy assertions that they had a perfect right to be here. She half thought of hiding. But where? The wardrobe was nowhere near big enough and she certainly wasn't crawling under the bed, not with her sciatica. Besides, *she* wasn't the one sneaking in – indeed, she'd been virtually corralled into coming here. Plus – well, Ffion would see the cherry-red hatchback, would know Jax was in the building . . . Thelma frowned. Where *was* she?

'Jax,' she hissed. 'Jax, Ffion's here.' There was no reply. Thelma crept out of the kitchen. She must be in the bathroom, or bedroom – but no. She was on her own in the Snuggery.

She became aware of voices outside.

'I'm doing the clean.' Jax's voice sounded high, almost fluttery with nerves.

'I never said I wanted no cleaning done.' By contrast Ffion's voice was as harsh as the morning sunlight.

'I thought it'd need it.' Jax was sounding shriller now, almost panicky. 'With it not being done.'

'Well, you thought wrong. I'm not letting it out anymore and no one has any right to be here. The very last thing I need is people gawping and sticking their noses in.'

'Honest, Ffion, I've just been in the flat cleaning, that's all. I swear on my mother's life.'

Thelma was aware of brisk footsteps receding across the gravel, and then Jax's nervous hiss: 'Thelma, we need to go – NOW.'

* * *

It was only later that it came to her. She was sitting in the relative cool of her living room, in her favourite wing-back chair, thinking about the afternoon's events. Teddy was having a lie-down before supper, recovering from a day's hot driving. Snaffles the cat was lying drowsily on the arm of the sofa, semi-alert to the smells and sounds of the deepening evening. In Thelma's hand was the unopened letter now retrieved from her desk drawer.

Father, give me courage, she said. She sighed, set the letter down unopened, and instead took out the scrap of paper she'd found at the Snuggery from where she'd safely stashed it in her purse. She looked at that curious symbol again. What on earth was it? Why that feeling of familiarity?

Her phone rang. It was Jax. Again. This was the fourth time she'd rung since that awkward, tense drive back from Hollinby Quernhow. For the fourth time, Thelma rejected the call. For the moment she had too much on her mind to speak to the woman, not after all the embarrassment of the afternoon.

She suddenly frowned. *Jax*.

Thelma sat upright in her chair. She'd heard Jax tell Ffion she'd been in the flat the whole time – but she hadn't. When Ffion had appeared, Thelma had been alone in the Snuggery.

So where had Jax been?

CHAPTER NINE

Wednesday 16th July

'So where did she go?' Liz frowned perplexedly.

'There's only one place I can think of,' said Pat, fumbling for the coral-pink handbag fan. 'The main house, right?'

Thelma nodded. 'It was the only logical place she could've gone,' she said. 'If, of course, she had a key.'

'But why?' Liz frowned.

Thelma shrugged. 'I don't know.' Grimly she swilled ice cubes round the remnants of her iced mango. 'I thought she simply wanted moral support. But now . . . well, I can't help wondering if there was more to it?'

'Like what?' said Liz.

Thelma shook her head. 'Again, I don't know,' she said. 'And for the moment I don't plan on finding out.'

Once again, it was almost as hot inside the garden centre café as it was outside, despite the presence of several large floor fans racketing away. Virtually every customer had ordered a cold smoothie or iced coffee. Outdoors a pink-faced employee could be seen watering the various ranks and stands of plants; almost as soon as the water hit the ground the stains began shrinking and fading in the relentless sunshine. They'd been there an hour, were on their second lot of iced drinks and were getting to the end of their 'debrief'.

'Maybe Jax knows something?' said Liz. 'About Ffion?'

Thelma shook her head. 'If she did, I'm sure she would have told me,' she said. 'She had plenty of opportunity. And there's certainly no love lost between her and Ffion.'

'You were lucky not to be caught!' said Pat. 'I'm telling you, if Madame Shally dares show her face anywhere near me, she'll get her cleaning brush shoved where the sun don't shine. Landing you in it like that.'

Liz cast an uneasy glance to the café entrance. 'Do you think she will?' she said.

'I wouldn't put anything past that woman,' said Pat, reaching down into her bag and getting out her phone.

Liz opened her mouth to speak but thought better of it. Not whilst her friends were in this bullish mood. Yes, Jax was all the things they were saying, but she remembered those tears in her eyes when she spoke about Neville. There never had been anyone else in her life. Surely the woman was bound to be upset, and in her considerable experience upset people did all sorts of silly things.

'As I say,' said Thelma again, 'I didn't answer her calls, nor did I ring back, so I'm hoping she's got the message.'

Pat snorted. 'You could spray-paint it on the walls of Fountains

Abbey and she'd still get the wrong end of the stick if it suited her, that one.'

She stole a surreptitious look at her Instagram – or more accurately Ms T.J. Rox's Instagram feed. The latest post was showing her and Justin sat in the garden brandishing sludge green drinks at the camera. *Enjoying some together time in the sun with these delicious organic O2H smoothies!* the caption read; already the post had had over seven hundred likes. All *seemed* to be well.

'Anyway, these rumours about Neville.' Liz's voice recalled Pat to the moment. 'Do you think Chris Canne has any idea who was spreading them?'

'If he did, he wasn't saying,' she said. 'But he seemed pretty bothered about the whole thing, which makes me think not.'

Her phone pinged and she dropped her eyes to yet another image of Justin and Tiffany, this time leaning on the gate across the lane from the house looking like something from a fashion shoot. Tiffany looked a world away from the bare-faced, peaky-looking figure Pat had glimpsed in Leeds – was it only two days ago? Had there perhaps been some row, which had subsequently been made up?

'The thing that strikes me about what Chris Canne was telling you,' said Thelma, 'is the nature of these rumours.'

Liz frowned. 'But there wasn't anything concrete, unless I'm missing something,' she said.

Pat took a gulp of her iced raspberry medley. 'I'm telling you everything Mr OBE told me,' she said in take-it-or-leave-it tones. 'Which is: a load of people getting in touch with Lodestone saying they'd heard bad things about Nev Hilton.'

'But *what* bad things?' persisted Liz. 'There's nothing specific.'

'Exactly,' said Thelma. 'That's exactly my point. There's nothing specific.'

Her friends both looked at her. 'Okay,' said Pat. 'I know I'm being thick here, but so what?' She resolutely turned the phone over to avoid being distracted by any more Instagram posts.

'Think about it,' said Thelma in her best Key-Stage-One-planning-meeting tones. 'If some *specific* accusation had been levelled at Neville it could have been investigated, countered – disproved, even. But with something as vague as this' – she gestured at her green planning book and the entry detailing Pat's account – 'there's enough to cast a shadow over Neville's reputation without giving any chance for any sort of redress.'

Liz frowned.

Pat sighed. 'And?'

'And,' said Thelma, shaking the ice cubes in her glass, 'it looks like someone was *deliberately* setting out to cause harm for Neville by spreading these unsubstantiated rumours. Especially when you take into account the way in which this rumour was spread.'

'Like all rumours are,' said Pat. She was beginning to feel decidedly exasperated; it was too hot a day to be playing Miss Marple. 'Someone told someone, who told someone else.'

Thelma drummed her fingers on the notebook. 'Yes, someone tells someone else, but no one ever knows who the first someone was.'

'Hearsay,' said Liz, light dawning.

Thelma nodded. 'It's quite simple,' she said. 'The person who started this rumour would tell it to a number of people but say they heard it from someone else . . .'

'So, you'd never find out who the original source of the rumour was,' said Pat.

'Exactly.' Thelma nodded emphatically. 'There was a case in our church some years ago – the last church warden but two – quite an upset it caused, and no one ever knew who was behind it.'

'I bet you had an idea,' said Pat.

Thelma shrugged modestly, failing to suppress a slight smile playing round her lips. Liz and Pat both knew exactly the sort of thing Thelma was talking about. Working in the community as they had all these years, it was impossible not to.

'It's bad enough when it's just folk talking,' said Liz. 'But once you throw emails and Facebook and whatnot into the mix, it'd be virtually impossible to work out what was behind it all.'

'*Who* was behind it all,' corrected Thelma.

'Okay,' said Pat. 'So, someone had it in for Neville. But didn't we sort of know that already?'

'But this with the emails all goes back months,' said Thelma. 'To February – long before Neville died.' She looked at her drink in mild frustration. Iced raspberry lemonade was all very well for a day like this, but it didn't really lend itself to indulging her favourite habit of stirring.

'At the risk of sounding like a stuck record,' said Pat, 'why do all this in the first place?'

'The answer to that lies with Neville himself,' said Thelma.

'That's what gets me.' The words burst from Liz with frustrated force. 'From *everything* we've heard – everything we *know* – Neville was more annoying than anything else. Not giving that kiddie her attendance award—'

'Objecting to the playing field,' agreed Pat. 'A bit of a pain in the arse.'

'But you don't kill someone for being a bit of a pain in the arse.' Liz spoke slightly louder than she intended and blushed slightly as more than one customer turned to look at her.

'You might,' said Pat. 'I can think of several people in Borrowby, off the top of my head.'

'But they're probably people you might suddenly lash out at,' said Thelma. 'Someone takes a parking space you're heading to, for instance – or rubs you up the wrong way somehow. You might say or even do something there and then, in the heat of the moment. But not when you've had time to calm down and think about it. And this with Neville – if I'm right – was very carefully planned.'

'Which brings us back to why,' said Liz.

'Sex,' said Pat, ticking off with her fingers. 'Money. Blackmail—'

'Surely not,' said Liz. 'Not Neville. I just can't see it.'

'Things happen,' said Pat. 'We all know that. He could have had an affair; he could have been helping himself to money from somewhere.'

'Yes, but if he *did* do something like that,' said Liz, 'I couldn't see him covering it up. Not Nev. With Nev Hilton – what you saw was what you got.'

Pat stepped out of the air-conditioned Yeti onto her driveway, heat washing over her. Her mind was puzzling over Neville Hilton and what it was he could possibly have done to warrant someone attempting to blacken his name, and then confront him in a life-ending way. Blinking in the afternoon glare, she fumbled in her bag for her sunglasses. The light really was brutal this afternoon. What she needed was a shower. It had become her habit since the really hot weather had kicked in, to have a long cool shower late in the afternoon. At the moment she was getting through two sundresses a day. Which reminded her, she needed to get yesterday's ones off the washing line.

Rounding the corner of the house she wondered if Tiffany-Jane would still be outside having some 'me time'. Surely not; after all it was a good few hours since she had made that last stylish post. But there she was, sitting alone on a sun lounger looking cool and fresh in a way that made Pat feel infinitely stickier and grimier than she was. She was sitting perfectly still, arms clasped round her knees, gazing out across the wide bleached fields that fell away from the house, and though her eyes were hidden by enormous (designer) sunglasses (*stylish, practical and VERY affordable, folks!*), Pat sensed something steady and fixed in that gaze.

She hadn't asked Tiffany about her trip to Leeds. Part of her reasoned that it was none of her business, but there had been something else, a bigger reason that had stopped her mentioning seeing the girl to anyone, even Rod. In the split second she'd seen her walking down Scott Hall Road, Pat had read *something* in her face. What she didn't know – and seeing her frozen on the sun lounger Pat sensed that significance again. Whatever was going on behind those sunglasses, Pat instinctively knew it wasn't something that would appear in her Instagram feed any time soon.

As her foot crunched on the gravel, the immaculate head jerked round and instantly the polished, sunny persona swung back into place.

'Pat,' she said brightly. 'It's such a *gorgeous* afternoon. I'm just treating myself to some time in the sun!'

Pat smiled. 'I've just got back.'

Tiffany-Jane nodded enthusiastically. 'Justy's at work. He'll be back around seven.' This was proving to be another feature of their close juxtaposition, Tiffany-Jane's need to explain where Justin was and when he'd be back – as if justifying her presence in the Taylor home.

'Do you two want to eat with us?' said Pat. 'It's nothing much, just salad, and farm shop quiche.'

The face composed itself into an expression of rueful regret. 'I've already eaten,' she said. 'And I know for a fact Justy's got to mug up for this interview.'

'He's got an interview?' Pat tried not to feel a surge of hope at the news.

Tiffany nodded. 'Didn't he say? That's typical him!' She shook her head. 'He probably doesn't want to needlessly stack up anyone's hopes.'

Pat tried not to feel slightly hurt by this; in her book, telling one's mother they had a job interview wasn't needlessly stacking up hopes but giving someone information they had a right to know.

'Is this the Manchester one?' she said, trying to make her voice enthusiastic.

'No, the Newcastle one. Eee Pet. The branding firm.' Tiffany spoke with enthusiasm. 'It should be a shoo-in, Justy was saying.'

Pat nodded, trying to give the appearance of someone who knew all about branding firms in Newcastle.

'Anyway, how was your afternoon?' asked Tiffany. 'Did you have a nice time with your friends?' Her tone made Pat feel exactly as if she, Liz and Thelma had spent the afternoon on the swings in Norby Park.

Without giving herself time to think, she found herself speaking. 'Actually, we were trying to think of reasons why someone would be murdered.'

Tiffany-Jane's eyes widened behind her big glasses and, for the first time in their relationship, Pat glimpsed something beyond the customary Instagram-veneer of their normal exchanges.

'Sorry,' said Pat. 'That was a bit "out there".'

But Tiffany-Jane was frowning in thought. 'I should imagine,' she said fingering the sunglasses, 'there's a whole number of reasons.'

Surprised, Pat nodded.

'I assume,' said the girl, 'that you and your friends discounted the obvious ones – money, sex, love.' She ticked the words off on those perfectly manicured fingers.

Again, Pat nodded. 'This person who died,' she said, 'seems to have been someone who – well, wouldn't steal money and wouldn't have an affair.'

Now Tiffany nodded. 'Oh-kay,' she said, considering. 'So maybe what you need to think about is *where* they were when they were killed – or what they knew . . . Either of those could be a reason someone would want to kill them.'

Pat frowned, puzzling this out. What Tiffany was saying was making sense. Had Neville maybe *seen* something? Or did he *know* something?

'Look,' she said impulsively, 'why don't I open a bottle of fizz? We can have a cheeky glass, and a proper chat.'

It was as if the sun went in. Without losing its friendly smile, the face became a mask.

'Not for me,' said Tiffany-Jane. 'But you go ahead. Actually, I think I need to get in. I've been out here way too long.'

She stood up and walked inside. Pat watched her, perplexed. Whatever momentary connection had been there was gone – the bubble burst. What on earth was the matter?

At about the same time, Liz was standing in one of the (thankfully) air-conditioned aisles of Tesco, staring in deep gloom at a packet of biscuits to help replenish her greatly denuded food cupboard. According to the link Jacob had sent her, they were both low in sugar and fat, whilst high in fibre and vitamin something or other. They were also, Liz noted, high in price, being over double the cost of her regular digestives. She put them down with a sigh and picked up another, less expensive packet of reduced-sugar biscuits, squinting at the discreet green squares on the back. Sugar 4.5 grams. Was that good? Jacob would no doubt know, but she could never be sure these days. She stared at them, irresolute. Sound substitute – or sugary time bomb? That was the problem, behind the facade of the packaging she just didn't know. Like with Neville Hilton.

Her mind made a sideways leap to her other preoccupation. There she was, saying to Pat and Thelma that Neville wasn't a bad person – but how did she know? How was she to know he didn't have a whole string of lovers plus a history of embezzling? Just because she couldn't imagine it, it didn't make it so, not by a long chalk. And then there was Jax, taking herself inside Neville's house like that. *Why?*

'I see. A goody two-shoes.' Zippy Doodah's grim tones barged into Liz's thoughts, bringing her rudely back to earth. How long had she been standing there, lost in thought? 'That's one healthy trolley you've got there,' said Zippy, openly regarding her rather drab collection of vegetables and brown pasta, even moving a butternut squash to see what lurked underneath.

Liz smiled thinly, wishing the other woman would neb out. For reasons she couldn't be bothered to unpack she found herself reaching for the more expensive biscuits and ostentatiously placing them prominently on top of a heap of broccoli.

'How are you?' she, said looking at Zippy's trolley with its brazen heap of crisps, white bread and biscuits.

Zippy Doodah followed her glance and smiled. 'I know – terrible, aren't I!? Don't go telling old Happy Harvey! Any road . . .' She leaned forward on the handles of her trolley with the air of someone settling in for a good chat. 'What *I* want to know is, are you and your mates any further on with finding out what happened to Nev Hilton?'

Liz stared at her. She was shocked and not a little outraged at the question. She knew Thelma had spoken to her the day of the festival. What had she said exactly? To have this woman with her trolley of disgrace refer to them as though they were three Jessica Fletchers, here, right in the middle of Tesco, for the whole world to hear!

'We're really not finding anything out,' she began to say but Zippy was shaking her head.

'I saw your mate Thelma snooping round the back of Nev's house, and Don and Jean said your other mate had been asking about the night Nev died.' She ducked her head confidentially and lowered her voice. 'I know people are talking about Ffion Hilton, but thinking about it, I reckon they might be barking up the wrong tree.'

To her chagrin, Liz found herself likewise ducking her head and lowering her voice. 'She told the police she was at some horse event, didn't she?'

Zippy nodded. 'Carlisle,' she said. 'And of course the police will have checked. Also, the thing about Ffion Hilton is she may be an arsey so-and-so, but with her – well, you get what it says on the tin.'

In spite of everything Liz was curious. 'You think she's telling the truth?'

Zippy shrugged. 'I think she'd be crap at lying,' she said. 'It's not exactly the same thing.'

Liz frowned. 'But if it wasn't Ffion shouting at Neville, who was it?'

'Not a clue.' Zippy Doodah spoke adamantly as she levered herself off the trolley. 'Sidrah were out in her garden most of the day and she reckons she didn't see anyone apart from Neville going into the place.'

'Sidrah?'

'Lass as lives opposite. The one you were speaking to at the village festival.'

An image of a flourishing hydrangea and a pink sparkly T-shirt came into Liz's mind: Sidrah with the CCTV.

'Anyway, flower, I must be making tracks. Keeping up with your food diary, I hope?'

Liz nodded, thinking of the blue and white tome by her bed. 'Are you?'

Zippy Doodah gave a little snort of laughter. 'Not a bloody chance,' she said. 'Life's way too fookin' short!' And taking her leave, she marched purposefully off to the frozen desserts.

Liz stared after her, feeling slightly shocked. Not because of Zippy's assumption that she, Pat and Thelma were actively investigating Nev's death, but because she realised she had been rather enjoying herself. All this finding out felt untold miles away from bleak choices about biscuits and salad cream. She smiled ruefully. What on earth would Derek say?

The buzz of her phone made her start guiltily, as if her husband had divined her thoughts. But it wasn't him. It was Jax Shally. Of course. Her first instinct was to ignore the ringing, but something . . . something to do with the memory of those tears, her feelings of sympathy – that and not wanting to face the bleak contents of her shopping trolley – found her taking the call.

'Liz. Thank God!' Jax's voice was shrill with need. 'Don't hang up on me. I know Thelma's mad with me, but please don't hang up! I need your help!'

CHAPTER TEN

Wednesday 16th July

Met Office weather forecast:

The Met Office has extended an Amber Extreme heat warning, as temperatures look to build later this week and early next week for much of England and Wales.

'Like I say, I know I put them down somewhere in the kitchen, when I were getting more cleaning spray,' said Jax, changing gear with brisk authority. 'I remember thinking: *put them there, Jax, and you won't forget them.*'

But you did forget them, thought Liz. Aloud she said, 'And these keys are for—?'

'The holiday lets,' said Jax grimly. 'All my Friday and Saturday cleans I tell you, Liz, without them keys I am up the proverbial creek without a paddle and that is somewhere I do not need to be, believe you me!'

'What were you doing in Nev's house in the first place?' said Liz, thinking of their speculation on the subject earlier that day. 'Weren't you and Thelma cleaning the Snuggery?'

'I needed more spray, didn't I,' said Jax smoothly. 'Nev used to say: "Jax, if you need more spray, just help yourself."'

Liz frowned, trying to remember if Thelma had said anything about cleaning spray running out. 'Don't you think you should ring Ffion – check it's all right,' she said. 'I know you say she's not in, but you thought that before . . . And what if Ffion found them and put them away somewhere?'

Jax swung the cherry-red Nissan into the driveway of the Old Barn. 'Liz!' she said, stopping the car with a sharp crunch of gravel. 'How many more times do I have to say it. *There's no one here*. And I need them keys for tomorrow. I have got to get into them holiday lets – I cannot afford to lose that contract – if not for me, then for Chelse.'

Liz duly nodded, feeling a tug to her heartstrings as she remembered the unhappy girl. And, she firmly reminded herself, upset people do impetuous things. She scanned the front of the Old Barn; there was no sign of the black four-by-four – indeed, aside from Sidrah watering her garden, Chapel Lane seemed utterly deserted. Maybe if they went straight in and straight out everything would be okay.

'We need to be quick,' she said.

The ponytail nodded energetically as Jax turned off the engine and snatched up her large tote bag. 'Thanks,' she said somewhat perfunctorily. 'I couldn't have done this on my own; I know I'm being silly, but I just cannot face going in that building alone.'

Liz felt like pointing out that the Old Barn wasn't where Neville's body had been found, but something told her she'd be wasting her breath. Like Thelma before, she couldn't quite rid herself of the feeling that there was some ulterior motive to this trip; but what, she had no idea. In Jax's voice, sneaking beneath the urgently professed need, there was a tone Liz recognised from their days in class together, when Jax would tell some convoluted tale outlining some dilemma – a missing reading record, a query about dinner numbers. These dilemmas had all had similar solutions: Jax absenting herself from the class for lengthy periods of time.

Looking over Jax's shoulder into the dim hallway of the Old Barn, Liz felt how most people would at the prospect of walking into a stranger's house uninvited: a sense of appalled guilt. 'I better wait outside,' she called.

'No, it's fine, come on,' said Jax, shifting her tote bag onto her shoulder.

Together they walked inside, Liz convinced Ffion would suddenly appear, possibly sliding down the bannisters, certainly with a shriek of rage.

'Oh my God,' said Jax, looking around. 'What a tip!'

She wasn't wrong. Coats and boots were heaped like brown and black fungi over and around what were presumably coat pegs. A sack of what looked like some sort of feed was propped against the bannisters and there was the faintly pervasive smell of stables. 'You can tell Nev isn't around; he'd never have stood for this,' said Jax in disgust. 'You wait here. I'll not be two seconds.'

Jax disappeared into what Liz could see was the kitchen, leaving Liz sighing and glancing nervously at the front door. *Two seconds!* Why did people always say 'two seconds' when they invariably meant considerably longer? She stood in the hallway, barely daring to move, but aware of another, growing feeling. Not two hours ago she had been stood in Tesco, wondering about the true nature of Neville Hilton – and here was an unexpected chance to find out. She looked round the hall with its jumble of jackets and bags. Not much to be learned here; the place to see would be Nev's study.

Jax appeared in the kitchen doorway and Liz felt a warm surge of relief. 'Found them?'

But Jax shook her head. 'Not yet. There's a few places I need to look,' she said. 'Just make yourself comfortable.'

Make yourself comfortable! Liz shook her head. Just how on earth was she supposed to do that? Use the feed sack like a beanbag? Again, her eyes strayed to the front door . . . and then to the door next to it. It was standing slightly ajar and through it she could just make out a bookshelf. Liz crossed to the door and peeked into a room that was as pin-neat as the hall was untidy. Two of the walls were taken up by shelves full of books and ring binders; the third was painted a sharp lemon colour and adorned with a plethora of framed photos and certificates. The polished gravitas of a large wooden desk and an adjacent smaller unit of drawers dominated the fourth wall. Here was a window with a view onto the drive and Sidrah's cottage across Chapel Lane.

It was definitely a home office of some description – Neville's? Dare she go in? She reminded herself of her earlier thought; here was a golden opportunity to find out more about Neville Hilton dropped right into her lap. What's more, she was pretty sure neither Thelma nor Pat would have hesitated; in fact, this could well be what Thelma referred to as a 'nudge from the Almighty'. And she need only have the quickest of quick looks – considerably less time than Jax's 'two seconds'. How many times over the years had she conducted the same sort of lightning fact-finding expedition into her son's bedroom?

Without giving herself time to think further she entered the study, heart pounding, fully expecting some sort of klaxon alarm to sound. She walked over to the desk, but it was locked; of course it was. Anyway – just what was she expecting to find? A folder of racy love letters from a mistress? A sheaf of receipts labelled 'embezzled fund'? She realised that her breathing was so rapid she was almost panting; she took a deep, shuddering breath, forcing down the rising feeling of panic.

Get a grip, Liz! She wouldn't find anything at this rate. But where to start?

Her eyes dropped to the cupboard next to the desk. No, not a cupboard – one of those wooden filing cabinets. *Dare she?* Looking over her shoulder she dropped (stiffly) to her knees and tugged at the handle. Like many wooden drawers it stuck slightly then opened in a series of scraping jerks, each jerk echoed by a panicky start from Liz's heart. Inside was a neat range of labelled sections – tax, insurance, Lodestone, Ofsted. She sat back, frustrated, again wondering just what it was she was hoping to find? A folder labelled 'Shenanigans'?

Hang on – *what was this?*

One of the folders was labelled 'Complaints'.

Intrigued, she extracted it from its divider and began leafing through the contents. These were – as one would expect – complaints. Chiefly from Neville, about various subjects: a faulty toaster, a blocked footpath, a substandard NightPrem Inn bedroom. Smooth words and phrases of displeasure curled up smoke like from the pages: *disappointed . . . unhappy . . . express my displeasure . . . direct contravention . . . failure on your part*. The latest one, dated only a few months previous, was a series of complaints about the dangerous state of the A171 moors road. There were some ten or eleven letters on this topic alone.

The feeling of sadness intensified as she stood looking at the litany of grumbles and complaints – trivial, piffling grumbles – all now made irrelevant by death.

Nice chap but nobody likes him.

It crossed her mind that maybe she should take some photos of the letters, but at that moment she heard Jax from outside calling her name. In a guilty burst of movement, she tried to shove the folder back into the divider, only to find something fouling it from going in smoothly. Feeling inside her fingers met the glossy surface of a photo, she pulled it out curiously. It was a picture of Nev and Jax, a much younger Nev and Jax. The word 'radiant' was one that in Liz's book was much overused but here it was spot on. The pair looked so *young*, so full of life. Nev, thinner and with considerably more hair, was alive with a happy smile and no trace of irritating smugness. And Jax – no ponytail, hair a natural colour – in that brief snapshotted moment alive with hope, joy and yes, love.

'Liz, are you there?' There was a tone in Jax's voice that brought a prickle to the back of Liz's neck. Relieved not to have been found in the study, Liz stuffed the photo back into the file, shut the drawer and hurried into the kitchen.

'Clichéd stunning' was a phrase that she and Derek had coined during their many hours of watching *Escape to the Country*. The beechwood units, the granite countertops, the gleaming steel hob and hood, were all exactly what you'd expect from a top-of-the-range North Yorkshire barn conversion – except like the hall there was more evidence of Ffion Hilton's priorities: another jacket, more boots, a rather smelly blanket and what appeared to be an old saddle.

Jax was at the far end of the room, by a back door, staring intently into a walk-in cupboard. 'Oh my God,' she was saying. 'Oh my God, I do not believe this.'

Liz hurried to join her and peered over her shoulder.

'I thought she might have stashed the keys in here maybe,' said Jax. 'Hung them up or something. And I saw these.' She flung out a dramatic finger.

Stashed at the back of the cupboard amongst a nest of toilet rolls was an object – a pair of objects – riding boots. Scuffed women's riding boots. Liberally splashed with pale-yellow paint.

'Oh my God,' said Jax. 'What should we do?'

'Don't touch them,' said Liz firmly, taking out her phone. Cursing silently as she grappled with unlocking it without her glasses, she eventually managed to find the camera app and took a couple of pictures (as well as nearly ordering more sugar-free biscuits off Amazon).

'Oh my God,' said Jax for a third time. 'Do you reckon you ought to tell someone?'

Liz shot her a glance at the use of the pronoun 'you'; there was that distinct 'Shall I leave it with you?' tone to Jax's voice. Liz opened her mouth to speak but at that moment there was a pistol-like click from the front door lock.

The two women stared in horror.

'I thought you said she was away,' hissed Liz angrily. Quickly, Jax stashed the boots back in the cupboard and shut the door; by the time Ffion appeared in the doorway the pair were stood by the counter, side by side, like naughty children.

'What the fuck?' said the second Mrs Hilton.

'I left my keys here,' blurted Jax. 'My keys for the houses in Pickhill. When I was in the other week.'

'Just what is going on?' said Ffion angrily. 'What are you doing in my kitchen?'

She's just said, thought Liz, but nevertheless said nothing.

'When I was cleaning the Snuggery earlier,' babbled Jax, 'I came in for some more spray like I do and I reckon I put some keys down.'

Ffion shook her head. 'So why didn't you ring and ask?' she snapped. Even without being seated on an enormous horse she had a powerful presence.

Why not indeed? thought Liz.

'I was just passing and I thought I'd drop by.'

'Listen,' said Ffion. 'I'm just gonna say this the once. I do not want you coming in here.' She emphasised each word with ice-cube hardness. 'I don't give a fuck about keys or spray. In fact—' A carmine-nailed hand shot out. 'In fact, give me the keys you've got. You cannot be coming in here; I didn't even know you *had* any keys.'

'Neville let me have them.'

'Yeah, well, Neville's dead. This is my house and I do not want you barging in here, especially not when I'm not in.'

Heart pounding and sinuses swelling, Liz regarded the angry figure of the second Mrs Hilton. Had this woman lied to the police? Had she not been in Carlisle but there, screaming at her husband?

'I'm so sorry,' she said, speaking for the first time. 'I do apologise. We'll go now.'

Ffion looked at her. 'You were at the funeral,' she stated flatly. 'And you were in the village the day of the festival.'

'I came with Jax because she doesn't like coming in here,' said Liz.

'There's a simple answer to that. Don't come.' Her hand closed over the key that Jax shamefacedly handed her. 'I'm serious – if I find any of you anywhere near the place again, I'm calling the police.'

Teddy was sitting in the backyard of number 32 College Gardens, back pressed against the warm brick wall, now alive with night-blooming honeysuckle, face relaxed and turned up to the sun under his battered white sun hat. Watching him from the kitchen window, Thelma could see again that blond rugby player she had married all those years ago. He was wearing what these days was his standard summer outfit: tan shorts and a blue polo work shirt, the orange and yellow of the WAMMP (Wait A Minute Mr Postman) logo bright on his left breast. She thought he might be asleep, but when she opened the back door his eyes immediately snapped open and his face broke into a warm smile. No two ways about it, her husband was looking way more relaxed, youthful even, than he ever did when working at Ripon and St Bega college – or 'the vicar factory' as he termed it.

'Having a pause?' she said, having clocked the stack of parcels in the hall waiting to be delivered.

'Something somewhat longer than that,' he said easily. 'It was so jolly hot in the car, even with the windows down. Each time I got back in, the seat was almost unbearable. So, I decided to call it an afternoon. One of the joys of this job.'

'I'm surprised you're so busy,' said Thelma, thinking of parcels piled high on his study desk.

'Holiday lets,' said Teddy simply. 'Predominantly. People go away from home and realise they've forgotten some necessity of life, which somehow cannot be managed without. That and, according to Big Cyn, self-help books. There's something about this heat that apparently makes people strive for perfection.'

'I'll make some iced elderflower,' said Thelma.

'Sit a moment,' said Teddy. 'It's so lovely. I was thinking of going for a walk presently.'

Thelma sat down on the warm bench, feeling the comfort of his cool fingers reflexively twining with hers. For a moment they sat in companionable silence enjoying the shade of the garden, the drone of insects, the various flowers and in the distance shouts of children on the college playing field.

'So,' said Teddy. 'How are things?'

Involuntarily Thelma felt her hand slacken and pictured the letter hidden neatly in her bag. She needed to tell him and she needed to tell him now. *Lord, give me the right words.*

But before she could grasp the sentences forming in her head, Teddy was speaking again. 'How did you get on this afternoon?' he said. 'Talking with Liz and Pat?'

Heart thudding at the reprieve, Thelma reached into her bag for her teacher's mark book. Opening it at the right page she handed it to her husband, who scanned her teacher's print with the same concentration he afforded scripture and his WAMMP delivery app.

'Murder, question mark,' he read. 'So, you do think Neville was murdered in some way, shape or form?'

'I honestly don't know,' said Thelma. She thought of that glinting steel knife nestling in the dishwasher with the three plates and the vegetable dishes. She shook her head, trying to clear her thoughts. 'The police are adamant he died of natural causes,' she said as much to herself, as to Teddy. 'They surely wouldn't get a thing like that wrong.'

'Of course, murder isn't necessarily a deliberate act of violently taking life,' said Teddy thoughtfully. 'It can just as well be the facilitation of a fatal act—'

Thelma looked at him. 'Oh?' she said.

Teddy nodded. 'Removing batteries from a torch, so someone is forced to walk in the dark – or the loosening of a rug at the top of a flight of stairs.'

'I suppose so,' agreed Thelma. 'But it's hard to see how a heart attack could be anything other than – well, a heart attack.'

'It could be something as simple as withholding medication. Remember Lesley Grey?'

Thelma nodded, remembering Mrs Grey in Teddy's first parish. That fatal heart attack after she apparently 'lost' her digoxin. And then Mr Grey remarrying so quickly afterwards . . .

'At the end of the day,' said Teddy, 'a man is dead. And as you say' – he indicated the green mark book with its neat writing – 'there does seem something very *deliberate* at play here . . . this rumour – and of course that yellow line – someone must have bought paint – and paintbrushes.'

'There was something else odd about that line,' said Thelma. 'Beyond the fact it was there. There was something almost slapdash about it. It certainly wasn't done as any sort of decorative feature, I'm sure of that.'

Teddy was looking at another part of the page in the green mark book. 'Have pity,' he read. 'For pity's sake.'

'That's important,' said Thelma. 'I know it is. I just don't know *why*.'

'And this.' Teddy's finger traced the scrap of paper with the curious symbol, neatly sellotaped into the book.

'Do you recognise it?' asked Thelma.

He slowly shook his head. 'No,' he said. 'And yet I know I've seen it before somewhere.'

Thelma took the book off him and bent her head, squinting at the white paper in the glaring sun.

'Come on.' Teddy stood up. 'I'm going to grab a quick shower and then let's walk out to Studley.'

'Do you not want to wait until it's cooled down a bit?'

Teddy shook his head. 'I'll just keep on thinking about all the parcels,' he said. 'And feeling guilty. Let people strive for perfection tomorrow.'

Thelma smiled. 'Talking of striving for perfection,' she said,

'Liz was in St Barney's – apparently it's poised in a constant state of excellence, waiting for Ofsted, even though it's the end of term.'

Teddy smiled. 'That's the thing about perfection,' he said, 'it's so utterly exhausting to maintain. Especially in hot weather.'

As he went indoors, Thelma had a strong feeling of missed opportunity. She fingered the letter in her bag. She needed to tell him; it wasn't like her to ignore an issue. In a way there was a parallel to be drawn with St Barnabus – they hadn't ignored the possibility of Ofsted arriving, even though it was the end of term.

She paused, frowned. St Barnabus!

Of course!

When Teddy emerged some fifteen minutes later, freshly showered and changed, his wife was pink in the face and stabbing at her phone almost frantically.

'What is it?' he said. 'Has something happened?'

'It's just come to me.' Thelma looked up, her eyes wide and unfocused. 'I know where I've seen that symbol before.'

Teddy regarded his wife.

'It's *Ofsted*,' she said. 'It's the Ofsted symbol. That's why it was so familiar. And that phrase Judy Bestall heard. It wasn't having pity or for pity's sake or anything like that – it was Pity Me!'

Teddy frowned. 'Isn't that a place near Durham?' he said.

Thelma nodded. 'It's a village,' she said. 'On the outskirts. A village with a school. And Neville Hilton led the last inspection.'

PART TWO

Pity Me

CHAPTER ELEVEN

Monday 21st July

Met Office pollen count:

Grass pollen on the rise. Nettle, dock and plantain too. Spores: a little Alternaria and medium Cladosporium when warm.

'I wanted the ground to swallow me up!' said Liz fretfully, shaking her head. Even though a weekend had passed, the memory of being found by Ffion Hilton was still painfully sharp. Her gaze ranged round the Costa Coffee, as if expecting the various customers sipping their iced drinks to give her looks of justifiable condemnation. It was relatively new, this branch, and thankfully had air-conditioning.

'If you will go listening to Jax Shally . . .' said Pat, not really trying to keep any trace of 'I told you so' out of her voice.

'I was mortified,' said Liz, vexedly clutching her tea. '*Mortified*! To be threatened with the police!'

Pat smiled but Thelma did not. Indeed, a fleeting wince crossed her features, as though she were suddenly assailed by a stab of toothache. Infinitesimal the look may have been, but Liz clocked it all the same.

'All I can say,' said Pat, 'is Ms Jax Shally better not try getting me to go round there.'

'I've blocked her number,' said Liz adamantly. 'And I won't be unblocking her any time soon.'

'Can you show me those boots again?' asked Thelma. Obediently Liz took out her phone and showed the photo of the two paint-splattered boots in their nest of toilet rolls.

'Definitely riding boots,' said Pat. 'And a fine old mess the Black Widow's made of them. The paint goes all the way up the shank.'

'If they are Ffion's boots,' said Thelma.

'Who else's would they be?' said Liz. 'They were hidden in her kitchen cupboard.'

'In which case,' said Thelma, 'why did she paint that line down the wall?'

'And why didn't she say she did?' said Pat. 'I mean, why bother hiding something like that?'

'Unless there's a reason behind it that you want to keep hidden,' said Thelma.

'Also' – Pat frowned, remembering the many, many walls she'd seen painted over the years – 'where are the brushes? And the dust sheets? And come to think of it, why wear riding boots to do the painting in the first place? I mean, I know people wear old clothes, but *riding boots*?'

'I'm just wondering about the paint on those boots,' said Liz. 'Is it even the same colour as the paint on the wall? Wasn't the wall a lighter shade?'

It was now Thelma's turn to take out her phone and they all scanned the images she'd taken of that yellow line on the back wall of the living room. In the streaming afternoon light, it looked pale, the colour of confectioner's custard.

'It's the sun,' said Pat dismissively. 'Coming in the room from the left like that. It makes the wall look lighter. What *I* want to know is what Jax Shally was doing looking in that kitchen cupboard in the first place. You're not telling me she thought she'd find her spare key stashed in amongst all the loo rolls.'

'There was definitely something going on with her,' agreed Liz. 'An agenda of some description. Something I didn't know about.'

'There always is, knowing her,' said Pat. 'Ms Ulterior Motive.'

Thelma nodded in agreement. 'I wonder what it was. Maybe something to do with whatever it was she was looking for?' she mused.

Both Pat and Liz looked at her. 'It stands to reason she'd have opened that cupboard for a *purpose*,' explained Thelma. 'So it seems logical that she was looking for something. Like when I was with her.'

'Anyway.' Pat drained her iced mochaccino. 'Isn't all this with Jax and Ffion and yellow boots a tad academic? Now that you've found this?' Her hand gestured to the printout of the Ofsted report they'd all been looking at earlier. Liz picked up the document. She'd been so worked up with the tale of her confrontation with Ffion Hilton that she hadn't paid as much attention to the Ofsted report as Pat had. She scanned the printed pages curiously. At first sight the phrases were warm, glowing even . . . *pupils enjoy coming to this vibrant and welcoming school . . . ambitious curriculum . . . strong vision . . .good quality of teaching* . . . But then, other phrases, decidedly *unglowing* emerged . . . *serious concerns . . . leaders unaware of weakness . . . significant failings* . . .

In the previous inspection the school had been judged to be Outstanding, the highest grade possible, but in this latest report the Leadership and Management were graded Inadequate, the lowest of the four grades. Even though the other areas were found to be Good, it was that one key word Inadequate that stood out, stark and uncompromising. However you looked at it, it was a dramatic drop, one that would bring ice into the heart of any educational practitioner. Liz shook her head and put the report back on the table.

'We were looking for a reason someone had it in for Neville,' said Pat. 'Well, here we are. Reading this report, I imagine there'd be a whole queue of people wanting to give him what for.'

'We *are* sure it's connected with his death?' said Liz.

'Pity Me!' pronounced Pat. 'Shouted in his face by someone, just before he had a fatal heart attack. I'd say that was fairly conclusive.'

Thelma put the report in her bag. 'I don't want this on view when they get here,' she said.

'Who is this we're meeting again?' said Liz.

'The Reverend Caro Miranda,' said Thelma. Liz looked none the wiser.

'She's the chair of governors from Pity Me school,' said Pat in her best 'keep-up-at-the-back' voice. 'Who just happens to be a pal of the Reverend Mare.'

'Who is in the same diocesan cluster as Mare,' corrected Thelma. 'I wouldn't say they were pals, but they do know each other. Fortunately for us. Mare said Caro was only too pleased to talk to us.' She thought back to the rapid sequence of events that had brought them to this Costa Coffee on the outskirts of Yarm: seeing the chair of governors' name in the report, ringing the Reverend Mare on the off chance she knew this Reverend Miranda, Mare's offer to reach out to her, and then, the almost startlingly rapid response, the phone call, the offer to meet. Why was this chair of governors so keen to meet them? Her eyes shifted across to the door of the coffee bar, and the two figures who had just appeared. 'Unless I'm mistaken, I think this is them now,' she said.

'So, this is the Reverend Caroline Miranda! Or as she is more commonly known, the Reverend Caro!' The Reverend Mare spoke with her trademark cheerfulness, sounding as if she were about to break into a cheer. In light of the hot weather, she'd swapped her usual sweater for a blue polo shirt, buttoned up to support the dog collar. She smiled encouragingly at the woman sitting next to her. Despite the laugh that punctuated

Mare's introduction, there was an air of restraint about her that revealed she wasn't unaware of the circumstances that had led to this meeting.

The Reverend Caro Miranda regarded them from under a fringe of glossy grey hair, styled in a rather unbecoming curtain round her face. Her appearance did not live up to the flamboyance of her name: the hair, the rather pointy nose, the pale rather glittery eyes that slid from side to side like something from an Oliver Postgate cartoon.

Miss Mouse, thought Pat, unsure of whether she warmed to her or not.

'Thank you for agreeing to see us,' said Thelma.

Caro Miranda nodded appraisingly. There was a brief pause before she spoke, her voice surprisingly deep with a faint Irish lilt. 'Mare tells me you knew Neville Hilton.'

'We knew his first wife more,' said Liz. Exactly how much they told this stranger about what they knew and what they wanted to find out was something they'd spent some time debating as Pat had driven them down the A19.

Again, Caro Miranda nodded.

'Well,' she said. 'What I need to say from the get-go is this: forgiveness is something I've preached for nigh on thirty years, and it's something I've never had much difficulty practising.' The pale eyes slid from side to side, looking at each of them in turn. 'Until now. I have to say in all honesty I am not sorry in any way, shape or form that that man is dead.'

After iced coffees had been brought, the Reverend Caro Miranda told her story. 'Pity Me Infants school,' she said, 'or Pity Infants as it's known locally – was a truly wonderful place to be a part of.' A wistful smile lightened the mouse-like features. 'The head teacher – Annie Golightly – was a wonderful, gifted person. *Is* a wonderful person I should say, though she's very ill, poor woman. She's a born teacher and at Pity Me she created somewhere that

111

was . . . truly special. In my time in the church, I've been into a number of educational establishments, and Pity Infants – well, it stands out head and shoulders.' Her face darkened. 'Stood out,' she corrected. She looked sadly out of the window at the cars whizzing past, sun blazing off their windscreens. 'It's hard to describe to someone who's not been there . . . It's a place shaped and driven by someone who loved young people and had a true vision of children's education.

'People used to come from all sorts of places to see the work Annie Golightly and her team were doing. I was only chair of governors, but I can say, hand on heart, it was a joy to be part of what was going on there.'

Caro Miranda sighed and once more her gaze slid to the passing traffic. 'Like many things,' she said, 'when something goes wrong, it goes wrong very, very quickly. First of all, Annie became ill – cancer, God bless her – and of course had to take time out. Davey Fletcher – he was the deputy – stepped up, but as he'd have been the first to say he wasn't Annie. But he absolutely worked his socks off, bless him.'

She stared at her iced mochaccino. 'We all knew the school was due an Ofsted, so it came as no particular shock when the call came. I saw the staff the day before, well, the night before. They were all there gone nine o'clock; it was that sort of place. They were all naturally tense, but no one felt they had anything to be especially worried about.' Her face darkened. Was she aware her fists were suddenly clenching?

'Then Neville Hilton set foot inside the building. And from the word go, nothing was right.' Caro Miranda took a deep, deep breath – almost a gasp as if steeling herself for what lay ahead. 'The first thing was the car parking. Why had a designated space not been set aside for him as lead inspector?' She looked up. 'We're only a small school; there's only a handful of spaces. Dolly in the office needs one, she's due a hip replacement and can't walk all that far. But try explaining *that* to him.'

Pat, Liz and Thelma, with their own memories of Neville Hilton, silently nodded.

'That was only the beginning. I won't go into all the ins and outs; I get too angry. Suffice to say, for the most part the points he raised were just piffling. It was obvious from the word go that the man had no appreciation for the many, many wonderful things the staff were doing. I honestly don't think he was capable.'

Caro Miranda paused and seemed suddenly choked on her words. The Reverend Mare laid a supportive hand on her arm. 'You don't have to go on,' said Thelma gently.

'No.' Caro Miranda shook off the hand and the comment almost fiercely. '*No*. It's important people know *exactly* what that man did to us.' She took a deep, almost shuddering breath before speaking again in a low, angry voice. 'The Leadership and Management were judged to be Inadequate, and despite the judgements in the other areas – the wonderful things the school was doing – that's all anyone took any notice of.' She shook her head as if unable to believe it, even after all this time. 'It was the safeguarding the school "failed" on.' She made bitter inverted commas with her fingers. 'The local press had an absolute field day . . . some *terrible* headlines they ran.' Caro Miranda shook her head in disbelief 'When I read some of the things they said – it'd be laughable if it weren't all so awful. Annie Golightly, Davey Fletcher – they knew each and every one of those kids and their families inside out and upside down and back to front. *Of course* they took safeguarding seriously!' Her voice rose again, shaking slightly and again the Reverend Mare put her hand on her arm. Caro took another deep, shuddering breath and continued.

'Both the days of the inspection were pouring wet,' she said, 'so of course the kiddies were indoors with all the issues that brings.' Pat, Liz and Thelma – three ex-teachers – nodded with deep empathy. 'But to say behaviour was an issue! Then there was this dance some of them were doing – something some of them had seen online, some game their elder siblings were playing. And it had become a bit of a craze, this dance.' Again, the three friends nodded with total understanding. '*Evidence of sexualised behaviour!* That's what Neville Hilton said. I couldn't believe it; I laughed out loud when he said that. I said to him that it was total garbage! You know what he said back to me? "I'm sorry and not a little concerned you find it amusing."' Liz thought of that awful line in the report: *leaders unaware of weakness* . . .

'What really sunk us was the paperwork.' Now Caro's voice was flat and weary. 'We had a new teacher – Chloe – a local lass, excellent teacher. And there was some error on her paperwork – something that wasn't in place. And then some of the safeguarding training wasn't completely up to date . . . Yes, technically we were in the wrong, but we could have sorted those things within hours . . .' She sighed. 'Looking back, it was a mistake to argue with the man. But he was just so blinkered and unfair! I argued, Davey argued. Davey's partner even turned up and collared him in the car park. Maybe that made it worse, I don't know.'

'I presume you challenged the report?' said Thelma.

'For all the good it did.' Caro Miranda's voice was bitter. She looked squarely at Pat, Liz and Thelma, eyes now still and strong. 'That report. That judgement of "Inadequate". It broke my heart. And it broke the heart of everyone in that school. And then after what happened to poor dear Davey and Annie not coming back – I suppose it was inevitable that the authority should hand the school over to a trust.'

'How *is* Annie?' asked Liz concernedly.

Caro shook her head, the grey eyes suddenly awash.

'Not good,' she said huskily. Mare placed a warm hand over hers and Liz wordlessly proffered a balsam tissue.

'You must forgive me,' said Caro. 'I just get so upset – seeing somewhere so good destroyed—'

'The school is closing, I believe?' said Thelma.

'Not according to the Angel of the North Academy Trust,' Caro smiled bitterly. 'According to them the Pity Infants school family is being welcomed to the Wearside Community Primary Academy. In other words, yes, it's closing; will close at the end of this week and all our "family" is being absorbed into some faceless, corporate three-form entry school. The site's already been acquired by property developers for housing. The bulldozers are all set to move in.'

There was a pause as she blew her nose with a loud, angry honk.

'Excuse me,' said Thelma. 'Can I just ask – you said just now *after what happened to Davey*. I wonder what you mean by that?'

Caro looked at her, her gaze bleak and clear. 'I thought you knew,' she said. 'It was in all the papers. But then, you didn't know him.' She paused, clenched her cup. 'He died,' she said simply. 'A car crash, driving over the moors. The day before the report was due out, his car went off the road. He was killed outright. And to my mind, it's all down to that man Neville Hilton.'

She shook her head again and, suddenly, thirstily drained her iced mochaccino.

'Evil,' she pronounced, 'is not a horned beast. Evil carries a clipboard and is totally secure in its own certainty.'

CHAPTER TWELVE

Tuesday 22nd July

Text sent from Hedley Lodestone Primary Academy to parents:

Because of today's extreme heat, children are allowed on this one occasion to come in non-uniform. PLEASE REMEMBER SUN HATS!

The white Fiat threaded cautiously in amongst the afternoon traffic on the Durham bypass.

'I'm still not really sure about this,' said Liz, frowning through her driving glasses. 'I mean what are we looking for?'

'The next roundabout but one,' said Thelma, frowning down at her phone. 'Signposted Pity Me and Framwellgate Moor.'

'I mean,' said Liz, not without a hint of exasperation, 'at the school. I just don't see what's to be gained by us going there.'

Thelma said nothing; the truth was she was none too sure either. She clasped her hands and mentally repeated one of her favourite lines of scripture: *seek and ye shall find.* Which was all very well – but seek what? And how could one know they'd found something if they weren't aware they were seeking it in the first place?

'I mean, how is it going to look?' persisted Liz. 'Us just turning up there – with the place about to close?'

'It's hardly a case of us just turning up there,' said Thelma. 'Caro Miranda was very insistent we went and saw the place for ourselves.'

'She was that,' said Liz rather grimly.

'Yes,' said Thelma. 'I'm not really sure what I made of her.'

'I was,' said Liz, still grim. 'I know she was upset, but she was a bit of a pushy so-and-so. She reminded me of Jan.'

There was a pause as they both pictured Liz's erstwhile friend and one-time colleague. Always so sure she was right.

'Here,' said Thelma. 'The roundabout coming up. Third exit.'

Liz nodded tensely, feeling a sneeze brewing. For her, unfamiliar roundabouts were one of life's trials.

They both stayed quiet as she focused. Roundabout successfully negotiated, Thelma said, 'I really do appreciate you driving.'

'How is your arm anyway?' asked Liz.

'Oh, you know.' Thelma sounded vague. 'A bit stiff.' She made a half-hearted demonstrative claw.

Liz said nothing.

About half a mile down the road she braked as the telltale speed bumps and green security fencing of a school materialised.

'Is this it?' she said doubtfully. The school itself looked large and corporate, more like an office block than a place of education. 'Wearside Primary Academy' announced a sign, 'Where young learners aspire!'

'That must be the academy school,' said Thelma. 'The one Caro mentioned. The school we want is about a mile further on, just beyond a church.'

'And have you been to the doctor's?' asked Liz. 'About that arm?'

Thelma shook her head. 'I'm going to see how it gets on.'

Again, Thelma sounded vague. Liz said nothing but continued driving down the long road of terraced houses that Pity Me seemed to comprise of. She felt worried, more than worried and not just about their imminent visit to Pity Me school. Thelma hardly ever lied, and when she did there was always some darker reason, making any untruth the more palatable option.

Some eighty miles away, Pat sat waiting in the lobby of Headley Community Academy listening to the sound of children singing: timeless, cheering and infinitely optimistic. Through the doors, her friend Victoria could be glimpsed at the front of the assembled school, a green-and-gold whirl of energy and encouragement.

Pat smiled and returned to studying the video on her phone: her son Justin, tanned, teeth bared in an easy white grin, confidentially speaking against the backdrop of books (her books) and drapes (her drapes).

'*It's all about facing these curveballs life chucks at us*' – on the phone his voice sounded tinny and insubstantial – '*and please note, folks, I'm not gifting these things with the term "setback" – which automatically bestows a negative energy. It's about saying, "Hey, universe: that's the way you're working and I make a conscious choice to go along with that."*'
Pat locked the phone. From all this talk about curveballs she was gathering that the job at 'Eee Pet' had not been such a 'shoo-in' after all, and that for the foreseeable future at least, the only place Justin would be gifting his positivity would be the Allied Insurance Call Centre, Northallerton. At least she hoped that was all the curveball was.

She thought back to those raised voices coming from the guest bedroom the other night, when Justin arrived home from work. Rod had quickly and easily put them down to pre-interview jitters, and normally, Pat would have too.

Except . . . She thought again of the figure on Scott Hall Road . . . Tiffany-Jane's tense unmade-up face . . . the faraway look in the girl's eyes as she'd stared out over the fields the other day . . .

'Pat! My best girl!' Victoria surged into the lobby like a benign tornado and encased her in a sweet coconut-scented hug.

118

'I'm so sorry to keep you! Leavers assembly – end of primary school . . . they're all on at least their *sixth* box of tissues, God love them!' Pat hugged back, drawing, as she always did, energy from her friend's very presence. As always with Victoria, the world seemed a brighter, more glittery place full of joy and hope.

'I've not got long, my darling,' said Victoria. 'Even though it's the last day of term the trust in their infinite wisdom have decided what all the staff need is some Goal Enabling. Thank you, Trust! Still, it's Bun Widdup, so it shouldn't be too bad, whatever it is. Anyway, how are you, my darling?' She held Pat at arm's length, surveying her critically, dark skin suddenly glowing in a girder of afternoon sunlight transecting the lobby. 'And what's all this about Neville Hilton?'

Back in Durham, the white Fiat pulled in directly in front of Pity Me Infants school. Where Wearside Primary Academy had been brash and new, this was Victorian old; twin gables of grey stone beyond an expanse of sun-baked asphalt, criss-crossed with the faded yellow and white ghosts of netball lines and hopscotch grids. Sharp and incongruous was a red-and-black sign fixed to the school wall: *Acquired by Berry Properties*.

Parked up, steering lock on, Liz put a restraining hand on her friend's arm.

'Hang on,' she said uneasily. 'We've still not agreed what exactly we're looking for.'

'We're looking,' said Thelma, undoing her seatbelt, 'for someone who could have had reason to confront Neville Hilton.'

'But what do we say?' There was a panicky edge to Liz's voice. 'It's not as if we can just walk in the staffroom and say, "Hi, we're just here to see if any of you caused your Ofsted inspector to have a fatal heart attack."'

Thelma wanted to quote from one of her go-to passages of scripture, from the book of Luke, words to the effect of the Holy Spirit will give the words to say at the moment they're needed,

119

but before she could put this thought into words, Liz nudged her arm and nodded in the direction of the school gate where the Reverend Caro Miranda had emerged and was walking purposefully towards the white Fiat.

'Just let me do the talking,' said Thelma.

'Oh my God!' Victoria's eyes were wide. 'An inspector croaks!' The mouth widened into a smile, hastily quelled as she slapped a generous hand over it, nails winking like jewels in the sunlight. 'Ignore me,' she said. 'Poor old Nev Hilton. Though we all have to go some time and I have to say there's worse ways.'

They were sitting in Victoria's office, which like the rest of Headley Primary Academy bore the unmistakable signs of the end of the school year; the noticeboard was a forest of thank-you cards, the desk was heaped with papers and no less than three crammed refuse sacks leaned lazily against the wall. Victoria's watch beeped and she quickly flicked it into view.

'It's okay,' she said. 'We've still a few minutes before we Enable Our Goals.' She laughed. 'I tell you, Pat, I remember the days when "Zoom" was a type of ice lolly. *Anyway*, the late Neville—'

'Did you know him?'

Victoria shook her head. 'No,' she said. 'That is to say I heard him speaking at some trust symposium on Ofsted awareness. You knew he was working for Lodestone?'

Pat nodded.

'Anyway, he managed to make his sessions as dull as old ditchwater, which takes some doing, given how worked up us mere mortals get about Ofsted. But I know Pete knew him. He spoke to me about Neville Hilton quite a bit after we heard he'd died.'

'Pete? This is your tame inspector?'

Victoria nodded. 'I'll let him tell you,' she said. 'It's his story. Though having sat through Nev Hilton talking about "What Ofsted want", I wish I'd shouted out *Blood*!'

'Are you due an inspection then?' asked Pat.

Victoria shook her silvery white head. 'No, praise be. We've a couple of years yet – and I'll be long gone by then.' She returned Pat's cynical smile. 'I know,' she said. 'How many times have you heard me say that? But I swear to God, Pat, it was bad enough before but now we're in Lodestone Trust – they get their knickers in a right old knot!'

Pat, remembering her meeting with Chris Canne, smiled knowingly.

'I tell you,' said Victoria. 'When you're due – the second that Ofsted window creaks open – the trust sends this team in. The Ofsted Action Support Team – T.O.A.S.T., I know!' She burst out into that rich chuckle. 'Popping up all over the place they are! Honestly, Pat, if schools put a fraction of the energy into teaching, they did into passing Ofsted inspections, education in this country would be transformed overnight.' Her face grew serious. 'And you think Neville Hilton may have died because of this Ofsted he did?'

'I honestly don't know,' said Pat. 'The police say he died of natural causes, end of.'

'But you, Thelma and Liz think otherwise?'

'We don't know what to think,' said Pat. 'But somebody was shouting at him about Pity Me school. And you say this inspector worked with Neville on the actual inspection?'

'Ex-inspector – Peter Powell – aka Dreamy Pete. He works here, on a Thursday. Not inspecting but helping out in our food bank.'

Pat stared. 'How long have you been running a food bank?' she asked.

'Since the powers that be axed the funding for the community outreach centre.' Victoria sighed a deep, weary sigh. 'We've been supporting families more and more, especially since the pandemic, so it seemed a natural next step. Bring on the baked beans! Honest to God, Pat, who'd have thought in 2025 we'd be needing food banks! She sighed again and glanced at her watch. 'I better take you through. As I say we've Bun Widdup Zooming imminently and there are some things in life you are not late for!'

'Who exactly *is* this, Bun Widdup?' asked Pat, following her through the school, walking round more filled refuse sacks and boxes. 'Chris Canne was talking to her; she seemed a bit fierce.'

Victoria smiled. 'The word is "passionate". Or "enthusiastic". She's an education consultant – one of the good guys, believe it or not. I could fill this school with people spouting on about education, but she actually leaves you *wanting* to do what she's talking about. My staff all love her, even at the end of term!' She grinned. 'And she has the most amazing red and orange African print drapes – what I wouldn't give for those babies!'

They had arrived at a locked door that would at one time have led through to more classrooms. 'Down there,' she said. 'On the left – shelf city, you can't miss it.' She gave Pat a final hug and held her at arm's length, her eyes suddenly dark and serious. 'Have a care, lovely girl,' she said. 'You and Liz and Thelma, with your detectivating. You know as well as I do how feelings run high with Ofsted and I'd hate for anything to happen to you.'

'A drink?' said the Reverend Caro Miranda, leading them into a room at the conclusion of their tour. 'You must both be parched. Tea? Coffee? Water? I'm sure I can rustle up some juice.'

'Coffee's fine,' said Liz.

'White no sugar,' said Thelma.

Caro Miranda nodded and darted out and the door closed behind her with a click. A sudden, blessed peace fell on the stuffy room, which seemed to be a mix between a library and a staffroom. The two friends exchanged glances. Neither woman was much of a drinker but after their tour of Pity Me Infants school they both felt in need of something considerably stronger than coffee.

'Well,' said Liz expressively.

'I think the word we're looking for,' said Thelma, 'is "bombarded".'

'I'll say,' said Liz.

No doubt the school *had* been good, wonderful, nurturing, inclusive – all the things Caro Miranda said it had been. Now, however, it was not.

Now it was dying.

With a few mere hours of existence left, Pity Me Infants school was a school approaching the end. Each of the school's three classes was barely half full, due to a steady exodus of children following the Ofsted report, and then the news of closure. Everywhere were signs of that closure – displays removed, resources boxed up, bulging bin bags, furniture stacked in the corridors and corners. There is always a melancholy air to a primary school at the end of the summer term, a sense of something dying away as classes prepare to move up and rooms are readied for the next year, but it's a temporary dynamic, underpinned with the comforting security that come September it will all start up again. Here things felt different; here the melancholy was deeper. Permanent.

In two of the three classes it felt very much as though the staff had given up, packing and sorting in a lethargic, listless way as the children chatted, coloured, played with Lego, dominated, as children are, by the here and the now, by Unifix and Pokémon and who was hogging the good red crayon. *Is this how the world will end?* Thelma caught herself thinking. *All of us going on with our business, day to day as the place dies around us?*

But in the third class it had been a very different story. Here the tables had been pushed back against the wall, and the resultant space filled with a castle constructed from cardboard cartons. The children were engaged with ferocious, purposeful concentration making brightly coloured flags and shields to Sellotape to the walls of their castle. 'We have to get this done, like, before the dragon comes,' explained one boy.

Their teacher, a thin blonde woman, not much more than a girl herself, was supervising a group of three children painting a further sculpture of boxes a lurid green. 'That's right,' she said with bright command. 'Give him lots and *lots* of scales!'

'This all looks wonderful,' said Liz enthusiastically.

The girl looked up and fixed Thelma and Liz with an appraising stare from wide, pale blue eyes. Then she stood up, pointedly turned her back on them and walked over to another group engaged in painting the castle walls with thick, black rectangles.

'You must forgive Chloe,' said Caro Miranda in an undertone. 'She's taken the whole thing very much to heart.'

Throughout the tour Caro kept up steady, bitter commentary of what had been and was no more – the Bookworm Club, parental coffee groups, the Hungry Caterpillar that had stretched right across the playground all the way to the neighbouring church. 'Every day the children would sing for fifteen minutes,' she said at one point. 'It's a Hungarian system called Kodály – apparently it readies the brain for the day's activity. And then they finish off the day with a final whole-school singing session.'

And now, left alone in the former library the two drew breath and looked around in reflective silence.

'I can't say we've found much out,' said Liz, peering in a box marked 'Skip'. It was full of books, thumbed, slightly battered tomes: *A Day with a Bus Driver, Tadpole to Frog, Topsy and Tim's Foggy Day.* 'How sad,' she said. 'How very sad.'

'Look at this.' Thelma was looking at a display on the wall, one of the few that had not yet been removed, a montage of photographs. Liz crossed to her side and looked. The photos had obviously been run off from a cheap photocopier and were arranged at rather crazy angles, the way these things generally are. Common to all of them was a man, somewhere in his thirties, with not much hair and an infectious if rather nervous smile.

Davey Fletcher 1989–2022 read the sign.

'This must be the man who died,' said Thelma. 'The deputy head.'

Davey Fletcher was caught in the many and varied poses that

form the lot of a primary school teacher: dressed as Professor Dumbledore, having a bucket of iced water tipped over him, on a rather precarious-looking raft with some wildly excited children and dressed as an elf standing next to a glittery grotto. Plus, others – on coaches, in classrooms, on staff nights out, smiling out at the world with energy and joy.

'*Fear no more the heat o' the sun, Nor the furious winter's rages . . .*' said a soft, sad voice. '*. . . Thou thy worldly task hast done, home art gone, and ta'en thy wages: Golden lads and girls all must, as chimneysweepers, come to dust.*'

Neither of them had heard the Reverend Caro Miranda re-enter the room with a tray of coffee. 'That inspection *broke* Davey Fletcher,' she pronounced, setting the tray down.

'I'm so sorry,' said Liz truthfully.

'When did it happen?' asked Thelma. 'The accident?'

'February 19th this year.' The words came out hard and prompt. 'The day before the report came out. Of course we'd all seen it – the staff, governors – we knew what it said . . . I think it was the thought of the parents and the community reading it that so upset Davey.' She stared bleakly at her drink. 'That must've been why he went out driving in that terrible blizzard.' Her voice trailed off as she stared at the man in the photos.

Looking at those smiling images, both Liz and Thelma found themselves remembering another car crash that past winter – though the circumstances of Terri Stanley's accident had been somewhat different.

'You mentioned Davey had a partner,' said Thelma eventually. 'Was he in the car with him?'

'No, thankfully,' said Caro. 'Davey was alone – though if Son had been with him, well, maybe it wouldn't have happened.'

'Sorry?' said Liz. 'Davey had a son?'

Caro smiled. '*Son*,' she said. 'That's his partner's name. Son Masters. There he is.' She pointed to one of the pictures, that of the staff night out. Davey was standing with his arm round a person of a similar age. With his amiable face and fluffy grey hair, Son Masters had a vaguely androgynous air.

'It's a lovely tribute,' said Thelma, stepping back from the mosaic of Davey Fletcher's life.

'Chloe put it up,' said Caro, almost absently. 'We had a little memorial service here in school a few weeks ago. Before everything got too sad and chaotic here. The staff were all here – and Son. Annie was able to attend, which was really special. Some authority people – even Bun Widdup – were able to Zoom in.' She caught sight of Liz's frowning face and smiled. 'Zoom, as in attend remotely.' She indicated a large, new flatscreen that dominated one of the library walls. 'The authority fitted these throughout school last summer,' she said. 'Before all of this. A complete waste of money as it turned out. They're heading straight for the skip.'

'Don't the new school want them?' asked Thelma.

'Nope,' said Caro bitterly. 'Apparently they're not compatible with their systems.' She shook her head and her eyes ranged unhappily round the warm, boxed-up room. 'See what that man did,' she said softly.

At that moment the noise of singing, sweet and clear, rose from the school hall. 'Bobby Shafto', sung together and then in parts, the sound sweet and yet at the same time mournful as if the dying school itself had found a voice.

Thelma's eyes flicked back to the display showing the life of the man whose world had been so brutally overturned by Neville Hilton and who shortly afterwards had overturned his own world on the A171. They had been looking for one person who might have had reason to confront Neville Hilton – and they seemed to have found a whole school full.

CHAPTER THIRTEEN

Tuesday 22nd July

Text sent from Hedley Lodestone Primary Academy to parents:

THREE handbag fans were left in the hall after today's end-of-year assembly. Please call at the school office to collect.

'So, you're a friend of Victoria?' said Dreamy Pete Powell. 'And you're some sort of detective?'

'I'm not any sort of detective,' said Pat rather hotly, thinking yet again she really needed to be careful what she told her old friend. *Detectivating!* It wasn't even a proper word! Perched between a box crammed full of carrier bags and a table littered with various forms and lists, she regarded the former Ofsted inspector turned food bank operative. Dreamy? She wasn't so sure about that. He was a slight, wiry man who could have been anything between fifty and seventy, one of those people who gave the impression of being someone younger, dressed up as someone older; the bright eyes made mockery of the lines on his brow and jaw; the wiry, white curls could have been a wig.

'I'm a former colleague of Neville Hilton's first wife,' said Pat.

'And she's wanting to find out a bit more about what happened to him before his death. Which,' she added hastily, 'was a natural death, so the police say.'

'But you think it might be something to do with what happened at Pity Me school?' Those bright eyes fixed her with a shrewd look.

'Somebody was overheard shouting the name of the school at Neville not long before he died.'

Peter Powell nodded slowly. He appeared to be making up his mind about something. 'Of course, there's only so much I can say – and all of it off the record. But, well, if what you say is right – I can't say I'm at all surprised.'

'I heard it was rather a brutal inspection,' said Pat.

Peter nodded slowly. 'It's the main reason I stopped working as an Ofsted inspector,' he said.

Crossing the sun-baked playground, a voice – clear and angry – stopped Liz and Thelma in their tracks.

'Excuse me,' it said.

Liz and Thelma turned to find themselves facing the blonde teacher, Chloe, who had turned her back on them earlier.

'Excuse me,' said Chloe again. 'Can I just say, what you people are doing is *disgusting*.' She was only short, barely five feet, but what she lacked in size, she more than compensated for in attitude. Visible on her upper arm was a black, spiky-looking tattoo of some fierce Celtic design.

'Pardon me?' said Liz, feeling a panicked sneeze building.

'How you people can sleep at night is beyond me.'

'I'm sorry?' said Thelma.

'Rona Middleton.' Chloe fired the words out with scornful power. 'Ro. My classroom assistant. I think it's *terrible* you're not giving her a job in your school. Okay, she's got a record, but it's only shoplifting and that was *years* ago. I am telling you she is an excellent classroom assistant; the kids all love her to bits.'

Standing there, face bright with righteous anger, silver-blonde hair blazing in the sun Chloe would, Thelma thought, make an excellent Viking goddess – a true Valkyrie.

Liz opened her mouth to speak but Chloe had not finished, not by a long chalk. 'All that *crap* about Wearside Academy welcoming the Pity Me family into your trust – absolute *bullshit*, with you picking and choosing staff like you are doing. And don't give me any of that guff about not having enough money because you know what, that's absolute bullshit as well. I've *seen* the money being splashed around by you people left, right and centre.'

'I think,' Thelma began.

'I know what it is,' drove on Chloe. 'You don't want someone with a criminal record. But that was years ago, and at the end of the day it was a nicked Mars bar. It should *not* debar you from working in a school. I've checked.'

'I think there's some crossed wires going on here,' said Thelma gently.

'How?' said Chloe angrily.

'We're not from Wearside Academy,' said Liz, voice muffled through a balsam tissue.

'We're acquaintances of Caro Miranda,' said Thelma.

Chloe frowned, her face dark and stormy. 'So why are you here then?' she said suspiciously. 'I were told some people from Wearside Academy were coming over.'

'I'm sure they are,' said Thelma. 'But we were asked here by Reverend Miranda.'

'Why?'

Liz and Thelma exchanged glances without actually appearing to do so, in the way that comes naturally to most primary school teachers. The simplest thing – perhaps the most sensible thing – would be to make up some excuse. But tempting as that was, Thelma realised it wouldn't help them in the purpose if their visit. She felt Liz tense beside her and knew her friend was reluctantly coming to the same conclusion.

'We're here,' said Thelma, 'because we're friends of Neville Hilton's first wife.'

Chloe frowned at them uncomprehendingly. 'Neville?'

'The man who ran your school's inspection last November,' said Thelma. She couldn't see Liz but knew her friend's hands would be clenched in a tight, nervous ball.

'Neville Hilton.' Chloe stared at them. Her face was blank but, in that blankness, both Liz and Thelma could sense a whole lava flow of emotion.

'He died suddenly,' said Liz nervously.

'Good.' The word was hoarse, almost a whisper, but behind it was an anger that was white-hot and frightening. '*Good.*' She turned to go, but paused, frowning. 'Wait a minute – you think someone from here *killed* him?'

'The police are very clear that he died of natural causes,' said Thelma.

'So why are you here?'

Again. Liz and Thelma exchanged that look that wasn't a look. 'We think,' said Liz, 'maybe someone from here saw him before he died. And wondered if they could maybe tell us a bit about how he died.'

'Slowly and painfully, I hope,' said Chloe sharply. She turned on her heel and walked back into the school.

'As a system Ofsted isn't at all bad – ninety-nine times out of a hundred.' Pete Powell spoke in clipped, energetic tones, as he spooned coffee into a chipped *Doctor Who* mug. Pat, mindful of her thirty-mile drive back home, had refused his offer. 'You need some system of accountability – some of the shitshows I've seen going on, you wouldn't believe.' They had relocated to a side room marked 'Office' which seemed to contain little beyond coffee-making equipment and an inordinate number of plastic bags.

'But it's a blunt tool.' Peter poured water into the mug. 'A hefty blunt tool. The proverbial sledgehammer to crack the nut.

And, granted, sometimes you need that sledgehammer, but in most cases a tap from a fingernail will do.' He turned and fixed her with those piercing blue eyes in a way that made her want to adjust her top. Maybe 'dreamy' wasn't so far from the mark after all . . .

'You mean Pity Me school?' she said, hoping he wouldn't detect any sort of blush on her face.

Peter nodded. 'What you have to remember about Ofsted,' he said, 'is that it's a series of guidelines – not a list of rules. Prompts for conversations, if you like. Only of course in practice they're treated exactly as a list of rules – especially by less experienced inspectors.'

'Like Neville Hilton?' said Pat.

'He was your prime culprit. To the Neville Hiltons of this world, the guidelines are a list of things to be ticked or crossed – no conversational prompts going on in any shape or form.'

At that moment the door opened firmly, pushed by a determined bottom and an elderly woman in a sari, the most gorgeous shade of sky blue, advanced towards Peter Powell with a cup and plate.

'Coffee, Mr Peter,' she said firmly, totally ignoring Pat.

'I have one thanks, Tania.'

Tania took one look at the strong brew, tutted in despair and tipped it down the sink, replacing it with one the colour of pale caramel. 'Cake,' she said setting down the plate with an unassailable clatter. On it sat two, glistening lokma fritters. 'You eat this, make sure you do. I shall look in the bins and ask the other ladies.'

'Bless you, Tania,' said Peter Powell, giving her a brilliant smile. Pat decided to have this man turning up in her classroom in search of conversational prompts would actually be no bad thing.

'God love her,' said Peter after the sky-blue figure had retreated. 'My diabetic consultant would have me sectioned if I so much as sniffed that. Where were we?'

'Neville Hilton and Ofsted guidelines,' said Pat.

Peter Powell nodded. 'With Nev, guidelines were rules – and he couldn't see beyond those rules. And with that school, Pity Me Infants, there were some pretty amazing things going on. Okay, there were some things wrong with the place – as there are in most places – but ultimately it was the sort of school consultants like Bun Widdup or Alison Phillipson would send people to as a model of good practice. But that said – there *were* some safeguarding concerns and Nev was absolutely right to raise them. There's some right evil bastards out there and you have got *to* be one hundred per cent watertight.'

He sighed, took a sip of the coffee Tania had made and pulled a face. 'If only the head teacher had been there,' he said. 'By all accounts she was one amazing woman – but she was off sick and her deputy was acting head. Nervy chap. From the get-go he got very defensive with Nev, really butting heads with him. How dare Nev be questioning their practice.' He shook his head. 'The staff – the governors – they lined up right behind him – and the more they kicked back, the more stubborn Nev became.'

Pat nodded; she could well imagine it. 'Could you not have intervened?' she asked. 'You were one of the inspectors.'

'But not the lead inspector.' He sighed despondently into his coffee. 'I tried,' he said. 'Believe you me, I tried – but at the end of the day, Nev was the lead inspector and there's some pretty hefty protocols around these things. I tried talking to Nev – but he wasn't for listening to me, or anyone for that matter.'

'It all got quite heated I heard?' prompted Pat.

Peter Powell nodded. 'I reckon,' he said, 'we were lucky not to get our tyres let down.'

'Was there anyone in particular,' started Pat.

'—who might go after Neville eight months later, driving him to an early grave?' finished Peter. Again, those eyes met Pat's. They really were a gorgeous shade of blue. He shrugged. 'Everyone was angry the Leadership was given that judgement of Inadequate. The chair of governors – well, I remember thinking it was a good job she was a woman of the cloth. At one point I thought she was going to go for our throats. One of the teachers, young lass – the one whose paperwork hadn't been there – she had a right go at us during the feedback. Stormed out in tears.' He shook his head sadly. 'It shouldn't ever need to be like that.'

'And the deputy's partner?'

Peter Powell's face broke into a sudden, sunny grin. 'I'd forgotten him,' he said. 'Do forgive me. I wouldn't say he confronted Neville so much as reasoned with him. Collared him by his car, asked him to find his inner peace and karma.' The grin broadened. 'He even asked Nev to hug it out.'

Pat, remembering Neville Hilton, found herself grinning too.

Peter's face grew sombre. 'I heard about the lad – the deputy who died,' he said. 'I felt very bad about that. He was in a terrible state by the time we left. And yes, I do feel responsible.' He took an absent-minded sip of Tania's coffee and again pulled a face. 'Teaching's so personal,' he said. 'Running a school – it's not about rules and spreadsheets, no matter how much the powers that be think it should be.'

Pat nodded, remembering her own years in school – so many memories, so many emotions, none of them boring. Noisy shouts made them both look outside. The end of the school day, nearly the end of the school year, children charging out of the doors, eager for whatever the summer afternoon had in store, followed more slowly by parents and grandparents fanning themselves and calling their charges to slow down.

Peter watched them, eyes far away. 'You take your energy and you use it to connect with others. *That's* what education is about. That's why I love coming to places like here – meeting people like Victoria. And that's why after the whole Pity Me inspection fiasco I decided that was it. I came home and said, "Sandy: that's me done." Which is why I find myself in places like this, manhandling the pasta sauce and the disposable nappies.' Again, the grin broke out, a rueful, reflective grin. Looking at this passionate, wiry and definitely dreamy man, Pat found herself wondering if Sandy – whoever she was – knew how lucky she was.

Thelma and Liz exchanged glances as Chloe stalked back into the school. 'That is one very angry young lady,' said Liz, shaking her head.

Thelma nodded. 'There seems to have been something about Neville Hilton that brought out that side of people,' she said.

Liz nodded her head again as she shaded her eyes, looking in her bag for more tissues and car keys. 'It seems to be my week for facing angry people,' she said, unlocking the white Fiat.

Thelma nodded. Watching the terraced houses of Pity Me slide by she reflected on the two angry people she'd encountered that day: Caro Miranda, bitter and outraged; Chloe Lord, hot and explosive. But for all that there'd been a common element underlying their anger. Rage. The rage, Thelma thought, that comes with grief.

As they approached the roundabout at the start of the Durham bypass, Thelma said, 'There's the road Davey Fletcher was taking when he crashed that day.'

Both thought of that smiling man from Chloe's memorial board, his fateful winter journey over the moor's road. On a day such as today it was almost impossible to conceive of any such thing as a blizzard. Liz looked at the road sign: *A171 Whitby and Scarborough*.

The A171.

'How very odd,' she said frowning.

'What?' said Thelma.

'That road – the A171. When I was looking through Neville's complaints file, that's one of the things he was complaining about ... the dangerous state of the A171.'

CHAPTER FOURTEEN

Wednesday 23rd July

From the Hambleton Amblers Not Ramblers Facebook Page:

Please be aware that due to the extreme heat, today's Abbey-to-Abbey Saunter has once again been postponed, this time until next month. Keep putting on that sunblock, Amblers!

'How about now?' The light behind Liz's head flared whitely, reducing her to a spectral silhouette.

'We can hear you fine,' said Pat. 'It's just the light.'

'The sun's all wrong in here,' said Liz crossly. 'Derek's in his study. I can't sit in the conservatory; it's like a sauna. The kitchen is the only place left with decent Wi-Fi—'

'As long as we can hear you,' said Thelma placatingly, but Liz wasn't listening. The picture juddered crazily, tilted, froze and unfroze showing blurred, tipped images of her hallway, stairs and landing. Finally, the picture settled and resolved, showing an expanse of white candlewick bedspread.

'I'm in the spare room,' announced Liz tetchily. 'Hang on whilst I pull the curtains.'

Pat could sympathise with her friend's frustrations. This Zoom 'debrief' had been urged by Thelma as an alternative to the garden centre, bearing in mind the temperature was forecast to, once again, nudge the forty-degree mark. Both Pat and Liz's reaction to her idea had been along the lines of 'so what?' but Thelma had been so grave, so insistent that the simplest thing had been to go along with the suggestion.

The picture of the candlewick bedspread shuddered, tipped and finally settled to reveal Liz in front of the drawn spare room curtains, pink with the sun behind them.

'Can you see me *now*?' she demanded in an irritated voice, which implied she'd rather face the heat than do battle with this means of communication. Both her friends responded in the affirmative and neither mentioned that in plain view behind her was an airer draped with Derek's powder-blue boxer shorts.

'So where were we?' said Pat. Behind her was a virtual backdrop showing one of the chateaus she and Rod had visited earlier that year. Not because she had any drying underwear to hide, but her kitchen counter was set up with an arrangement of fat, lavender candles, which Tiffany was planning to photograph, and Tiffany-Jane was a subject she wanted to keep her friend's thoughts all the way away from. There had been more raised voices last night after Justin had got home, following which she'd seen neither her son nor his girlfriend – not even ducking in and out the bathroom.

'The A171,' said Thelma. 'I was wondering just where Davey Fletcher was driving to when he had his accident.' Behind her could be seen the sober, olive-green tones of her living room, with Snaffles the cat eyeing them fixedly from a patch of sunlight. It looked the epitome of tidiness and order, but to move the laptop slightly to the left would reveal a whole stack of Teddy's parcels waiting to be entered in his WAMMP app.

'The A171,' said Liz in brisk, business-like tones. 'I've been checking. I reckon the poor lad would have been heading to

Whitby or Scarborough, or even Bridlington – anywhere round those parts. Any place else and he'd have taken the York road.'

'Did he have to be going anywhere?' said Pat. 'Maybe he just wanted to drive?'

'In a blizzard?' said Liz, incredulous.

'Maybe,' said Pat. 'If he was upset.' She thought about her own periodic sojourns to the lay-by above Borrowby when life got fraught. 'It was the day before the Ofsted report came out, remember.'

'He crashed at a place called Wentworth Bank,' said Thelma. 'A bit of an accident black spot apparently. Hang on.' Deftly, she operated the screen share and a page from the *Cleveland Herald* appeared showing an image of a stretch of snowy road, taped off with a number of attendant police vehicles parked at angles. WENTWORTH BLIZZARD CRASH. LOCAL TEACHER KILLED. HOW MANY MORE? SAY APPALLED RESIDENTS. Pat and Liz read the brief summary of the crash, the fourth in sixteen months, plus a police appeal for careful driving in bad weather.

'It doesn't tell us anything we didn't know,' said Pat.

'I wonder,' said Liz, 'why Neville Hilton was writing to complain about the same road.'

'If it *was* the same road,' said Pat. 'You said yourself you only got a quick look.'

'A171,' said Liz stubbornly. 'I remembered the 171 because that was my code for the photocopier.' There was a momentary respectful acknowledgement of this from her former colleagues. Evidence of this nature was, Pat and Thelma both felt, as watertight as it got.

'It's a long road, the A171,' said Thelma. 'Some fifty-odd miles.' She killed the sad image, and the three faces appeared once more on the screen. 'It doesn't have to have been that particular bit.'

'Well, one thing's certain,' said Pat, 'it wasn't Davey Fletcher who was in Hollinby Quernhow shouting the odds at Neville.'

'No,' said Thelma. 'The question is who could it have been?'

'Caro Miranda,' said Liz promptly. 'Hold on.' There was a pause as she shared a picture. The first attempt showed her Amazon Prime page (low-sugar salad cream), but the second showed the lady herself, smiling a rather glacial smile. 'It's from the school website.'

'So, you think it's the Reverend Nemesis in the Snuggery with the attitude,' said Pat. 'Dreamy Pete said how hostile she got. She certainly looks as if she's got an axe to grind.'

'Maybe,' said Thelma neutrally.

'Come on,' said Liz. 'You saw how she was. Really angry. You can't discount her just because she's a vicar.'

'That's nothing to do with it,' said Thelma shortly. 'Like you, I saw an angry, upset woman. But it doesn't necessarily follow she was angry and upset enough to track Neville down to his house and confront him.'

'Talking of confronting,' said Pat. 'There's that Chloe you met. She sounds a right piece of work.'

'She was really upset,' said Liz, sounding slightly defensive. 'Sticking up for her friend who hadn't been given a job.'

'She was still angry,' said Pat. 'And by the sounds of it angry enough to have a go at Nev.'

Thelma said nothing. She was remembering that glinting kitchen knife in the dishwasher in amongst the jumble of plates and serving tureens. Those plates – three plates . . . *Why three?*

'I've been wondering about Davey's Son,' said Liz, breaking into her thoughts.

'His son?' said Pat. 'I didn't know he had any kids.'

'No,' said Liz. 'His partner – his name is Son. Hang on.' Pat sighed as Amazon Prime appeared yet again (sugar-free madeira cake) to be rapidly replaced by an image of fluffy clouds and pink and purple sky. Over this were Comic Sans letters in a bold tangerine colour: *Are you the best you that you can be?* (Pat had to read this through twice before finding the correct phrasing.) To one side of the screen was a picture that Thelma recognised from the montage at school. Despite all the advantages of posed studio photography, Son Masters still retained that air of slightly androgenous amiability.

'He does these talks,' said Liz. 'Self-help stuff.'

'There's one today,' noted Thelma. 'Seven steps to success. Ingleby Barwick library, wherever that is.'

'Remember, it was a woman that Judy Whats–her–face heard,' said Pat. 'Not that I don't think he had a good reason to be mad with Neville. But from what Dreamy Pete was saying, this Son person was more into hugging. At least on the surface.'

'I think he looks rather sweet,' said Liz. 'Harmless.'

Pat clicked her tongue impatiently. 'Liz Newsome, what are you like?' she said. 'It's not about how people look. Remember Jason Riley in my class? Mr Butter–wouldn't–melt himself. We lost half our tadpoles thanks to him.'

'The thing to remember,' said Thelma, 'is that the nicest people, the most well-meaning of us – well, we're all capable of doing the most terrible things. And just because someone has done something terrible, it doesn't automatically make them a terrible person. Sometimes they're just as good and principled as ever they were.'

'So, what are we going to do?' asked Pat. There was a slight tumbleweed moment, one that made her feel frankly irritated. 'Come on,' she said, 'Victoria called us detectivators – we might as well detectivate.'

Thelma coughed slightly. *Here we go*, thought Pat half considering doing a drum roll on her coffee table. *Just spit it out.*

'I've had an email,' said Thelma, once more sharing the screen. The email was brief.

Dear Mrs Cooper, it read, *I understand from Caro Miranda you visited Pity Me Infants school yesterday. I wonder if you would have the time for a conversation very soon? We could speak on the phone or via Zoom. Alternatively, we could meet face to face, although due to ill health I am unable to travel very far. I live near Middlesborough in a village called Newton-under-Roseberry.*
King regards,
Annie Golightly

'Who,' said Pat impatiently, 'is Annie Golightly?'

'She's the head teacher at the school,' said Liz, mildly reproachful. 'The one who's been ill.'

'So, are we going to see her then?' said Pat.

'*I* am,' said Thelma with a slight emphasis on the first word. 'I'm going later on.'

'Today?' said Liz. 'Don't you need someone to drive you? With your arm?' If there was a certain ironic inflection on the last part of this sentence, Thelma ignored it.

'Teddy's taking me,' she said. 'I don't think going in mob-handed is such a good idea.' There was another bit of a tumbleweed moment, this one more pronounced.

Quite how the exchange would have played out was unclear; however, at that moment Snaffles the cat decided to assert his authority by walking casually across the keyboard, treating Liz and Pat to a flash of bottom. By the time Thelma had removed him the call had timed out and ended.

Pat shut the laptop with feelings of vague irritation. *Mob-handed*? What was that supposed to mean? Like she and Liz were going to barge in shrieking with laughter and start wrecking the joint? Larson, seeing that she was done with the call, nosed hopefully round her ankles in that way he had when announcing he was about ready for his walk. Pat was just reaching for her sun hat when the door to the kitchen opened to reveal Justin, dressed for work in short-sleeved shirt and cargo shorts, leather satchel over his shoulder. It was the first time she'd seen him in two days.

'Hey, Ma,' he said, walking purposefully to the back door.

'Never mind, "hey, Ma",' said Pat, standing up. 'I want a word with you—'

'Just heading off to work, can't stop,' said Justin with a dazzling smile.

'I wanted to say I was sorry about Newcastle.'

The smile flickered, but only briefly. 'Ah well,' he said. 'Plenty more nets to shoot.' He started to move but with the ease of experience, Pat transposed herself adroitly between her eldest son and the back door.

'Justin,' she said.

'Ma! On a deadline here!'

'What's going on?' she said firmly. 'With you and Tiffany?'

'Er – nothing!' Justin's tone was an upbeat, sunny blend of the questioning and mocking.

When there was something wrong with her eldest son, he'd invariably present his parents with one of two faces: either bright and chirpy or abandoned misery. His sunny appearance now didn't fool Pat one jot, having seen it used over the years to mask exam disasters, a stolen credit card and any number of weeping girlfriends.

On the whole Pat preferred abandoned misery.

'Justin,' she said firmly. 'Why have you two been rowing?'

There was a pause and Larson pointedly absented himself from the room.

'Okay.' He let out a breath. 'Okay, I'm really sorry – and I'm sorry on behalf of Tiff as well.' He made to move, as if this explained everything. Pat, however, did not shift.

'Ma, we were just having a bit of a head-butt. Like you and Pa used to have.'

The attempt to widen out whatever was going on into an inevitable fact of existence was another of Justin's tried and tested tactics, one that also failed to cut any ice with his mother.

'What about?' said Pat standing her ground. 'This bit of a clash – what was it about? And don't be saying "nothing".' The direct approach was always the best way with Justin; at least that way she could tell if he was lying.

Justin sighed, ran his hand through his hair in the way that reminded her so strongly of Rod.

'Okay, Mother,' he said. 'So we're both working really hard to make this thing work. Losing the job, the apartment – it's not been easy – not that we're both not massively grateful to you for letting us stay here. But we're both busting a gut to get things back on track. And it's bound to generate – a certain amount of friction.'

So, lying then.

At the back door he paused, as a warm gust of air and light flooded in from the baking morning.

'Mum,' he said seriously. 'Promise me – *promise* me you won't say anything about this to Tiff.'

Watching him bounce out into the hard light, satchel jauntily over his shoulder, Pat felt her heart break just a little bit more.

Wearily she sat back at the table. What on earth was going on? Had one of them been unfaithful? Tiffany-Jane? She thought of her that day in Leeds, bare face set. Where had she been going? She didn't look as if she was going to – or coming from – any sort of lover. Pat found herself remembering Thelma's words: *Just because someone has done something terrible, it doesn't automatically make them a terrible person.*

She opened the laptop to turn it off and found herself looking at the amiable face of Son Masters. Amiable he might look, but was there also a shrewd, almost watchful quality to that gaze? *Jason Riley – Mr Butter-wouldn't-melt* – and something else, something lurking at the back of her mind . . . What *was* it about that face that chimed off a faint chord of something?

A nudge on the ankles announced the presence of Larson, lead in his mouth.

'Two minutes,' she said focusing on the laptop. Where was that seminar again? Ingleby Barwick library? Where was that when it was at home? Pat brought up Way Finder on her phone . . . There was another, more pointed nudge.

'Hold your horses,' she said to Larson. 'We'll go for your walk, but it'll be a quick one. I'm going on a bit of an expedition later on.'

She studied the route flashing up on the screen. Thelma wasn't the only one who could take herself off detectivating.

CHAPTER FIFTEEN

Wednesday 23rd July

Hambleton Council: Hot tips for hot weather:

In very hot weather, keep an eye on the elderly who may struggle to keep themselves cool and hydrated.

Carrying the laptop back downstairs, Liz was also reflecting on Thelma's expedition, but for different reasons. Going to see Annie Golightly? *With Teddy driving her?* Why was her friend suddenly so reluctant to drive? Had there been some sort of accident or something?

She pushed the speculations aside. Tonight was her pre-diabetes awareness class and she needed to fill her food diary in, a task she never relished, no matter how 'good' she'd been. There was something about seeing that sensible spreadsheet of low-sugar this and high-fibre that, that never failed to give her a feeling of grey flatness, despite the undoubted good it was doing her beta cells. She was glumly tapping in 'low-sugar biscuit' (right enough, it had tasted like cardboard) as Derek pottered gloomily into the kitchen.

'It's like a sauna in that back bedroom,' he announced fanning his red face with a sheaf of papers.

Her husband presented an odd appearance: on the top half, a white shirt and red tie, which was very much his North Yorkshire County Council persona, witnessed by everyone on the Zoom meeting he'd just been in. His lower half, however, was altogether more summery – flip-flops and a pair of baggy shorts, red faded to pink, which Liz remembered him buying when their son Tim was at the paddling pool stage.

'Good meeting?' she asked.

Derek didn't immediately answer, as he spooned coffee into his favourite Bispham mug; he wasn't much of a one for multi-tasking. Eventually he spoke. 'The usual,' he said in tones of deep gloom. 'Dishforth Lea.'

Liz nodded understandingly. Part of Derek's job at the council involved assessing land for potential building there. Dishforth Lea was a pretty field, by a pretty village; feelings were running high, with people making lengthy and outraged social media posts on a daily basis.

Derek pulled his white shirt out of his shorts and flapped it against his stocky frame. 'It'd save half the argy-bargy if only people would look at the pictures and the plans – they're all on the website . . . Instead, they're asking a load of totally unnecessary convoluted questions.' He sighed, a deep sigh. 'Anyway – how's your morning going? How were the gruesome twosome? What were you talking about?'

'This and that,' said Liz, angling the laptop round to avoid any unnecessary questions about potential killers. Yes, the various faces and newspaper headlines were hidden by the food diary, but you never knew and her husband was looking stressed enough already. 'I was just updating my food diary. Don't forget it's pre-diabetes tonight so we'll need tea earlier.'

Derek rumpled her hair in an understanding way. 'You can tell old Happy Harvey we've the food police descending on us tomorrow. Our Jacob's planning to try a new recipe on us and wanted to know if we have any frozen spinach.'

They smiled, a smile of mutual adversity, and Derek picked up his coffee and retreated to the door.

'If you want me,' said Liz, 'I'll be down in the allotment.'

Derek stopped dead in his tracks, turning all the way round to face her. 'The allotment?'

'Billy's bench, remember? I said I'd do it ages ago.'

Billy's bench was a feature much cherished by the various allotment holders, a memorial to one of its best loved and long-standing members. The holders all took it in turn every six months to treat it with wood preservative and this time it was Liz's turn.

Now Derek was looking at her as if she'd said 'minefield' not 'allotment'.

'Liz, have you not heard any of the warnings they're giving out?' He sounded gravely horrified. 'About staying out of the direct heat for long periods of time?'

'It won't be a long period of time,' she started to say, but Derek was in full anxious flight, face furrowed with concern.

'Older people – that's us – need to stay out of the direct sunlight.'

Liz knew better than to argue. She merely nodded obediently, fighting to keep the exasperation from her face. Derek crossed the kitchen, touched her shoulder. 'It's vital us old gimmers stay safe,' he said earnestly. 'If you want, later on when I've finished work, you can maybe do twenty minutes and I'll stand over you with an umbrella.'

Liz nodded without speaking and Derek smiled again.

'We've Jacob's Spinach Surprise, remember,' he said, and Liz smiled brightly to hide her feelings.

Older people! Old gimmers!

She watched the shorts-and-shirt-sporting figure retreat and found herself thinking about the night they'd met all those years ago, at her cousin Janice's wedding. That hotel place in Kirkstall . . . meeting, talking – having one too many Babychams . . . and then walking down to the abbey, watching the night sky growing paler and paler over the stark, smoke-stained stones. Realising, with a feeling as wonderful and unspectacular as the grey dawn that this was the man she was going to spend the rest of her life with.

She sighed, for days long gone by when her beta cells could cope with as much Babycham as she cared to drink. Of one thing though she was certain. She'd been looking forward to space and peace and thinking time down the allotment repainting the bench: no way would she find any of those things with Derek hovering behind her with an umbrella.

She sighed again. The food diary could wait. She reached to shut down the laptop, saw the photos smiling blandly out at her – Chloe and Caro . . . Two hurt, two angry people with a lot more to feel upset about than Spinach Surprise or an untreated bench. A thought struck her. Had it been either of *them* visiting the Snuggery the night Neville died? Derek's words popped into her mind. *If only people would look at the pictures* . . . then they'd KNOW.

Pictures . . .

Suddenly life felt a little less grey and old-gimmery.

Derek was deep into a phone call, spreadsheet on his PC, duvet cover draped over the window to further block out the light and heat. He was barely aware of the Post-it Note his wife carefully affixed to his Dishforth fields ring binder.

Gone to shop: out of frozen spinach – will go STRAIGHT inside.

She didn't feel especially guilty about the lie, because it wasn't a lie – it just wasn't the whole truth.

Today the headscarf was purple, not pink, but still as bright and sparkly as the smile that had welcomed her. 'Here we go, my lovely!'

The ice clinked invitingly in the jug of elderflower Sidrah carried in. Liz smiled and decided that Derek would agree that the benefits of hydration on such an afternoon definitely outweighed the potential drawbacks of a sugary drink. Sidrah's welcome had been warm, fulsome even. One that Liz recognised instantly: the welcome of a lonely person who knew all too well what it was like to feel the hours stretching away. Liz felt awkward and not a little guilty at this; making conversation about the plants in the garden was one thing, asking her about the various comings and goings at the Old Barn felt like quite another. However, Liz Newsome non-gimmery detectivator had come here for a reason.

As Sidrah poured the drinks, Liz looked round the opulent room, unlike any Yorkshire cottage interior she'd ever seen. The kitchen and living room had been knocked into one, the walls stripped back to the stone, and what had probably been a rather conventional fireplace replaced by an altogether flashier affair of slabs and beams. The decor was a makeover show's dream of white carpets, leather sofas, a positively enormous wall-mounted TV, state-of-the-art kitchen appliances, including a wine fridge – and yet for all the opulence the room felt awkward, slightly out of place – much like Sidrah herself. The main window – like the garden – gave an almost flawless view of both the Snuggery and the Old Barn. Liz could see the window of Neville's study and remembered with a stab of embarrassment her fevered fumbling through his filing drawers.

'I'll just shut this lot down,' said Sidrah, indicating a laptop on the kitchen counter flanked by ring binders and a magazine box; presumably this was the home business.

'What is it you do?' asked Liz.

'CVs,' said Sidrah. 'As in write them up for people.' Her voice was brisk and professional.

'I'm sorry, I interrupted your working,' said Liz.

'You didn't. I wasn't,' said Sidrah. 'I was looking on Rightmove as it happens.'

'You're thinking of moving?' said Liz.

Sidrah nodded. 'This place,' she said and stopped.

Instinctively Liz glanced out the window, across to the Old Barn. 'Because of what happened?' she said.

'Oh no!' Sidrah shook her head. 'No, nothing to do with

Neville – and yet, maybe it made me think how lonely this place is . . . Nick and I.' She cast a reflexive glance at the mantel where sat a photo of herself entwined round a cheery-looking rather red-faced man. 'It was our dream – move out here, run the business from home. Nick was from York originally; he always loved it round here. And we had an idea living in a village would be like it is on the telly.' She sighed a deep, sad sigh. 'But now it's just me.'

Liz nodded understandingly. 'There's some really nice places in Ripon and Thirsk,' she said. 'Sowerby, just down from us has some lovely properties.'

'Actually,' said Sidrah, 'I'm more looking round Solihull. Home. With my family and my bezzies. Where all the Prosecco bars are! Don't get me wrong – I'm sure it's lovely here.' She smiled sadly. 'But knowing what I know now – well, moving here was a mistake. Anyway.'

She set her glass down and looked expectantly at Liz. Liz braced herself. How on earth to manoeuvre the conversation round to the subject of the Old Barn and its late occupant? As it turned out, however, there was no need.

'I'm guessing you're here about Nev?' said Sidrah.

Liz felt flustered, opened her mouth to deny this, then all of a sudden realised the woman was smiling at her.

'One thing you learn in the CV business, babes,' she said, 'is how to cut out the see are ay pee. I've been gabbing with your mate Zippy. She said you were asking questions.'

Liz wanted to say something along the lines of 'she's not my mate', but then realised Zippy Doodah had, in her own way, undoubtedly done her a favour. 'We were just wondering one or two things,' she said. There was now no pretence whatsoever of this being a visit about hydrangeas, so Liz Newsome Detectivator reached into her bag and brought out the photos she'd printed off.

'These people,' she said, arranging Chloe and Caro Miranda on the sparkling glass coffee table. 'Have you ever seen them before?'

'Oh my God!' Sidrah's eyes widened and she bit back an excited laugh. 'Are these the people who were shouting at Neville?'

'Possibly,' said Liz.

Sidrah stared at the two photos with avid interest. 'No,' she said, almost sadly, Liz thought. 'No, I've not seen either of these two.' She held up the picture of Chloe, as if willing some spark of recognition to ignite. 'No,' she said again. Putting it down she noticed a third sheet, still in the folder, the picture of Son. 'Is this someone who knew him too?' she said.

Liz nodded, was about to say it was a woman they were looking for but Sidrah was looking at Son's amiable image with a puzzled frown.

'I don't think I know him,' she said, 'Just for a sec he reminded me a little bit of that funny woman.'

'What funny woman?' said Liz Newsome Detectivator.

'The woman who had been staying in Nev's holiday let,' said Sidrah. Liz recalled what Thelma had told her. 'You spoke to her, didn't you?' she said.

'She spoke to me,' said Sidrah. 'When she was leaving. About four o'clock. The afternoon when it all happened. I was in the garden and she came over and started talking to me about my plants.'

'She didn't,' said Liz, 'say anything about seeing anyone watching the house? Maybe hanging round the snicket?'

'She didn't say anything about seeing anyone,' said Sidrah. 'But that doesn't mean she didn't. Mind you, I'm more likely to see anyone hanging around. I'm out in the garden that much.' She shook her head and took a reflective sip of her elderflower. 'She was a funny little thing.'

'Oh?' Liz Newsome Detectivator took a glorious sugary gulp of her drink. 'Funny in what way?'

Sidrah frowned. 'It's hard to say,' she said. 'There was just something about her. She was a bit drab, if you know what I mean – greeny-brown-coloured clothes,' she said, unconsciously fingering the scarf. 'Like an old person would wear.'

Or a gimmer. Liz thought of her beloved olive-green gardening fleece but said nothing.

'And the garden!' Sidrah frowned. 'That was weird. She came over and started saying how nice it looked and how hard I must work, and how she had a garden at home – and then she said she liked my hydrangeas.'

'Your hydrangeas?' Liz frowned. 'Surely it's the wrong time of year for them?'

'Exactly, babes! They weren't hydrangeas at all, they were gladioli! And if she was as loved up on gardening as she cracked on she was, she'd have known that!'

'And this lady was the last person you saw?'

Sidrah nodded. 'The last person driving in or out of the Nev's place until he got home. I checked the CCTV, remember.'

'And that would show anyone driving in or out?'

'It just shows the front gate,' said Sidrah. 'And when it swivels round you get a teeny-tiny glance of the front of the house. But yeah, you can definitely see people driving in and out of the gate. I mean I can send the file across to you, but like I say there was no one. No one coming in the front that is . . .'

Back outside Liz braced herself for a baking dash to the car, but for whatever reason the heat didn't feel quite as oppressive as before. Standing in Chapel Lane, in front of Sidrah's house, she was suddenly struck by the smell of lavender. Ignoring the throb in her sinuses, she inhaled, finding herself remembering a long-ago holiday in Corfu, how carefree she had felt (until Derek's dickie tummy had kicked in). For a moment she stood, luxuriating in the baking blue and gold day, inhaling the heady warm scent. She should of course go back to the car – the heat was rapidly changing from warm to oppressive and she was aware she'd no sun hat. But still she lingered, smelling the heady lavender and looking at the honey stone frontage of the Old Barn.

Sidrah had promised to send the CCTV footage over later

but had been adamant it had shown no one leaving or entering the property – apart from Neville and the tenant of the holiday cottage. But what about the *back*? What about that unlocked back gate Thelma had mentioned? On impulse Liz Newsome Detectivator found herself heading to the snicket next to the Old Barn, the one that led to Hollinby Quernhow playing fields.

Her first, dominant thought on seeing them was *what a sad place . . .* A carpet of limp, thistle-strewn grass, amidst which two ageing goalposts sagged wearily. She found herself imagining autumns past, the village football team playing Pickhill or Rainton or Marley, the mud, the shouts, and afterwards everyone repairing to the now boarded-up pub. But no more.

She saw the black wooden door set into the hedge, but lacked the courage to try it – besides, she knew from Thelma it had been open even if it was locked now. Shading her face, she scanned the playing fields. The distant borders were tangled hedgerows, bright with wildflowers, meadow stock, cow parsley – and was that heartsease? She ignored a mental image of a descending cloud of golden pollen and focused on the distant boundary. Towards the east, next to a clump of trees, was a gate; as she looked at it a tractor went past. Judging by the sound of its passage, Chapel Lane must loop round the back of the playing fields after leaving the village, the way country lanes do.

As quickly as the grass and thistles (and her knees) allowed, she crossed the field. Now the sun was starting to weigh heavily, clamping the back of her neck and bare head. *Never mind the pollen – where's your sun hat?* said her inner reproving voice. *Heatstroke! People our age are especially vulnerable!* She really shouldn't be staying out here any longer than she needed to. (*Derek! It's me! I'm in the Friarage with heatstroke!*)

At last, she came to the gate. Pushing it open, Liz could see a pull-in, off the lane, in the shade of the trees, largely concealed by bushes and vegetation. Perhaps somewhere in times past where the roller for the playing field would be stored.

The grass, Liz noted, was crushed and broken. Obviously in the recent past a vehicle had been parked up here. But it could have been anyone, surely.

Except . . . A splodge of artificially bright yellow in the vegetation caught her attention. Frowning, she picked up the object, which was a crumpled yellow paper flower . . . A paper flower? How odd – and yet a tickle of recognition supplanted the feelings of surprise. Where had she seen a yellow flower recently? She forced herself to pause, let the images come . . .

Not one yellow flower but several . . . being worn by people.

Of course! *Davey Fletcher's memorial!*

Chloe, Annie, Caro, Son – all of them bearing those splodges of bright yellow . . .

Excited, Liz Newsome Detectivator carefully put the paper flower in her bag, and then braced herself to brave the long hot walk back to her car.

As she crossed the playing field, she cast an idle glance at the back of the Old Barn.

She was being watched.

With a chill jolt she clearly saw a figure in an upstairs window staring in her direction. And despite the heat, despite the distance, Liz knew that stare was icy cold.

Ffion Hilton.

CHAPTER SIXTEEN

Wednesday 23rd July

From the Thirsk and Ripon Green Fingers Gang Facebook Page:

Don't worry about watering the lawn! Grass is very good at dealing with a lack of water. Even if it's brown, it'll bounce right back!

'Left here,' said Thelma. Obediently and concisely, Teddy turned the mussel-blue Corsair up Church Lane and into Newton-under-Roseberry with its wide bone-dry verges and set-back houses.

'We're looking for a bungalow called Bretton Hall,' she added.

'Isn't that the sculpture place near Wakefield?' commented her husband, peering at the passing houses.

'It was a teacher training college,' said Thelma. 'Back in the day. I did a course there once, many moons ago.' She spotted a sign on a gate. 'There!' she said.

Teddy stopped the car just beyond an imposing five-bar gate. Some way back sat a bungalow, south-facing, the wide windows bouncing back the fierce afternoon sun.

'Not very hall-like,' said Teddy, turning off the engine. 'I wonder if it's where she went to college?'

'Maybe,' said Thelma, distracted. She paused, slightly awkward, and took his hand. 'And thank you again for driving me, for giving up today's deliveries.'

'Listen.' Teddy's voice was serious, his blue eyes fixed on her, his grip tightening. 'It's like this. Today is an absolutely glorious day, and I get to spend it all with my lovely wife. Which is a win-win in my eyes.'

Thelma smiled, unclipped her belt. 'I hope you still feel like that after we've seen Ms Golightly.'

Teddy retained his grip. 'Before we go in,' he said, his voice becoming serious, 'you know what I'm going to say to you – about what you told me.'

'I do,' Thelma broke in hastily. 'I do – but for now, let me focus on Ms Golightly.'

Teddy nodded and likewise unbuckled. 'Why do you think she wants to see you?' he asked.

Thelma shrugged. 'One would guess,' she said, 'that it's to do with my visit to Pity Me school. Most probably Caro Miranda told her.'

'And you're sure it's all right, me coming in with you?' said Teddy. 'I can easily go and find some shade and listen to the cricket.'

Thelma gripped his hand; there was something she was finding very reassuring about her husband's presence this morning. She looked over to the south, where Roseberry Topping was shimmering in the heat. Her conversation with Annie Golightly was very possibly not going to be an easy one.

'Please,' she said, 'I'd like you with me.'

They walked up the lane hand in hand. As the drought deepened, Thelma had noticed a number of trees shedding leaves in response; here in the lane it was quite pronounced, drifts of shrivelled brown spinning downwards in the hot breeze. As they approached the neat frontage of Bretton Hall the door fairly sprung open, ejecting a trim, frowning figure sporting a purple medical uniform and an enormous single plait, which swung with energy. A name badge announced her as Oorja.

Even though pausing at the sight of Thelma and Teddy, she still managed to exude the air of someone marching full pelt onto the next of life's tasks.

'Ah,' she said and turned her head. 'Annie, your visitors are here, my lovely woman!'

There was a faint answering call from somewhere within the house.

'You better go through,' said the woman, setting off up the path. 'She's in the lounge. First door on the left.'

'A moment,' said Thelma. Reluctantly Oorja halted, giving the air of someone who was, so to speak, pausing on the clutch. 'Ms Golightly,' said Thelma. 'She *is* up to having visitors? Only I've heard she's very ill.'

Oorja gave a short shout of laughter. 'I would very much say so,' she said, 'God bless your hearts.' The smile faded slightly. 'That isn't to say of course that Annie is not a seriously poorly lady. And she sometimes comes over all wearisome. But some days like today – well, I ask myself the question, just who the nurse is and who is the patient here?' She appeared to notice Teddy for the first time and her eyes narrowed as she focused on his dog collar. 'A vicar,' she said almost to herself. 'Well, good luck with that one!'

She smiled briefly and took herself off up the path at a great rate of knots.

Thelma and Teddy exchanged glances and entered the hallway of Bretton Hall, a wide, light space, the walls dominated by small panels of vivid blue and orange art, which looked, to Thelma, African. On the hall table stood an enormous arrangement of yellow flowers, roses, marigolds, chrysanthemums.

'I'm in here,' said a voice. A clear, authoritative voice. The voice of a head teacher.

* * *

155

There was something remarkable about Annie Golightly, they both agreed afterwards. Whilst not conventionally attractive, with a slight figure and cropped grey hair, she had a pleasant, face free from make-up, and yet there was something about her, the crisp, carefully chosen words, the piercing grey-eyed stare, the sharp attention that radiated a force of personality. Thelma, with her love of theatre, found herself mentally casting the woman in a variety of roles: St Joan . . . Eleanor of Aquitaine, Mother Courage – yes, even Lady Macbeth. Someone, she felt, who drove the action rather than reacted to it.

Like Nurse Oorja, Annie Golightly immediately noticed Teddy's dog collar. 'A vicar?' she said. There was a hint of amusement in the voice, as well as a definite tinge of challenge. Teddy smiled the respectful but glowing smile that had won Thelma's heart all those years ago.

'A vicar yes,' he said. 'But today, first and foremost a chauffeur. One who is more than happy to wait outside, should you so wish.'

'Not at all.' Annie still sounded amused, but now there was a note of apology in her voice. 'You must forgive me. When one is facing death, one finds all sorts of people heading your way, presenting a bewildering array of offers, memorial benches, wicker coffins – untold joy for all, if one gifts money to any number of organisations. And yes, in amongst them all, offers of paradise.'

Teddy smiled. 'As I say,' he said, 'a chauffeur and' – he took Thelma's hand – 'husband to this remarkable woman.'

Annie nodded, as if Teddy had passed some sort of test, and spun her attention to Thelma.

'Yes,' she said, 'Caro Miranda was telling me a bit about you.' Her eyes, Thelma noted, were a clear grey with minute flecks of amber. 'I understand you're finding out about the death of Neville Hilton.' It was an expertly placed remark, concise, accurate, non-confrontational but at the same time leaving Thelma little option but to tell the truth. It was a comment that showed the expertise of a highly experienced leader.

Thelma nodded. 'I believe,' she said, 'before Neville died, there was some sort of confrontation, which may have contributed to his death.'

'His death from a heart attack,' said Annie mildly, but very definitely.

'A heart attack that could well have been brought on by that confrontation.' Thelma held firm.

Annie nodded slowly, considering. The wide grey eyes regarded Thelma thoughtfully. 'Go on,' she said.

Concisely, calmly, Thelma outlined the facts as she knew them. Annie did not interrupt, merely listened, her gaze unwavering, and Thelma knew beyond the shadow of any doubt that every word was being taken in and assessed by a calm, deliberate mind.

After Thelma finished, Annie regarded her, obviously turning things over.

'You think it was someone from my school who came to confront Mr Hill that night?'

Thelma nodded. 'Someone angry enough to shout the words "Pity Me" at him,' she said.

'But surely you can't be sure of that?' said Annie. 'And this wall, the wall with the yellow line. You think that had something to do with whatever happened?'

Thelma nodded. 'Possibly,' she said. 'Though what exactly I don't know.'

'It couldn't be, just as the police said, something Mr Hilton maybe did himself?'

'I don't think so.'

Another pause. 'And you want to find out what happened that night?' said Annie.

'Yes,' said Thelma.

'*Why?*' The question was rapped out firmly and deliberately. Almost instinctively Thelma found herself sitting up. 'What can it possibly achieve?' said Annie Golightly. 'Neville Hilton's death was natural. Why go into it at all?'

Thelma found her mind echoing Annie's question – and as it did an image came to her, a frightened girl with a puffy, tear-stained face.

'Chelsey,' she said simply. 'She's the girl who found him. She's been very, very shaken by the event, to the extent of not working anymore. She feels that maybe in some way she's to blame. Knowing exactly what happened might help put the poor soul's mind at rest.'

Annie Golightly nodded. 'Poor lass,' she said. For a moment she was silent, again considering. When she spoke again her voice was calm. 'You've heard, no doubt, that Neville Hilton was the devil incarnate – excuse the phrase.' She smiled across at Teddy, who bowed his head. 'And I've no doubt that he was a very foolish, narrow-minded man who did a great deal of damage. But even so, I refuse to consider the fact that any of my staff had anything to do with his death.' She nodded firmly and turned to look out of the window across to the distant drowsing mound of Roseberry Topping. All at once she seemed tired and Thelma found herself remembering Nurse Oorja's words.

'I often look at that hill these days,' said Annie almost to herself. 'It's been there millions of years and will be there for millions of years more, long after me, my school – even Ofsted – have gone. I find that an increasing comfort. Nothing lasts.' She turned back to face them. 'It makes me smile; all these ridiculous hoops teachers have to jump through nowadays – targets, data profiles, rolling programmes . . .' She shook her head. 'I taught in Mombasa for a while – there were none of these straitjackets. It was all about connecting with the children.' She sighed a deep sigh and glanced at the clock. 'You know today is the last day of term? As of thirty minutes ago, Pity Me Infants school is no more.'

'I am very sorry,' said Thelma. 'It must be hard to hear your school has closed.'

Annie smiled. 'That's just it,' she said. 'It isn't my school; hasn't been since that day I came home ill. And' – a faint but wicked grin stole across her face – 'and truth be told, the egoist in me doesn't want to think of the place going on without me. In all of this, there's only one thing that really preys on my mind.' She reached, with noticeable awkwardness, across to a nearby small table and picked up a framed photo, which she regarded sadly. 'Davey Fletcher,' she said softly. 'He's the one who comes to me when I can't sleep at nights.'

She handed the picture to Thelma, who found herself looking back into a happier, simpler past, a time that positively radiated hope and life and energy. Annie, a fuller, more vibrant Annie, and Davey Fletcher, alight with a smile and a gloriously yellow shirt with rich purple braces.

'Yellow.' Annie smiled sadly. 'Davey Fletcher's signature colour.' She deliberately and carefully took that picture, as if treasuring a thing of fragility, and replaced it on the table. 'When he was interviewed for the deputy headship,' she said, 'I honestly thought he was going to pass out, he was so nervous. But then when he was in front of a class . . .' She smiled at the photo. 'He had such connection with the children. Something I've only seen very rarely.'

Thelma nodded, thinking of Sam Bowker at St Barney's: gangly, awkward and yet able to hold a whole class mesmerised.

'Of course, he was totally unsuited to management,' said Annie. 'I could see that from day one, not that that mattered to me; I could do all the managing necessary!' She smiled, then the smile faded. 'So, when I was off sick – I know how he must have struggled. And when Ofsted came, I can only imagine how he panicked when Mr Hilton started working his way down his tick sheet.' She shook her head. 'Despite what everyone said, including me, he blamed himself for that Ofsted report.' She sighed. 'That's what I feel so terrible about. There were things I knowingly overlooked, which came back to bite us.'

Thelma frowned slightly. What was she referring to?

Annie looked at Thelma. 'So, going back to what you were

saying,' she said, 'You really believe one of my staff came round to Neville Hilton's house the night he died?'

Again, as a question, it was expertly pitched; again Thelma found herself nodding. 'It does seem likely,' she said.

'And what night was this exactly?' asked Annie.

'Friday June 13th,' said Thelma.

Annie frowned. 'Are you sure?' she said. 'Are you one hundred per cent sure of that?'

Thelma nodded. Annie reached for her phone and peered at it for a moment. 'Friday June 13th,' she said, 'was when we had the memorial service in school for Davey Fletcher.'

Thelma frowned. 'About what time was this?' she said.

'About an hour or so after school finished.' Annie's voice dropped. 'That was the last time I set foot in the building.' She looked at Thelma. 'I daresay you're thinking that one or more of my staff were fired up by the service into an emotional frenzy and drove over to Neville Hilton's house, pitchforks in hand. But I can reassure you, Thelma Cooper, it wasn't like that at all. That gathering was about celebrating all that Davey was and all that he meant to us. *Not* about denouncing Neville Hilton.'

She slumped back and all at once it wasn't difficult to see how ill Annie Golightly really was.

'We'll leave you in peace now,' said Thelma gently.

Annie nodded. 'Remember,' she said insistently, 'it wasn't any of my staff went over there.'

As Teddy stood up, she raised a hand in his direction. 'As you might have gathered,' she said, 'I'm not a particularly religious woman. I'm afraid to me the Almighty has been largely confined to Nativity plays and Easter baskets ... But sitting here ... looking out at that remarkable view ...' She gave the faintest twitch of her head in the direction of Roseberry Topping. 'One thinks ... and I wonder, if at some point you would mind saying a prayer for me?'

* * *

160

Annie insisted on showing the two of them out, even though Thelma was sure she'd have been better off staying where she was. In the hallway Annie paused by the yellow flowers, as if getting her energy up.

'I was thinking before,' said Thelma. 'What gorgeous flowers.'

Annie nodded. 'For Davey,' she said. 'I know I keep saying it, but I feel so very bad for him. I can somehow bear whatever comes my way. It's other people's pain I find so very distressing.' Was that a tear or two brimming in the clear grey eyes? She gently fingered the petals. 'The nights I can't sleep . . . I keep thinking of how it must have been for him – tearing off in a total "Davey Fletcher" state—'

'Where was he going?' said Thelma suddenly.

Annie frowned. 'He was going—' She stopped herself. 'Somewhere. Where, I have absolutely no idea,' she said airily.

There was a curious note in her voice that Thelma couldn't fail to pick up on. That was the thing about totally straightforward people like Annie Golightly, she thought, walking down the path.

When they lied, it was so glaringly apparent.

She was standing by the five-bar gate, hand on the latch, bunch of yellow carnations tucked under one arm, a slight figure with white-gold hair. In one swift transformation, her face turned from recognition to surprise to anger.

'What the fuck d'you think you're doing here?' demanded Chloe Lord.

CHAPTER SEVENTEEN

Wednesday 23rd July

Hambleton Council: Hot tips for hot weather:

*If you have to go out during the day, try and walk
in the shade and ALWAYS wear a wide-brimmed hat.*

Cooling the inside of the white Fiat by a combination of door wafting and waving her handbag, Liz was aware that her earlier excitement had evaporated like water in the sun. What if Ffion Hunter *were* to come out and confront her? What if Derek *had* noticed her prolonged absence and was even now scouring the baking streets of Thirsk looking for her? And what if her thumping headache wasn't just due to the pollen but was in fact the precursor to full-blown heatstroke?

Taking a mouthful of water she checked her phone: no panicky texts from Derek, thank goodness. She cast an uneasy glance back up Chapel Lane – no signs of a vengeful Ffion Hilton. But the headache still remained, defiantly pounding.

Get a grip, Liz! Drive home now, and everything will be fine. She could pick up some frozen spinach, lie down in the cool and then update her food diary all ready for pre-diabetes awareness.

But looking at the postcard cottages drowsing by the village green, she became aware of a growing sense of something left undone, some question unasked ...

She scanned the baking street, the deserted, grass-fringed pavements.

What question? Asked of who?

The place looked the stuff of calendars and tea towels and *Yorkshire Living* magazines – but the sad reality was that, despite all the rural loveliness, there was hardly any community here to ask anything. Driving off, she passed the scaffolded structure of the pub, being converted (according to an excited billboard) into four luxury apartments. Beyond that: 'The Old Post Office', then what had obviously been the village school – somewhere in the place was the deconsecrated parish church. All now expensive holiday accommodation for people who came and went but knew nothing of the actual soul and life of the village.

On the outskirts of Hollinby Quernhow were two pairs of semis, obviously one-time council houses. These did at least have some signs of real life – a washing line, a rabbit hutch, a cluster of garden furniture. This must be where Zippy Doodah lived, one of the last fragments of the village community. And that was what she needed – community. People who had known Neville.

It was then she saw the cherry-red hatchback parked on the verge opposite in front of a Sixties semi, which declared itself to be the Old Police House.

Jax? Liz frowned. What was she doing here? Wednesday wasn't a changeover day as far as she knew... but even so. She braked as she was seized by one of those flashes of inspiration particularly common to lady primary school teachers.

Liz's lips tightened; she was still angry about the incursion into the Old Barn to find those keys . . . and yet—

She braked as she was seized by one of those flashes of inspiration particularly common to lady primary school teachers where various events and elements coalesce into one shining course of action. Someone who knew Neville. *Jax* . . . They'd spent so much time and mental energy being annoyed with the woman, blocking her calls and generally fending her off – yet here she was, one person who arguably knew Neville better than anybody and to whom he might well have talked.

'What are *you* doing here?' Chloe Lord repeated the words in a voice heavy with aggression. She stood on the verge directly between them and the mussel-blue Corsair, hands on her hips, her white-blonde hair gleaming, body a study of anger and accusation. Discreetly Thelma nudged Teddy who equally discreetly nudged her back and retired to the nearby bus stop where he appeared to become instantly absorbed in reading the timetable.

'Good afternoon, Chloe,' said Thelma. 'I presume you're here to see Annie.'

'I asked you the question,' said Chloe angrily. This afternoon she was wearing a sheath of a silver-blue dress. It did not take too much imagination for Thelma to see in her mind's eye it armoured with steel-plated shoulders, silver wings sprouting from the back.

'I'm here,' Thelma said. 'We're here – my husband, Teddy, and I – at the direct request of Annie.'

'You're trying to tell me she asked you here?' The words throbbed with scorn.

Thelma nodded.

'What for?' Chloe almost spat the words into the thick, warm air, two angry barks.

'She'd heard about our visit to your school,' said Thelma. 'And emailed me. I imagine Caro Miranda gave her my email address.'

Chloe half closed her eyes and threw back her head. 'And you thought you'd come here and bother her an' all?' she said. 'You do know I suppose she's a very sick lady?'

'I do,' said Thelma. 'And I'm very sorry. But as I say – she called me and asked to see me face to face.'

'Hasn't that woman been through enough?' blazed Chloe. 'What with being ill, and Davey and that inspection and now you and your friends nosying around?'

164

Thelma tried hard not to resent being seen as the equivalent of a terminal illness, a bereavement or an unfair Ofsted inspection. 'I know how much she's been through,' she said.

'Do you? *Do* you?' Chloe seized on the words and fired them right back at Thelma. 'You know our school – *her* school – closed today because of that bastard Ofsted inspector? You should've seen everyone today – staff, parents, kids, everyone was in bits.'

'I'm very sorry,' said Thelma. 'I can imagine how upsetting that was.'

'No, you can't!' Chloe's eyes brimmed with tears and she abruptly turned away. Thelma wondered about offering her a tissue but before she could, Chloe had rounded back on her again. 'So let me see if I'm getting this right,' she said in a low voice. 'You think someone from our staff drove over to this inspector's house and told him where to go?'

'Possibly,' said Thelma gently. 'But Annie's just told me that the day Neville died was the day you held your memorial service for Davey Fletcher.'

At the mention of his name Chloe's eyes filled once more. When she spoke her words were hoarse. 'And what? You think one of us ran off from the ceremony to go and tell the bastard what we thought of him? Well, let me tell you, Mrs Whoever You Are, that we were too busy thinking about our friend who died in a car crash caused by that evil git of an inspector.'

By now she was breathing as though she'd just completed a sprint, her words short and spiky.

She scrabbled for her handbag and produced her phone, stabbing at the screen, eyes screwed against the sun. Thelma moved near and likewise screwed her eyes up as she focused on the small rectangle. Dimly she could just make out a striking woman with a buttercup yellow scarf twined round her hair, wearing a yellow paper flower, sitting against a backdrop of red and orange drapes. Chloe pressed play and the image came to life.

'Golden lads and girls all must,' the woman spoke in a soft, sad contralto voice. 'As chimneysweepers, come to dust.' As she spoke

165

the sun blazed in from the left of the picture, making her amber earrings wink madly.

Thelma looked at Chloe. Now the tears were running down her face, unchecked.

'That's how we were all feeling,' said the girl, her voice breaking.

Thelma nodded. 'Was that from the service?' she asked gently.

Chloe nodded, wiping her eyes. 'It's from some poem,' she said. 'That's Bun reading it out on the Zoom.'

Thelma nodded, remembering Caro Miranda quoting the same words in the staffroom at Pity Me School.

'Poor Davey,' the girl said, brushing tears from her face.

'I'm so sorry the school has closed,' said Thelma quietly, finally passing her a tissue.

Chloe took it and looked squarely at her, pale blue eyes firm and clear. 'If it weren't for that school,' she said. 'That school, Davey and Annie – especially Annie – God knows where I'd be.'

'Annie helped you?' asked Thelma.

Chloe nodded. 'She gave me a chance. She believed in me when I didn't believe in myself. I started going in see, when I dropped our Mirrel off, when she started in Reception. I used to help out and Annie encouraged me to go for a TA's job. And I used to catch her watching me, and I was worried I was doing something wrong, till she called me in her office and said, "Chloe, you are a born teacher and I want you to train." She got me doing this in-service training at the school – and she give me a job.' Her voice was quietly proud as she gazed over to Roseberry Topping drowsing in the late afternoon sun. 'I loved that job,' she said simply. 'And I love her and I loved Davey Fletcher – so yeah, if anyone were going to drive over to that Hollinby place and give that man what he had coming to him – it was me.' There was a trace of defiance in her voice.

'But you didn't?' prompted Thelma.

Chloe didn't answer for a moment. 'What that man said about us – in that report – it were pure crap,' she said.

'Safeguarding is important,' pointed out Thelma mildly.

Whatever it was she said, it was the wrong thing.

The body tensed; the head snapped up. 'Just what do you know about *anything*?' she said angrily and stalked off down the path to the front door of Bretton Hall.

'I can't stop to talk,' said Jax, retreating to the bathroom. 'I shouldn't even be here, only the people left early leaving the place a right old mess. I've had to dash here from Helmsley.' Her voice was brusque, annoyed – in keeping with the cool 'Hello, Stranger' with which she'd greeted Liz. Had Jax cottoned on to the fact her number had been blocked? And if she had, Liz wondered, would she be able to tell it had only been unblocked five minutes previously?

'I'm guessing,' said Liz following her, 'that Chelsey is still off?'

'What do you think?' said Jax, snapping on a pair of rubber gloves. 'I can't see her coming back any time soon. So that's yours truly up shit creek without a paddle.'

The ponytail bobbed moodily and she plunged a yellow-gloved hand into the bath. 'Oh my God!' she said, 'That is *disgusting*!' She held up some greasy-looking white and orange strands.

'What on earth is it?' asked Liz.

'Coleslaw,' said Jax.

'Coleslaw?' echoed Liz. 'What's that doing in the bath?'

'Oh, come on, Liz,' said Jax not bothering to hide the exasperation in her voice as she contemplated the mess. 'You know what weird stuff people get off on.'

Liz did not know. In forty years of marriage to Derek, coleslaw had only ever appeared on a plate, accompanied by tomatoes, lettuce and cucumber.

Jax shook her head. 'I tell you; you don't want to know the things people get up to on holiday! I think to myself: what is it

167

about being in a holiday cottage that turns people into feral beasts. The stuff I find, you would not believe!' She looked in the bath and gave a yelp of frustration. '*And* it's all in the plughole. And there's all smears round the tub! It'll take me forever; I'll never get done!' She sighed a deep, angry sigh. 'I tell you, Liz, I can't be doing with it anymore.'

'The cleaning business?' said Liz.

'Every weekend I says to myself: "Jax: this is no life." Every Friday and Saturday cleaning like a blue-arsed fly, dashing from pillar to post, cleaning up everyone's ess aitch eye tee.' Her tone was one Liz recognised of old. She'd sounded exactly the same when quitting St Barnabus – and for that matter when she'd left Neville.

'Come here.' Liz took a cloth out of the bucket of cleaning things and sprayed the sink. Jax being Jax didn't say thank you, but resumed her work on the bath, picking out strands of cabbage and carrot with a loud, disgusted commentary.

'Anyway?' asked Jax eventually as Liz scrubbed vigorously at the beautiful porcelain sink with its ornate brass taps. 'I thought you and your mates had fallen out with me.'

'Not at all,' said Liz mildly (and untruthfully). 'Though it was a shock being confronted by Ffion like that.'

'That wasn't my fault,' said Jax self-righteously.

Liz could've replied that actually, yes it was, but that wouldn't help her find out what she wanted to know.

'I was talking to Sidrah,' she said, 'the woman as lives opposite Neville. Trying to find out if anyone had been to see him the night he died.'

'And she said she saw Ffion,' supplied Jax.

Liz shook her head. 'No, actually. She said no one went in apart from Nev. And that's with her checking in her CCTV.'

Jax gave a scornful snort as she put the last bits of offending vegetable matter in a bin bag and began running taps. 'CCTV! That shows nowt! She'll have gone round the back, I'm telling you.'

Liz nodded, thinking of that black door in the hedge – and that yellow paper flower.

'Did Neville ever say anything to you about Ffion?' she asked. 'Like she was threatening him or angry with him?'

'He didn't have to.' Jax stood up and applied spray to the glass shower screen. 'I knew Nev. He didn't love her – and from what I've seen of her, she weren't capable of loving him. He'd say to me, all jokey like, "She only married me for my money."'

Jax resumed rubbing the shower screen. 'You only have to look at their house to see there's a shedload of money they must have.' Her rubbing intensified; her voice was high and angry. 'And now it's all hers.'

'Did you talk much to Neville?' asked Liz gently.

Jax didn't look up. 'A bit,' she said. 'From time to time. When I'd bump into him.'

She sighed, her eyes suddenly distant, and Liz found herself remembering the photo of Jax and Neville taken so many years ago.

'I tell you something, I talked to him more than that Ffion ever did. All she cares about are those blumin' horses of hers.' Jax absently squeezed her cloth, her eyes sad. 'I tell you something else,' she said, 'I know he was there for me. Whatever had gone on – he was looking out for me.'

She wrung out the cloth.

'I was wondering,' said Liz, 'whether he'd ever mentioned anyone else being angry with him?'

'Apart from Ffion, you mean?' said Jax. 'Like who?' The thought had obviously never occurred to her.

'I don't necessarily mean in the village,' said Liz. 'I mean through his work. The Ofsted inspections he did, for instance.' She deliberately didn't mention Pity Me; she didn't want Jax posting the suspicions she and her friends had all over social media.

Jax frowned. 'I don't think so,' she said. 'I thought it was Ffion you were finding out about.' She picked out the last of the coleslaw and stood up. 'Because I tell you, Liz, it was her! Had to be. She didn't care about him – she certainly didn't care about what he wanted. And' – she snatched up the bin bag with a quick, angry flick of the ponytail – 'she was the one shouting in Nev's face and she's the one got all his money.'

How you hate all this, thought Liz in a moment of insight. *How you hate all this cleaning up after people.*

'Everything okay?' The interior of the mussel-blue Corsair ventilated, Teddy and Thelma sat side by side letting the stale, cool air play over their necks and faces. 'I wasn't sure whether to intervene,' he said.

'You did exactly the right thing,' said Thelma. 'She was angry and needed to vent; hopefully she feels a bit better.'

'And she's a teacher from the school?'

Thelma nodded. 'The school that closed today,' she said.

'I think,' said Teddy, turning on the satnav, 'that all in all you did very well. With her, of course, but with Annie Golightly too. What a remarkable woman. Having spoken to her, I can absolutely see why her school was outstanding.' He placed the key in the ignition. 'Now,' he said, voice firm, 'I think you should drive us home.'

Thelma's head dropped. 'No,' she said in a small voice. 'No, I'm sorry.'

'You can stop if you want to,' he said. 'Just try a few miles?'

Wordlessly Thelma shook her head.

'I'm going,' said Teddy with an edge of impatience in his voice, 'to say another prayer.' For the second time that day he took her hand. 'Loving Father,' he said, 'thank you for my beautiful, lovely wise wife. You know what a good person she is, and the shame she feels. You love her and you know the truth, that being caught doing thirty-seven in a thirty-mile zone does not make her a bad or dangerous person. Stand alongside her and help her confront the fear, shame and guilt she feels at having to attend a speed awareness course. Amen.'

CHAPTER EIGHTEEN

Wednesday 23rd July

From the Ripon and Thirsk Local History Society Facebook Page:

Tonight's talk: Mental maths and a robust bladder! Twenty-five summers of manning the ice-cream stall at Newby Hall by Geoff Hall.

At about the same time as Thelma and Teddy were setting off home, Pat was waking from a sweaty doze, mouth dry, to find the bleached fields of North Yorkshire giving way to one of the brick and concrete estates fringing Stockton-on-Tees. In spite of the air-conditioning in the car, the mere sight of the sun-baked pavements and bleached pockets of lawn was enough to bring back that dull woozy surge behind her eyes. She closed them again.

'And you're sure you're feeling okay?' Tiffany-Jane shot her a concerned glance from the driving seat.

'I'm fine!' Pat snapped her eyes open and spoke firmly, brightly, as if the strength of her words could drive away the remnants of that muzzy head.

'Just let me know if you need to stop.'

'Thank you, but I'm fine,' she said, because she was, of course she was. It really had been nothing – entirely her own silly fault – walking in the sun with Larson, her sun hat forgotten at home. Was it any wonder she'd suddenly come over all faint on her return? She remembered that horrible dizzy feeling, the blobs of violet and green blotching out her vision.

The offer from Tiffany to drive her to Ingleby Barwick library wasn't one she'd have accepted in the normal way of things – the prospect of making conversation for the fifty-minute drive – or rather making conversation without referring to the row with Justin that left her with an engrained weariness. However, Tiffany had been so matter-of-fact – it really wasn't any trouble, she'd welcome a run-out, they'd be inside an air-conditioned car – it'd been hard to refuse. Plus, Tiffany had been strongly supported in this scheme by a concerned Rod.

'It's forty-three point two degrees in Cambridge,' he'd kept saying.

So what? Pat wanted to say *This isn't Cambridge, it's Thirsk* – but the bleariness had been too all-consuming.

'Anyway, why exactly do you want to go and see this life guru?' Rod's tone had made it clear he equated 'this life guru' with one of her episodes of *The Real Housewives of Tampa Bay*. 'Surely it can wait?'

There'd been a panicky concern in her husband's eyes, which she'd found rather unsettling.

Honestly! She hadn't fainted – just stumbled a bit . . . Throughout this Tiff had said nothing, merely handed her a large glass of iced water and Pat had wearily realised if she were to stand any chance of making it to Stockton to check out Son Masters, the girl's offer was one she needed to accept.

Contrary to her fears, the journey had proved to be fine – more than fine. After Tiffany had fed the postcode of Ingleby Barwick library into the satnav, she'd put on Classic FM leaving Pat free to close her eyes, caressed by the gentle waft of the air-conditioning and the strains of Medleys for a Summer Day (Sponsored by Specsavers).

'About ten minutes, Pat.' Tiffany's voice roused Pat from what she realised had been another shallow doze.

'It really is very good of you to drive,' said Pat.

'No problem.' Tiff frowned as she slowed for a right-hand turn into one of the estates. 'So – this Son Masters we're going to hear.' There was a bright curiosity in her voice.

'Yes.' Pat felt a resurgence of the muzziness. *What should she say?*

'He's a sort of life coach,' she began rather lamely. Was she going to have to fabricate some story about redefining her life goals or some such? She really didn't have the energy. However, for the second time that day a conversation she was expecting was not to happen.

'Would this,' said Tiffany-Jane carefully, 'be anything to do with reasons someone might kill someone?' At that moment a large leisure centre loomed before them, glowing a dull blue in the sunlight. 'This looks like the place!'

'Ingleby Barwick library?' said Pat. Was this the right place? She'd been expecting a low pleasant building, perhaps surrounded by flowers, not this glass-and-steel edifice.

'The library is part of the leisure centre,' said Tiff, neatly negotiating the car into a parking space. 'Anyway.' She turned to face Pat. 'What is it exactly you need to find out from this Son Masters?'

Pat sighed. 'It's complicated,' she started but stopped herself.

Actually, it didn't have to be very complicated at all. Suddenly by far the simplest and the best option was the truth. Briefly she outlined the story of the demise of Nev Hilton, Pity Me school and Davey Fletcher. Once again, Tiffany listened well, nodding a few times but not interrupting.

'And you think Son Masters might be something to do with this woman who came to this Nev's house?' she said when Pat had finished.

'Davey died in a car crash the day before the Ofsted report

came out. People are saying he only drove off in a blizzard because he was in a state about it all. I want to see what Son thinks.'

Tiffany-Jane nodded, opened the car door and let the warmth of the afternoon heat roll in. 'And this yellow line down the wall?' she said, 'Where does *that* come in?'

Pat shrugged. 'I have no idea.'

'I just feel like it's all closing in on me – and I think, *Just calm yourself down, you silly sausage.*' The bald man with the enormous damp patches under his arms shook his head in bewildered self-disgust.

'Step four point three,' said Son Masters mildly. 'Step back and *look.*'

The man nodded. 'That's why your plan is *bob on*!' he said enthusiastically.

'So many people feel . . . y'know, um . . . a bit of a failure.' Son Masters' slightly high, nasal voice was pleasant enough without being in any way stirring. 'But these feelings – failure, embarrassment, fear even – they're these like invisible *handcuffs* – um, holding us back, y'know.'

Pat shifted uncomfortably in the plastic chair, her sweat cold in the small of her back. Surely handcuffs were more for restraining than holding back?

'But with my simple five-point plan – sorry, *six*-point plan – you can, y'know, free yourself up and crush it – professionally and personally!'

Son Masters smiled amiably at the half-dozen or so people sitting in the Stephenson room of Ingleby Barwick library. He didn't sound much like someone delivering a life-changing message. With his slight drawl, prominent front teeth and general laid-back demeanour he was reminding Pat irresistibly of Dylan the Rabbit from *The Magic Roundabout*. She glanced at Tiffany, trying to gauge what she thought of all this. The younger woman was sitting, slightly inclined forward, eyes wide, smile bright as though this were the most amazing thing she'd ever heard.

'Okay, so that's about everything I've got to say,' said Son Masters, biting back a yawn. 'Has anybody, like, got any questions? I will be signing books afterwards if anyone wants to ask me anything or chat about something.'

He waved a copy of a thick book titled *Smash It! Six Significant Steps to Change your Life* with a half-hearted smirk.

In the event there was only one person ahead of them in the queue – the man with the armpits. He, however, had as much chat for Son Masters as a whole queue full of people.

'What you were saying – it could have been *written* for me . . . I just can't get over it – it was bob on! I kept saying, "Col, this man's got a direct line to your life!"'

Son Masters grinned amiably, seemingly oblivious to Pat and Tiffany queuing behind. At this rate, Pat thought, they'd still be here when the library shut. If Tiffany was getting impatient, she wasn't showing it in her face, she was alternating between scrolling on her phone and listening to Col's excited chatter with an expression of keen attention. Could it be, Pat wondered, she was actually finding all this guff interesting?

To take her mind off her irritation Pat picked up a copy of *Smash It! Six Significant Steps to Change Your Life*. Self-published, she noted. Inside the glossy volume there seemed to be a lot of complicated-looking flow charts more suited to a boiler manual than a self-help book. Plus, a lot of lurid green captions – *Remember: no is yes! Look at what IS, not at what ISN'T!'* All in all, £17.99 seemed a lot to fork out for a book about life mastery written by a man who couldn't even stem a flow of enthusiastic burble from an admirer. Thumbing through to the front something on the title page hit her, two simple words that grabbed her attention more effectively than any one of the flow charts or captions.

To Davey.

'I mean work at the moment is just so horrendous.' Col's plaintive tones made her look up. 'A real culture of toxicity.'

The amiable smile froze. Without changing, Son's face changed. Suddenly there was a sadness, as palpable as the air-conditioning. 'Society,' said Son in even tones, 'can be so – you know – *judgy*, so . . .' He shook his head and his words tailed off. Pat found herself wondering: could this amiable man be capable of bringing about a man's death in some way, shape or form?

'Hi, guys!' Col was, at long last, retreating (carrying no less than three copies of *Smash It! Six significant steps to change your life*) and Son was looking at them, face once more relaxed and amiable. Pat felt a stab of shock that she had absolutely no idea what to say to him.

On this point, however, she needn't have worried.

'Son! Hi! That was *amazing*!' Tiffany took a step forward, bright, confident, young – all the things that Pat wasn't. 'OMG!'

'Thanks,' said Son placidly.

'I have *got* to have a copy!' Tiffany whipped out a credit card and Pat found herself wondering fleetingly what the balance on it was. 'Can you sign it to Justin? He's my partner – he's the one who recommended I come. He's worked with some people you know.' She said two names that sounded like Fig Dicky and Oink Fee. Pat watched this performance in an awed silence. That must have been what all the scrolling on her phone was about.

Son was equally transfixed, eyes wide and bright under this torrent of affirmation.

'And can I just say . . .' Tiff's face suddenly looked troubled, she dropped her hand lightly onto Son's upper arm in a butterfly touch. 'I *hope* you don't mind me saying – we both wanted to say, Pat and myself – how very sorry we were to hear about Davey.'

Once again, the face changed without physically changing. Now there was a lost quality to the smile, an emptiness behind the eyes. Whatever wonders six significant steps could bring to someone's life it seemed none of them involved dealing with grief.

'Thanks,' said Son quietly.

Pat was flushed by a sudden impulse to take the lead in a comforting hug and she noticed Tiffany's butterfly touch grow firmer.

'I wonder,' said Tiffany, 'have you time for us to take you for a coffee?'

The absolutely heartbreaking thing was that Son Masters didn't actually seem aware of how sad and lonely he was. Even now, some six months on, he didn't seem to have done much beyond actually cremating his husband. Sitting with Tiffany and Pat in Jemima's Pantry (the kettle's always on, folks!), he spoke about moving forward and moving on, of the need to bag up Davey's clothes, to box up his possessions, but he spoke as though as these were vaguely desirable life goals – not the bleak necessities that occur in the aftermath of death. Even Davey's ashes were still in his utility room waiting for 'the right head space' for Son to go to Hisehope Reservoir. Pat felt more than a little awkward at this intrusion into someone's obvious grief and could think of little she felt comfortable saying; Tiffany-Jane, however, had no such scruples.

'It's just so awful,' she said. 'Such a horrible, *horrible* thing to happen. Going off the road like that ...'

Son took a sip of rather pale coffee. 'He wasn't in a good place,' he said softly.

Tiffany nodded. 'Justin was saying he'd had a bad time at work.' She spoke gently and her expression was soft and shining with sympathy. 'I thought that was so awful—'

Son nodded. 'He worked in a school and they'd had this inspection, and it hadn't gone to plan,' he said mildly. Pat mentally shook her head – talk about understating things! Was Son Masters always this laid-back?

'I used to teach,' she said. 'Inspections can be awful things—'

Son shrugged. 'I told Davey he shouldn't let external judgements touch his inner validity.'

177

'Very true,' said Tiffany.

'This adviser friend we know said the school should appeal, but his boss – Annie – she was very ill. She said to leave it. That was what bothered Davey. He felt he'd let her down.' He shook his head.

'I heard one of the inspectors was really awful,' said Pat.

Son shrugged. 'He was doing his job,' he said. 'He said what he had to say, I guess. I said to Davey, "Look, this is where the universe *is*."'

Pat felt a sudden impulse to shake the man. No wonder Davey Fletcher had gone driving off in a blizzard!

'Poor Davey,' said Tiff softly. 'I wonder *where* he was driving off to?'

For a third time Son shrugged. 'I wasn't there,' he said quickly. 'I was doing a book event.' Pat had a sudden vision of a bleak function room with seven people, snow falling past the windows. 'I didn't know he was planning on going anywhere.' Son put his hands out in a gesture of resignation, with no discernible change to his amiable, slightly vacant expression. *Too amiable? Too vacant?*

'Complete change of topic here.' Tiff's voice, whilst still sympathetic, contained a distinct 'life moves on' tone. 'I don't know if you can help me, Son – and this is horrendously cheeky of me – but I was reading on your blog how important colour is in the workspace.'

Son nodded. 'Yes,' he said placidly.

'Only I'm realigning my home office, and I'd really welcome your view,' said Tiffany. She spoke with such sincerity that for a panicky second or two Pat wondered if she was planning to redecorate the spare room.

'Oh?' said Son.

'Colour,' said Tiffany-Jane. 'At the moment it's this dove-grey, which is fine, but some days it like, you know, saps the energy – and I was thinking I needed a change.'

Son nodded. 'What did you have in mind?'

'A red?' said Tiff. 'A purple?'

Son shook his head. He was showing, Pat thought, the most animation he'd shown all afternoon. 'No,' he said. 'The stimulation has to come from *within* not from without. You need something that soothes and nourishes.'

'I like the sound of that,' said Tiff. 'What would you suggest?'

'Personally,' said Son, 'I'd go for a soft, pale yellow – something like that.'

'That,' said Pat as they crossed the car park, 'was brilliant!'

'It just came to me,' said Tiffany, looking pleased and modest.

'Clever old you!' Impulsively Pat put her arm round the younger woman. Tiff instantly stiffened. It wasn't as though she was repulsing the gesture, rather as if she couldn't allow herself to relax into it. Awkwardly Pat let her arm drop as Tiff fumbled for the car keys.

'So, what do you think about Son?' asked Tiff, turning on the air-conditioning. 'Do you think he was involved in what happened?'

Pat frowned, wafting her side door in order to cool the interior. 'It's hard to imagine him doing anything out of anger,' she said. 'You saw how he was.'

Tiff nodded, and the two gingerly slid onto the roasting car seats. 'He reminded me of Mavic,' she said thoughtfully. 'A friend from Manchester. Quite quiet, but when he was up on stage – honestly, Pat, you should have seen him.'

'A singer?' said Pat, as Tiff's mobile began shrilling out Lady Gaga.

'Sort of,' said Tiff, frowning at the display. 'A drag artist. Hey, Justy – I'm just out with your mum.' She spoke brightly into the phone. There was a pause. 'Stockton,' she said, a frown clouding her face. From the tone of her voice, it was clear something was the matter. 'Justy, I'm *fine*, your mum's fine. We've just been to this talk; we've been inside the whole time. I've been outside

179

three minutes tops when I got out of the car.' Her voice sounded reassuring – almost soothing. Why? Tiffany smiled apologetically at Pat and got out of the car, moving a way off to under the shade of a tree. From her body language it was clear this wasn't an easy conversation. What was the matter? Had they maybe arranged to go somewhere? Or for Tiff to do something? Or – and the force hit her with a chill despite the heat of the day – or was he quizzing her about who she was with? Should she maybe intervene?

No, Pat, neb out. It was as if Rod was sitting next to her. And it was true – whatever was going on there was very little she could do unless asked. Only – and she realised the thought gave her a pang – only she found the thought of her eldest son splitting up from this beautiful, clever girl quite distressing.

With an effort she turned her mind away from the earnestly gesticulating figure back to the question of Son Masters. There was something Tiffany had just said – something about Manchester ... her friend Mavic – *he's a drag artist.*

Pat sat up. What if the woman confronting Neville Hilton that night hadn't been a woman, but a *man* ... ?

CHAPTER NINETEEN

Wednesday 23rd July

Voice of the Vale, Thirsk FM Radio: Today's beat-the-heat tip!

Sizzle sizzle, Thirskians! For a heat-busting snack try chomping on a cucumber! This has a high water content and can be key in keeping you properly hydrated!

With a flourish worthy of a stage magician Harvey pulled a packet of chocolate digestives from out of his plastic crate. 'Triggers!' he cried with a broad grin. 'That's what it's all about! Things that get the old brain thinking naughty thoughts!'

'Ey up,' said Zippy Doodah in a deadpan voice. There was an explosive snigger from the coven.

Harvey didn't react but it was noticeable the tips of his ears turned rather red. 'If you know you've got these in your cupboard' – he brandished the offending packet – 'is it any *wonder* your brain is going to be tapping you on the shoulder every ten minutes saying, "Er, excuse me, what about those bad boys we've all got stashed away!"'

Liz felt a flush of shame remembering those two packs of

Vegan Moments. It'd been just after she'd come back from Hollinby Quernhow, as her headache was subsiding and she'd been getting Jacob's room ready. After the exertions of the afternoon, she'd been assailed by a sudden powerful craving for something sweet – and as if in answer to a prayer they'd just fallen out of his Greenpeace duvet cover, two glossy brown packets . . . Even now she could taste the glorious chocolatey sweetness on her tongue. Surely, it couldn't have caused any real harm. With a shock she realised Zippy Doodah was looking directly at her, a significant glint in her eye. It was almost as if she knew in some way. Which was, of course, ridiculous . . .

It had to be that other thing – whatever it was.

Liz thought back to the start of the session. As she had been on the scales being weighed by Happy Harvey, Zippy Doodah had come up almost offensively close – so close Liz suspected her of sneaking a glance at the reading.

'At the end, don't disappear,' she'd said grimly, giving Liz's arm a firm little shake.

Don't disappear indeed! Liz had felt indignant, not just because of the invasion of her personal space, but the tone of her voice – as if Liz was in the habit of running out of the sessions, hand clapped to her mouth sniggering in mischief! What on earth could the woman want anyway? Presumably to ask her how she was getting on with finding things out – in the same way she had in that brazen way in Tesco. Possibly in the normal way of things Liz might have stayed and talked to the woman, but she was feeling tired and drained after her expedition to Hollinby Quernhow, sorely in need of some space and peace to reflect on the afternoon's events.

So tonight, despite the muzzy vestiges of her earlier headache, she was determined to stop off by the allotments to give Billy's bench that long-promised coat of preservative. Everything she needed was stashed in the boot; she could be at the allotments and painting in less than ten minutes without any need for Derek to stand over her with an umbrella. It'd take, she reckoned, the best part of an hour so the last thing she needed was any interrogation from Zippy slowing her down.

'Okay, peeps!' Happy Harvey smiled round at the group. 'That's a wrap! Avoid those triggers. Keep those food diaries and step counters going, folks, and I'll see you in three weeks' time when we'll be immersing ourselves in the dizzy world of Carbs Carbs Carbs! I'd say maybe *the* most important session so far.'

'More bad news,' said Zippy Doodah in a gloomy undertone.

Even as Harvey had been speaking Liz had been discreetly gathering up her things – notebook, food diary, pen – in order to make a quick getaway. While Zippy was talking to the coven she was able to duck out of the room unnoticed, stifling down any feelings of guilt with the thought that that bench really did need its coat of green preservative.

Don't disappear indeed!

The white Fiat was where she'd left it in the car park, now partly obscured by a large, black four-by-four. There was something off though, and it took her a second or two to register what it was. The black four-by-four wasn't just obscuring the white Fiat – it was parked close against it, making it impossible for Liz both to get in, and manoeuvre it out of the library car park.

A flurry of panicky thoughts swelled up in her mind. There would be no one in the library, no one official, not at this time. She certainly didn't want to alert Zippy or even Harvey. She could ring Derek, but what could he do? The AA ditto? Could some crane or truck pull the offending car away? Alongside these thoughts she was aware of a growing, blooming flower of familiarity.

Black?

The door of the four-by-four opened with a chill waft of air-conditioning.

'I wanna word with you.'

Black hair, black T-shirt, black leggings – bronze smooth face, eyes obscured by black shades, and an aura as deep as the lengthening

183

shadows. Ffion Hilton was obviously not in a good place. Looking at her, Liz was reminded of the Bad Fairy in a pantomime; all that was needed was a puff of purple smoke and a clap of thunder.

'You and I.' Ffion jabbed an accusing purple-taloned finger at Liz. 'We need to talk.'

Liz felt icy adrenalin kicking in, as one of her all-time dreads materialised – a scene. 'What about?' she said weakly.

'What about?' Ffion kicked the words scornfully back at Liz. '*What about*?'

Yes, what about? Liz didn't dare utter the words aloud, and besides she had a pretty good idea.

'I want you to tell me one thing,' said Ffion. 'Why are you going round my village sticking your nose in where it doesn't belong? Why are you spreading rumours about me? And why have you been coming into my house?'

Liz could have pointed out that this was in fact three things, but of course she didn't. Ffion's angry questions, her accusatory tone, her stunt with the car – were all designed to wrong-foot and fluster. And whilst Liz fully recognised this, she was still both wronged-footed and thoroughly flustered.

'We're not—' she began to say but Ffion cut her off, which was just as well, as Liz had no idea how she was going to finish that sentence.

'Are you trying to tell me it wasn't you round the back of my house today? Not you sneaking round my kitchen? Putting all them lies on the village website? Coming in when I'm not there?' Ffion lobbed the words with the force and precision of cricket balls aimed at pads and stumps. Liz shut her mouth and regarded Ffion, hands on hips, shades glinting in the fading sun. What could she possibly say to someone who wouldn't let her speak more than two words together before angrily interrupting?

'So go on then,' said Ffion. 'What have you got to say for yourself?'

'What lies on the village website?' asked Liz.

'Do not give me that!' The words were hard and scornful.

'Do *not* give me that! Do not pretend you don't know what I'm talking about!'

'I don't,' protested Liz.

Ffion raised her half-shut eyes to the sinking sun. 'Give me strength!' she said.

We're going to stay here forever! thought Liz wildly. *Her rolling her eyes and me not knowing what to say!*

'Everything okay here?' Liz had not heard the approach of Zippy Doodah and neither, judging from the slight start she gave, had Ffion. The larger woman regarded the scene, car keys in hand, with, Liz thought, the aura of some inner-city bouncer.

'I'm not being funny,' said Ffion. 'But keep out of this, Zippy. This is between me and her.'

'Maybe it is, Ffion,' said Zippy Doodah. 'But at the end of the day you can't go round blocking people in car parks. At least' – she cast a glance upwards – 'not while it's on CCTV.' Both Ffion and Liz nervously jerked their eyes upwards.

'How would you like it?' said Ffion angrily to Zippy. 'Someone going into your house when you're not there?' She gave Liz a raking, angry glare. 'So, what were you up to? Looking for something?'

'I really don't know what you mean,' said Liz.

'You were in my kitchen!' The words came out as an angry shout. 'It's bad enough having my husband die on me, but then on top of that, to have people thinking it was something to do with me! *I did not see Nev the night he died.*' There was an odd quality to the statement, an odd emphasis, a defensiveness – and something else . . . a certain tone to her voice . . .

'Listen, Ffion love,' said Zippy Doodah. 'Everyone knows you've been through a lot—'

'So why is everyone looking at me funny?' broke in Ffion. 'Saying stuff about me?'

'People would be a lot nicer to you if you didn't walk round like you had a stick up your backside,' said Zippy Doodah in a surprisingly gentle voice.

The effect was dramatic. Ffion seemed to pinch herself in at the waist whilst at the same time puffing her torso up and out. Again, Liz fully expected a puff of violet smoke and a clap of thunder.

'Don't you *dare* talk to me like that,' she screeched. 'Anyway' – again the talon jabbed towards Liz – 'it's *her* I'm talking to. Her who's been coming into my house.'

Liz regarded her. Zippy Doodah's timely intervention had done two things. First it had shown some definite chinks in Ffion's angry, enamelled carapace. Secondly it had given her a much-needed opportunity to step back, calmly assess the nature of Ffion's wrong-footing tactics and react accordingly.

'First of all,' she said, 'I only came into your house that once, because Jax was looking for her keys – and I said then how sorry I was about—' Ffion opened her mouth but it was Liz's turn to drive on. '*If* you'll just let me finish.' There was a steely blade in Liz's voice, the uncompromising tone of a primary school teacher on the attack.

'Yeah, for fook's sake, give the lass a chance to speak,' said Zippy Doodah. Was that a grudging note of respect in her voice?

'Go on,' said Ffion warily.

'Someone *was* in your flat – the Snuggery – the night Neville died,' she said.

'Well, it wasn't me!' said Ffion.

Liz disregarded this. 'Whoever this person was, I think they parked up at the back of the playing field and came in through your back gate.'

'That's kept locked,' said Ffion. 'And I did not see Nev.' Again, there was that strange quality in her voice.

'Are you not curious who *was* shouting at him?' asked Liz.

'Why should I be? The police said Nev's death was natural causes – a heart attack, for God's sake. Can you not get that into your head?'

'Look.' All at once Liz's tone became crisp and uncompromising. 'You can shout at me and box me in all you want, but I am not going to stop nebbing in until I've found out who was there and what exactly happened in an effort to give that poor girl some peace of mind.'

'What poor girl?' said Ffion suspiciously.

'She means that cleaner,' said Zippy Doodah with a trace of exasperation. 'The one who found your husband. In a right state she is, tablets and everything.'

Liz regarded the two women. There was, of course, a good deal she wasn't saying – about a yellow line down a wall and yellow paper flowers, Pity Me Infants school – she had no desire for any of that to end up whizzing round such a scanty grapevine as existed in Hollinby Quernhow.

'I know,' she said, 'how perfectly horrible all of this must be for you, and you have my deepest deepest sympathies—'

'I've not got time for this.' Ffion wrenched open the car door and climbed in. 'It's not your sympathy I want – what I want is for you and your mate to stay out of my house and keep your big noses out of my business!' Once more that curious tone. What was it? Ffion Hilton slammed the door and the engine gunned grumpily into life.

'Ffion love,' said Zippy Doodah, but the windows were down and the door remained firmly shut.

If it had been an episode of *Emmerdale*, Ffion would have driven off with a dramatic roar and squeal of tyres. Thirsk library car park, however, did not lend itself to such dramatics and there followed a good deal of complicated manoeuvring as Ffion extricated the black four-by-four whilst Liz and Zippy Doodah looked on.

'I was going to warn you she was on the warpath,' said Zippy Doodah in I-told-you-so tones. 'She collared me as I was setting off tonight.'

Liz nodded, more worried about the jerky manoeuvres of the black car. How would she explain to Derek a large black scrape on the side of the white Fiat?

'What are these messages she was going on about?'

'They appeared on the village Facebook page,' said Zippy. 'Saying all this stuff like "where was she the night Nev died" and "she knows more than she's letting on".'

They both took an involuntary step back as the black four-by-four revved, shot forward two feet, narrowly missing their feet and a crash barrier before returning to its tortuous manoeuvring.

'So, they didn't actually say she'd killed Nev?' asked Liz. 'These messages?'

Zippy shook her head. 'They didn't need to,' she said. 'Folk are more than capable of taking two and two and making fifty-six.'

Liz nodded. This was all reminding her of something – those vague rumours someone was spreading about Neville Hilton when he joined Lodestone. No specific accusations but plenty for people to make fifty-six out of.

'I thought,' said Zippy Doodah, 'that she'd eat you for breakfast. But I was wrong.' There was a grudging tone of respect in her voice that for whatever reason gave Liz a faint gleam of pride.

'Thanks for your help,' she said.

At last the thousand-point turn was complete – no scrape but it was a pretty close call. However instead of finally squealing off, the black car paused and with an expensive whine the driver's window slid down.

'You need to stop coming into my house! I said before I'd call the police and I wasn't lying!'

Then she drove off with a dramatic squeal of tyres.

'*Are* you going into her house?' asked Zippy Doodah looking after the retreating black 4 x 4.

'Only that one time,' said Liz.

'It sounds like it's happened more than once,' said Zippy.

'Yes,' said Liz thoughtfully. 'Yes, it did.'

She'd finally worked out what that strange tone in Ffion's voice was.

Ffion Hilton was afraid.

CHAPTER TWENTY

Wednesday 23rd July

From the Carlton Miniot Allotments Facebook Page:

Could ALL allotment holders please note the current hosepipe ban and also try and be mindful of the number of times they fill watering cans from the central tap. Your cooperation in this matter is appreciated.

As the heatwave persisted ('it's with us awhile yet, folks!' the *Look North* weatherman had cheerily announced that teatime) the people of Thirsk and Ripon had grown accustomed to snatching at their outdoor jobs in the mid- to late evening. It was between the hours of seven and ten that dogs were walked, gardens watered, strolls taken, albeit at a slower pace through the lengthening shadows and pungent smells of baked grass and pollen.

This evening, sometime before eight found Pat and Rod sitting on their teak love seat, watching the sun just beginning its dawdling descent over the distant Pennines. Between them stood the remnants of a bottle of a particularly fruity Merlot. Normally this was one of Pat's favourite summertime things, feeling the sun-warmed teak against her back, savouring sips of red as she and Rod gently chit-chatted the day to rights, or just sat in a companionable silence.

Normally.

She glanced up uneasily at the window to the guest bedroom. It had been eleven minutes since the shouting had stopped and the curtains had been tightly pulled.

When they'd returned from Ingleby Barwick library around six, her son had been out in the drive, oblivious of the heat, waiting for them.

'Hey up,' Pat had said. 'We've a welcoming committee.' She hadn't felt especially alarmed, but Tiffany's face had become set and tense, hands gripping the steering wheel as she negotiated the red Mini into the space between Pat's Yeti and Rod's pickup truck. Justin had strode over, feet angrily scrunching on the gravel, face set behind his mirrored shades.

'Where have you been?' he said, eyes wide with unaccustomed anxiety.

'Good afternoon to you too,' said Pat pointedly.

'Stockton,' said Tiffany reasonably. 'I *did* tell you, Justy.'

'There's roadworks on the A1 at Leeming Bar,' said Pat. 'That's why we're a bit later back.'

'You need to be indoors,' Justin said to Tiffany, eyes still wide. Looking at his face, wet and blotchy in the heat, Pat rather thought he was the one who needed to be out of the sun.

Tiff nodded. 'I need to grab a shower,' she said.

As they retreated into the house, Pat could hear her son talking – not the words, but the tone, stressed, almost panicky, quite unlike his customary easy voice. He was obviously worried about something – but what? Surely, he couldn't be concerned about her in the heat – after all it was she, Pat, who had had the funny turn. Tiffany was a lot healthier and younger than she was.

And surely if he was worried about infidelity, shouldn't Justin have been reassured that his girlfriend was out with his mother? She looked after them, puzzled.

What on earth was going on?

About twenty minutes later Pat was distractedly preparing another non-meal for her and Rod (salad and farm shop burgers) when Justin came downstairs.

'Tiff tells me you've been out doing your sleuthing.' His voice was quiet and firm.

'We were talking to a man—' began Pat.

'A man you think might have killed someone,' interrupted her son.

'Hardly.' Long practice of dealing with emotional sons had taught Pat to keep her voice pleasant and neutral in such situations. Inside, however, the butterflies were stirring. She wasn't sure she could remember Justin ever talking to her in this cold, steely tone. She faced him, mind groping for the words and thoughts, refusing to have her child speak to her in this way. But Justin was powering on in that awful, quiet voice.

'I don't care what you and your mates get up to,' he said. 'But don't you ever involve Tiff in anything like this, ever again—'

'I wasn't—' she began to say.

'*Ever* again,' interrupted Justin, anger warming the steel.

Rod had walked in in time to catch the tail end of the exchange. 'Hey – don't you speak to your mother like that,' he rapped out in a tone that was a carbon copy of his eldest son's. Which was of course as it should be, but not particularly helpful as Justin simply ignored the pair of them and stormed back upstairs.

Tea was a largely silent meal but as she began loading the dishwasher Rod held her from behind.

'Come on,' he said. 'Leave that. Let's sit out for a bit.'

Outside in the love seat, as the first tang of red produced the stirrings of an uneasy peace, Rod said, 'You were taking a bit of a chance though. Justin had a point.'

'We were talking to a life coach in a public library,' said Pat. 'Not shadowing him down some dark alley.'

'And you think he had something to do with Nev Hilton's heart attack?'

Pat shrugged. 'Maybe,' she said. Now, in the warm peace of the evening the concept of Son Masters dressing as a woman and shouting in Nev's face seemed as remote and far-fetched as a winter frost.

'He shouldn't have spoken to you like that,' said Rod. 'But then you weren't that clever yourself – dashing off doing your sleuthing when you weren't well.'

Pat opened her mouth to speak, but then closed it again.

Rod took her hand. 'Hey,' he said seriously, 'I don't know what I'd do if anything happened to you.' She smiled but said nothing; what was there to say? She let her gaze rest on his profile a moment. When had he got so grey? Time really did speed past at an alarming rate.

It was then that the shouting had started, three bursts from Justin, two from Tiffany. Rod and Pat had sat tense, looking up, instinctively holding hands as they had been when Liam was in the incubator that first time.

When the shouting had died down Rod said, entirely predictably, 'Let them sort it out themselves,' as if Pat had been on the point of running up the stairs and bursting in the bedroom.

There was a pause, with both of them holding their breath expecting the shouting to resume. But it didn't.

'I thought,' said Pat eventually, 'when they all grew up – all left home – I mean I knew it wouldn't be plain sailing, but it would all be . . .' She paused.

'. . . not under our roof,' finished Rod.

Pat nodded. 'First our Andrew and now Justin . . .'

'And I wouldn't be at all surprised if Liam doesn't land back on us at some point,' agreed Rod.

At this point the back door opened and Justin swept out, marching towards his car.

'Son.' Justin paused at his father's voice. 'Son, where are you off to?'

'Out.' The voice was terse and uncommunicative as he turned away.

'Justin,' said Pat. He stopped once again and faced them. Writ clear on his face was the upbeat motivator battling their scared, hurt little boy. 'Justin, what on earth is it?'

The upbeat motivator won. 'Er – nothing?' he said brightly. 'I'm just going to check in with Taj.'

Pat looked at him. She had no idea who Taj might be and what form checking in with him might take. 'Is everything all right?' she said.

'Yes?' The tone was classic Justin, upbeat with an element of surprise that anyone could think there could conceivably be anything wrong in his sunny world. It was a response he'd grown adept at when faced by unfinished course work, sobbing girlfriends and on one famous occasion a used condom suspended from the tree by his bedroom window. On the whole Pat thought she preferred his anger.

As the car drove off, Pat said, 'I'm going upstairs and don't tell me not to.'

Rod shrugged: anything building-related he was happy to sort, the messier aspects of Taylor family life he was equally happy to leave to Pat.

Tiffany opened the bedroom door on the second of Pat's oh-so-tentative knocks. Her face was a flawless impenetrable wall. 'Pat,' she said in tones of warm surprise.

'I just wanted to see if you were all right,' said Pat.

'You heard?' Tiffany smiled ruefully. 'Oh, I am *so* sorry!'

'There's no need to apologise,' said Pat, 'I just wanted to see if you were okay—'

'We were just venting,' said Tiffany in tones that might have been describing a game of table tennis. 'And I'm *so* sorry about the way Justy spoke to you earlier. He should never ever have spoken to you like that and he's very sorry.'

'It's fine,' said Pat. 'Having sons vent at me is part of the job description.'

Tiffany's smile widened. Was it about to crack? Pat had a sudden impulse to take the girl in her arms but didn't dare.

'Listen,' said Pat. 'It's so lovely outside. Why don't you come out and join me and Rod. Have a glass of wine. Or juice. Or water. I can even make a herbal tea – I promise venting will be *off* the topic of conversation—'

Again, that flicker was there, just briefly.

'I'd love to!' But there was regret in her voice. 'Only I promised to treat myself to an early night! I'm pretty much done in!'

And the bedroom door shut.

Painting Billy's bench that warm July evening was something Liz found immeasurably soothing, after the confrontation with Ffion. The wet slaps of the brush calmed her sharp and agitated thoughts. For once the pollen levels were low, almost negligible. She felt only the slightest discomfort in her eyes and sinuses as she worked.

Of course, the easy, instinctive thing to have done would have been to retreat straight back home, back to the safety of the curtain-dimmed interior with fans whirring over bowls of iced water. But she knew that if she did that, everything that had just happened would, like the fans, whirr round and through her thoughts. Plus, Derek would be there in the background, back from his evening run, with his uncanny knack of divining when she was bothered. She needed the time and space to process the confrontation, and here at the allotments with Ruth and Norinna watering beans and courgettes, with the sky a burnished peach, with the soft chink of Norrina's windchimes – here was the perfect space.

The surprising thing she found was that although she was disturbed by the angry scene, she didn't feel in any way guilty, in spite of the fact that Ffion undeniably had a point. And she realised that she didn't feel guilty because, at a very deep level, she knew it was important to find out what had happened to Neville Hilton. Not so much for his sake, as for that of those around him, the women who had in different ways been a part of his life.

There was Chelsey, her dark, crippling fears effectively putting a headlock on her life. And Jax, upset and troubled by her ex-husband's sudden death. And then there was Ffion. Having to face down online rumours was undoubtedly distressing, but after their conversation, Liz knew that the woman was also scared. But of what? And why did she seem to think Liz had been repeatedly in her house? What had been going on *there*? Each of these very different women were connected not just by Neville Hilton – but by a shared sense of unresolved disquiet.

Yes, for all sorts of reasons, Liz felt without any shadow of a doubt that the truth about what happened and why needed to be uncovered. And she was quite certain that figuring out the truth would begin with discovering just *who* it was that had been shouting so angrily to Neville Hilton before he died.

She gave one of the legs of the bench a firmer stroke than she intended and felt a spray of droplets on her gardening wellies. So – what did she know? What did she have to share with Pat and Thelma when she saw them tomorrow? She re-dipped the brush in the oily green wood preservative and began tackling the back of the bench.

Someone had parked up by the edge of the playing field, then approached the Old Barn and the Snuggery from the gate at the back. Who? The person who had been going into Ffion's house? Or Ffion herself, having somehow faked her trip to Carlisle? If it was Ffion, it didn't explain that yellow paper flower she'd found, which seemed to link the whole thing to Pity Me school and

Davey Fletcher's memorial. But what about those paint spattered wellies – where did they fit in? They did seem to link everything back to Ffion somehow . . .

As her neat brushstrokes covered the back slats of the bench, Liz sighed in frustration. Like the fans at home, her thoughts were going in circles.

'Here she is.'

She looked up to see Derek approaching from the main gates.

'I'm just doing the bench.'

'I can see.' He touched her arm in a friendly, unspectacular way. 'It's such a lovely evening I thought I'd walk on and see how you were getting on.' He stood back, surveying the bench. 'How was the dreaded pre-diabetes awareness?'

She frowned, applying no-nonsense strokes to the offending part of one of the legs. 'I have to avoid triggers,' she said. 'Knowing there's biscuits in the cupboard, that sort of thing.' She thought of those Vegan Moments, rich on her tongue.

It was as if Derek could read her mind. 'The Food Police'll sort it,' he said. 'If he's not too busy saving the planet that is. It was today our Jacob broke up, wasn't it?'

Liz nodded pushing back those guilty thoughts. She'd replace the Moments first thing. 'Our Tim rang earlier; he's bringing him over around nine.'

Now her grandson was older (year 6 next year! Where did the time go?) he was a lot more self-sufficient, and although the Wensleydale Railway, Lightwater Valley and the local maize maze were all written in red on the calendar, he was also largely content to amuse himself. At the moment this seemed to consist of either going through his grandparents' food cupboards or having endless, serious online meeting with his group of activists from school (BCCDAG – Boroughbridge Climate Change Direct Action Group).

'Right.' Liz gave a final, determined stroke to the slats and Derek stood back surveying her work. Watching him Liz suddenly knew he was remembering another time, a wild autumn night when they'd found Billy's grandson slumped and barely conscious on this very bench.

'Love you,' she said.

He made a not unfriendly noise in his throat and nodded. 'There's a couple of bits on the side you've missed,' he said.

Liz clicked her tongue in impatience, re-dipped the brush and gave a couple of hasty strokes.

'Careful!' said Derek warningly. 'You're getting it on your wellies.'

Tutting, Liz looked down, remembering the spray of droplets earlier. How much had she got on her wellies? But there were only a few droplets round the toes.

Hang on . . . What did that make her think of? *A pair of riding boots liberally spattered all on the toes and up the front with yellow paint!* She looked at her own boots, with only a few drops of paint on the toes – and she'd painted virtually a whole bench, not just a single vertical line . . .

Odd.

About the same time, Thelma was sitting in the space behind number 32 College Gardens. Not really a garden, certainly bigger than a backyard, she was never quite sure how to refer to it apart from 'out the back'. Whatever, this brick-paved space of pots, outhouses and a pocket handkerchief lawn was a place she loved, a favourite place to sit in the summer months. Now she sat on the bench, breathing in the heady scent of the night-blooming honeysuckle cascading down the back wall. Away in the west the muted glow of the sun, obscured by the wall and by Ripon and St Bega college was firing the sky. On the bench beside her Snaffles the cat was staring with focused intent at the open laptop in her knees.

On the laptop was the answer to a prayer.

The email was short and to the point.

Dear Mrs Cooper,

Due to the ongoing challenges posed by the current heatwave, we are pleased to offer an online option for your Speed Awareness course.

Online! Attending from her own front room as opposed to the Villette suite at the Harrogate Heights Hotel – with all the attendant risk of running into someone she knew. Of course, there was still some risk of there being some familiar face online, but there were things she could do about that.

'Thank you, Father,' she said, inhaling a deep, deep breath of sweetened air. She thought again of the actual offence. Her fingers tightened slightly on the laptop at the word 'offence'. It was all so unfair. That hill out of Ripon needed some welly to get up it, and it wasn't as if there were any houses or even pedestrians there as a rule. So why was it a thirty-mile-an-hour zone? Thirty-seven she'd been going! It wasn't as if she'd been some young buck out to impress his mates. She'd been dashing from the charity shop to the Friarage to visit Contralto Kate from the choir. A mobile camera mounted in a van had taken to haunting the pull-in where the old feed mill had been, and it had been this that had caught her. According to the local online bulletin, the *Wakeman*, this van had netted untold thousands of pounds for the powers that be in what was a notoriously accident-free area.

So unfair.

But her reaction had taken her by surprise – a crippling shame at being judged and found guilty. So strong was this feeling it had sapped her confidence to drive at all. She had expected the feelings to diminish over time, but if anything, they had grown until it towered in her mind out of all proportion to the actual offence. When she had done the course, even in the less threatening surroundings of her own living room, would this feeling of disquiet ever fade? What if she never felt comfortable driving again?

Thelma took another scented breath, reminding herself of her favourite go-to passage of scripture at times like this – *Let tomorrow worry about itself, sufficient to the day is its own trouble.*

The sound of the back door and the chinking of ice heralded the arrival of Teddy with two tumblers of elderflower cordial. He stood a moment, luxuriating in the peace, eyes slightly squinted against the last rays of the sun. 'Man goes forth to his work, and to his labour until evening,' he quoted.

'Were there many parcels?' said Thelma, referring to the stack of brown packages in the porch that had greeted them on their return.

'A fair few,' said Teddy. 'About thirty fans of varying descriptions. I'll clear it tomorrow.' He set the drinks down, sat next to Thelma and took her hand. 'It's good news about the course-that-dare-not-speak-its-name,' he said.

Thelma returned his grip and said nothing.

There was a pause filled only by the lazy noise of an evening game of cricket on the college recreation fields.

'Thank you for coming with me today,' she said.

Teddy nodded. 'I was glad to come with you,' he said. 'Glad to be with you, glad to be with Annie on her journey.'

Teddy had never referred to 'death' – only to people being at the end of their journey. In her darker moments this was something Thelma found very comforting.

She closed the laptop. With a disgusted stretch Snaffles got up and padded off into the kitchen.

'So where,' said Teddy, 'will you go next?'

'I don't know,' said Thelma. 'Annie was very definite none of her staff were involved – but then we've only her word for it they were all at the memorial service and not in Hollinby Quernhow. And I don't see how I can possibly go asking them, not without causing a lot of upset.'

Teddy nodded absently, and his wife realised he was in all probability contemplating the logistics of delivering thirty fans.

The ping of the laptop stirred them both. 'That'll be the email,' said Thelma, reopening the lid, 'confirming my online registration.'

But it was not the course.

The email was brief to the point of curtness.

Dear Mrs Cooper,

I received your contact details from Ms Annie Golightly. I wonder if we could schedule a Zoom call as a matter of urgency.

Kind regards,

Bun Widdup

BUN WIDDUP EDUCATION SERVICES

PART THREE

Fear no more the heat o' the sun

CHAPTER TWENTY-ONE

Thursday 24th July

Hambleton Council: Hot tips for hot weather:

Two people in a bed means twice the body heat. Stretching like a starfish with a fan on nearby may be the coolest option.

The Northern Lights took Ripon and Thirsk by surprise that night. Between one thirty and three, a time when most people were snatching what fitful sleep they could, the skies beyond the moors were washed with dazzling, shimmering sheets of turquoise, amethyst and lime green. By three thirty when many people were stirring more no matter how wide open the windows, how big the fans, how thin the sheets, the spectacle had largely faded and by four thirty when Pat, Thelma and Liz were if not exactly wide awake, certainly far from peacefully asleep, all that remained were a few pale smears away in the pearly-grey north-east.

Pat lay in that semi-conscious state common to mothers waiting to hear the noise of a child's return home from a night out. This was something that had become second nature to her during her son's teenage years; like Larson she'd used to sleep with one ear open until the click of the back door, the flush of the toilet announced a safe arrival home. This instinct had been something Pat thought gone for good, but that night it had slammed back prompt and strong when she realised she had not heard Justin come back home from his 'catch-up' with Taj.

Now she lay in an uneasy doze wondering whether to wake Rod or Tiffany, or text Justin or even go the whole hog, ring all the hospitals and inform the police that her son had stormed out in a strop and failed to come back.

Thelma was sitting yawning at her kitchen table. Spread out before her lay a veritable jigsaw of prompt cards plus two pretty, thick booklets and a boxed-up computer programme – all her prep for the speed awareness course in two days' time. Where on earth to start? When she took her driving test – her mind shied away from just how long ago that had been – there'd been none of this. Just one, holly-green Highway Code booklet, which she'd duly memorised. And now . . .

Blinking her tired eyes, she looked blankly at the untidy heap of information consisting of current rules for motorists. Of course, the speed awareness course hadn't said anything about mugging up on the Highway Code but she wanted to do something to address this icy nag of anticipation she still had, despite now being able to attend by Zoom.

Liz was also sitting at her kitchen table enjoying the relative cool flooding in from the open window. These days whenever she woke early, she'd got into the habit of opening the downstairs windows when the heat (and the pollen) was at its lowest ebb. Now, luxuriating in the cooler air on her face and neck, she was looking drowsily at footage of Chapel Lane, Hollinby Quernhow, date-stamped Friday 13 June. The footage alternated between looking up and looking down the lane, punctuated by a dizzying swivel as the camera swung from right to left.

Earlier, idly scrolling through her phone, she'd seen an email from Jacob (what was he doing sending emails at 12.43 a.m.?) outlining the ingredients needed for spinach and kale risotto. She made a note of them – plus a guilty memo to replace the Vegan Moments – then, lacking the energy to go back upstairs, listlessly flicked through her junk folder. She'd nearly deleted the crucial email – *CCTV 4 U!* – along with yet more offers for solar panels and discreet hook-ups with Estonian hotties. It was the name that had stayed her finger – Sidrah? *Sidrah!*

The CCTV from Chapel Lane!

She'd now been staring at the screen for some ten minutes and excitement was rapidly giving way to boredom and drowsiness. It looked like Sidrah had been right. Aside from the lone figure of the tenant from the Snuggery crossing and recrossing the lane and then driving off at 4.03, there had been nothing and no one entering the Old Barn. Indeed, if it hadn't been for the odd vehicle passing, the views of the honey-stoned front wall, the banks of lavender, plus that brief glimpse of the building's frontage when the camera swivelled, the views could have been photographic images.

Liz found herself thinking of Ffion, her sense that the woman was scared. But of what? Or who? Those wild rumours on the village website? Or being a target of whoever shouted at Neville? Or was there a darker reason? Ffion . . . on horseback . . . in the car park . . . framed in the window . . . Outside the kitchen window the sky was paling from slate grey to mauve; from the fuchsia bush by the back door could be heard the first business-like peeps and cheeps of the dawn chorus. Soon it would be time to close the windows against the onslaught of the day's sun.

She jerked upright in her chair. What had she just seen? What was that beige flicker on the screen that had dimly registered on her sleepy vision? She rewound the CCTV and there was Neville's beige hatchback pulling smartly into the driveway of his house. Annoyingly it was just after the camera had swivelled up the street, so Liz had to wait a frustrating twenty-five seconds until it pivoted back. It took a couple of goes to freeze the image at the exact moment when the front of the Old Barn was in view – showing no signs of Neville or the car, both now out of sight round the side of the building. Liz tutted in frustration, abandoning the wild hope of catching a glimpse of whoever it was who had called Nev into the Snuggery.

She took a note of the time stamp – 18.52 – and was about to close the window when she saw the shape in Neville's study window. Too dim to be distinct, the face shrouded but the body language unmistakable.

A body language Liz had seen similarly framed in a window only that afternoon.

Ffion Hilton.

'Are you sure it's her?' Pat squinted at the vague, blurry outline on the screen of Liz's phone. 'It's not very clear.'

'That's her,' said Liz obstinately. 'It's how she stands. It's how she was standing when I saw her watching me from the back window yesterday. She must've come in round the back; she's not on any of the CCTV film—'

'So,' said Pat in her best 'let's get this straight' voice, 'Ffion Hilton dashes into her home, shouts at Nev, maybe paints a yellow line down the wall, dashes out and hot-foots it off to Carlisle.' She stifled a yawn; it had been gone five when Justin had finally arrived back and she'd not managed to get any proper sleep since then.

'It's what must've happened,' said Liz. 'When she ranted at me last night she was scared, I know she was – and now we know why.'

Pat looked across at Thelma who was stirring her coffee and gazing thoughtfully out of the window at the baked car park. Thankfully the garden centre had taken steps to combat the worst excesses of the heat; hefty linen blinds were muting the sun's glare into something more bearable and a number of silver floor fans were racketing away sending blasts of cooler air round the ankles of the customers. Once more the round table in the corner was usable.

'You're very quiet,' Pat commented.

Thelma looked back at them, with the air of someone waking up. 'I'm sorry,' she said. 'I was just thinking. If it was Ffion who was shouting at Neville – and it does make sense because Ffion *was* there – I was just wondering—'

'Wondering what?' cut in Pat.

'Wondering why Ffion was in the house and not the Snuggery. After all – that's where all the shouting took place.'

'Well, she'll have seen him drive in,' said Liz. 'And followed him over to the flat and had a go at him there. Or' – her voice grew excited – 'or she maybe deliberately wanted him in the flat because she didn't want suspicion to fall on her.'

'She couldn't have known he'd have a heart attack,' pointed out Pat.

'The thing is Ffion was there – at the property – when she said she wasn't,' said Liz, emphasising her words with a briskly tapping fingernail.

Thelma nodded. 'I know,' she said. 'It just doesn't seem to fit somehow.'

Liz bristled at this damp dismissal of her theories. 'Well, who else could have been there?' she said combatively.

In reply, Thelma looked at the open page of her green book and the neatly printed names: *Chloe . . . Rev. Caro . . . Son Masters.*

'As far as I can see, any of them could have turned up at Neville's shouting the odds,' said Pat, peering into the book. 'And having met Son I do think his voice could possibly be mistaken for a woman's – especially if he was upset.'

Thelma frowned and added another name to the list in her neat script: *Annie Golightly.*

'The head teacher?' said Liz. 'I thought you said she was very ill.'

'She is,' said Thelma. 'But this was five weeks ago, remember; she could well have been a bit stronger then. She was well enough to attend Davey Fletcher's memorial service. Oh! Of course!' She gave a soft exclamation. 'And there was someone else—'

'Who?' said Liz.

'The tenant of the holiday flat,' said Thelma.

'The tenant who left at four p.m.?' said Pat.

'The tenant who made a point of announcing she was leaving at four p.m.,' corrected Thelma. 'The one who spoke to your friend Sidrah, claiming to love gardening and then making some totally inaccurate comments about her plants.'

The other two looked at her.

'You mean,' began Pat slowly.

'People don't generally make a point of announcing their departure from a holiday cottage,' said Thelma. 'They just go.'

'So, you think what?' said Pat.

Thelma stirred her coffee. 'I suppose it just feels to me a bit like she was drawing attention to the fact she was leaving.'

'Is she on this CCTV?' said Pat to Liz.

Liz nodded, and with a bit of difficulty wound back the video to show the slight figure in a fleece and beanie trotting across the road.

'There she is,' she said. 'And there she is coming back – and there she is driving off – and the time stamp's saying four oh three.' She rewound the video and froze it as the figure was crossing the lane. 'It could be Caro Miranda,' she said. 'Or Chloe even. You just can't tell with her in that fleece and hat.'

'It could even be Son Masters,' said Pat. 'Tiffany did say he reminded her of someone she knew who worked as a drag artist. A touch of make-up, that higher voice – and remember a fleece is a fairly androgynous garment.'

'Not always.' Liz's lips thinned as she thought of her beloved green garment hanging on the back of the utility room door. Her mouth opened. 'Oh,' she exclaimed. 'It's just come to me.'

'What has?' said Thelma.

'My fleece,' said Liz. 'I've not worn it for weeks now – it's been hanging on the back door all this time—'

'So?' said Pat.

'So,' said Liz triumphantly, 'Friday 13 June was right at the start of the heatwave. Why wear a fleece and hat?'

'Unless they were disguising themselves,' said Pat in excitement. 'So, it could have been Caro or Chloe *or* Son!'

'Except,' said Thelma. She was speaking in her best Key-Stage-One-planning voice, which told Liz and Pat she was about to roundly rain on their parade.

'Go on,' said Pat long-sufferingly.

'The time.' Thelma pointed at the time stamp on the screen. 'Four oh three p.m. Chloe would certainly have been at school, Caro too – Son and Annie would have been arriving around then for the service.'

'So, it must've been Ffion after all!' said Liz triumphantly. 'Don't forget those boots in the kitchen cupboard.'

Thelma looked at Liz and frowned as she stirred her coffee. 'You said those boots had too much paint on?'

Liz nodded. 'I only got a few specks on mine. But Ffion might have been in a hurry – or upset or drunk or something – and splashed paint everywhere.'

'In which case,' said Thelma. 'Why wasn't there paint on the floor and walls?'

'Someone put a dust sheet down?' said Pat.

'Or maybe,' said Thelma, 'it was a fake.'

'But I saw the boots,' said Liz.

'No,' said Thelma. 'I mean maybe someone splashed them with paint and put them in the cupboard. Someone who wasn't Ffion.'

'You mean planted them?' said Pat excitedly. 'To implicate Ffion?'

Thelma nodded. 'And those rumours that have been posted about her on the website,' said Thelma. 'Those vague accusations – just like happened with Neville.'

They looked at each other.

'It strikes me,' said Pat, 'we've lots of questions but precious few answers.'

'Maybe we'll get some off this Bun Widdup person tomorrow,' said Liz.

'I wonder what she wants?' said Pat.

'Your guess is as good as mine,' said Thelma. She checked her watch. 'Just to let you all know, Teddy's picking me up in twenty minutes.'

'You better both come over to mine tomorrow,' said Pat. 'Justin can hook my laptop up to the flatscreen; don't ask me how. That way, we won't all be squashed round someone's laptop.'

Liz nodded. Thelma didn't.

'Actually,' she said, 'would you mind coming over to me? There's some parcel deliveries I'm expecting that I need to be in to sign for.' Her voice was low, diffident, quite unlike her normal self. Pat and Liz looked at her.

'Right, Thelma Cooper,' said Liz briskly. 'This has gone on for far too long.' She faced her friend, a well-known glint in her eye. 'You might as well tell us.'

'Tell us what?' said Pat, bemused.

'Tell us why I had to drive you to Pity Me, why Teddy had to drive you here and why you're all of a sudden nervous about driving. And don't give me any guff about a bad arm; you've been stirring that coffee off and on for the best part of twenty minutes.'

Thelma sighed and looked at them.

'It's not good,' she said quietly. 'What I've done—'

'What you've done?' echoed Pat in alarm.

'Whatever it is,' said Liz, 'it can't be half as bad as the things I've been imagining.'

Thelma took a deep breath and laced her fingers. 'Right,' she said. '*Right*.'

As she told them, Pat found herself biting back a smile. Thelma, of all people, in trouble with the law! And typical her – all that guilt about a mere speeding ticket! She remembered the various brushes with the police her own speeding had engendered over the years. She looked at her friend, frowning unhappily, hands clasped, and felt a well of sympathy. As if Thelma could read her mind, she looked back at her imploringly.

'*Tell me* I'm being stupid. Tell me I'm overreacting,' she said.

Pat put a comforting hand over one of her friend's. 'Of course you're not being stupid,' she said. 'It's an upsetting thing. I'm just glad it's nothing worse.'

'Hear, hear,' said Liz, taking the other hand.

'You're a much better driver than me,' said Pat.

'Exactly,' said Liz. 'Think of all the tickets Pat's had over the years!'

Pat ignored the prickle of irritation she felt at this comment. This was one of those times when the ties of friendship transcended personal pride.

'Even though I can do the speed awareness course on Zoom, I'm still all over the place about it,' said Thelma. 'I've made a start looking at the Highway Code but that seems to be making me feel worse.'

'It's really upset you, all this,' said Liz, squeezing her hand.

'It's knocked my confidence,' admitted Thelma in a confiding burst. 'I keep thinking: what if I don't ever feel comfortable driving again? Living round here – you need a car. What if that's me done with driving?'

'Come on,' suggested Pat. 'See how you feel after the course. Take it from one who knows – it really isn't anything to get your knickers in a twist about.' Silently she hoped Thelma wouldn't have the same instructor she had last time, the ex-territorial army instructor who persisted in describing the attendees as Speed Sinners.

'But we'll come to yours for the Zoom with Bun Widdup,' said Liz. 'Won't we, Pat?'

But Pat wasn't looking. Her surprised gaze was fixed on the brightly smiling girl who was threading through the tables towards them.

'*Tiffany*?' she said in alarm. 'What are you doing here?'

'Liz! Thelma!' Having sat down and taken a sip of iced water, Tiffany-Jane bestowed both of them with a white-teethed wide-eyed smile. 'I've heard so much about you both!' She turned to Pat. 'Rod said if I'd find you anywhere he'd lay money it'd be here.'

'Is Justin all right?' said Pat. The spark of alarm in her voice wasn't missed by her two friends.

'Pat, he's *fine*.' Impulsively Tiffany took her hand. 'He came back about five. He just got talking with Taj and thought it best to stop over. We'd have let you know, but we thought you must both have been asleep.'

Fat chance, thought Pat. She regarded Tiffany. The girl was wearing a loose, white top and although the smile, the hair, the make-up were as immaculate as ever, she had a tired air about her – almost one might say peaky. Presumably she hadn't had much sleep either.

'Anyway, folks, I'm *so* sorry to gatecrash your coffee session,' said Tiffany. 'But last night – well, I couldn't sleep waiting for Justy to get back, so I ended up doing a spot of online sleuthing.'

Pat, remembering yesterday's fireworks, wondered if Justin was apprised of this fact. 'Right,' she said noncommittally, stifling yet another yawn.

'Anyway, I found out something that seemed pretty significant and I thought you'd want to know about it.' She looked round the three faces, eyes bright. The three faces looked back at her.

'What have you found out?' asked Thelma.

'Son Masters.' Tiffany paused. 'It's not his real name FYI. "Son" is a name he adopted when he became a life coach, apparently his real name's Barry.'

'What about him?' interrupted Pat, trying to stifle another yawn.

'He's got a criminal record,' announced Tiffany-Jane.

'Son?' said Pat, now wide awake. 'Son Masters?'

'He was Barry Masters back then,' said Tiffany. 'I was as amazed as you. And you'll never guess what he got it for.'

You're rather enjoying this, thought Thelma.

'Fraud?' said Pat.

'Shoplifting?' ventured Liz.

'Robbery?' wondered Thelma.

'GBH,' said Tiffany-Jane, with the distinct air of having trumped every other statement uttered.

'Grievous bodily harm?' Liz spoke the words in a shocked undertone. 'I thought you said he was quite amiable—'

'He was,' said Pat. '*Is*.'

Tiffany nodded in agreement. 'Every comment unthreatening, very unassuming body language,' she said. 'But – well, I was reading his book and it talked about patches of darkness in his life – so I got to thinking *what* patches? And I went online, and there it all was.'

'When was this?' asked Thelma. 'And where?'

'Newcastle, seventeen years ago,' said Tiffany, efficiently handing printouts to the three. 'I've done you each a copy.'

The three read the account of how a row in a nightclub, over a drink, had spilled over into a fight outside which resulted in the other person losing the sight in one eye.

'Neville wasn't assaulted,' pointed out Liz, scanning the printout. 'He was shouted at.'

'People can carry round all sorts of negative emotions,' said Tiffany. 'And if they fail to vent them properly, they can burst out all over the place.' All at once her face froze. 'Two seconds!' She smiled a bright smile – or tried to – and stalked rapidly off across the garden centre in the direction of the ladies.

'That,' said Pat, 'is Tiffany-Jane.'

'She seems charming,' said Thelma genuinely.

'She's been a bit peaky lately.' Pat frowned in the direction of the ladies' toilets. 'She was telling Rod it's some sort of stomach bug. I hope she doesn't pass it on to the rest of us.'

Liz and Thelma exchanged glances.

'You do realise,' said Liz gently, 'that the girl's pregnant?'

CHAPTER TWENTY-TWO

Friday 25th July

Met Office weather forecast:

A Met Office Amber weather warning has been declared for the Yorkshire and Humber region. The current high temperatures are set to continue over England and Wales extending across the weekend and into next week with highs of 43 degrees possible in the Vale of York.

The curtains of Teddy's study were drawn tight, admitting only the faintest chinks of sun. Pat and Liz were sitting side by side in front of Teddy's laptop. From high on the back of Teddy's armchair Snaffles regarded the screen with steely intent.

'Have you spoken to her?' Liz's voice was low. 'Tiffany?'

'No.' Pat also spoke quietly. 'I mean, I've not really had the chance.' *Not really had the chance because I've been avoiding her*, she thought.

'Remember, I'm no expert,' said Liz. 'I could be wrong.'

Pat shook her head. 'I don't think so,' she said. 'It all makes sense – her avoiding alcohol and looking so wan.'

Plus, she thought, *seeing her on Scott Hall Road . . .* Three minutes on the internet had revealed to her it was close to the location of a termination clinic. Had Tiffany arranged a termination? She was obviously pregnant now – that *had* to be what all the rows were about surely? What did she want? What did Justin want? It all seemed so huge, it felt safer – and certainly easier – to stay all the way away from it.

'Have you mentioned anything to Rod?' asked Liz.

Pat shook her head. 'God no,' she said. 'There's no point saying anything to him till we know something. I didn't even tell him *I* was pregnant until I was cast-iron sure.'

As Thelma came in, Pat and Liz instinctively fell quiet. Discussion of all things childbirth-related was something they steered well clear of when around their friend, remembering Thelma's own heartbreaking history of failed pregnancies.

'Here we are,' said Thelma, putting down a tray of glasses. She nodded at Liz. 'Apple and mango, only three per cent sugar, which makes it a green traffic light. And I do hope it's not too unbearable in here. I've had the curtains shut and the fan on all afternoon but even so . . .'

She jiggled the mouse and the laptop flared into life, revealing a tranquil vista of the Lake District. At the sight Snaffles tensed and took a flying leap at the laptop only to be neatly intercepted by Thelma mid-air. 'Goodnight, sweet prince,' she said, depositing the cat firmly outside and shutting the door on his disgusted yowl. 'And thanks to you both for coming here.'

'That's no problem,' said Liz, sipping her drink, trying to ignore her craving for full-fat lemonade.

'But don't think you're off the hook, lady,' said Pat. 'The minute that speed awareness course is done and dusted you're driving us out to Masham for a cream tea.'

A faint alarm from the laptop made them look at the screen. 'Four fifty-seven,' said Thelma. 'That's our three-minute warning.'

'Tell me again, who exactly is this Bun Widdup?' asked Liz. 'I mean I know she's something to do with Lodestone Academy Trust.'

'She's an education consultant,' said Thelma.

'A passionate, committed education consultant, according to Victoria,' said Pat. 'With a pretty fancy website. Here.'

She brought up an image on her phone and held it out for the others to see, squinting in the dim room. It showed a series of images of the striking woman both Pat and Thelma had seen before, smiling happily out at the world from atop a windy-looking clifftop, a restless blue sea behind her. Cerise words arched over her head: 'Bun Widdup Educational Vistas'.

'I see.' Liz sounded and looked both suspicious and wary – as she always had when any sort of consultant or inspector or adviser crossed her path.

'She runs online courses and staff training,' said Thelma.

'According to Victoria,' said Pat, 'people tune in from all over the world. She has this studio at her home in Robin Hood's Bay. Hang on.' She adjusted her phone to show the same woman in front of the background of vivid red and orange drapes against a buttermilk wall. 'She does this podcast,' she continued. '*Simply Ed*. I did think: here's someone else making money out of education.' She adjusted the phone again and handed it to Liz. 'Here—'

'Children first and last,' Liz read aloud. 'Ditch those tick sheets.'

'I heard her really giving Chris Canne a hard time,' said Pat. 'Telling him education was about more than getting schools through Ofsted inspections.'

'She spoke very movingly at Davey Fletcher's memorial service,' said Thelma. 'Chloe showed me a video of her reading out a sonnet.' In her mind's eye was a sudden image of that striking figure in the halo of sunlight. *Fear no more the heat o' the sun . . .*

'But why does she want to speak to us?' asked Liz, breaking into the memory.

'We're about to find out,' said Thelma indicating the screen, which was suddenly filled with a window declaring the meeting was about to start.

★ ★ ★

'Pat, Thelma, Liz,' the warm deep voice said each of the three names with a pleasant but authoritative tone. Today Pat noted that Mrs Kohl Panda was wearing vivid shades of cyclamen – a sundress, a scarf twined round her head. Round her neck amber beads winked in the afternoon sunlight streaming in from the right of the screen.

Bun Widdup shielded her eyes against the rays. 'Excuse me,' she said. 'Don't get me wrong, I love the sun but it can be a bit of a nuisance in summer – at this time of the afternoon, it shines straight in from the west.' She half stood and reached for something off screen, adjusting what must have been a blind or curtain. The sun's glare muted to a uniform warm glow that seemed to make the red and orange drapes pulsate with colour, vivid against the sliver of wall visible behind.

'It looks a bit on the warm side,' said Pat.

'No, honestly, it's fine.' Bun had a way of making every statement sound like a sort of stirring pronouncement. 'We're right on the cliffs above Robin Hood's Bay, so there's always some breeze going on.' She smiled. 'I once worked in Kenya, believe you me what we're experiencing now is nothing like the heat there! Anyway, I'm blessed living in this lovely place. These days I do all my work from home, with its sea views.' She looked appreciatively over to her left. 'I wish you could see it!' She smiled contentedly. 'You know, I haven't had to set foot outside of Robin Hood's Bay for four months or so!' she said. 'Gone are the days of belting up and down the country from staffroom to staffroom! *Anyway*—'

Now there was a crispness to that pleasant voice, a tone that unmistakably said, '*Down to business, ladies!*' Pat found herself remembering Chris Canne nervously pulling at his collar.

'Thank you for agreeing to see me. Especially so late on in the afternoon. I understand from Annie Golightly that you're asking questions about the death of—' She looked down at an iPad in front of her.

'Neville Hilton,' supplied Thelma.

'The man who led the Ofsted at Pity Me school,' said Liz.

Bun Widdup nodded. 'Of course – apologies, it's been a long day.' She yawned slightly. 'I did speak to the gentleman myself a few times, in the course of my work,' she said. 'Neville Hilton was ...' she paused delicately, a frown clouding her face, '... someone with interesting views. However, didn't he die of a heart attack or have I got that all wrong?'

'He did,' agreed Thelma.

'So the police say,' put in Liz.

'Well, he either did or he didn't!' There was faint laughter in her voice.

'He did die of a heart attack,' said Pat. 'But he had a visitor beforehand.'

Bun frowned, nodded, as if to say '*and?*'

'There was a lot of argy-bargy going on,' said Liz. 'A lot of shouting.'

'And whoever it was, was heard saying the name of Pity Me school,' said Pat.

Bun nodded as if light was dawning. 'So you think this person was from the school and might have been in some way responsible?' she asked.

'We don't exactly know what to think,' said Thelma.

Again, Bun nodded. 'And you say someone saw this confrontation?'

'No,' said Liz. 'They heard it. They were in the snicket outside.'

Bun smiled at them. 'Well, all I can say,' she said, 'whoever this person in the snicket is, they've got jolly good hearing!' She looked at them for a long moment, allowing the point to register.

'Okay,' she said finally. 'So I think I see where you were coming from. Assuming it *was* the name of the school this person heard being said.' She smiled and they smiled back. 'Suppose that someone did confront this Neville Hilton. And okay, suppose he subsequently had a heart attack? So what? I mean, it's all very sad and tragic, but it's not like any actual crime's been committed?'

Such was the sheer common sense in Bun Widdup's tone that it was hard to disagree with her. Pat was reminded of INSET training days, when she found herself being told what she was doing was not up to scratch, and what she needed to do instead.

Hey, Mrs Kohl Panda, what do you see? I see three retired lady primary school teachers making tits of themselves!

She glanced at her friends. Thelma was frowning and Liz looked like she was on the point of apologising and ending the call.

It was Thelma who spoke. 'Can I ask,' she said, 'why it was you wanted to speak to us?'

'Cutting to the chase!' Bun Widdup gave a merry laugh. 'I like that! Well, it's about Pity Me school – the late, much-lamented Pity Me school. Or rather the staff. I gather you visited there?'

'Thelma and I did,' said Liz.

'Well, you don't need me to tell you what a brutal – and I chose the word deliberately – what an absolutely brutal time they've all had of it recently, what with Annie, and poor Davey Fletcher and that awful Ofsted inspection and now the school closing and those lovely people being scattered to the four winds. I just can't but help feel a bit protective of them. As someone who's worked with them, I'm telling you, ladies, the very last thing they need is a lot of questions about some deceased Ofsted inspector.'

The three nodded in silence.

Bun nodded back, satisfied her point had been made, then picked up her tablet.

'So, this all happened . . . Neville Hilton died on' – again Bun looked at her iPad – 'Friday June the 13th?'

Thelma nodded. 'He did.'

The contralto voice sharpened with excitement and interest. 'And does anyone know about what time exactly he was reckoned to have died?'

'About seven o'clock,' supplied Liz.

Bun nodded. She almost looked relieved.

'I just wanted to be sure,' she said. 'I think I might be able to help you there. You heard there was a memorial service that day for Davey Fletcher?'

The three nodded.

'You spoke at the memorial,' said Thelma.

Now Bun nodded. 'I did,' she said. 'I knew Davey Fletcher quite well. As I said just now, I've done a fair bit of work with the school over the years. Not that I could tell them anything.' There was a sudden bleak sorrow haunting those features and despite the halo of sun and the vibrant colours of the drapes, it was as if a frost had fallen. 'Annie was – *is* – a phenomenal leader. It was more a case of me saying "here's somewhere that's getting it right!" As my old tutor at Bretton used to say, "Good news needs to be shared!" And she was dead right. Pity Me was a school people needed to see. But I digress.' Her voice regained its customary crisp energy. 'You say Mr Hilton died around 7 p.m.?'

The three nodded.

'And this was in—?'

'A place called Hollinby Quernhow,' said Liz. 'It's about nine miles from Thirsk.'

The woman on the screen bowed her head in affirmation and touched her keyboard.

'I'm going,' Bun Widdup said, 'to share a couple of pictures.' All at once the screen was filled with two images, obviously the screenshot from a Zoom call. One of the images was Bun Widdup as Thelma had seen her on Chloe's phone, earrings afire and vibrantly red against the backdrop of the African print. The other larger one showed the room Thelma remembered from her visit to Pity Me, the school library. It was full of assembled staff. At the front were Annie, Chloe, Caro Miranda; at the back of the room was Son Masters. All four of them were sporting bright yellow paper flowers.

'Davey Fletcher's memorial service,' said Bun. 'Friday June 13th. As you already know, I Zoomed in; it was way too far for me to come, as at this time of year it takes me a good hour plus to get anywhere, pretty much. But anyway – I want you to have a look at the clock on the wall.'

Pat, Liz and Thelma squinted at the clock visible on the back wall of the library. It was showing a little before six thirty.

'About half an hour before Mr Hilton died,' said Bun. 'So, you see there's no way it could have been anyone in that picture who shouted at him. At six thirty they were all listening to me – and I'd say it's impossible to get from Pity Me to Thirsk in half an hour.'

'I feel,' said Pat, 'like we've been ticked off, in the nicest possible way.'

Her friends didn't immediately respond. There was something about Bun Widdup's energy, even over Zoom, which left them all feeling slightly subdued.

'What she told us,' said Thelma eventually, 'it changes things.'

Liz nodded. 'With the clock *and* the time stamp,' she said, 'There's no getting away from it. *None* of them could have driven over to Hollinby in the time after the service.'

'Unless one of them has a TARDIS,' agreed Pat. 'Which means they're all ruled out – Son, Caro, Chloe, Annie—'

Thelma nodded. 'It seems to me,' she said, 'we've taken six almighty steps back.' She stood up and opened the door. Immediately Snaffles shot in and leapt territorially onto the keyboard. Absently Thelma scooped him up and deposited him onto the floor, where he stalked over to the curtains, which he clawed in an affronted manner admitting a chink of light as strong as a spotlight.

Thelma frowned.

'What?' said Pat.

She shook her head as if trying to clear her ears. 'I don't know,' she said. 'There was something – just for a second – but it's gone.'

'What?' echoed Liz.

'I don't know,' said Thelma again.

CHAPTER TWENTY-THREE

Friday 25th July

Voice of the Vale, Thirsk FM Radio: Today's beat-the-heat tip!

Shine on, Thirskians! Did you know sitting on the floor can lower the temperature by a few precious degrees? Hot air rises, so hitting the deck can help keep things a bit more bearable!

After her friends had gone, Thelma found herself weighed down by that peculiar lethargy that comes after any intense meeting; a sense of a task accomplished coupled at the same time with a total lack of energy or motivation to do anything else. She should, she knew, go through the conversation with Bun Widdup, jotting down salient points in the green mark book. Failing that she really should make a start on those Highway Code facts – but somehow, she ended up doing neither. Instead, she found herself sitting in her favourite wing chair in the front room, thoughts buzzing feebly round her head like so many weary, trapped bluebottles.

The fact that no one from Pity Me school could conceivably have been at Hollinby Quernhow for around seven o'clock, when Judy Bestall heard that shouting, lay heavy and dull across her thought processes, like a wrong word in a crossword puzzle. All her thinking had been thrown by this one, fundamental fact. Surely it *might* be better to let the whole thing drop? And yet *someone* had been shouting at Neville Hilton. But who? And why?

From a patch of sunlight by the window Snaffles stretched and drowsed, regarding her sleepily. She felt her own eyes growing heavier, her thought processes as heavy and dull as the afternoon outside.

A stir of movement, a clatter of claws, a frenzy of rapping feet jerked her awake. Snaffles. Her eyes sprung open, just in time to see a panicky blur of black as the cat exited the room. *What had disturbed him?* That was her first thought. The second, with a judder of fright, was *Someone's looking in the front window . . .*

A figure was standing at the window, perfectly still, staring into the room at her.

The Reverend Caro Miranda.

'I did ring but your bell didn't seem to be working.' The Irish voice was soft but authoritative as she followed Thelma into the kitchen. 'Oh my!' She stopped at the threshold, eye sliding appraisingly over across the Aga, the dresser with its sky-blue plates, the ceramic sink with the lovingly polished brass taps. 'Oh my, what a *wonderful* kitchen.'

Unbidden she began scampering curiously around the room, looking at the fixtures, studying the Eric Ravilious calendar, running a finger over surfaces, eyeing cupboards and drawers, almost as if she wanted to open them and ferret around inside. 'Of course—' She stopped abruptly and faced Thelma. 'Of course I could never afford anything like this.' There was a queer tone to her voice, one that Thelma couldn't quite identify but instinctively disliked. It made her want to say that what Caro was seeing was the result of years of hard work and doing without, cheap margarine, jumpers instead of heating, holidays in Brummie Maureen's static near Withernsea. Of course, she said none of these things, merely offered her tea – or a cold drink.

'Thank you, no.' Caro didn't sit down but stood with her back to the Aga. 'I was going to say something along the lines of "I was just passing" – but I think we'd both know that was a total lie.'

Seated at the table, feeling somewhat at a disadvantage, Thelma regarded her visitor.

'I understand from Chloe Lord that you've been to see Annie Golightly.'

Thelma nodded. 'She asked me to.'

'So I understand.' Caro broke restlessly into passing movement, crossing to the countertop where she regarded Thelma's knife block. 'Goodness me,' she said, half pulling out the largest knife. Almost reverently she pushed it back, before swinging round to face Thelma again.

'I know she asked you,' she said. 'And I know I invited you to come to the school. But' – she fixed her with muddy grey-brown eyes – 'I want you – I need you – to let this drop, Thelma.'

'Let what drop?' asked Thelma mildly.

'Whatever it is you're on with investigating – you and your friends.' She held a stubby hand up, as if warding off any denial Thelma should choose to make. 'I've spoken to Mare,' she said. 'She told me how you and your friends are gifted at – well, finding things out.' Her muddy stare became intense. 'But in this case, I'm telling you there's nothing to find out.'

'Someone did confront Neville Hilton the night he died,' said Thelma.

'Yes, that's as may be.' Caro shook her head impatiently. 'But it wasn't one of us. Thelma, Annie Golightly is a very sick woman. Chloe's a young lass at the very start of her teaching career. They don't need this aggravation.'

'Annie – and Chloe, for that matter – approached me,' interjected Thelma.

'Because they wondered what it was you and your friends were doing.' Caro's voice was fraught. She paused, a trickle of sweat running unbecomingly down that pointy nose. 'And as I say, Mare believes you have certain gifts: of observation, of deduction. "God given" was how she described them. But Thelma' – she clasped her hands – 'Jesus didn't use his gifts all the time. He picked and chose the times he acted.'

Thelma was about to say that any gifts she possessed couldn't begin to compare with those of the Almighty – and besides there was no way Annie, or Chloe – or even Caro for that matter could possibly have been in Hollinby Quernhow. But Caro was on something of a roll. 'Chloe Lord,' she carried on, 'is an exceptional teacher. And yes, okay, she can be a little hot-tempered – but only about things that matter to her.'

'Jesus himself turned over the tables in the temple,' pointed out Thelma.

'Exactly!' Caro seized on her words. 'One hundred per cent! But you need to know' – she took a deep breath – 'that night – after the ceremony – she drove straight home. If you're asking me how I know that – well, I followed her. I was a bit concerned about her, so I drove after her to make sure she got home safely. I saw her pull up outside her house. Anyway, I had a PCC meeting over at church, so I went on there after – and when I was driving back that way an hour later her car was still there.' She took a deep breath and abruptly all the energy seemed to go out of her. With her hands clasped at the waist and her head bowed, Thelma wondered if she was praying.

'Caro.' Her voice was gentle yet authoritative. 'Caro.' The face looked up and the grey-brown eyes met hers. Thelma was shocked by the unhappy misery ravaging those pointy features. 'At six thirty,' she said gently, 'you were all in the ceremony for Davey Fletcher; I know that for a fact. There's no conceivable way any of you could have been in Hollinby Quernhow for seven o'clock.'

She fully expected the woman to take some comfort,

225

reassurance from her words, but Caro's face remained stricken. She took a deep shuddering breath, her hand straying abstractedly to the knife block.

'People think,' she said in a low voice, 'that being clergy confers one with an automatic goodness.'

'I don't,' said Thelma calmly. 'My husband has worked for the church in some shape or form for decades, and I've seen for myself clergy have struggles just as much as anyone else.'

Caro nodded. 'This has all shaken me to the core of my being,' she said. Her fingers, Thelma noted with disquiet, had begun to caress the handle of the largest knife. 'To find oneself struggling with such . . . anger.'

'Scripture is populated by people who struggled,' said Thelma, eyes warily on those stubby fingers. 'Adam, Eve, King David. Saint Peter, betraying Jesus.'

'I worked in a prison once,' said Caro, gazing mesmerised at the knife. She seemed almost to be speaking to herself. 'It was a very . . .' she paused as she selected the right word '. . . rich experience. And the men there – all of them – they owned whatever it was they had done. Whatever their attitude to their crime, they knew it was a crime.' Her eyes met Thelma's. 'Neville Hilton. I wonder if he really ever knew the pain he caused?' Her knuckles whitened as she gripped the knife. 'I need to know,' she said. 'I need to know that on some level that man understood the havoc he wrought.'

Suddenly she looked down at her hand. An expression of horrified surprise flashed across her face as she snatched her hand back as if the knife were burningly hot. The moment seemed to shock her back to some semblance of normalcy.

'Thelma,' she said in a normal if rather shaky voice. 'Thelma, thank you for your time, but I need to be going.'

At the front door she paused, eyes pleading. 'Please, Thelma,' she said. 'Please – leave us alone.'

Thelma watched the retreating figure walking down College

Gardens until she was out of sight. A thought crossed her mind, and she reached round the lintel and pressed the doorbell. Instantly the hall was flooded with a pealing double chime. And yet Caro said the bell wasn't working . . .

With shaking hands, Liz opened up the food diary on her laptop. Shocked – almost tearful even – she typed 'TWO BAGS VEGAN MOMENTS' into the entry for the day before. A low rumble from the direction of the dining room told her that the online meeting of the Boroughbridge Climate Change Direct Action Group was still in progress. There'd be no point in even trying to talk to Jacob until it had finished.

He'd been so angry! Liz had thought as he'd become older, he would grow out of those volcanic episodes the family termed 'Jacob's meltdowns' – but no . . . On learning what she'd done he'd stared at her, eyes wide with a bewildered outrage that had taken both of them by surprise.

'*Grandma!* Don't you *know* how much sugar there is in *one single* little Vegan Moment?'

Liz hadn't, but he had and had proceeded to tell her in an outraged squawk. He'd also know how much sugar there was in one hundred grams of them, and how much therefore there was in the two bags Liz had scoffed down the night before. '*Gazillions*, Grandma! And your beta cells have to hoover *all* that up out if your bloodstream!'

Had she been silly to own up? But then – he had asked her directly, a suspicious gleam in his eye, and lying to her grandson's face was something she found she simply couldn't do.

Liz sighed, staring unseeingly at the grids of the food diary. She was shaking and upset in a way she hadn't been after either of her run-ins with Ffion Hilton. Throughout Jacob's many childhood meltdowns Liz had always found herself a step back, hardly ever the target and always, always the rock of security and stability to which he'd eventually turn and cling to. This almost savage anger towards her was something new and frightening; now she was the one who wanted someone to cling to.

Why had he been so angry? Was it maybe some worry about being in year 6? Or some fallout with the Boroughbridge Climate Change Direct Action Group? Or was it something else? Something to do with his parents perhaps? Of one thing she was sure – behind these meltdowns there was always some underlying reason responsible for triggering his violent operas of rage. And for him to lose it with her like that . . . it must be something significant.

How much longer would this meeting go on for? The rumbling from the conservatory had grown slightly higher in pitch, telling Liz that now Anna-Marie Lister-Brooks, self-appointed leader of BCCDAG was having her say about something and Anna-Marie was someone who liked to make her points long and loud. Ms Lister-Brooks was a person obviously destined for a life of confrontation; only a few months ago she'd had to be forcibly removed from a pelican crossing in Boroughbridge where she'd been lying down in a protest against proposals for fracking.

Liz sighed in frustration. She needed to talk to Jacob, see if he'd calmed down. Derek always said where Jacob's meltdowns were concerned the trick was to ride out the storm and wait for calmer waters, but how could she tell if this storm had abated if she couldn't talk to him? At the thought of her husband, she glanced upwards listening for the noise of his post-run shower. When he was done, she'd need to talk to him and tell him the sad story of what had happened, see if he knew of anything bothering him.

The noise of her phone ringing was such a welcome diversion from these unhappy thoughts, that she only vaguely registered it was an unknown number as she answered.

'Is that Liz? Plant lady Liz?' The voice was familiar. 'It's Sidrah, from Hollinby Quernhow – you came by the other day.'

'Yes of course! You sent me the CCTV film – thank you so much! Is everything okay?'

'To be truthful I'm not sure, Liz.' The voice was troubled and urgent. 'I'm a bit bothered about Ffion Hilton and couldn't think who else to ring. But you know her—'

Liz thought of those two fraught encounters. 'I wouldn't say know her as such,' she said.

But Sidrah was talking again, her voice even more troubled. 'The thing is, Liz – I think something's happened to her.'

CHAPTER TWENTY-FOUR

Friday 25th July

From the Thirsk and Ripon Green Fingers Gang Facebook Page:

It's best to water first thing in the morning or late at night, as when the sun shines on water it can act like a magnifying glass, burning the leaves below. And remember that hosepipe ban! Watering cans only, folks!

Thelma was sitting at her kitchen table. Once again, set before her were the books and prompt cards of the Highway Code and her laptop was open showing two androgynous purple cartoon characters promising an Easy-Peasy Guide to Highway Awareness. From the windowsill Snaffles regarded the two figures with grim, determined purpose.

Focus! She needed to forget – or rather put to one side – the complexities of the afternoon's events and concentrate on the complexities that represented the Highway Code.

She took a determined breath. *Speed* – that seemed a relevant place to start . . . There were sections in both books on the subject, plus a whole swathe of prompt cards. She picked one up.

What is the speed limit for cars towing a trailer on a single carriageway road?

She sighed bleakly. *No idea!* But then did she need to know that? They hadn't had a caravan in tow since that disastrous week in Alnwick some thirty years ago.

She looked again at the mosaic of facts that lay before her. *So many!* Just like with Neville Hilton – so many facts, both contradictory and unresolved . . . The fact that someone was shouting at Neville Hilton about Pity Me school and the fact that no one from Pity Me school could have actually been there. And then Caro's urgent insistence that Chloe had gone straight home after the service. What was it again? She'd seen the car on her way to a PCC meeting – and then again on the way back.

Thelma frowned. The way Caro's hand had clasped almost absent-mindedly round the knife . . . Her words – *I wonder if he really ever knew the pain he caused.*

A knife . . . *glittering in the dishwasher . . . that jumble of plates . . .*

She shook her head. *Come on, Thelma, focus on the job in hand.*

Taking a deep breath she said a prayer. 'Father, you say your word is a light for my feet. Make that light shine brightly now and show me the bits of the Highway Code I need to get my head round before tomorrow.'

Her phone rang. Thelma felt a pang of irritation. She had to make headway with absorbing at least some of these facts before Teddy came in, she wanted a quick supper so that she could have another go before she got too tired. She shook an impatient head at the ringing phone – it was probably Verna asking her to change shifts at the charity shop.

But it wasn't Verna.

'Thelma Copper?' The accented voice was familiar. 'Am I speaking to Mrs Thelma Copper?'

'This is Thelma Cooper,' said Thelma cautiously.

'Mrs Cooper, this is not a cold call. This is Oorja Kaur. I'm nurse to Annie Golightly.' An image of a plait waving determinedly between the shoulder blades of a marching figure appeared in Thelma's mind's eye.

'Oorja,' she said. 'How can I help you?'

'You can't help me,' said Oorja. 'I'm fine. It's Annie. I'm ringing on her behalf; she gave me your number. I have a message from her. She wants to see you.'

'She wants to talk to me?' The distance between College Gardens and Newton-under-Roseberry spooled out remorselessly in Thelma's mind. 'Can I call her?'

'No.' Oorja was emphatic. 'She has to see you – face to face. I think she's too weak to speak on the phone, my poor angel.'

'Would some time tomorrow be convenient?' She could always ask Teddy to rearrange his deliveries again.

'No.' Again the voice was emphatic. 'I would not leave it that long. You need to come now!'

'Now?' Thelma could feel the panic swelling at the thought of the long drive. Could she maybe call Liz or Pat? But how long would it take for them to get here?

'Yes please,' said Oorja. 'I fear time is short for my lovely woman.'

'Have you any idea why she wants to talk to me?' she asked.

'All she said to me several times was: "I have to see Thelma Cooper. I need to speak to Thelma."'

Although way down the sky, the sun still hammered relentlessly on the back of Liz's neck as she cupped her hands and peered through the glass frontage of the Old Barn.

'It's the milk see.' Sidrah hovered anxiously behind her. 'Delilah – she's the lady as brings the milk – she said the milk she left yesterday hadn't been touched, and had gone off so she left some more. Only when I was out doing the watering just now, I saw it was still there ... I thought maybe Ffion had gone away but the car's sitting on the driveway, and there were lights on last night ...'

Liz peered into the dim hallway. Should she ring the bell again? She took a step towards the study window but paused. Knocking on

a door was one thing, looking through windows quite another . . .
She steadied herself and peered in cautiously remembering that
figure framed in the glass on the CCTV. The study looked very
much as it had that last time she'd seen it – no, hang on . . . She
leaned in closer until her forehead was touching the warm pane.
There was something different about the drawers. Whereas before
they'd been flush with the unit, now they were slightly pulled out,
and stuffed paper could be seen in the gap – as if someone had
pulled paper out and then stuffed it back in again.

'D'you think everything's okay in there?' asked Sidrah
worriedly.

Liz moved back to the front door and gave a smart double
ring accompanied by a sharp rap on the iron-studded wood, again
expecting the appearance of an angry Ffion breathing smoke and ire.

But no one came.

'I'm getting a really, really bad feeling about this,' said Sidrah.

Liz frowned, worry overtaking her trepidation at once again
upsetting Ffion. Where was the woman? Was she even inside?
She considered the options. Calling the police at this stage very
definitely felt like overkill. But on the other hand, walking away
didn't feel right either. If only Hollinby Quernhow were different!
She thought of the Old Police House, the deconsecrated church,
the converted pub – all hubs of activity where one could have
gone for help and advice. All now a series of anonymous holiday
lets full of oblivious strangers.

'Is everything all right there?' Liz turned at the sharp interrogative
tones and felt a wave of unexpected relief at the sight of Zippy
Doodah accompanied by the ludicrously small shape of Buddy Dog.

It was just after seven thirty when once again the mussel-blue
Corsair pulled up on the wide brown verge in front of Bretton. More
parched leaves were drifting down, giving the lane an autumnal
atmosphere, eerie in the baking afterglow of the day. Thelma
turned off the engine and the air-conditioning. For virtually the

whole drive from Ripon, her mind had been turning over and probing the same question – what could Annie Golightly possibly have to say that was so important that it seemed to amount to some sort of death-bed confession? There was obviously something very important she wanted to share. Could *she* somehow be the person who had confronted Neville that night? Fired up by the memorial service, driven at implausible speed from Pity Me to Hollinby?

Mind still turning Thelma got out of the car, feet crunching on the scattered leaves and all at once she was struck by the stillness of the early evening's advent, the peace as tangible as the fading heat of the day. The fierce sun had mellowed into something more tranquil, sweeping the early evening sky with strokes of lilac and tangerine, bathing the bulk of Roseberry Topping and the surrounding patchwork of fields. She locked the car, breathing in the scents of cut grass and cow parsley – and all at once the thought hit her—

I drove here . . . !

She had driven the thirty-five miles from Ripon with barely a thought of unease or insecurity. It was as if the whole crippling doubt and lack of confidence of the past few weeks had broken like a fever. What on earth had she been making such a fuss about? But then, she reflected, how many, many times in life the mind built fears up, and equally how many times the feared realities proved to be so much less than the dark imaginings one had?

'Father,' she said, 'thank you. Thank you for easing my fears – and give me grace and wisdom to respond to whatever it is Annie has to tell me.'

She turned to walk up the lane to the five-bar gate of Bretton Hall – and stopped. With a surge of déjà vu, she saw the powder-blue Mini parked in by the bus stop, brown leaves dotting the bonnet and windscreen. Had Chloe Lord not even moved her car since their encounter a few days ago? With some trepidation she scanned the lane beyond – and sure enough there on the bench by the bus stop was the slight figure with white-blonde hair ruddy in the lengthening rays of sun. Chloe Lord was sitting, head bowed, face pressed into her hands. This time the sheath dress was an emerald green and the spiky tattoo was muted under the redness of the skin on her upper arms. Thelma approached and she looked up, face puffy and blotchy and so very tired.

As Thelma sat down beside her, Chloe began scrabbling self-consciously in a crammed and jumbled bag, presumably for tissues. Thelma's bag, benefitting from forty years more organisational skill, was considerably more accessible. Before the older woman had fully sat down, she was able to offer the younger one a pack of tissues.

'Ta.' Chloe tore out a tissue and opened it out. 'Annie said she'd asked you to come.'

'You've been to see her? How is she this evening?' asked Thelma.

For an answer Chloe shook her head, burying the tissues into her sore eyes.

'I'm so very sorry,' said Thelma gently. 'I know how much you care for her.'

'She believes in me.' Chloe's voice was little more than a whisper. 'She's the only one who does.'

'I don't think that's true at all,' said Thelma, but still in the same gentle tone.

'I mean as a teacher,' corrected Chloe rather hoarsely. 'Her and of course Davey – he believed in me.'

'As do your class,' pointed out Thelma.

'My class?' Broken as she was, Chloe sounded puzzled.

'Of course, your class,' said Thelma. 'Those thirty-odd children you teach. They believe in you, that's very obvious – both Liz and I noticed it straight away, when we saw you in school that day. That castle with the shields and flags – and that wonderful dragon. The children were all totally absorbed.'

Chloe shrugged. 'They're a good class,' she said grudgingly.

'Believe you me,' said Thelma. 'Even the very best group of children can and will run amok if they don't believe in or respect their teacher. Annie believes you're a good teacher because you are.'

Again Chloe shrugged and finished wiping her face. As she did Thelma prayed that her words had lodged and would in time take full root. She was wondering whether to get up and continue on with her visit to Annie when Chloe spoke.

'You don't know everything,' she said in a sad, small voice. It was the sort of comment that equally may or may not lead to something more, some revelation or confession. Thelma recognised such moments from of old, and knew they were as fragile and unpredictable as soap bubbles. She breathed in the still, scented air and waited.

'It's all my fault,' said Chloe eventually.

'What is?' asked Thelma.

'The inspection!' The words came out in an anguished sort of bark. 'The Ofsted. It's my fault the school's been shut down.'

Accompanied by the substantial presence of Zippy, Liz felt a lot more confident knocking on doors and peering in windows; even the prospect of being confronted by an angry Ffion didn't seem as bad.

She pressed her face against the Clichéd Stunning kitchen window. It was looking less stunning than before; fast food cartons and a couple of empty Prosecco bottles were scattered about, clutter on clutter all but obscuring the granite worktops.

'Fookin' hell,' said Zippy. 'That's a tip and a half.'

'Denby plates though,' said Sidrah in awe. 'Lush.'

The living room curtains were pulled, leaving only the narrowest of gaps through which Sidrah, Zippy and Liz all peered.

'OMG! That rug!' exclaimed Sidrah. 'I'm sure that's Orla Kiely.'

But neither Liz nor Zippy were paying any attention to the rug.

They were looking at the pair of feet, unmoving at the end of the sofa.

CHAPTER TWENTY-FIVE

Friday 25th July

From the Ripon Community Facebook Page:

A word to the wise! The River Ure by Skel Bridge is NOT a designated clean water zone. Even paddling is likely to bring a nasty surprise or two!

'When I was younger, I was all over the place.' Chloe spoke dispassionately, hair stained ruddy gold by the evening sun. 'The usual thing – Mum and Dad split up; I didn't get on with her new partner. Anyway, I was just a gob on legs me – couldn't be bothered with school, got in with the wrong crowd. I'm not excusing myself, Mrs Cooper – I'm just saying. And then . . .' She paused as if summoning up the will to go on. 'Then, I got in a fight. Stupid. Like I say – gob before brains – and the upshot was I got a criminal record.' Chloe sighed, a reflective Valkyrie, wide pale eyes looking into a troubled past. 'Then I had our Mirrel. Well, her dad was a no-hoper but she was – she *is* – the best thing that happened to me. Calmed me right down. Still does – sometimes I catch myself thinking, hang on, which one's the parent here?

'Anyway, Annie got me on that scheme – the one where you do your teacher training in school – but when I started on at the school, I had a criminal record. And I know for a fact Annie covered it up. I'm not sure how. She's like that – all that matters to her is the person. But when that—' Here she stopped herself. 'When that inspector, that Mr Hilton, started going through things, it all came out. And that's why we failed the Ofsted. *Because of me.*'

'No,' said Thelma.

'Yeah, okay there was other stuff,' said Chloe. 'But that was the main reason. That's why we were Inadequate, not Requires Improvement.'

'No,' said Thelma again, taking Chloe's hand. 'The school didn't fail – the school *was* failed . . . Failed by a clumsy, rigid system of monitoring, carried out by an inflexible man who should never have been doing the job in the first place.'

For a moment Chloe said nothing, then she took a deep, shuddering breath.

'Thank you,' she said, and Thelma sensed that again the tears were not far away.

She handed her another tissue and stood up.

'You are an excellent teacher,' she said to Chloe. 'Remember that.'

'Do you not think we should just call 999?' asked Zippy, for what felt like at least the tenth time. For once she was lacking her usual confidence, indeed one almost might say she was looking agitated.

'Let's just check ourselves first,' said Liz, more calmly than she felt. She looked at the glass of the kitchen door. It should be easy enough to break, and with her hand and arm wrapped in the tea towels Sidrah had just run across the road to fetch. 'The sooner we can get to her . . .' She let the words tail off.

'You mean the sooner we can see if she's carked it,' supplied Zippy gloomily.

'The sooner we can see if she's okay,' said Liz. 'Or not.'

Zippy shrugged. 'She didn't wake up when we banged on the window.'

Liz nodded. It was a miracle the glass was still intact after Zippy and Sidrah's vigorous efforts to get the woman's attention. She looked at the window in the kitchen door. It should be easy enough to reach the key she could see visible, as long as the door wasn't bolted. She didn't think any alarms would have been set, not with Ffion in the state she must have been in. She pictured the unmoving figure on the sofa and shuddered despite the evening heat.

Zippy shook her head. 'Back in the day,' she said, 'there was the Police House, the district nurse down Back Lane, Doctor Heathcote over in Pickhill.'

Liz nodded, remembering her earlier thoughts. 'How many people actually live here now?'

Again, Zippy sighed. 'Fewer than thirty, I reckon. And I'm not being funny, but a number of them aren't that long for this world.'

'Okay!' Sidrah sounded excited as she appeared with an armful of tea towels. 'I've cotton and I've linen. Which do you think would be best?'

From where he was tied up by the front door, Buddy Dog emitted a sharp bark, as if to say, 'Here goes.'

The living room door was ajar and the noise of flies from within made them slow their already cautious progress and instinctively clutch at each other, whilst outside Buddy Dog howled mournfully. Once again there was the faint smell of stables but this time it was overlain by something else, something Liz's scared mind shied away from identifying. Breath sticking in her gullet somewhere, Liz gingerly pushed at the door. An overpowering, sickly sweet smell wafted out on a cloud of warm air and angry flies.

'OMG,' said Sidrah in a small voice. 'The smell of death!'

Zippy Doodah sniffed suspiciously. 'More like Prosecco,' she pronounced. 'Very cheap Prosecco.' She crossed the room and opened the curtains, revealing an irregular, discoloured stain on the edge of the carpet. At the edge of this was an overturned bottle of KostKwik Fizz-tastic, with purple lipstick stains just discernible around the neck. It was around this stain where the flies clustered and buzzed.

As one, they reluctantly turned their eyes to the sofa.

Ffion Hilton lay on her back, eyes wide open, staring, face slipped, T-shirt rucked unbecomingly up round her middle. Feeling as if she were in some fevered daydream, Liz approached the supine figure, watched by Zippy and Sidrah who were clinging to each other. She bent over the figure, laid a cautious finger against the side of the neck.

Ffion screamed.

Liz screamed.

Sidrah screamed.

'Fookin' hell,' said Zippy Doodah.

Annie Golightly's room was flooded by the same early evening sunshine, the window opened wide to admit the smells of cut hay and the distant noise of cattle being led homeward. On the threshold Nurse Oorja spoke to Thelma in a discreet murmur. 'She is sleeping a lot,' she said. 'That is the way it is with these times. Occasionally she wakes, but then she sleeps again. Soon she will no longer wake.'

Thelma nodded, remembering her own experiences with her parents and various parishioners over the years. She approached the bed, which had been turned to face the open window; propped up against a cluster of purple pillows, Annie was a still, small presence.

Thelma sat by the bed. 'Annie,' she said gently. 'It's Thelma Cooper.'

Annie's eyes opened revealing that calm grey gaze.

'Thelma,' she said her voice barely a murmur. 'Thelma Cooper.'

'I'm here,' said Thelma.

Annie nodded slightly, satisfied. Her eyes closed but Thelma sensed rather than being asleep, the woman was mustering the very last fragments of her energy. Without opening her eyes, she spoke again, in that same hushed voice.

'The truth,' she said. 'The *truth* . . .'

Thelma took her hand, as if by doing so, she could imbue the woman with some of her own life force.

'The truth . . . *important* . . .'

'What truth, Annie?' said Thelma.

The eyes snapped open, gazing into the amber evening light. 'Love . . . it doesn't excuse,' she whispered.

'I agree,' said Thelma.

'There have to be . . . limits . . .' A single tear trickled down her shrunken cheek. 'I know.' There was agonised passion in the tiny weak voice.

'What is it you know, Annie?' prompted Thelma.

'The service . . . for Davey . . .'

'What about the service?'

'Golden lads . . .' she murmured. 'Fear no more . . . I *saw* . . .'

'Annie, what did you see?' asked Thelma as gently as she could.

Annie murmured something, barely breaking sound with a breathed whisper.

'Annie, can you repeat that?' Thelma bent her head close to that of the dying woman.

Again, that faint murmur.

Thelma frowned. She looked at Annie, but Annie had slipped back into that deep sleep from which it was unlikely she would wake.

'Father,' said Thelma softly. 'Hold Annie's hand and welcome her into your eternal kingdom.'

When Nurse Oorja came in some time later, Annie had not woken again. Thelma offered to stay but the nurse shook her head.

'People want to be alone at this time,' she said compassionately but firmly. 'Besides, I will be here with her till the end.'

Thelma nodded, looking at that still figure on the bed, her face growing ever more relaxed and at the same time strangely radiant. Annie Golightly was peaceful, of that Thelma was sure.

But as Thelma walked away, she was frowning. Those last murmured words . . .

What on earth had Annie meant?

From the kitchen window Liz watched the retreating figures of Sidrah, Zippy and Buddy Dog. From the rear, silhouetted against the evening light, they rather resembled something from a child's picture book. They disappeared out into the lane. Liz suspected they were only heading as far as Sidrah's house where she was sure the events of the past hour would be discussed and dissected (possibly to the accompaniment of alcohol, though probably not Prosecco).

'They've gone,' she said, carrying a cup of strong black coffee into the living room. 'And I'd better be making tracks as well. My husband and grandson are going to be wondering what's happened to me.'

'Actually,' said Ffion, 'I wonder – could you hang on a sec, Liz.' It wasn't so much a question as an instruction, gruffly delivered.

Liz sat down. She'd half expected this, which was why she'd not made her excuses and gone with the other two. She knew she should be wary; after all, here was a woman with whom she'd had two angry encounters and who had been in the near vicinity when her husband had mysteriously died. Yes, Liz probably should be wary – but for whatever reason she wasn't. She regarded the figure swathed in a fluffy white dressing gown. Without the carapace of make-up, Ffion looked a lot younger – almost pretty.

After Ffion's dramatic resurrection, a hectic interval had ensued when iced water was poured, black coffee made. Zippy started bagging up the detritus from the kitchen and Sidrah had insisted on having a Good Go at the Prosecco stain on the carpet. (It's Orla Kiely for God's sake!)

At one point in the midst of all this, Ffion had suddenly shouted out, 'Weetabix!' This turned out not to be a cry for cereal, but the name of her horse, and how she needed to head down to the stables to see to her, because Lib who was in charge was short-handed. Ffion had been so distressed that she seemed on the point of charging off down the lane barefooted, white fluffy dressing gown notwithstanding, until Zippy had said in firm tones that she'd get Piggy Paul to have a look-down – an arrangement that seemed to put Ffion's mind at rest. Evidently there was still some fragment of community in Hollinby Quernhow that could be called upon in times of crisis.

Liz had helped with mixed feelings. Once she had established Ffion was very much in the land of the living, she had wanted nothing so much as to head home, talk to Jacob and hopefully repair some of the damage caused by the Vegan Moments. She'd had the quickest of conversations with Derek to outline the bare bones of their falling-out, and now she needed to go back and see if calmer waters had been achieved. But then another part of her had to be sure Ffion was all right to be left, and to do that she needed to talk to her alone, away from busy chit-chat about specialised cleaning sprays and the scandal that was North Yorkshire Council recycling.

Ffion took a sip of her coffee, staring moodily into the dark depths. For all her asking Liz to stay, she seemed to be in no hurry to talk.

'I'm sorry for screaming like that,' said Liz to break the silence. 'You just gave me a bit of a scare.'

'I've always slept with my eyes open like that,' said Ffion. 'The Living Dead, my mum used to call me.' She looked fixedly at the black coffee.' I suppose it'll be all around the village by now.'

'They were both worried about you. Sidrah rang me, she was that concerned.'

'Ffion Hilton.' Her voice was bitter. 'Not only has she a stick up her backside, but now she's dead drunk. Can't cope with killing

243

her husband—' Ffion looked challengingly at Liz. 'That's what everyone's going to be saying. Don't think I don't know. You've seen the website – don't pretend you haven't.'

'The website doesn't actually accuse you outright of anything,' said Liz.

'You see the thing is—' Ffion's fixed gaze didn't leave the steaming coffee. 'The thing is – you might as well know – I *did* come back to the house the night Nev died.'

Liz could have said words to the effect of 'Actually, I know', but of course she didn't.

'I did go to that horse event in Carlisle like I told the police. I'd got Weetabix in the horsebox all ready, got the box hitched up, and I realised my driving licence was in Nev's study. He'd been looking at getting new insurance.' She took a sip, staring darkly into past events. 'I didn't want to drive the horsebox up the lane; I'd never get it turned round, so I nipped across the field and in the back. I got the licence off Nev's desk and went back. I swear I wasn't there more than thirty seconds.'

Liz nodded. 'I see.'

'I mean if I'd heard something – or seen something – I could've called 999—'

'But you *didn't* see or hear anything,' pointed out Liz gently.

'No.' There was regret in the voice. 'I saw Nev's car come in the drive – and I didn't want to talk to him. I was in a hurry. I didn't want to get into any long conversations about car insurance. I was running late.' Her voice was louder now, salted with guilt. 'So, I rushed off out the back praying he wouldn't see me.' Her hands whitened as she clutched the mug. 'I'd no idea . . . Afterwards – when I was told what had happened – I felt terrible. I swear to God, Liz, if I'd known . . .'

'There's not much you could've done,' explained Liz.

'I could've been with him!' The words came out in an anguished shout. 'Held his hand! And spared that poor lass. The one who found him.' Liz put a hand on her arm, but almost angrily Ffion shook it off. 'Whoever posted those things on the website – they must know what I did. And now everyone else knows.' She sighed a deep, exhausted sigh.

Liz looked at the woman. Was she telling the truth? Or merely a half truth, to cover a darker reality? She had no way of knowing. She stifled a pang of guilt. Whilst Ffion had been in the shower, and the cleaning operation in full swing, Liz had taken the opportunity to have another look in the kitchen cupboard. There had been no sign of the yellow-stained boots. Which meant either Ffion had discovered them and removed them, or Ffion had actually put them there in the first place and subsequently disposed of them. Or . . . someone else had both put them there *and* removed them.

'Can I ask you something?' said Liz.

The dark eyes slid from the coffee to meet Liz's gaze. 'Go on,' she said noncommittally.

'When I saw you yesterday . . .' There was a sheepish pause as they both acknowledged the previous night's encounter in the car park. 'You said that someone had been coming into the house? I mean since you found me and Jax that time.'

Ffion turned her head to look at her, full on. 'That's right.'

'You think you've been burgled?'

'No,' said Ffion. 'It's more subtle than that – nothing's been taken, at least not that I can see. I'd come home and things would have been moved – only slightly. Drawers a bit mussed up.'

'Mussed up?' Liz remembered the crammed drawers in the study.

'Like I say, really subtle, but once I started looking for it, it became more and more obvious.'

'How many times has this happened?' asked Liz.

Ffion shrugged. 'I can't be sure. Three or four. Defo once on a Saturday when I was out with Weetabix—'

'And you've no CCTV or anything like that?' Liz thought of the jerky figures on Sidrah's laptop. Could she have captured the intruder?

245

Ffion gestured wearily to a large unopened Amazon Prime box. 'After it happened with Nev, I knew being on my own, like, I needed something. But I can't get my head round setting it up. I'm no good with that sort of thing. I keep catching myself thinking I need to get Nev to sort it—' Abruptly she stopped.

'If you want,' said Liz gently, 'I could get Derek – he's my husband – to have a look at it. He's very good with that sort of thing.'

Ffion nodded, with acknowledgement or agreement Liz couldn't be sure. 'So was Nev,' she said.

'You must miss him very much,' said Liz, still in the same quiet voice.

'That's just it – *I don't!*' The passion of the words startled Liz. 'I'm such a horrible person,' wailed Ffion.

'No,' protested Liz.

'I am! I don't miss *him*. When he was here, we were like – what's that phrase? Ships that pass in the night. Him off with work, me off with Weetabix. But that night, he must have been lying there in pain, afraid. And there was I, off necking Merlot with my horse-riding mates!' She brushed brimming tears from her eyes with a wadge of toilet roll.

Liz said nothing. What was there to say? Nothing she could think of. She looked at the younger woman. Was now the time to make her departure?

'And there's something else,' said Ffion abruptly. She jumped to her feet. 'D'you mind? Can I show you something? I don't understand it – but I think it's got something to do with what happened to Nev.' She jumped up, tore off another length of toilet roll and headed out of the room.

Liz followed her, noting that once again that frightened tone was present in the woman's voice.

CHAPTER TWENTY-SIX

Friday 25th July

From the Twitter feed of Rainton Farm Shop:

Friday night is barbecue night! Here at Rainton Farm Shop we've a two-for-one offer on ALL burgers and sausages in our Summer Sizzle range. (NB due to the extreme heat customers are urged NOT to barbecue outdoors.)

In the event, confronting Tiffany-Jane proved easy. Not wanting to face the girl, Pat had deliberately lingered on the way back from Thelma's, calling in first at the leisure centre for a swim, then the farm shop for a totally unnecessary shop. By the time she pulled up at home, it had gone seven, a time when she could be reasonably sure that both Justin and Rod would be at home.

However, they were not.

Walking into the kitchen she had found Tiffany, squinting through her phone at Pat's Tuscan platter, which was bearing two poached eggs artistically arranged on a bed of watercress, zig-zagged across with dribbles of brown. Next to the platter were posed two ornate glass bottles of balsamic vinegar.

'Hello, love,' she said, more cheerily than she felt.

'Hiya. Rod and Justy have gone down the Wheatsheaf to watch the cricket,' said Tiffany, photographing the eggs. Pat sighed to herself as she deposited her keys in the Moroccan bowl – the repository for all the household keys. Of course, in an ideal world Justin would have fessed up to Rod over a few pints and by the time they got home everything would be out in the open and sorted out. However, this wasn't an ideal world, this was two Yorkshiremen watching cricket; personal conversation of any description would be way down the agenda. She'd maybe go upstairs and have another shower, then by the time she came down Tiffany might well have removed herself and her bottles of vinegar.

A sudden clatter caught her attention. Tiffany had dropped her phone on the floor. She was looking away from the eggs, frowning worriedly at the wall – before bolting off in the direction of the downstairs toilet from where rather graphic and unmistakable noises could be heard. Larson gave Pat a resigned shrug and padded off to the lounge.

When Tiffany returned, Pat had tactfully moved the eggs out of sight.

'Pat! I'm so sorry!' she said chirpily. 'Like I said – I think I've got a spot of gastric trouble.' She was heading towards the stairs but Pat's matter-of-fact voice stopped her.

'With our Justin,' said Pat, 'I was sick as a dog twenty-four seven. With Andrew it was heartburn. But our Liam – I wouldn't have even known I was carrying him.'

Tiffany turned, the perfect face frozen. Frozen – then slipped – then puckered before finally, *finally* giving itself up to tears. And at last Pat was able to hold the girl. At last, she saw that face, open and honest, blotchy and damp with the degradations wrought by tears.

'It's all right,' she said, patting her back as she used to do with Liam.

'It's *not* all right!' The strength of Tiffany's reaction shook them both.

Pat stepped back. 'Is something . . .' *How to find the words?* 'Is something not . . . right?' she said tentatively, 'I mean with the baby?'

'No.' The word came out as a weary exhalation. 'No, the baby's fine – at least it was last check-up . . .'

'And Justin?' Again, that tentative tone in Pat's voice. The baby was Justin's surely? 'He's all right with it?'

'Justy's fine. I mean, surprised and very overprotective – but yeah, he's really pleased – and so am I . . .'

'But?'

'But we've nowhere to live – nowhere near enough money!' Tiffany's voice was almost shrill with panic.

'Stop right there.' Gently Pat led the girl to sit down at the kitchen table. 'Now listen,' she said firmly. 'You and Justin and the baby can live here – *live* not stay here – as long as you need to. Justin's got a job; he's looking for another—'

'I can't work though,' said Tiffany in anguished tones, looking forlornly at the green plate. 'At least not influencing. It's taking all my headspace to do just one or two photos . . . and even then . . .' Her voice tailed off as she queasily eyed the bottles of balsamic vinegar. 'But if I do step back, even for a couple of months, there's a hundred other influencers out there just waiting to step into my shoes—'

'We'll manage.' Pat stemmed the flow with the firmness and certainty that six decades of life and all its trials had afforded her.

'But it's not what I planned!' said Tiffany with a wail.

'Newsflash, love,' said Pat with a faint smile, 'life seldom is.'

Tiffany smiled back, an uncertain, watery smile.

'Tiffany, listen to me.' Pat took both her hands. 'This is wonderful, *wonderful* news!'

The younger woman's eyes met hers and for the first time Pat thought she detected a faint light of hope in them.

She'd think of what to say to Rod later.

The heat came as an unwelcome blast after the relative cool dimness of indoors. Liz shaded her eyes as, with a mighty clatter, Ffion hoisted up the garage door of the Old Barn. Following her inside, inhaling those garage fumes of chemicals and oil, Liz stopped dead.

There was none of Ffion's equine detritus here. Without being told, she knew instantly that this was as much Neville's domain as his study had been. The space was nothing less than a love letter to order and organisation. Shelves were stacked with plastic boxes, a shelf of red, of blue, of yellow – each bearing a printed, laminated label: cross-headed screws, LED bulbs, misc. hinges. On the wall hung a dizzying array of tools clipped on a templated background. It was beyond tidy, beyond organised, it was so many things but the one overwhelming thing it was, thought Liz looking at the array of tools and labels – was heartbreaking. *Oh, Neville Hilton . . .*

'Here,' said Ffion urgently, indicating a jar on the lower shelf. '*Look*.'

Liz frowned at the jar, feeling a familiar prickle growing on the back of her neck. 'Did Neville not leave this here?' she asked.

'No!' Ffion's cry was explosive, almost passionate. 'No! That's just it! Nev would never ever leave anything like that! He used to play pop with me if I ever did! You might as well chuck that straight in the bin – that's what he'd say.'

'Do you have any idea when this appeared?' said Liz, knees creaking as she bent down for a better look.

Ffion shook her head. 'I hardly come in here,' she said. 'DIY and stuff – that was all Nev's department.' She hugged herself, staring at the object on the bottom shelf. 'It was when I was thinking about setting up that CCTV; I came in here and it was the smell that got my attention.'

Liz nodded; indeed, the smell of white spirit was pretty strong in the stuffy dim space.

'All along I reckoned it must've been Nev doing that weird decorating – what other reason could there be? But then I found this!' She looked at Liz. 'He'd never *ever* have left it like that.'

Liz nodded and looked at that jar half full of a cloudy liquid in which a paintbrush was soaking. The liquid was a cloudy yellow, the colour of butter.

The colour of a certain line on a certain wall.

* * *

When Liz arrived back from Hollinby Quernhow, she felt a bit nervous about facing Jacob. Was he still angry with her for eating those wretched Vegan Moments? Derek clearly knew this as he was waiting for her. 'He's in the sitting room,' he said quietly. 'The storm has abated and I rather think he wants to talk to you; he's kept on asking when you'd be back.' He squeezed her shoulder in a gesture of solidarity and Liz nodded. *Talk to me – or shout at me again?*

Jacob was sitting on the sofa, staring sightlessly at a SpongeBob SquarePants cartoon, a sure sign of worry and preoccupation. Steeling herself, she sat beside him, fully expecting him to shrug himself away and stalk off.

However, he didn't. After a moment – to Liz's warm, blessed relief – he snuggled up against her as he'd done so many, many times before.

'Grandma,' he said in a small voice, eyes not leaving the screen. 'Grandma, you *have* to keep your beta cells working. They *have* to keep hoovering the sugar up out of your blood.'

And all at once Liz understood. Heard the fear in his voice – and understood the root cause of his anger. She felt a sudden, warm, swell of realisation that here was one person who loved her, and out in the kitchen was another who loved her, and that both of them cared for her enough to try and keep her out of direct sunlight and away from sugary snacks.

'I know,' she said sensibly, putting her arm round him, so he could snuggle still further. 'And one of the reasons I know is that you've explained it all to me so well. And what I want you to do now is go online and find me a reasonably priced gizmo for testing blood sugar so we can keep checking how I'm doing.' She expected him to nod, leap up in search of his tablet, but instead her merely nodded, eyes fixed to the screen.

'Is there something else worrying you, lovey?' she said, knowing full well there was.

Finally, Jacob looked at her, eyes magnified and troubled behind his spectacles. 'It's Anna-Marie,' he said.

'Anna-Marie from your direct action group?' said Liz. 'Why, what's she done?'

Jacob took a deep breath, marshalling his words in the way he'd done ever since he'd learned how to talk.

'So, you know our blog, *Climate Change Devastation*?' he said. Liz did, of course she did. Barely a day went by when she wasn't WhatsApped some photo of parched trees and browning vegetation. 'She's *lying*.' He brought up a picture on his tablet showing a flower bed, earth cracked, plants brown and very, very dead. 'That's her garden,' he said.

'Oh dear,' said Liz, wincing at the sight of such horticultural devastation. She looked at Jacob. 'Her garden?'

'Oh yes.' Jacob nodded. 'But it's only like that because she deliberately hasn't watered it, not even with a watering can. She's just left it, so people will think it's like that even with watering.'

'That does seem rather extreme,' agreed Liz.

'I mean I know how bad climate change is, but isn't it wrong not to be truthful about it?'

Liz thought of the Vegan Moments. 'Yes,' she said firmly. 'Yes, it is. Deception is not right.'

As Jacob got up to fetch his tablet, Liz remained sitting there. A train of thought had started flickering in her mind, just beyond sight but definitely there. A brush left soaking in white spirit . . . someone going in Ffion's house, going through drawers – and boots liberally splashed yellow . . .

Direct action . . . telling a lie to support a truth or something you believed was true . . .

When Jacob appeared twenty minutes later with three blood sugar monitors to show her, she was still sitting there, frowning.

CHAPTER TWENTY-SEVEN

Monday 28th July

From the Surviving Hay Fever: A Guide for Sufferers website:

Tip 9: Wearing wrap-around sunglasses can effectively prevent pollen getting in your eyes when outdoors

'And you're *sure* the boots weren't there?' said Pat. Today she wasn't even bothering to hide her yawns. How many restless nights had it been? Four? Five? 'I mean they could've been hidden away at the back of the cupboard, behind all the cleaning stuff?'

Liz nodded her head firmly. 'Positive,' she said. 'While Ffion was in the shower, I had a good poke around and those boots were not there.' She turned to Jax who was sipping a mango smoothie through a straw. 'And they weren't that well-hidden, were they?'

Jax shook her head, ponytail swinging, swallowing down a mouthful of smoothie. 'The minute I opened that door I saw them,' she confirmed. 'I thought: aye aye – what's that? But Ffion'll have put them somewhere else, as soon as she got wind that people knew what she'd done. That or chucked them.'

'Unless,' said Liz, 'it's like Ffion says – someone's been in the house.'

The ponytail shook emphatically from side to side. 'She's

bound to say that. We know she lied about coming back to the house – so why not lie about this?'

Pat bit back another yawn. It didn't feel quite so blisteringly hot that morning. The rays that penetrated the linen drapes on the windows of the garden centre café were hot but maybe not quite so scorching in their power. Which was just as well – if it'd been any warmer, she'd have had serious trouble staying awake.

The previous night after Justin and Rod had come back from the Wheatsheaf, they'd had a family conflab. Rod (hastily pulled to one side and primed by Pat) had said the couple could stay with them as long as they needed – *live, not stay*, Pat had corrected. Justin had said that was Mega and Amazing, and implied it wouldn't need to be for very long as he had several Irons in the Fire and Projects in the Pipeline. Tiffany had said very little. For once she looked lost, a little girl in a world of grown-ups.

'A baby,' Rod kept saying, later on when the two of them were in bed. 'A *baby*. How's that going to work?'

'The same way it worked the last three times,' Pat had said with an ease and assurance she didn't in any way feel. The image of a gentle, joint retirement had recently taken so many knocks through illness and the demands of family and had now taken yet another. But . . . *a baby* . . . The thought glowed bright throughout that wakeful night and early hours.

She forced her mind back to the here and now, to her hurried conversation with Liz first thing this morning. *Get a grip, Pat! You're not just here to yawn.*

She forced some brightness into her voice. 'What I don't get,' she said, 'is why Ffion – or whoever it was – painted a yellow line down a wall in the first place. It's just such a random thing to do.'

'I can think of a reason.' Jax rolled her eyes significantly. 'It's just the sort of thing that'd wind Nev up. A big yellow line down the wall – that'd stress him out big time.'

'Painting a wall to provoke a heart attack,' mused Pat. 'As ways to dispatch someone go, it's novel.'

'And, as I say,' persisted Liz, 'there's all that Ffion was saying about how someone had been in the house.'

Pat forced her tired eyes wide open. 'You mean like a burglar?'

'No, not exactly,' said Liz. 'Nothing's been taken, as far as she can tell. It's more like there's been someone having a good look through things.'

'I'm telling you – she'll be making all that up,' said Jax, sucking up the last of the smoothie with a dismissive slurp. 'To cover up what's she's done!'

'What has Ffion done though?' said Pat. 'We don't know anything, not for a fact.'

The ponytail gave an irritated twitch. 'We know she shouted at him, don't we? And then he keeled over with a heart attack. God knows what exactly that woman said to him. It'll have been something vicious I'm telling you!'

'Going back to this person who's been going in the house,' said Liz. 'I was thinking maybe they were looking for something in particular. After all, nothing's been taken, and Ffion thinks they've been in a few times.'

'How?' said Pat.

'How what?' said Liz.

'How did they get in?' said Pat. 'I mean did they break in every time? Or had Ffion kept leaving windows open or something?'

'Nothing like that,' said Liz. 'Ffion reckons they must have had a key.'

'I gave mine back,' said Jax. 'You saw me, didn't you, Liz?'

Liz nodded. 'I did indeed.'

'It's a good job you hadn't gone and got another one cut!' said Pat with a cheerful laugh. 'Or you'd be right in the frame, Jax!'

Jax smiled tightly. 'Anyway,' she said, 'I have to ask – where's Thelma? I thought when you asked to meet, she'd be here an' all.'

She looked around the garden centre as if expecting to see their friend peeping out from behind one of the displayed sun loungers.

'She's got something on this morning,' said Liz vaguely. Neither she nor Pat had the slightest intention of mentioning the speed awareness course.

'So, Ffion reckons someone's been in the house?' said Pat, taking her turn to get the conversation firmly back on track.

'She would though, wouldn't she?' Jax was now sounding impatient, as she fished her car keys out of her bag. 'She's going to be making all that up. I mean it's not like she can prove it one way of the other, so she can say what she wants.'

'Oh, she can,' said Liz. 'Prove it, that is. Thanks to the CCTV.'

'CCTV?' Jax's voice was sharp. 'Sidrah's camera doesn't show the front of the house.'

'Not Sidrah's, Ffion's,' said Liz. 'She ordered one of those internal systems and got it all set up. She just needs to work out how to get it to play back.'

'Well, good luck with that one,' said Pat. 'It took us forever and a day to get our heads round the system at the Yard.'

'And even if she does,' said Jax, 'it won't show anything.'

'It might,' said Liz mildly.

Jax looked at her. 'It won't show anything up because Ffion Hilton's making the whole thing up.'

'Why though?' Pat's question sounded innocent enough as she took a bite of her Melmerby slice. 'Why make something like that up?'

'I keep telling you,' said Jax, rolling her eyes. 'To cover up what she did. Shouting at Nev – bringing on his heart attack. Bottom line: the woman didn't love Nev and now he's dead, and she stands to get all his money.' She stood up. 'Look, are we done now?'

'How d'you mean "done"?' asked Liz.

'When you messaged me – you said you had something to tell me. Was that it? I'm not being funny; I've stuff to do. So, if there's nothing else, I need to be heading off.'

'No, there's nothing else really,' Liz said.

'Er – the messages?' prompted Pat, as Jax turned to go.

'Oh goodness me,' said Liz, clapping her hand to her forehead in a way that was almost theatrical. 'I nearly forgot – how silly of me! The messages!'

Jax turned back. 'Messages?' she said.

'The ones on the village website,' said Liz. She smiled at Pat. 'Well remembered!'

'What about them?' said Jax suspiciously.

'Nothing really,' said Liz. 'It'll keep – you've got to get off.'

Jax sat back down. 'I thought those messages had been taken down.'

Liz nodded. 'They were,' she said. 'At least that's what Zippy told me.'

'It's more a case of who put them up there in the first place,' said Pat.

Jax frowned. 'I heard they were anonymous.'

'Ah, but that doesn't mean they can't be traced,' said Pat. 'Our Liam was telling me all about it; it's really very clever.'

'How is Liam?' broke in Liz brightly. 'How's the trip round Europe going?'

'He's reached Bologna,' said Pat. 'You know he and Bern are staying with Bern's cousin?'

Liz nodded. 'She has a house out there, doesn't she?'

'Think villa,' said Pat. 'Think very plush villa. He Zoomed me last night – and Bern's sent me some amazing pictures—'

'What about these messages?' interrupted Jax.

'Oh yes.' Pat frowned in a visible effort of remembrance. 'Liam was saying apparently all messages leave some sort of footprint.'

'A footprint?' said Liz.

'A digital footprint. Don't ask me to explain it,' said Pat. 'Our Liam's the expert. But apparently you can see where the messages originated from.'

'You mean you can find out who sent them?' asked Jax.

'The police can,' Pat corrected.

'The police? They not going to be bothered, surely?' said Jax uneasily.

'They were some pretty nasty messages,' said Liz grimly. 'Insinuating all sorts of things. Very upsetting for Ffion.'

Jax stood up, slightly flushed. 'Look,' she said. 'I've got to go.' She paused. 'Listen,' she said. 'Thanks for all you've done, you two and Thelma. But I've been thinking. I reckon it's all best left alone now, don't you? Stop finding stuff out. People want to move on.'

Liz nodded. 'I'd agree,' she said, looking Jax firmly in the face. 'One hundred per cent, I'd agree. As long as *all* the messages and *all* the goings-on in Ffion's house stop – well, then there'd be nothing *to* find out.' Her tones were crystal sharp and uncompromising.

Jax nodded. 'Yes,' she said quietly, looking at the ground. 'Of course.'

As the subdued figure retreated across the garden centre, Pat let out a laugh. 'You enjoyed that, Liz Newsome,' she said.

Liz nodded grimly. 'After all that woman put us through,' she said. 'All the confusion she caused – all she put Ffion Hilton through – it'll do her no harm at all to have something to think about.'

Pat grinned and stifled another yawn. 'So go on, Liz Newsome Detectivator,' she said. 'Explain – because I'm feeling very slow on the uptake here.'

Liz half shut her eyes, gathering her thoughts.

'It all comes down to triggers,' she said.

'Triggers?' Pat took a thoughtful bite of Dishforth meringue. 'Like in a gun? Or that man off *Only Fools and Horses*?'

'Mental triggers,' said Liz, doing her best to avoid looking at the sugar on her friend's lips. 'Harvey was telling us about them at pre-diabetes awareness.'

'So, what were Ms Shally's mental triggers?' asked Pat.

'Money,' said Liz sombrely. 'Or rather the lack of it. She is working all hours she can, cleaning up after other people – and there's her ex and his wife doing very nicely, thank you, with a very plush property, plus a holiday let to rent out.'

'Jax was the one who left Neville,' pointed out Pat.

'Which is Jax all over,' reminded Liz. 'Giving something up in the hope of something better. And then, after all these years she's suddenly back in touch with her ex and sees that maybe she'd have been better off staying with him all along. Every time she set foot in that holiday let, she was reminded of how much money Neville and Ffion actually had.'

Pat frowned. 'But it's a bit of a leap – going from envy, to actively besmirching his widow's name,' she said. 'I presume those boots were her doing?'

Liz nodded. 'I think she must have taken them from one of the charity bags Ffion would leave outside the house. Maybe she took them for herself and then realised they'd come in handy,' she said. 'Whatever the case, I think she genuinely believed Ffion had in some way caused Neville's death, so when she planted the boots, she felt she was planting evidence about something she thought was a fact. But of course, she put too much paint on them, and in slightly the wrong colour. But that's Jax all over – she never thinks things through properly.'

Pat nodded. 'And that was her going through the house?' she said. 'Letting herself in with a copy of the key?'

'I'm completely guessing here,' said Liz. 'I rather think after she went in with me and Thelma, she started letting herself in on her own, with a key she must have got cut.'

'So, what was she looking for?' said Pat.

'Guessing again,' said Liz, 'I think she was looking for his will.'

'His will?' said Pat. 'Did she think Nev was leaving her something? That seems a bit unlikely.'

'Maybe not,' said Liz. 'She'd been talking to Neville a fair bit ever since she took on cleaning his holiday let and, knowing her, she'll have made it quite clear how hard up she is. When I saw her yesterday, she was hinting how Neville always looked out for her. I wouldn't be surprised if Nev had even given her some money from time to time. And Jax being Jax would've drawn her own conclusions—'

'And was he, d'you think?' Pat mused. 'After all, at the end of the day, she left him.'

Liz didn't answer for a moment but looked out of the window where two young people in garden centre polo shirts were laughing together as they wrestled down the table umbrellas. In her mind was a creased photograph of two other young people laughing, happy, carefree, with it all stretching out in front of them.

'Feelings,' she said reflectively, 'are funny things. They flare up and then they die back down. And then years later they can flare up all over again.' She sighed and thought about her son, Tim, and the whole sorry saga of him and the barmaid from Dishforth, and how after many years she'd resurfaced in his life, almost upending his marriage. With a determined shake of the head, she pushed the past away. 'Anyway, I don't think there's going to be any more anonymous postings or visits to Ffion's house.'

'Liz Newsome,' said Pat, 'I take my hat off to you, you ace detectivator, you—'

But Liz was not looking at her friend, she was looking at the determined figure crossing the garden centre café towards them.

'Thelma?' she said. 'But surely today's her course?'

Pat turned and looked. 'Maybe it's finished?' she said.

Thelma reached the table and sat down.

'Good morning,' she said. 'I can't stay long; I have to be logged on by noon. But there's something I have to tell you.'

CHAPTER TWENTY-EIGHT

Monday 28th July

From the Thirsk Garden Centre website:

These top 5 drought-tolerant plants will thrive in dry conditions and longer hot summers, which will ultimately mean you can have a low-maintenance garden with the environment in mind. Check out our display stand next to Garden Ornaments.

'Son was wrong,' said Thelma.

Pat and Liz looked at her. 'That's what Annie said. That the truth was important, love doesn't excuse us and there have to be limits – then she mentioned the memorial service for Davey, quoted from that sonnet Bun Widdup read out, and finally that – those three words . . . *Son was wrong.*'

There was a frowning pause as the three considered.

'What bit of the sonnet did she quote?' asked Liz eventually.

Thelma got out her green mark book, even though she knew those muttered words by heart. '"Golden lads" and "fear no more",' she said.

'It sounds like she was leading up to saying something,' said Pat. 'But never got to what it actually was.'

'What she said – it doesn't make sense.' Liz shook her head in frustration.

Thelma sighed. 'It did to Annie. After she'd spoken . . . she looked peaceful – as if she'd got something off her chest.'

'But what though?' said Liz.

'Son was wrong,' mused Pat. 'Wrong about *what*?'

'This is Son, Davey Fletcher's partner?' said Liz.

'Who else could she have been meaning?' said Pat a trifle impatiently. 'There's no one else called Son in the mix and no one else had children – any sons – not Neville, or Caro or Davey Fletcher or even Annie—'

'Chloe has children,' said Liz. 'A child rather.'

'A daughter,' said Thelma. 'Not a son.'

There was a pause. Pat sighed, shook back her hair. It felt like straw in this hot weather. How she longed for cooler days, so she could return to her baggy tops. She was sick of sundresses and T-shirts were only really good for the Tiffanys of the world. She stopped, with a jolt of feeling. Soon Tiffany would be needing to wear tops as baggy and loose as her own.

'So, what did he say?' Liz's voice cut into Pat's reverie, bringing her back into the here and now. 'You saw him.'

'I'm sorry,' said Pat. 'I was miles away. What did who say?'

'Son Masters,' said Liz. 'When you saw him. Did he say anything he might have been wrong about?'

Pat frowned, recalling that amiable, sad figure in Jemima's Pantry. 'He said he was at the memorial service,' she said counting the memories off on her fingers. 'He said he was away on a book event when Davey set out on his drive in the blizzard. And he said how Davey was in a bad place about the report coming out.' She frowned again, looking into space. 'My main memory,' she said. 'My overriding impression is that he didn't seem to bear Neville Hilton any particular ill will. Which felt a bit strange, seeing how it was Neville's Ofsted report that caused Davey to drive off that day.'

'Of course, Son could have been pretending,' observed Thelma.

'He could well have been pretending,' said Liz, more forcefully. 'Remember he has a criminal record for GBH.'

'I know that' said Pat. 'I just don't think he was lying to me. He was one of those people who wears his heart on his sleeve.'

'But if he was hiding his anger,' said Liz, a skip of excitement in her voice. 'That's what Annie could have been referring to. Son was wrong. Meaning he was angry and he confronted Neville.'

'Only . . .' Thelma frowned as she stirred her coffee.

'Only what?' said Pat.

'Only that's not how you'd say it,' said Thelma, frowning up at the ceiling fan. '"Son was wrong" implies a mistake – a wrong choice or decision – not that he was lying about something.'

'Annie was very weak, poor lady,' said Liz impatiently. 'You said yourself. People say all sorts when they're not thinking straight.'

'But that's just it,' said Thelma. 'She *was* thinking straight, I'm sure of it.' She sighed, thinking of that still figure on the bed. Was Annie even still alive? Hopefully the peace she'd seen had remained with the woman.

'Of course,' said Liz, 'it could have been Son who somehow confronted Neville and Annie thought he was wrong to do it. Son was wrong to shout at Neville . . .'

'But even if it *was* Son who did it,' said Pat, 'you can't get away from the fact he was an hour's drive away at six thirty. Half an hour before Neville had his shouting match. They all were – Son, Annie, Chloe, Caro – all of them. According to Google Maps, Pity Me is a fifty-seven-minute drive away from Hollinby. Rod said you might just make it in forty-five if you break the speed limit – but remember you're talking the tail end of rush hour round Durham.' She sighed. 'It's a pity Ffion's been ruled out – at least she was actually in the building even if it was only for five minutes.'

'Ruled out?' Thelma looked interrogatively at her.

'Oh yes.' Pat gave a grin. 'You missed some right fun and games earlier on. *CSI: Thirsk* starring Liz Newsome.'

'Give over,' said Liz, flushing slightly. 'It was as much you as it was me.'

'It was not!' said Pat. 'I was just the heavy backup.'

After Pat had finished telling the tale, Thelma took Liz's hand. 'Well done you,' she said, and Liz flushed. 'Anyway . . .' Thelma stood up with the sombre air of someone heading for the gallows. 'I must be away. As I say, I need to be logged on to the speed awareness website by midday.'

Pat stood and gave her friend a rare hug. 'You'll be fine, my love,' she said.

Thelma nodded. 'I know,' she said. 'I drove all the way to Annie's and back, and I drove here and really, I'm okay. It's just the whole thing – I feel so judged . . .'

There was a sympathetic silence. They both knew exactly how she felt. So many times, as classroom teachers they had been judged and found wanting in some way. It was an experience that had never grown any easier. Indeed, as they had grown old the fear of being judged seemed to have grown more powerful rather than the reverse.

'You're a good driver,' said Liz. 'Just focus on that and ignore whatever pantomime they make you sit through.'

Son smiled; the amiable face slightly blurred on the screen. Tiffany-Jane smiled warmly back. 'It's good to see you!' she said. 'How are you, Son?'

The question was – despite the ulterior motive behind it – warm and sincere. Pat reflected that it had been very fortunate that Tiffany had been sitting rather aimlessly around when she arrived home. The girl had listened attentively – almost avidly – to her account of the morning's events, shaking her head, widening her eyes and at one point exclaiming, 'No way!' Jax had been labelled a 'misguided soul' and Annie had prompted a cry of 'Bless!' When Pat had told her about Annie's murmured, cryptic words she'd nodded and said decisively, 'We need to Zoom Son Masters.'

'And say what?' asked Pat doubtfully. 'It's a bit out of the blue don't you think?'

'Oh no,' said Tiffany airily. 'I've messaged him a few times since we met him, poor love.' She frowned considering. 'I think,' she said, 'this is one of them times you need to ask someone point-blank.'

It was with this sentiment in mind Pat sat now, watching Son nodding at them from in front of a pale-yellow virtual sunrise.

'I'm doing good,' he said. 'I'm in phase – and in tune.' He made a little punching movement with his fists and Tiffany clapped her hands.

'Excellent,' she said.

'And thanks for the mention you gave me,' said Son. 'I've had six, seven reach-outs.'

'That is so brilliant!' said Tiffany. '*Now*.' The voice changed into something more assertive. 'Son, I have something to ask you. And if it's in any way intrusive I must apologise.'

'Okay.' Son frowned, looking puzzled.

'It turns out,' said Tiffany, 'that a friend of ours knows Davey's boss.'

'Annie?'

Tiffany nodded. 'You know she's ill?'

A cloud crossed over the amiable face. 'I do,' he said. 'I mean she's been ill a long time; I keep meaning to check in on her.'

'Now, the thing is,' interrupted Tiffany, 'Annie mentioned Davey's memorial service – but said there was something *wrong* – maybe to do with it . . . and we were wondering what she could mean?'

Son frowned. 'The service they held at the school?'

Tiffany nodded. 'Do you remember *anything* about it that seemed in any way *wrong*.'

'Wrong?' Son sounded doubtful as he slowly shook his head.

'Or something that struck you as strange,' put in Pat. 'Out of place?'

Son looked at them, perplexed. 'No,' he said.

Tiffany looked at Pat, who sighed in frustration. 'Was anyone missing who should have been there?' she asked.

Again, the shake of the head. 'The only person who wasn't there was Bun Widdup,' he said. 'But she was never going to be there; it's two hours from where she lives.'

'Our friend told us the service was quite emotional,' said Pat tentatively.

Son nodded slowly. 'There was a bit of darkness,' he said. 'But people moved their souls to the place where they needed to be.'

Pat nodded. 'Was one of those places Hollinby Quernhow?'

'The poem,' said Son suddenly. '*That* helped everyone.'

'Poem?' said Tiffany.

'The poem Bun read out . . .' Son smiled remembering. '*Fear no more the heat o' the sun,*' he said. 'It was . . . special. It brought light into the space we were all in.' Son nodded, remembering. 'When she read, the sunlight was coming into her room. It was like she had a halo, like an angel—'

As they were saying goodbye Tiffany said, 'We'll Zoom again – and maybe meet up sometime?'

'That was good of you,' said Pat as she shut the laptop. Privately she wondered what her son would have to say about his pregnant partner visiting someone who might had a criminal conviction for GBH; indeed, thinking about it, she was none too happy herself. A conversation for another time, she thought.

'I feel sorry for him,' said Tiffany. 'Besides' – she looked blankly round the kitchen as if it were a top-security cell – 'I'll have enough time on my hands.' She sighed a deep sigh.

'Yes, about that,' said Pat, 'I've been thinking. About you, about your influencing . . . I mean what is it you and Justin are saying? Don't get down – *get right back up!*'

Tiffany looked at her, tired and pasty.

'It just occurred to me,' said Pat. 'How about something along the lines of Ms T.J. Rox the Cradle?'

'Sorry?' Tiffany frowned.

'Motherhood with pizazz!' said Pat. 'Feng-shuied nurseries, holistic lullabies – bath bombs for birthing pools.'

She went over to the counter to start preparing Angela Hartnett's yellow bean, fennel and tuna salad. There'd be a houseful tonight. Andrew and Simone were coming for supper so that the news could be broken to them. Plus, they were going to Zoom Liam and Bern away in the Bolognian villa. Looking up from the recipe, she could see Tiffany's face in the reflection from the glass cupboard door, frowning, mouth slightly open, and Pat could tell with a thrill of satisfaction that this wonderful, bright creature, the mother of her first grandchild, had been stopped short by an idea that wasn't her own.

CHAPTER TWENTY-NINE

Monday 28th July

Voice of the Vale, Thirsk FM Radio: Today's beat-the-heat tip!

Hot in the office? Ditch the darkness! Dark clothes absorb the heat, so go for loose, light garments! Better still – strip off! (If you have your own office or work from home, that is!)

'Come on, Noah. Frame thissen', lad!' The hearty Yorkshire voice vibrated through the speaker on Thelma's laptop. 'Tell me one reason you might be caught speeding the old brum–brum? We've had been late; we've had having an urgent appointment.' Thelma was glad it wasn't her being asked the question because the only answer she could think of was something along the lines of 'driving from Pity Me to Hollinby Quernhow in half an hour flat'. She stole a glance at the open page of the green mark book. Now Ffion was removed from the equation it seemed that Neville's visitor had to be someone from Pity Me school.

'Come on, Noah, we're waiting, lad!' The owner of the voice – Jim Whitlaw, their course leader – was one of those people who made a virtue of their Yorkshire accent, implying through its blunt, colloquial nature a quality of down-to-earth common sense.

Yawning, the young man wrapped in a duvet looked out, a sleepy face amongst the other panels of faces.

'How about there being a totally unnecessary speed camera in a place no one can see it,' interjected another voice, crisp and decidedly tetchy.

'Now then, Cheryl love, let Noah speak,' said Jim Whitlaw easily. 'We're all here to muck in and learn, remember.'

'If you drive when you're upset' – Noah spoke up suddenly and clearly – 'you can lose concentration and end up going fast without thinking about it.'

'Nice one, Noah lad!' said Jim Whitlaw approvingly. 'Remember, chaps and chappesses, when you're upset avoid getting behind the wheel if at all possible. There's being over the limit alcohol wise, and there's being over the limit emotionally.'

In an instant Thelma's mind once again slid away from speed awareness, this time to a newspaper picture of a wrecked car on a snowy moorland road. Davey Fletcher, very definitely driving unsafely, very definitely over the emotional limit, thanks to Neville Hilton's damning Ofsted Report.

She forced her mind back to the screen. She was finding Teddy's John Lennon glasses a shade too weak and consequently was having to squint rather ferociously at the other ten faces of the course attendees. She peered at the clock in the bottom corner of the screen and with a slight jolt of surprise realised they were not too far from the end of the two-and-a-half-hour session. The realisation fuelled the sense of relief that had been growing inside her since the start of the session, which had been nowhere near as bad as she feared.

For a start, Jim Whitlaw had been at great pains to emphasise how the course *wasn't* about judgement. The glossy website of the course providers gave much the same message. *You are not being judged!* it said, more than once. This in itself hadn't quietened

Thelma's fears because of course she had been judged. She knew it in a very private and primal part of her soul – just as, she guessed, all the other attendees did – and just as the staff of Pity Me school must have known it, following Neville's report. But five minutes of listening to Jim Whitlaw's cheery common sense had quietened her upset and when he'd said it was all about moving forward safely, and maybe learning a thing or two on the way, she'd believed him.

And there'd been a number of things she'd learned – how lamp posts in a street automatically meant a thirty or even twenty-mile-an-hour zone. And how adding even an extra mile an hour to your speed had a massive impact on your ability to brake. Jim was, Thelma recognised, a good teacher. He had a lively way of speaking and she felt sure some of the more complex aspects of the course would have been decidedly dry without his cries of 'nay, chaps' and his habit of marking any significant point regarding motoring by hitting a fist in his palm with a solemn bark of 'doof'.

Then there were the people on the course, with their fascinating square glimpses of their various lives – the bookshelf, the wallpaper, the curtains. 'No virtual backdrops allowed,' Jim had said cheerfully when they logged on. 'We need to know you're at home and not in a TV studio! So, hide them drying pants, chaps and chapesses!'

And then there was Noah. The first sight of him had been a mounded duvet, a bleary face and a glimpse of a *Jurassic Park* T-shirt.

'Hey up there, Noah,' Jim had said. 'Good of thee to join us!'

The screen had briefly tipped crazily before the image resolved on Noah, obviously sitting cross-legged on his bed, duvet wrapped round him.

His background – the background to his be-duvet-ed form – was by far the most interesting aspect of the course. The space behind him looked to be some sort of attic, sloping ceiling painted a vibrant shade of blue, on the walls and ceiling were modern art posters – Tracey Emin, Davey Hockney, on the table beside him were a stack of what looked to be books on art and philosophy; his handwriting when the course held up their answer pads was clear and well formed. A young person's room.

Golden lads and lasses . . . Why did that sonnet from Davey's memorial service suddenly pop into her mind? She thought again about the extensive text Pat had sent just before the course began, about the conversation with Son Masters . . . How Bun had resembled an angel with the light around her . . .

She looked at the figure swathed in a duvet. Noah could hardly be described as an angel, and certainly no sort of golden lad – he looked way too bleary that . . . Who was he? An artist perhaps? A student? And why, given the culture of his surroundings, was he sporting *Jurassic Park* pyjamas? So much, Thelma thought, could be gleaned from the background of someone's Zoom. She found herself thinking about Bun Widdup – those African drapes, gloriously red and orange against the visible sliver of buttermilk wall. Kenya, wasn't that where she'd said she'd worked? And then that image of the staffroom at Pity Me, that time-stamped image freezing those people into that precise moment. Caro, Annie, Chloe – sporting those yellow flowers. And Son . . . *Son was wrong* . . .

What *had* Annie meant when she said those words? Wrong about what?

'Okay, chaps and chappesses, that's about a wrap!' Jim's cheerful tones broke into her different trains of thought. 'I hope tha's learned a thing or two. And I have to say, because the company tell me to, but I do happen to think it's a fact worth sharing, that some eighty per cent of people who take this course do not go on and reoffend. So, let's hope tha's not one of the twenty per cent that presumably do!'

It was with a huge feeling of lightening relief that Thelma shut down the laptop and replaced Teddy's glasses with her own. She unwound the green and purple scarf from round her head and changed the garish lemon-yellow blouse for her own white one. Both scarf and blouse were ones she had 'borrowed' from the charity shop where she worked. Both were going straight back there at the first opportunity. With any luck even if she came face to face with Noah, Jim or any of the course members they would not equate her with the gaudily dressed woman she'd been five minutes before.

She picked up the hairbrush to restore some order to her greying bob, and frowned, brush poised in her hand. Quite unconsciously something had flitted across her mind, something she knew to be of importance. What? Brushing her hair she reviewed her recent thoughts: judgement, Davey's crash, golden lads and lasses, Noah's room . . . *What was it?*

With a sigh she opened the door and Snaffles shot in and took a bold leap onto the dressing table, sniffing the laptop before walking firmly and territorially across the keyboard, realising it had been turned off and turning away in disgust. Thelma turned her phone on; whatever the thought had been it had gone, for now.

Her phone buzzed. Three missed calls from Caro Miranda.

With a dropping feeling of sad anticipation, she dialled.

'Hello? *Thelma*?' Caro's voice sounded different . . . broken.

'Caro, you called me?'

'Yes . . .' It sounded as if Caro was having trouble putting her words together. 'Yes, thank you for calling me back. I thought you'd want to know, Annie Golightly died early this morning.'

'I see.' Although the news wasn't totally surprising Thelma found herself sinking down on the bed, hands trembling. 'I'm so very sorry,' she said. There was a pause. 'Hello?'

'Yes, I'm still here.' Caro's voice was cracked and congested. 'You must forgive me.'

'Not at all,' said Thelma. 'There's absolutely nothing to apologise for.'

'Of everyone I've ever known, Annie had so much life—'

'I only knew her at the end,' she said. 'But I know exactly what you mean.'

'Sometimes,' said Caro, 'as a person of God, I find there's what I know in my heart and what I know in my head. And sometimes the two don't connect.'

'I completely understand,' said Thelma.

'I believe you do.' There was a pause, a muffled sob. 'It's just . . . I've known so many people, so many people who have died in all sorts of ways – but with Annie, she had so much life . . . there's a real sense of loss . . . of a light gone out before its time.'

'Yes,' said Thelma.

Again, that image came before her, a wrecked car at the side of a moorland road.

Golden lads and lasses.

There was a sigh down the end of the phone. 'There's something I need to say,' said Caro. 'I lied to you. I mean I could try and dress it up because I know there's no way Chloe Lord went to confront Neville. I just know, but—'

'But you didn't actually follow her home, did you?' supplied Thelma. 'Yes, I rather thought so.'

'Am I such a bad liar?' There was an ironic tone in Caro's voice. 'Maybe that's something to be thankful for.'

'It was what you said to me,' said Thelma. 'How you went on to a PCC meeting after the ceremony. I know PCC meetings – and I don't know of any that start any later than seven thirty. People are so prone to ramble on. And I've certainly never heard of any that last just an hour.'

'I see,' said Caro. 'Well, I'm sorry anyway, but you have to trust me – there is no way Chloe confronted Neville.'

'I wonder, Caro,' said Thelma. 'Could I ask you something? It may seem unconnected but believe me it's important.'

'Of course.' The voice sounded slightly sharpened by curiosity.

'The memorial service. That sonnet Bun Widdup read out.'

'Yes? What about it?'

'Did you happen to film it?'

There was a pause. Then: 'Yes, I did.'

'I'm wondering, could you send me a copy? I can't say why, but it's important.'

'I can't, I'm sorry,' said Caro. 'I deleted it.'

'I see,' said Thelma.

'I'm telling you the truth,' said Caro. 'Annie asked me to.'

'Annie did?'

'It was the last time I saw her – a couple of days ago – she asked if I had it on my phone. She said how Son didn't want any recordings of the service and asked me to delete it. So, it's gone. But I can remember the poem. I could send you a link if you want to read it.'

After the call had ended, Thelma stayed sitting on the bed, hands no longer trembling but folded.

Son didn't want any recordings of the memorial? *Why?*

CHAPTER THIRTY

Tuesday 29th July

Met Office weather forecast:

A cool front bringing cloudy and patchy showers will make its way down from the north during the later part of the night, bringing lower temperatures across England and Wales.

During the small hours, welcome clouds gathered over the moors, hills and rooftops of Thirsk and Ripon.

In the grey of that cool early morning, Thelma dreamed.

She dreamed she was back at St Barnabus, the school she'd worked at for all those years, walking through its empty corridors and classrooms. In her heart and throat was the most terrible aching sadness, for she had the knowledge that soon the school was to close, that the miniature chairs, the stacks of reading books, the plastic trays of glue sticks were to be removed, leaving the rooms where she'd spent so much of her life bare and empty shells, stripped of purpose and meaning.

And then she was in the staffroom – with staff from the old days, Pat and Liz, Feay and Topsy. They were watching a Zoom call, not on a laptop but on the old school television on its cumbersome, wheeled stand. They were all looking at Noah, who was gazing blearily back, duvet hunched round him. Only Thelma knew Noah wasn't in his attic room, but in Teddy's study with its thick drapes, and that for some reason it was vitally important no one watching should know this. If only she could close those thick drapes no one would know . . .

Then, as was the way with dreams, she was suddenly in the study, trying to force the drapes shut. Only, try as she might, she couldn't close them fully. There was a telltale gap where the material wouldn't meet; she was afraid to pull too hard in case the whole lot came crashing down.

She woke, with a sleepy feeling of receding sadness, and some muddled notion of ringing Liz and Pat to explain that Noah wasn't in fact present in her husband's study. Shifting into wakefulness she became aware of another sensation, both welcome and unfamiliar. She was chilly. Getting out of bed she padded over to the curtains, stirring in a wafting breeze, looking outside at clouds, blessed, big fluffy castles and continents and galloping horses, billowing lazily over Ripon and St Bega college. At long last, the heatwave had broken.

Dressed and waiting for the kettle to boil, Thelma became aware that the memory and sensations of her dream had in fact stayed with her . . . That sadness wandering the corridors of the school . . . The need to conceal Noah's location . . . Why? She took her camomile tea and sat in her favourite wing chair; taking up her prayer journal she began to jot down the details . . . *St B closing . . . Sadness – with staff – watching Noah on Zoom . . . he's in T's study, have to hide this – curtains won't shut.*

She stopped; pen poised. All at once she was convinced that somewhere, just beyond conscious coherent thought, lurked something very, very important.

'Guide me in your truth and teach me,' she said quietly to the grey morning. 'You are my saviour and all my hope is in you.'

But nothing happened. No thought, no revelation, just Snaffles

276

standing plaintively at the French windows as if to say, 'Are you going to let me out or what?'

Opening them she drank in the cooler air. Maybe the garden was duller, maybe the sunflowers and hollyhocks weren't as enamelled, perhaps the cobwebs weren't bejewelled but all the same there was a blessed quality to the cool cloudy morning drenched in the whistles and chirps of birdsong.

But still her dream niggled.

If anything, it was growing in its intensity.

Ten minutes later saw her crossing the playing fields, fists clenched in her cardigan pockets. As the soothing noise of soughing trees filled her mind, Thelma recalled and replayed her dream – the empty school, the Zoom call, the frantic tugging of the curtains. *What did it mean?*

As she crossed Trinity Road, a spike of sun hit the red brick frontage of Ripon and St Bega college, turning the windows gold. Even though it was barely six, there were signs that Ripon was waking to face another day: Myra Bennett's son was delivering papers, that friend of Contralto Kate was kneeling discreetly by her labradoodles, hand swathed in a plastic bag. Behind each window, kettles and showers and electric toothbrushes were doing their work to a background of the *Today* programme or Georgey Spanswick on *Radio York*.

But Thelma was still lost in her dream. That sense of there being *something* just beyond her thoughts, was like the clouds, swelling and billowing.

She hadn't any particular destination in mind, so it was with mild surprise she found herself approaching the benign Georgian edifice of St Catherine's church. The door wasn't locked. Dot and James, the church wardens, had fallen into the habit of 'forgetting' to lock the building in order to afford some of the local homeless a place to sleep on the strict understanding they didn't leave any sort of mess. Whether there had been any such visitors last night

277

Thelma couldn't tell. The narthex was swept and tidy as it always was.

With a feeling of relief, she slipped into her favourite pew (left-hand side, halfway down) breathing in the comforting scents of the church, paper, must and lavender furniture polish.

'Father,' she said aloud. 'Father, if it be your will, give me guidance. There is something my mind is trying to tell me, but I don't know what it is.'

She took the prayer journal from her cardigan pocket and again read the words aloud.

St B closing . . . Sadness – with staff – watching Noah on Zoom . . . he's in T's study, have to hide this – curtains won't shut.

As was her practice, she sat back, breathed deeply and allowed the cool peace of the church to soothe her tangled thoughts.

Neville, his foolish, smug grin – confronted in anger, doing so much damage – Annie's school, Son's partner, the people Chloe cared for, the community Caro Miranda was part of. Four people who would have felt no sorrow at the man's death.

And yet all of them too far away, each with an immutable alibi . . .

But then, was Neville's death even connected with the school? As Annie herself had pointed out, that shout of 'Pity Me' could have been misheard . . . that paper flower Liz found, just a coincidence.

Father, guide my thoughts . . .

All at once she was back by Annie's bedside, struggling to hear those whispered words . . . *the truth important . . . Son was wrong . . .*

Annie. Thelma opened her eyes. Blinking in the dim light, she walked to the iron stand of candles to the left of the altar rail. Retrieving the green plastic lighter that lived there, she rasped a flame into life and lit one of the plain white tea lights.

'Father,' said Thelma quietly. 'Father, bless your child Annie Golightly. Hold her hand and take care of her.'

At that moment, a beam of pure, clean sun, as powerful

as a spotlight, hit the east window, bringing the cross and the assembled saints into brilliant, glowing life and scattering bright jewels of colour – ruby, sapphire, emerald – across the altar steps and Thelma's upturned face.

Thelma stood bathed, haloed by the coloured lights winking across her glasses.

Image after image, word upon word, came crowding into her mind . . .

Like an angel . . . A yellow line . . . vivid red and orange . . .
Fear no more the heat o' the sun . . .

The sun . . .

Of course!

CHAPTER THIRTY-ONE

Thursday 31st July

Voice of the Vale, Thirsk FM Radio:

Hey there, Thirskians! Time to put those fans away. Normal service has resumed with cloud and rain forecast! If you want the heat back, better buy yourself a plane ticket somewhere sunny!

'Is this such a good idea?' Pat's gaze roved uneasily round the half-full garden centre café.

'You really don't have to stay,' said Thelma. 'I was the one she asked to see.'

'Of course we're staying,' said Liz robustly. 'We wouldn't dream of leaving you on your own!' She set her chin defiantly.

Pat nodded, but she had more than a few doubts about this meeting, not least the speed at which it had been set up. Thelma had sent an email, which had provoked an immediate request to meet, face to face. And if what Thelma had supposed was true – which Pat instinctively felt it was – there was no knowing how this person might react. She was suddenly assailed by an irreverent mental image of Thelma and their visitor rolling over and over between the tables, locked in grim combat, and had found herself biting back a grin. At least, she thought, the weather had cooled down. At long last she was back to wearing her baggy tops! Once again there were summer jackets on the backs of the chairs and the air admitted by the patio windows was fresh. Everyone seemed to have lost that slow, droopy listlessness. It was as if the whole world was breathing one huge, cool sigh of relief.

Thelma touched her arm. 'You really don't have to stay,' she said again. 'Honestly, it's perfectly safe here with so many people around.'

Fighting down images of brawls between the tables Pat smiled at her friend, her very clever friend. 'No,' she said with a confidence she didn't feel. 'No, of course I'm staying.'

'Here we go,' said Liz nodding across the garden centre. 'But who's that with her?'

In the flesh, Bun Widdup cut no less a striking figure than she did on Zoom. Today she had presented herself in shades of green, a holly-green scarf twined round and through the auburn hair, a sage green skirt and loose-fitting top, emerald glass beads glinting round her throat. But close to, without the filter of Zoom, it was possible to notice other things, wires of white at the uncoloured roots of the coppery hair, lines around the jawline and the uneasiness in those dark-ringed eyes.

Hey, Mrs Kohl Panda, what's a-botherin' you today?

With her was a neat, slight woman of about thirty, dressed – expensively, Pat noted – in a charcoal grey suit and cream silk. She appeared to be one of those people who maintained a firm screen between whatever they were thinking and whatever was happening in the world.

'This,' said Bun Widdup, sitting down, 'is Sarah Botha of Meredith and Bray solicitors.'

Sarah Botha gave a detached, professional nod and took a tablet from her bag – her Prada bag, Pat spotted.

'My client,' she said formally, 'has a statement she wishes to share with you.' She nodded at Bun, who took a brightly coloured A4 wallet from her bag, from which she extracted a printout. Her hands, all three noticed, were shaking slightly but when she raised her head to face the three her gaze was steady.

'When we leave here in a few minutes,' Bun said, 'we're going to Northallerton police station where we'll be attending an interview with Chief Inspector Ian Blakley of North Yorkshire Police. In that interview I will tell him the following.'

She looked at the statement and began to read. 'On Friday June 13th last, I was staying at the property known as the Snuggery, Hollinby Quernhow, belonging to one Neville Hilton. I had been staying there during the previous week and had also stayed there for some ten days at the beginning of April this year. I left the property at approximately four p.m. as was witnessed by the neighbour across the road living in the property called "SidrahNick". To the best of my knowledge Mr Hilton was perfectly fine when I left the property and indeed, I believe he subsequently attended a Rotary meeting later that day.' Her voice was clipped and formal, somehow less confident than normal and certainly more subdued than her usual rich tones. She looked at Sarah Botha, who gave her a brief, approving nod. 'And that,' said Bun Widdup, 'is all I have to say.'

The two stirred, obviously preparing to go. Sarah replaced her tablet in her bag. Pat sat back, feeling relief mingled with surprise. Whatever she had expected, it wasn't this.

'Except—' Thelma's voice as mild and quiet as it was nonetheless felt as powerful as a thunderclap. 'Except we all know it wasn't like that at all.'

Bun sat back down, eyes fixed uneasily on Thelma.

'Bun, I suggest we leave now.' Sarah Botha's voice had the clipped, smooth precision of a cut diamond.

'I want to know exactly what she means by that,' said Bun, her voice slightly hoarse.

'We have an appointment,' said Sarah warningly.

'I want to know what she means.' Now it was Bun's turn to have an undercurrent of strength in her voice.

Maybe, thought Pat, *the prospect of a punch-up wasn't off the cards after all*.

Bun looked at Thelma. 'Go on.'

'For a start,' said Thelma, 'you saw Neville Hilton later on.'

'My client has already said, she left the property at around four p.m.,' interjected Sarah Botha smoothly.

'Maybe she did.' It was Liz's turn to speak, a distinctly frosty edge to her voice. 'But she came back later. She parked up behind the house, by the playing fields and entered through the back way.'

'When Neville returned home from Rotary,' said Thelma. 'You called him into the Snuggery. You confronted him about his actions regarding Pity Me school. You shouted the name of the school in his face.'

'When my client last saw Mr Hilton, he was alive and well—'

'Hardly well,' interjected Pat, 'if he was on the verge of a massive heart attack.'

'You were there when Neville Hilton died,' continued Thelma. 'You confronted him, he had a heart attack and he died.'

There was a pause – brief and yet at the same time infinite. When Bun spoke again there was a distinctly nervous quickness to her voice. 'Even if that was the case' – she gave Sarah a quick glance – 'which it wasn't. But even if it was, *so what*? The guy died of natural causes. I've really got nothing to hide.'

'So why didn't you tell the police before that you were staying at the Snuggery in the week leading up to Neville's death?' asked Pat.

'Because I wanted to avoid exactly this type of ridiculous Miss Marple pantomime,' snapped Bun. 'It was all a coincidence. And coincidences do happen.'

'So, you're saying you didn't know the property belonged to him?' asked Liz flintily.

'Funnily enough,' said Bun, voice heavy with sarcasm, 'it wasn't mentioned on the White Rose Country Cottage website. I wanted a bit of a break, so I hired the cottage – as I had a few months previously. I liked the place; I was able to shuttle between

Robin Hood's Bay and there in a couple of hours. I could still keep up with the Zoom calls – I'm all set up at home – but then I could zip across here and have a complete break.' She gave a simple smile and held out her hands in a 'there you have it' type gesture. 'I know it sounds convoluted – but hey! It worked.' She nodded at Sarah, who obediently stirred and again the pair seemed on the point of leaving.

The three women looked at her. It was Liz who spoke this time.

'So why do that to the wall?' she said.

'Do *what* to the wall?' The simple smile became puzzled.

'Paint a yellow stripe down it,' said Pat.

Bun shook her head. 'I feel like I've walked into some bonkers episode of *Murder, She Wrote*,' she said, standing up. 'Good day, ladies.'

'You painted a stripe down the wall,' said Thelma. 'So you could hang your drapes in front of it and pretend you were at home in Robin Hood's Bay when you did your Zoom calls. You hung your red and orange drapes – there are visible holes at the top of the wall where you fixed the hooks – and painted a small strip of yellow paint where they don't quite meet. So, to anyone on a Zoom call with you would automatically think you were in your studio back home.'

'Bun,' said Sarah. 'We really need to go.' But there was less conviction in her voice, and she made no effort to stand up.

'Now I've heard everything,' said Bun, sinking back down. 'Why on God's green earth would I carry out such a ridiculous conjuring trick?'

'So people would think you were at home in Robin Hood's Bay,' said Liz. 'Like you'd told us you had been for the past four months.'

'Giving yourself a cast-iron alibi,' added Pat.

'An *alibi*?' Bun's voice was soprano with incredulity. 'Why on earth would I need to give myself an alibi?'

Thelma fixed a sorrowful, steady gaze on the woman. 'Neville might have died of natural causes,' she said. 'But you intended to kill him.'

There was another pause. Pat was struck by the sudden thought that to the other clientele of the garden centre café they must look like ladies of a certain age passing the time of day over coffee and cake.

Bun's voice was low and firm. 'I absolutely refute that one hundred per cent.'

'Bun.' Sarah's voice was urgent. 'Bun, as your legal representative I'm advising you to leave now.'

But again, it was as if she hadn't spoken. 'What on earth makes you think for one moment I planned to kill a man I barely knew?' Bun tried to laugh incredulously and very nearly succeeded.

'This is what I think must have happened,' said Thelma. 'You left the property as you say about four p.m., making sure Sidrah across the road saw you go. Then later on, you came back. 'You'd left the wall set up with your drapes to look like your wall at home – so when the time came for Davey Fletcher's memorial service you were able to log in with everyone believing you were taking part from your house in Robin Hood's Bay. Then you phoned Neville – I'm not sure what you said exactly – at a guess I'd imagine you pretended to be one of his neighbours saying something like smoke was coming from the house, to ensure that he came back at the right time. As he got out of his car you called him over to the house.' Thelma drew breath and the three friends fixed Bun with a steady, remorseless gaze.

'Once inside – you confronted him. Told him exactly the damage he'd caused at Pity Me school. And how he was responsible for Davey Fletcher's death.'

'Knowing Neville Hilton I imagine he completely rejected what you were saying,' said Pat. 'Which would make you angry enough to shout at him.'

'You shouted the name of the school in his face,' said Liz.

'You probably read to him from the Ofsted report,' said Thelma.

'I'm guessing he must have tried to snatch it off you – which is how a corner came to be ripped off.' She paused, looking almost sympathetic. 'I do realise how angry you must have been – after all, the man had done terrible damage—'

'He should never have been an Ofsted inspector in the first place,' agreed Pat.

'And because of what he did,' said Thelma quietly, 'you decided he had to *die*—'

'What, you think I somehow managed to induce a heart attack?' scoffed Bun. 'How? Maybe I had a voodoo doll and stuck pins in it?'

'What induced the heart attack,' said Thelma, 'was a knife. A knife he believed you were going to stab him with. You moved towards him with the knife, and he must have finally realised the danger he was in – and that was when he had his heart attack.'

'Bun!' Sarah's voice was sharp. Several people at adjoining tables turned their heads.

Bun stood up. 'I need to make it clear that I totally deny any of the suppositions put forth, one hundred per cent. None of this has a word of truth in it,' she added shakily.

Pat, Thelma and Liz said nothing, just gazed impassively as Sarah Botha and Bun gathered their things. Bun fumbled slightly with her coat and all at once looked immeasurably older and sadder.

'We're all truly sorry about Annie,' said Thelma, almost impulsively. Bun's hands trembled slightly as she picked up her bag.

'What can you possibly know about it?' she said, her voice weak with exhausted sadness.

As they left, Bun Widdup paused, her look to Thelma was almost pleading. 'What that man did was nothing short of appalling,' she said.

Thelma nodded. 'I agree,' she said. 'But what you planned to do was worse.'

CHAPTER THIRTY-TWO

Tuesday 5th August

From the Hambleton Amblers Not Ramblers Facebook Page:

Please be aware that due to today's wet weather, the Abbey-to-Abbey Saunter has been postponed until next week.

'So, the fact is, Chelsey, Mr Hilton – Neville – had been there for hours before you even went into the property.' DS Donna Dolby's voice was calm and matter-of-fact. 'And even if you *had* been there when he was taken ill, there was very little you could have done.'

Except maybe stop Bun Widdup from waving a knife in his face, thought Pat.

Chelsey nodded. 'I mean I had been told that but you can't help wondering, *what if—*'

'Well, you can stop wondering.' Ffion's voice was surprisingly gentle. 'Nev had suffered with his heart for years. Since before I knew him. He used to say, "I'm a ticking time bomb, me."' She sighed, and looked at a photo, newly fixed to the wall. The smug and, yes, frankly irritating features of the late Neville Hilton smirked back.

Eyes wide, Chelsey looked round at the others sitting in Ffion's living room, which was a sight tidier today and smelling strongly of furniture polish (apparently Zippy and Sidrah had been in). Pat, Liz and Thelma smiled reassuringly at the girl, and she nodded again, seeming to grow in confidence. Outside, the August rain hissed and dribbled down the washed wet glass; the grass was green and lank. 'It's just hearing someone official say it,' she said.

Donna smiled grimly and tapped a document on the coffee table next to her. 'Can't get any more official than a forensic report, love,' she said.

Chelsey nodded. 'I just have to get a hold of myself,' she said. She sighed, and the shadows returned to her face again.

'Are you not back at work yet, lovey?' asked Liz. Since their encounter a few days previously, none of the three friends had heard from Jax.

Chelsey shook her head, shuddering slightly. 'No,' she said. '*No way*. I mean, I know it's daft, but I just can't face going into all of them different houses on my own.'

'It's not daft at all,' said Pat.

'It's the most understandable thing in the world,' said Liz.

'I mean I'm sleeping a bit better,' said Chelsey. 'And all that talking with the therapy lady does help. It's just—' She shuddered. 'I keep thinking about putting my key in that lock and pushing open the door.' She stopped abruptly, eyes filling with tears.

'So, if you don't go back to work with Jax, what will you do?' asked Thelma. None of the three friends liked to say it, but they all felt losing the cleaning work would inflict a financial hit that Chelsey could barely afford. Plus, it was seeming more than likely that before long Jax would ditch the business and move on to something else.

Chelsey shrugged. 'I dunno,' she said. 'Something will turn up.'

'What are you like with horses?' Ffion's voice was back to its usual brusqueness.

'Horses?'

Again, Chelsey shrugged. 'I mean, I used to have riding lessons when I was little,' she said.

'Only Lib needs someone on a weekend to help out,' said Ffion. 'Mucking out and so on.'

'Like cleaning stables?' said Chelsey.

'It's not for everyone,' said Ffion. 'And I suppose if you gave up riding—'

'Only because my dad lost his job and we couldn't afford the lessons anymore,' said Chelsey. 'I used to love it.'

'It's a lot of mucky work,' said Ffion. 'Shovelling ess aitch eye tee.'

'I wouldn't mind that,' said Chelsey. 'It can't be worse than some of the stuff I've found when I was cleaning. I mean aside from dead bodies. Oh God—' She stopped, clamped her hand to her mouth. 'I'm so sorry, Mrs Hilton, that came out all wrong.'

'Don't worry, love,' said Ffion with a grim smile. 'And it's Ffion.'

On her way out, having taken Lib's phone number and said a nervous goodbye to Donna Dolby, Chelsey paused in the doorway. 'So, it's *really* okay then?' she said. 'About Mr Hilton?'

'It's fine,' said Ffion. 'Don't worry about it.'

'And that yellow line on the wall? What was that about?'

The remaining five women exchanged glances.

'Nothing important,' said Ffion. 'Nev must've been trying out colours to repaint or summat.'

Chelsey nodded. 'I am sorry,' she said to Ffion. 'About Mr Hilton. I'm sorry he died on his own like that.'

Ffion nodded but no one spoke. After all, what was there to say?

* * *

289

Once Chelsey had gone, and Ffion returned with a fresh cafetiere of coffee. DS Donna slapped her hands on her knees. 'Right,' she said. 'I have exactly twenty-two minutes before I need to be heading elsewhere. And remember – I am not here; I never was here.' She reached for her cup and spooned in brown sugar. 'So, speak.'

'Well,' said Thelma. 'Whatever Bun Widdup might have said to you, she had this whole thing meticulously planned. From booking an earlier stay at the cottage, to setting up the whole fake Zoom scenario.'

Donna nodded. 'When do you think she decided all this?' she asked.

Thelma stirred her coffee. 'Probably when Neville got the job at Lodestone. Here was the man who had effectively destroyed Pity Me school, landing a top job with one of the leading academy chains in the country.'

'And a top-whack salary,' put in Pat. 'When there were people like Chloe Lord potentially facing being out of work when the school was closed.'

'She had tried a smear campaign,' said Thelma. 'Spreading rumours about Neville, but that didn't work. Neville still landed the job. So, I imagine it was around then, in her rage and grief over everything that had happened – the school, and then Davey Fletcher's death – she decided she was going to kill the man.' She looked at Ffion. 'I can imagine this must be very hard for you to hear,' she said, 'So just say if you want me to stop.'

Ffion shrugged. 'It's not easy,' she said, 'but then it'd be harder not to hear it, if that makes sense.'

Thelma nodded and continued. 'Remember,' she said to Donna, 'this is for the most part supposition – there's very little actual proof.'

'Which is okay as technically a crime hasn't been committed,' said Donna. 'FYI seventeen minutes.'

'Bun would have used the time she spent here in March finding out the lie of the land, as it were,' said Thelma.

'She'd have found out about your weekends away with the horses,' said Liz to Ffion. 'And the fact Neville went to Rotary on a Friday.'

'She'd also have worked out she could disguise the living room to look like her studio,' put in Pat. 'So she was all set. Your typical primary school practitioner.' She smiled grimly. 'Planned up to the hilt.'

'I think if you ask Caro Miranda,' continued Thelma, 'she'll tell you that the memorial service in school was Bun's idea. She'd have said it needed to fit in with her diary, so it'd have been relatively straightforward to book a week here in June and arrange it so the service would be on the Friday. At any rate she managed it. All she needed to do was check in, fit the drapes and paint that line of yellow where they didn't quite meet in the middle. She could then do all that week's Zoom calls and no one would know she wasn't at home in Robin Hood's Bay. And of course, the same thing applied to the memorial service – everyone thought she was sixty-odd miles away on the coast.'

'Only one person realised that she wasn't,' said Liz.

'Annie Golightly,' said Pat.

'I think when she saw Bun on the Zoom at the memorial, she might have had some idea something wasn't quite right but she wasn't sure what,' said Thelma. 'It was only when I mentioned the yellow line on the wall of your holiday let' – she nodded at Ffion – 'that the pieces fell into place and she worked out what Bun must have done. Her first instinct was to protect her friend – which is why she told people to delete the film of Bun from their phones – but as she neared death, she realised it was important to her that she told someone what had happened, and she sent for me.'

'Excuse me,' said Donna. '*What* was it that made her realise Bun wasn't at home?'

'The sunlight,' said Thelma. 'When Bun was reciting the sonnet, the curtain slipped, letting in the sun.'

'Son Masters said she looked like an angel haloed in the light,' said Pat.

'Only Annie realised the light was coming in from the wrong direction,' said Thelma.

'The Snuggery faces a different direction to her studio in Robin Hood's Bay,' said Pat.

'Not the west but the east,' said Liz. 'Or the other way round, I'm not exactly sure. But the sun was coming in the wrong side for the time of day.'

'Annie tried to tell me,' said Thelma. '*The sun was wrong*, she said. Only I thought she meant SON – *ess oh en* – as in Davey's partner – when really, she was saying SUN – *ess you en*.'

Ffion and Donna exchanged glances.

'Blumin' hummer,' said Ffion. 'How you lot worked this out is beyond me.'

'I've been on a number of Zoom calls lately,' said Thelma delicately. Both her friends tactfully looked down at their coffee cups. 'It's such a recent phenomenon, everyone having these virtual meetings. And one time when I was on a call, I realised that what I was seeing was what people wanted me to see . . . Things they wanted hidden could all stay neatly off camera.'

'And Bun was able to hide the fact she wasn't in Robin Hood's Bay,' said Pat.

'Yeah, but why didn't she use a virtual background?' said Ffion. 'Like a photo or something?'

'Or even blur the background?' said Donna.

'Bun's red African drapes are very distinctive,' said Thelma. 'If they suddenly disappeared, people would notice—'

'And remember she did all this when she was planning to *murder* Neville,' said Liz.

'So, she needed an alibi?' said Donna.

'Partly,' said Thelma. 'After all, Robin Hood's Bay is at least a good hour and a half from here. But also, it was very important to her that she protected all the staff and friends of Davey Fletcher.

When Neville was to be murdered, she wanted them all together, a safe distance away so they would be beyond suspicion.'

'What I don't get,' said Ffion, 'is how come Nev didn't clock this woman and know who she was. I mean she was staying here the best part of three weeks.'

'Do you often see your tenants?' asked Pat.

Ffion conceded the point. 'Only in passing,' she said. 'Some you don't see at all.'

'And anyway,' said Thelma, 'when Bun was staying here, she altered her appearance.'

'How?' said Donna. 'Like a disguise – a wig or something?'

'It was simpler than that,' said Pat. 'It wasn't so much what she did as what she didn't do . . .'

'Here we have a striking woman,' said Thelma. 'Scarf in her hair, bright clothes, heavy make-up—'

'Kohl eyeliner,' added Pat.

'Take away those things,' said Thelma. 'No make-up, no bright clothes – hair under a beanie hat – what do you have? A nondescript late-middle-aged woman – the type of person who passes largely unnoticed.'

There was a brief, understanding pause.

'When Friday came,' said Thelma, 'Bun made a big point about being seen checking out from the Snuggery, making sure Sidrah saw her.'

'Making some cock-eyed comment about hydrangeas,' added Liz.

'Then she parked up out of sight behind the playing fields and returned to the house by the back way, joined in the memorial service, phoned Neville – and waited for him to come home,' said Thelma. 'When he did, she called him into the flat and she confronted him, telling him what he'd done, producing the knife—'

'And completely out of the blue, Nev had a heart attack and dropped down dead in front of her,' finished Pat.

'Really,' said Thelma, 'it must have seemed like providence to her. She didn't have to go through with her plan after all, so a lot of her preparations – like cleaning the flat – were unnecessary. If she'd stopped to think she could have called 999 and no one would have been any the wiser.' She looked at Ffion. 'But then you came home unexpectedly. Bun must have panicked. She thought you'd gone away for the weekend – she'd no way of knowing you were only popping in and out. All she knew was she had to get out as quickly as she could, which is why she didn't paint the wall back grey again and stuffed the knife in the dishwasher.' She nodded. 'It puzzled me did that dishwasher.'

'What did?' asked Donna.

'The contents,' said Thelma. 'The fact it had vegetable dishes and three plates – not the sort of washing up a person on their own would generate. And then I realised – it was all stuffed in at random to camouflage the fact Bun wanted that knife washed clean of her fingerprints.'

'Even though she hadn't used it?' said Donna.

'She was panicking, remember,' said Liz. 'You do all sorts of daft things when you're in a fluster.'

Donna frowned. 'Suppose everything you say is true – and incidentally I have no problem believing it is – but why do all this in the first place?'

'That's what I was gonna say,' agreed Ffion. 'I mean okay, she sounds off her chunks this woman, but it's all a bit extreme—'

'Okay Neville did a bad Ofsted report, which ruined this school and led to the death of that poor lad,' said Donna. 'But it's not like she was the head teacher. She has her own very successful business. Why put all that in jeopardy?'

Pat, Liz and Thelma exchanged glances. It was Thelma who spoke. 'Annie Golightly,' she said. 'They'd been friends since college days. They were both at Bretton Hall together – Bun mentioned one of her tutors to us, Annie named her bungalow after the place.'

'They'd been friends for over forty years,' said Liz. 'Nearer fifty. She was right cut up when Thelma mentioned her at the garden centre.'

'They'd both been working as teachers in Africa together,' said Pat. 'Mombasa, in Kenya. It wasn't hard to find out with a bit of digging online.'

'And what – they were having a thing?' said Ffion bluntly.

Thelma shook her head. 'Not latterly,' she said. 'Though they might well have been lovers at some point. But they had a shared passion – *education*.'

'*Primary* education,' amended Liz.

'It's a stronger bond than you might imagine,' said Pat. The three ladies shared a smile.

'You'd have to be a teacher to understand,' said Thelma. 'Over the past twenty years in this country there've been some trends in education that many people have viewed in a very negative light.'

'Academisation,' interjected Liz darkly.

'Suits and money over ideals and playdough,' put in Pat.

Thelma looked sombre. 'Neville's almost casual attack on the school her friend had built – a school that embodied their ideals and beliefs – must have been very difficult, especially when that attack resulted in the destruction of the school. And, even worse – the absorption by a hated academy. It would have felt personal.'

'More so for Bun,' said Pat. 'Annie was facing her own destruction.'

'And then to cap it all, Davey Fletcher died,' said Liz.

'That was the lad who went off the road? In a blizzard?' asked Donna.

The three nodded.

'Being close to Annie, she knew how much her friend cared for him,' said Thelma. 'How Annie worried about how Davey would cope when the report came out, when the whole world would read what Neville Hilton had written. I believe she felt she almost had a duty to protect him.'

'When Davey had that crash, he was on his way to see Bun,' said Pat.

Donna frowned. 'How do you work that out?'

'He crashed on the A171,' said Liz. 'Which if you look at it on the map, you'll see it leads almost directly to Robin Hood's Bay.'

'Son told me they had a friend who was an adviser,' said Pat. 'And that was Bun. Davey probably rang her up the day before the report was due out, and she'd have told him to come over. So, despite the bad weather he set off.'

'I could tell Annie knew where he'd been going,' said Thelma.

There was brief, sad silence.

'That poor lad,' said Ffion.

'When Neville heard about the crash,' said Liz, 'he must have felt very bad himself.'

'Only, Nev being Nev,' said Pat, 'he just carried out a letter-writing campaign complaining about driving conditions of the A171.'

Ffion nodded. 'That sounds exactly like Nev,' she said sadly.

Liz flushed slightly, hoping Ffion wouldn't ask exactly how they knew about Neville's letter-writing campaign.

'So, what'll happen to this crazy woman?' said Ffion. 'I mean, is she going to be charged with anything?'

'Like what?' said Donna. 'Painting a wall? Loading a dishwasher inappropriately? I mean we could look at charging her with not reporting a death – but it's all circumstantial. She spoke to Ian, my colleague.' She shrugged. 'But as I keep saying, no crime was committed.'

'But one was planned,' said Liz.

Donna nodded. 'But they're very different things,' she said. 'And – as we keep coming back to – we haven't got much evidence.'

'So, she'll just get away with it, I suppose,' said Liz, lips thinning.

'In her own eyes she's done nothing wrong,' said Thelma. 'Especially as she hasn't actually killed anyone.' She shook her head. 'I'd imagine she feels totally vindicated. That's the trouble with committed, passionate people – they often have very strong self-belief, which can dull their sense of what's right and wrong.' She sighed. 'And particularly in this day and age, I'm afraid there's many such people in positions of power in our society.'

'But then,' said Pat, 'her best friend is dead, remember, the friend she loved and was inspired by, plus the lad she was looking out for.'

Hey, Mrs Kohl Panda, what can you see from your lonely house on a cliff?

A shrill peep disturbed the still of the room. Donna Dolby clapped her hands to her knees again and stood up. 'I must be away,' she said. 'And remember, I wasn't here.' She looked at Thelma, Pat and Liz. 'Which means,' she said, 'I haven't heard any of this, so course I can't say *well done, that's amazing work*.'

After she'd gone, Pat, Thelma and Liz looked in concern at Ffion.

'And you,' said Liz, her voice warm. 'How are you?'

'Oh, you know,' said Ffion and shrugged. 'Getting there.'

'Will you be all right?' asked Pat.

Ffion nodded. 'I'll be fine,' she said. 'There's Sidrah and Zippy coming round in a bit. They want to talk about some idea for reopening the village playing field. Though who's going to play on it, God only knows.'

'Won't that be a bit noisy for you?' asked Pat.

Again, that shrug. 'I dunno,' said Ffion. 'Be nice to hear a bit of life going on. This village can be like a bloomin' morgue sometimes.'

At the front door as the three were taking their leave, Thelma said, 'I imagine that was all quite hard to hear.'

'It was,' admitted Ffion. 'I mean typical Nev, Mr Pedantic and all that. It was always the same – his way or the highway. What he did to that school—' She looked at the three of them. 'But hearing how he died. I mean, I make no secret of the fact that he wasn't the love of my life, but even so. Talking of lack of love, I'm going to give Jax some money.'

The three tried not to look surprised.

'That's very good of you,' said Liz. She could have added *and it's totally undeserved* but naturally she didn't.

'I dunno.' Ffion looked awkward. 'I reckon it's what Nev would have wanted,' she said. 'Like I say, I never loved him, not really, but at least I can do this one thing for him.' She sighed. 'I don't reckon I knew what love was till I bought my first Cleveland Bray.'

More than once whilst driving through Hollinby Quernhow, the mussel-blue Corsair hit a puddle, sending curtains of muddy water over the straggly verges.

'I can't get over how different it is,' said Liz.

'One extreme to the other,' said Pat. 'They're giving out flood warnings in York. What's that all about?'

Outside the Old Police House, a bedraggled-looking family could be seen dashing in out of the rain.

'Poor things,' said Liz. 'I hope they're having a good holiday.'

'It wouldn't suit me,' said Pat as the last houses faded into the rain. 'I like somewhere with a bit of life going on.'

Thelma laughed. 'I rather think,' she said, 'that Hollinby Quernhow has had more than a bit of life going on recently.'

'I tell you something,' said Pat. 'It's good to see you back driving again.'

'And thanks for picking us both up,' said Liz.

'Not at all,' said Thelma. 'More than happy to. And run you back home.'

'Unless . . .' said Pat. 'I was wondering if you had time for a coffee at the garden centre?'

'I'm in no rush,' said Liz. 'Our Jacob's doing something with courgettes.' She rolled her eyes mournfully.

'I'm not due at the charity shop until three,' said Thelma. 'Why, was there something you wanted to tell us?'

'Not about Neville Hilton,' said Liz. 'I've had about enough of dark goings-on for now.'

'Nothing like that,' said Pat. 'It's just we've had the first sonogram of the baby. I wanted to show you, but it didn't seem right before.'

She was about to say more but Liz and Thelma interrupted with that noise lady primary school teachers are so good at: a joyful exclamation at the anticipation of coffee and some exciting news to celebrate and mull over.

EPILOGUE

September

The school was large, the school was ultra-modern – *This is a place where children strive and thrive!* screamed out the school logo. The corporate identity was everywhere, the Airforce blue colour scheme, the logoed sweatshirts and books, the identical fonts on the hessian-backed noticeboards, in the endless signs exhorting all young learners to push themselves on to that next level.

To stand in one classroom was very much to stand in all of them – with the exception of the corner room on the ground floor. Yes, there were the notices, the hessian, the fonts – but there was also so much more. A display of books about elephants presided over by an enormous multicoloured Elmer. A mound of rainbow-coloured beanbags in one corner, in another a wobbly construction of painted cartons proclaimed itself to be the Wearside Longship.

The intense heat of those July days was a far-off memory. Indeed, as Chloe gave out writing books with the well-practised precision of a card shark that cold, gusty late September morning, she wondered whether the rain would hold off or bring an abrupt end to playtime. She knew, as all primary teachers do, a focused five minutes is a precious resource. Once all the books were given out, she should just have time to trim the Viking artefacts in readiness for that afternoon's 2D Viking ship burial.

'Excuse me?' The tentative voice accompanied by a tentative knock arrested her just as she was reaching for the paper cutter. Looking up, she saw Thelma Cooper in the doorway accompanied by her two friends, the worried one who'd been with her at the school that day, and the hennaed one who she'd met at Annie's funeral.

'The office did say as it'd be all right to come down,' said Liz, anxiously fingering her dull blue lanyard.

'Hello!' Chloe smiled in the slightly abstracted way primary school teachers do when interrupted mid-task.

'We're so sorry to interrupt,' said Thelma.

'No, it's fine,' said Chloe. 'Only the kids'll be in, in five minutes—'

'—and you've nine million things to do,' supplied Pat.

Chloe smiled. 'Something like that,' she said.

'We won't keep you,' Thelma told her.

'We just wanted to wish you well in your new job.' Pat smiled.

'How's it all going?' asked Liz. 'It all looks *lovely* in here!'

'Well, we're getting there,' said Chloe, a wistful sadness softening her features. 'I mean it isn't Pity Infants.'

There was a brief pause of acknowledgement.

'And how's your class?' asked Thelma.

'Lively,' said Chloe.

'Good lively or not-so-good-lively?' asked Pat.

'Both, God love 'em,' said Chloe, raising her eyes with a grin. 'Again: we're getting there!'

'Anyway, won't hold you up,' said Thelma. 'We just wanted to give you a little something.'

'A sort of hope-it-all-goes-well present,' said Liz.

Confusion and embarrassment clouded Chloe's face. 'You didn't have to do that.'

'Wait till you see what it is,' said Pat.

Liz handed her a pair of what looked like scissors but with thick, serrated blades. 'Pinking shears,' she said. 'They give a zigzag edge. They're ideal when you do Mother's Day and Christmas cards. Give that extra bit of pizzazz.'

Chloe looked doubtfully at the heavy shears.

'Who's Topsy Joy?' she said reading the label on them.

The three women exchanged smiles of love and sadness. 'She was our nursery nurse,' Thelma told her. 'Sadly no more.'

'Could get through a stack of mucky paint pallets quicker than anyone I know,' said Pat, handing her a second object.

'I've got a stapler already,' objected Chloe, looking at the scarred orange tool.

'Not *this* stapler you've not,' said Pat. 'These plastic ones you get these days last five minutes. This is the real deal – and here's some staples to go with it.'

'A tip,' said Liz. 'When you staple – don't hold it flat against the wall. Hold it at an angle – that way it's so much easier to get the staples out when the time comes.'

A rather insipid hooter sounded.

'That's the end of playtime,' said Chloe. 'The kids'll be here any second—'

'This is from me,' said Thelma, handing over a new, A4 sage green notebook. 'Not to put too fine a point in it, this is your bible. You record everything in there—'

'Spelling tests,' said Liz.

'Maths tests,' said Pat.

'All the times you hear the children read,' said Thelma. 'I've set it all up for you, all you need is to enter the names of your class.'

'We're meant to do all of that online,' said Chloe. 'Only sometimes the system's slow, and one time it wouldn't even come on.' She leafed through the book. 'I was thinking I could do with some sort of hard copy.' Those clear blue eyes looked at her visitors. 'Thank you,' she said.

The hooter sounded again.

'That's our cue, ladies,' said Pat. 'Best of British—'

'Not that you'll need it,' said Thelma.

'One sec,' said Chloe as the three turned to go. 'I don't suppose you've heard anything about Bun Widdup?'

Without looking at each other, the three exchanged glances in that way lady primary school teachers do.

'Not as such,' said Thelma.

'Just that she's thrown everything up and gone to work in Africa,' said Liz.

'Nairobi,' specified Pat.

None of them mentioned the brief but rambling email Thelma had received a week earlier, saying how at Pity Me school, Annie had created something truly special, a unique environment for children to learn, and that to destroy that was a crime of the darkest order.

'It was just all so sudden, her going like that,' said Chloe. 'I couldn't understand it.'

'Sometimes in life that's the way things happen,' said Pat. 'Suddenly.'

'Miss!' The voice was shrill, outraged, not far from tears. 'Everyone's pickin' on me!'

'What's happened, Nirmal?' said Chloe. She crossed quickly to the small figure in the doorway, face screwed up against the injustice of the world. 'Come here,' she said. 'And the rest of you—' She raised her voice to the others hopping and stamping and skipping into the classroom. 'The rest of you, dates and learning outcomes at the top of your next clean page.'

She looked up to say goodbye, but her three visitors had gone. She knew that they must have just walked out of the door, but it felt as if they'd simply vanished. And in days and weeks and years that followed – when stapling, when entering spelling scores, when adding pizzazz to Christmas cards and Easter baskets, she would reflect that maybe this was how a visitation from angels perhaps must feel.

ACKNOWLEDGEMENTS

It's ironic that in a year when I've formally retired from teaching, learning has played a major part in my life, as I've negotiated the change from a busy, structured routine, to an unstructured (but no less busy!) one. In acknowledging the people who have played such a big part in the creation of this, the fourth outing for Pat, Liz and Thelma, I find I'm wanting to thank them for the things they've taught me, as much as for their help and support.

First off, I want to thank the team at Avon for their tireless, top-of-the-range hard work and for the many lessons I've yet again learned from them. Thanks to my two editors, Sarah and Emma, plus Jess and Helena for all their advice, suggestions and insights with the text (memo to self: check and recheck names! *And don't overuse italics!*). Thanks to Angela and Katie for their sterling work on sales (it's no accident I keep seeing the books all over the place!), to Toby for another terrific cover and the wonderful Becky for being an absolute powerhouse of a publicist.

Thanks also to my agent, Stan – yes, for his hard work, but also the invaluable ongoing reminders there *is* a wood even if I can't see it for all the trees.

Then there's the people who also helped with the book, my team of readers – the Grammar Police! Peter Dodd, Maureen from church and Sandra Appleton (more on her later): thank you! And I want to give an extra special thanks to Audrey Coldron, 100 years old this year and the best lesson I know for living life well. It's been wonderful working with you over the years, Audrey; the things you've taught me about storytelling have made such an impact on my writing life.

Big thanks as well to Gary Brown from the BBC, another five-star teacher of all things text-related, who's taught me so much about sharpening and refining text, and also one of the most invaluable lessons in writing: to 'arrive late and leave early'!

Plus, a special shout out to the incomparable Julie Hesmondhalgh, whose warmth and talent and sheer humanity teaches me again and again that storytelling is about SO much more than words and chapters and scenes.

I'd like very much to thank my group of 'technical' advisors, who have been so patient and helpful: Peter Marsh, for his insights into the life of an OFSTED inspector, and Pippa Davies and Isobel Ashmead, for their expertise on school inspections.

Thanks as ever to my fellow creatives, the people in my life who 'get it'. Louise Fletcher and Catherine Johnson – the things I've learned/am learning/will learn from you about the creative process would fill more books than I could ever possibly write. And Jonathan Whitelaw and Mark Wright, my cosy crime bros-in-arms, who are always ready with advice and support, plus provide a much-needed respite from writing in the form of discussions about all things *Doctor Who*.

I make no apologies for shouting out to the very special people who make up the community of independent bookshops. Their warmth of welcome, their enthusiasm and interest in me as a writer, help me learn and relearn the value of that quirky, enchanted world of books. You get a sense of it in the shop names: the White Rose in Thirsk, the Stripey Badger in Grassington, Darling Reads in Horbury, Wonky Tree in Leyburn, the Grove in Ilkley, the Beverley Bookshop and the St Ives Bookseller. These places provide communities with much-needed oasis of peace and meaning in a world driven by the instant and the digital and are a life lesson for all of us. Three special mentions: the new and the terrific Criminally Good Books in York (go visit!); my original cheerleader and supporter the Little Ripon Bookshop; and the very special place that is Truman Books in Farsley, a place that gives again and again the lesson of how beneficial an impact bookshops can have on their communities.

And – as always – thanks to my huge, lovely family. My amazing crime-o-pedia sister, Judith, and my niece Caitlin, a.k.a. the Agatha Christie book club. My wonderful aunties Lee and Mary. To Babs and Tracey, Sally, Maisie, Elise and Trevor, Dan, Anja, Robin and Lawrence. Andy, Conor, Tais, Niall and Jess, to John and Rozzi, to Pippa, Paul Matthew and Adam.

To my cousin Ruth for teaching me about life since we were in the playpen together.

To Simon for teaching me on a daily basis that there's so much more to me than someone who sits for hours in the attic trying to write.

And to my late lovely Auntie Catherine who taught me more about humour and light and life than she ever knew.

Finally, in a novel that focuses so much on all things education, I want to give a mention to some of the amazing practitioners I've been fortunate enough to have been taught by or worked with over the years, who have given Pat, Liz and Thelma life in so many many ways.

Sandra Appleton, of course, and always, still marking my text with an unsentimental but *so* helpful eye. My lovely much-missed history teacher Jean Cherry. To Hazel Jones and Ian Carroll, Doreen Hunt, Margaret Lane, Tina Brace and Angela Anning to name but a *very* few.

And to all those I've worked alongside across the years. Averill,

Anne N., Cheree and Liz. Anne S., Julie and Gill. Hilary, Olga and Mary. Anne M., Chris, Sally and Kathryn.

And, as ever, the whole team at Foxhill Primary school, past and present. With a special cheer for the new leadership team of Sarah and Amanda, who are driving forward a place that strives to give the very best in primary education.

**Introducing the three unlikeliest sleuths
you'll ever meet . . .**

Every Thursday, three retired school teachers have their
'coffee o'clock' sessions at the Thirsk Garden Centre café.

But one fateful week, as they are catching up with a slice
of cake, they bump into their ex-colleague, Topsy.

By the next Thursday, Topsy's dead.

The last thing Liz, Thelma and Pat imagined was that they
would become involved in a murder.

But they know there's more to Topsy's death than meets
the eye – and it's down to them to prove it . . .

**Don't miss J.M. Hall's debut cosy mystery –
available now!**

Signed. Sealed. Dead?

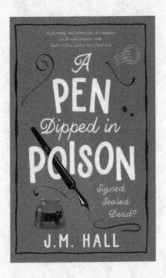

Curious white envelopes have been delivered to friends
and neighbours. Inside are letters revealing the
deepest secrets they have tried to hide.

As one by one, careers are ended, marriages destroyed
and no one is beyond suspicion, the three friends decide
enough is enough. They must take matters into their
own hands before more damage is done.

But as they work to uncover the truth, they begin to wonder
just how far someone will go to silence this poison pen . . .

Could a murderer be in their midst once again?

**The second addictive and page-turning cosy
mystery from J.M. Hall – available now!**

Tick. Tock. Time's up.

Retired teachers Pat, Liz and Thelma are happiest
whiling away their hours over coffee, cake and
chat at the Thirsk Garden Centre café.

But when their good friend tells them about an unsettling
experience she had in a sinister-feeling charity shop,
they simply can't resist investigating . . .

Because the entire shop has vanished into thin air.

Before long, our trio of unlikely sleuths find themselves
embroiled in a race against the clock to get to the bottom
of this mystery – but who has a secret to hide and
how far will they go to keep it concealed?

Only time will tell . . .

**The third wonderfully witty and gripping cosy
mystery from J.M. Hall – available now!**